Corinne

Corinne

A Novel

Rebecca Morrow

ST. MARTIN'S PRESS
NEW YORK

First published in the United States by St. Martin's Press, an imprint of St. Martin's Publishing Group

www.stmartins.com

Designed by Jen Edwards

Library of Congress Cataloging-in-Publication Data

Names: Morrow, Rebecca, author.
Title: Corinne: a novel / Rebecca Morrow.
Description: First edition. | New York: St. Martin's Press, 2022.
Identifiers: LCCN 2022005249 | ISBN 9781250279996 (hardcover) |
    ISBN 9781250280008 (ebook)
Subjects: LCGFT: Erotic fiction. | Romance fiction. | Novels.
Classification: LCC PS3613.O77853 C67 2022 | DDC 813/.6—dc23/
    eng/20220303
LC record available at https://lccn.loc.gov/2022005249

ISBN 978-1-250-27999-6 (hardcover)
ISBN 978-1-250-28000-8 (ebook)

Our books may be purchased in bulk for promotional, educational, or business use. Please contact your local bookseller or the Macmillan Corporate and Premium Sales Department at 1-800-221-7945, extension 5442, or by email at MacmillanSpecialMarkets@macmillan.com.

First Edition: 2022

10 9 8 7 6 5 4 3 2 1

1992

Chapter One

All the good Bible names must have been taken when Enoch Miller was born.

"Can't we do 'Daniel'?" his dad would have said.

And his mom would have been like, "'Daniel'? So that people think we only go to church on Easter? We may as well name him 'Matthew.' Or 'James.' Next you'll suggest 'Thomas.'"

"My name is Thomas, sweetheart."

"Your mother was Episcopalian. I rest my case."

"What about 'Jacob'?"

"This congregation already has three 'Jacob's."

"'Isaac'?"

"It's a little try-hard. I'm looking for a name that's try-really-*really*-hard. Like—not quite 'Zebediah,' but close."

Enoch Miller.

Enoch, Enoch, Enoch.

He looked terrible in that brown suit. He'd looked terrible in it two years ago, back when it fit, and now he looked ridiculous. The pants were too short, and the buttons strained on the jacket. He should just wear it open, who was he kidding. He was built like a front door, no waist at all. Imagine a rectangle with legs, crammed into a brown suit. That's what Enoch Miller looked like. (*Enoch, Enoch.*)

He was walking up the church aisle, counting people, standing up extra straight like he was doing something really important. Like, *"Jesus said I was the only person who could handle this. Better give me some space."*

It wasn't fair that the boys got jobs to do during church services. They got to take attendance and manage the audiovisual equipment. Some of them, the older boys, even got to watch the parking lot. Imagine getting to skip half the service to stand outside in the sunshine—or the rain, Corinne wouldn't mind the rain. She'd take any job at all.

Enoch got to read the Bible sometimes. As a job. He got to stand onstage and read the selected passage for the week, before an elder led the discussion. Enoch would go up there, and another boy would come up behind him to adjust the microphone to Enoch's height. Because that was a job, too. Microphone boy. (Enoch used to be a microphone boy; he'd graduated.)

Corinne could adjust microphones. She was able. She could read the Bible out loud. She could stand outside in the parking lot and chew gum. She could walk up and down the aisles verrrry slowly with a pencil and a notepad, mouthing the headcount to herself.

Put me in, Coach. (Where "Coach" is "Jesus.")

Not in this lifetime, girly. (Jesus would say.)

The Sunday service was two hours long. (Tuesday and Thursday services were shorter.) Corinne was allowed to go to the bathroom twice on Sundays—but only because her family was trashy and sat in the back of the church.

The un-trashy people sat up front, and their daughters were expected to hold their water, and their sons got to hold the microphones.

Corinne's family were serfs. Her dad was an unbeliever, and her mom was a convert, so they all bore the stink of the outside world. Her family had been coming to this church three times a week for a decade, but the word was still out on them.

Maybe they deserved it.

Because even though Corinne never broke any spoken rules, she sort of hummed over lots of unspoken ones. And her mom let her. Her mom was soft; she let the younger kids run wild, too. That's why they all sat in the back row—because Corinne's brothers wouldn't stay in their seats, and they drew pictures instead of taking notes. The whole family was kind of embarrassing.

So who cared, really, if Corinne went to the bathroom twice in two hours, and if she always went to the bathroom downstairs, even though she knew you weren't supposed to be downstairs without a reason.

"I don't like the upstairs bathroom," she'd tell her mother. *"People can hear you flush."*

The church basement had thick, emerald-green carpeting left over from the 1970s. There were small study rooms down there, and a library, and a room for the furnace and the cleaning equipment.

If you used the downstairs bathroom, you could sit in the stall as long as you wanted. There was never a line. Sometimes Corinne would sit there so long that she peed twice. Then she'd wash her hands like a surgeon and spend a few minutes examining herself in the mirror.

She always looked bad. She was fat, and her face was broken out, and she wasn't very good at putting on makeup—and you had to be *really* good at makeup to wear it to church, because it had to look like you weren't wearing any at all.

She wore long skirts with elastic waists, and solid-colored crew-neck sweaters.

The girls upstairs in the front rows wore dresses.

They had bodies for dresses. Waists that would take a zip. Arms like *Seventeen* magazine models—the same circumference from wrist to shoulder.

The girls upstairs had *money* for dresses. And matching tights. And low-heeled pumps that their mothers let them wear when they turned fourteen, but not a day earlier.

Corinne would look at herself in the downstairs bathroom mirror. She'd suck in her stomach, stick out her tongue. Pull the ends of her dishwater-blond ponytail to tighten it. (It never looked the same after you fixed it that way.) She'd pick at her nail polish (no one explicitly said that you couldn't wear nail polish to church) and scrape at it with her teeth.

And then she'd peek into all the study rooms . . . The one with the green chairs that used to be upstairs before the church was re-modeled. The one with the mural of Noah's ark. The library. Corinne would walk along the bookshelves, running her fingers thump-thump-thump over the spines. She wouldn't turn on any lights. She wasn't supposed to be down here.

She'd peek in the furnace room, too. It smelled like store-brand Pine-Sol.

Sometimes, when she'd run out of distractions, she'd linger on the staircase, listening to the services happening on the other side of the lobby. Standing. Bouncing on the edge of a step. Making lines in the thick green carpet with the toes of her black flats.

Enoch Miller had caught her there before.

"What are you doing out here, Corinne?"

"I went to the bathroom."

"Yeah, well, what are you doing now?"

"Standing. I had a leg cramp. What are you doing?"

"It's my job to check the basement."

"You must be very important. Brother Miller."

"You're missing services, Sister Callahan."

"Well, you don't miss a beat. No wonder they trust you with the base-ment."

Corinne had already used the bathroom twice during today's ser-mon. Once upstairs and once downstairs. And she'd already exam-ined the back of everyone's heads. And read her favorite scriptures . . .

Why couldn't you get lost in the Bible the way you could in a book? The Bible *is* a book. It has stories. Pretty raunchy stories. With be-headings and floods and so much adultery. But Corinne's eyes would glaze over every time she tried.

Her favorite passages were the lists. Especially the lists of names. She liked to say them out loud in her head. *Abraham begot Isaac, Isaac begot Jacob, and Jacob begot Judah.* (Matthew, chapter 1.) It wasn't all guys' names—occasionally one of them begot a child "by" a woman. David got the verb, and Bathsheba got the preposition. (God, Enoch Miller was lucky. If his mom had read Matthew 1 as much as Corinne had, he would have been named "Rehoboam." Or "Zerubbabel.")

Enoch Miller was still walking down the aisle in his terrible brown suit, counting heads like Christ and the Father had anointed him for the job.

Corinne stood up and straightened her long skirt. Her mother frowned at her. *"I think I'm starting my period,"* Corinne mouthed. She headed for the stairs.

Chapter Two

Sunday services were supposed to be two hours long, but Brother Dawes always went over. Because he could. Because no one would stop him.

After services, people would gather in the lobby and, if the weather was nice, out on the steps. If you drove by on a Sunday morning, you'd think about what a nice place this must be, with people of every color all dressed up and smiling at each other. All the men in suits. All the women in dresses and hats and hair ribbons.

Corinne liked that view of it.

She liked the way they sounded, too, during the hymns—everyone so joyful and harmonious.

Corinne's mom didn't have a car, so after services, her family was at the mercy of whoever had driven them to church that day. Usually it was the Merediths, an elderly couple with a minivan. Sister Meredith liked to sign up for cleaning duty, so Corinne's family would stay and clean, too.

It meant waiting for everyone else to leave. It meant chasing after her littlest brother, Noah, while he chased after all the other little kids. Corinne used to have to chase after both her brothers—but Shawn was twelve now, and got in trouble for things like stealing their dad's cigarettes and showing them to the other twelve-year-old boys out in the parking lot. It wasn't great, but it was out of Corinne's hands.

She had a little sister, too. Holly. Holly never got into any trouble anymore. She was fourteen, and after services, she'd stand in a circle with the other girls her age, talking about all the boys their age and a little older.

The girls and boys Corinne's age stood in a circle together on the other side of the lobby. There were more girls than boys.

More girls than boys, more women than men. At every level. Those were the breaks, demographically speaking. Boys were more likely to opt out of church as teenagers (lured off the path by girls who weren't waiting for marriage), and women were more likely to opt in as adults.

That made boys hot property.

Even a boy like Enoch Miller, with his big nose and his ugly brown suit.

Enoch was eighteen, and a trusted servant of the Lord. He got to take attendance and read the Bible during services. Pretty soon he'd be monitoring the parking lot. He'd be an elder someday; his dad was an elder—or had been, before he died a couple years ago of cancer. Enoch Miller was going places.

Well, he wasn't *going* anywhere. That was the point. That's what made him desirable.

That's why Shannon Frank desired him.

Shannon Frank was a bitch.

And Corinne didn't think that just because Shannon was beautiful. Though Shannon might be a bitch *because* she was beautiful. Because when you looked like Shannon Frank, you could be a bitch, who even cared? (Nobody cared that Corinne was a bitch either. But that was because nobody cared about Corinne. There was a difference.)

Shannon Frank was tall and slim and wore fitted dresses from Laura Ashley, with puffed sleeves and long, full skirts. She had red patent leather pumps with bows. She had a pair of pink pumps with actual ribbons. And she wore hats sometimes in the summertime— which you'd think would look lame on a teenager. But it didn't. She looked beautiful. She looked like someone who would be friends with Anne of Green Gables.

She was not friends with Corinne.

She never spoke to Corinne, she never had—but whenever

Corinne walked by, Shannon would whisper something into one of her friends' ears, and then they'd laugh.

Corinne had gone to a slumber party at Shannon Frank's house in fifth grade, only because Shannon's mother made Shannon invite every girl in the congregation. All the other girls whispered funny things to each other all night. Shannon made everyone take turns with her Barbie Dreamhouse, and Corinne never got a turn, and then Shannon put it away.

Maybe Corinne should get over it. But it was hard to get over hating people when you saw them three times a week, and they never got any better.

Shannon Frank and Enoch Miller were going steady. They went on dates with chaperones. They had each other over to their families' houses for Bible studies. They went roller-skating with groups on weekends. They'd probably get married next year.

Corinne knew all this because her mom was close to Enoch's mom. Sister Miller was the one who brought Corinne's mom into the church ten years ago—she'd seen Corinne's family at a park and offered her mom a Bible tract.

Corinne's mom was the sort of person who was just waiting for someone to hand her a Bible tract. Gagging for it. She didn't have any extended family, and her husband was an alcoholic. She was broke, and overwhelmed, and had three terrible kids.

Who in that situation *wouldn't* want to hear some good news?

Who wouldn't want to be part of something bigger and better and closer to God? Wouldn't you want to come to church three times a week if everyone there loved you? If they *had* to love you? Because those were the rules? Couldn't you put up with all the other rules? All the other bullshit?

(Corinne never said words like "bitch" and "bullshit" out loud. But she thought them sometimes. She thought all sorts of things.)

You couldn't start vacuuming the church until everyone was gone. Corinne stood at the edge of the lobby with the vacuum plugged in and ready. Enoch Miller was standing with Shannon Frank and their circle on the other side of the room. Shannon leaned over and whispered something into her best friend's ear. Enoch looked up and caught Corinne watching them. Corinne turned on the vacuum.

Chapter Three

One side effect of going to church every Tuesday and Thursday night was that you never got to see any of the good shows. Corinne only got to watch Must See TV when someone in her family was sick, or if their ride to church fell through.

On most Thursday nights, their ride would show up five to ten minutes into *The Cosby Show*. Corinne had watched the opening credits of *The Cosby Show* hundreds of times. She'd watched the Cosby kids grow up that way. But she never got to see them do anything.

"I'm a modern-day Sisyphus," she told her mother.

"How does Jesus feel about false gods?" her mother replied.

"Sisyphus was mortal," Corinne said. *"Initially."*

Her mother was totally sincere when she talked like this. Sometimes Corinne wondered what her mother was like before she found God. Her dad said her mom used to be really into astrology and palm-reading. Corinne couldn't imagine it. Her mom wouldn't even say "Good luck" because luck was too close to magic. She wouldn't let them watch *The Smurfs*.

Today was Thursday.

Which usually meant Corinne would take the bus home from school and have a couple of hours to herself before it was time to change into church clothes and watch the first ten minutes of *The Cosby Show.*

But instead she got called to the office in the middle of the afternoon.

Her mom was there to pick her up.

Chapter Four

Sister Miller was standing at the head of the table, with her head covered, because a woman had to cover her head when praying in front of a man. Even if the man was her own son.

"And thank you, Lord, for blessing us with this opportunity to support our brothers and sisters. Please help us show the Callahans how welcome they are in our home."

Corinne opened one eye. Bonnie—Corinne didn't have to call Enoch's mom "Sister Miller" when they weren't at church, she was allowed to call her "Bonnie"—had pulled folding chairs up to their dining room table. Enoch and his little brother sat in their usual chairs, with their heads bowed and their hands folded. Corinne and her siblings sat on the folding chairs, squeezed in at the corners. Her six-year-old brother, Noah, was already eating his spaghetti.

"Help us lead with love and generosity," Bonnie said. "And please, Lord, we beg of you, help us to stand when we feel weak. Everyone at this table knows what it feels like to lose an earthly father. Let us not forget that we have a heavenly Father, who will never abandon us."

Enoch's fox-brown hair was hanging over his eyes, but Corinne knew what he was thinking: His father didn't abandon him; he died of lung cancer.

Corinne's dad maybe didn't abandon her either . . . Sure, he left— but he'd left before. And he'd come back before. Her mom always took him back. Because God doesn't recognize divorce, her mom said. (Because she wanted to take him back, Corinne knew.)

This time her dad had really made a mess of things. He'd been gone for two months, and they'd been behind on the rent even before he left. Their landlord sent the county sheriff around today to evict them.

"Where would we be," Corinne's mother said, when she'd sat them down to explain it, "without our brothers and sisters?"

The sheriff had given her mom two hours to clear out. Bonnie came with her station wagon, and they stuffed it with clothes. Someone else from the congregation, Brother Fiala, came by with a pickup truck and took their beds—and maybe some other things, Corinne's mom wasn't sure. It was all in the Fialas' garage for now, thank the Lord.

They were going to be okay. God was looking out for them. God had sent His angels to protect them—her mother had felt their presence. Why else would Bonnie Miller have decided at the last minute not to go grocery shopping today? The angels had intervened. Bonnie was home when Corinne's mother called—and had offered to take in their whole family. There was plenty of room in the Millers' basement.

"God watches over every sparrow," Corinne's mother had said, sitting on the basement couch with Noah in her lap and her arm around Shawn. "He's watching over us, too."

Corinne and her siblings had all gotten out of school early. They stayed in the basement while Sister Miller had a family meeting upstairs with her own children—who must not have taken the news with good grace, based on how instructional this prayer was.

Enoch's twelve-year-old brother, Japheth, was frowning at Corinne over his folded hands.

Corinne closed her eyes.

"We ask these things with love and humility," Bonnie said. "In Jesus's name, Amen."

"Amen," they all said. Corinne opened her eyes.

The Millers had to eat fast; they were going to church that night. They were already dressed. Corinne's family was staying home—well, was staying here—to deal with their trauma.

"Why don't they have to go?" Japheth said, when Bonnie was rushing her boys out the door.

Enoch knocked him on the back of the head. Enoch was wearing his gray suit. It was newer than his brown one, it covered his ankles. He still looked like an evangelical rectangle.

"We'll be home soon," Bonnie said. "Make yourselves at home."

Corinne and her mother cleaned up the dinner mess, then they all went downstairs. There was a sofa bed down there, and a shower, and a big old-fashioned console TV.

They'd missed most of *The Cosby Show*, but they got to watch *A Different World*.

Chapter Five

Corinne waited by the flagpole after school.

"You'll walk home with Enoch," her mom had told her that morning, after they'd gotten Corinne all registered for classes.

"Did he agree to that?"

"Corinne."

Enoch hadn't said a word to Corinne since she'd moved into his basement.

He wasn't exactly ignoring her—they didn't really see each other. Corinne's family spent most of their time in the basement, even when the Millers weren't home. And her family ate dinner an hour earlier than the Millers did. *"So we won't be crowded around the table,"* her mom said. But Corinne knew that her mom was trying to disrupt the Millers' household as little as possible. They didn't even all ride to church together. The Merediths still came to pick up Corinne's family in their minivan.

The basement was fine. It could have been so much worse. The floor was carpeted, and the walls had wood paneling. Corinne's mom and Noah and Holly slept on the sofa bed. Shawn slept on a La-Z-Boy. Corinne slept in a fancy nylon sleeping bag on the floor. (Apparently Enoch's older brother, Jed, had been really into camping before he became a missionary. He and his wife served in Africa. Now they were in Arkansas, trying to start a new church there.)

Their first week at the Millers' house, Corinne's mom let every-body stay home from school. Corinne suspected her mom was wait-ing for her dad to come back and fix everything. There was no sense in getting them registered at new schools if they were just going home again—or going somewhere with their dad.

But after a week, Bonnie told Corinne's mom that she was break-ing truancy laws. And now Corinne was finishing her senior year at the high school over the hill, where Enoch Miller was a senior, too.

Corinne was waiting for him by the flagpole.

School was fine. It would be fine. This school was in a better neighborhood than her old school. The kids wore more expensive polo shirts. Corinne had changed schools a lot over the years—she was used to starting over. She was smart. She'd adjust. And in a few months, she'd be done.

"Hey," someone said. She knew it was Enoch. She knew his too-deep voice. His voice that had dropped so low it didn't sound like it fit in his body anymore. Like it was straining against his suit buttons.

"Hey," she said.

Enoch was standing next to her in a generic green polo shirt and jeans his mom probably bought at Target. His black parka was hang-ing open. He looked big and pale and plain.

He squinted down at her, like he was maybe going to ask her a question, but then like he'd changed his mind—and he started walking.

Corinne followed him. She only generally knew where they were headed. "Do you walk home every day?" she asked.

"It's not far. A mile."

She nodded. She followed him. Enoch walked with his head down, looking at the sidewalk, a no-brand black backpack slung over one shoulder.

Corinne didn't say anything else for the first ten minutes or so. She tried to pay attention to where they were walking. (She was try-ing to stay out of Enoch's hair.) "You don't have to walk with me tomorrow," she said, eventually. "I'll remember the way."

He didn't look up. "Whatever, Corinne."

They walked another block in silence.

"I mean," she said, "I didn't mean to crash your senior year."

"What do I care about my senior year." He kicked a rock into the street. "Besides, we don't even have any classes together."

"I'm in your study hall," she said.

"Oh. I didn't see you."

They walked another block, uphill. Corinne was breathing heavy. Enoch could definitely hear it. He was still frowning at the sidewalk.

"I didn't mean to crash your house either," she said.

He shrugged. "It's not your fault," he muttered.

"You don't have to be my friend just because I live with you."

Enoch looked up at her, finally. Dismayed. "You don't live with us. You're just staying with us."

"Your mom wants us to stay through the school year, so we don't have to switch again."

His chin dropped. "That's four months."

"I know. I said I'm sorry."

"You didn't."

"Well, I am. I don't want to be there either."

"I know."

"So I'm telling you—you don't have to be my friend."

He jerked one hand in the air. "No one said I had to be your friend."

"Your mom is making you walk home with me."

He stopped walking. Frustrated. There was an angry crease between his eyebrows. Enoch Miller had a caveman forehead, a ridge that hung over his eyes like a shelf when he was frowning. His shoulders were hunched. The top button of his polo shirt was unbuttoned, and his neck was full of cords. "You're my sister in Christ, okay?"

"Okay," Corinne said. "Right."

"And"—angry crease, caveman ridge, hunched shoulders, cords— "you're practically my sister."

"I wouldn't say that," she said right back.

Enoch glanced over at her and rolled his eyes. He started walking again. "Yeah, well . . . I can't seem to get rid of you."

Corinne didn't reply. Because he was right. And she was never going to tell him he was right about anything. It would mar her stainless record of always disagreeing with him.

But he was right.

This wasn't the first time he'd been stuck with her. This wasn't even the hundredth. Ever since Bonnie started studying the Bible with Corinne's mom, Enoch and Corinne had been stuck together, and stuck entertaining their younger siblings.

They'd played so many games of Monopoly, they had their own house rules. Enoch's dad used to travel for work, and Corinne's family would come over on the weekends, and their moms would make dinner together while the kids played board games in the living room. They'd eat popcorn with Junior Mints and stay up late. Then Bonnie would drive Corinne's family home.

Enoch used to have a crew cut. His mom would cut it with clippers on the front porch. Now his hair was long enough to brush his ears and fall in his eyes. It was the color of a Burnt Sienna crayon. (The crayon itself. Not the color that came out of it.) And his eyes were Russell Stover brown. Like terrible chocolate with too much sugar.

"Whatever," Corinne said.

⁓

Corinne walked home by herself the next day. And she only sort of got lost. Enoch was in the kitchen drinking milk when she walked into the house. She went straight down to the basement.

The next day, a girl from her English class asked Corinne if she wanted to walk home together. For part of the way.

You get a new-kid bonus when you first start at a school, especially if you start midyear. You're fresh and interesting, and everyone looks at you and sees a fresh start for themselves.

You should really press your advantage that first week or two. Make friends with people before the shine has worn off.

Corinne walked home with the girl, and they saw Enoch along the way, and Corinne wondered whether he was going to turn her in for associating with worldly people. Corinne hadn't seen Enoch associate with anyone so far. He kept his head down in study hall—and the few times she saw him in the hallway, he was always alone.

A week went by, and her mom didn't mention the worldly girl, so Enoch must not have told on her. Corinne wouldn't have gotten in trouble, anyway. Her mom just would have encouraged her to talk to her new friend about the Bible and the Lord's promise for mankind.

"Do your friends at school know you're one of God's people?" her mother would ask her.

They know I go to church three times a week, Corinne would think, *and that I'm not allowed to listen to "Thriller."*

Heck no, she didn't talk to people at school about the Bible. Corinne didn't think you should hit people with the Bible when they were just trying to live their lives. It's not like the Bible was some big secret they'd never hear about otherwise. Most of the kids at school had churches of their own.

The wrong churches, according to Corinne's mom. Going to the wrong church was worse than going to no church at all. Serving God inappropriately was way worse than ignoring Him—it was disrespectful. It was dangerous. If you're weren't heading the right way, you were heading the wrong way. There was no neutral movement. There was no standing still.

On Thursday nights, their church services were all about how to talk to people about the Bible. How to make the most of different scenarios. *"What if a coworker has a question about hell?"* Or—*"What if your neighbor is considering an abortion?"*

Why would your neighbor ever talk to you about having an abortion?

(Once, in tenth grade, one of Corinne's friends *did* tell her that she was pregnant and considering an abortion. Corinne brought her a Bible tract about the miracle of life. Her friend took it, but she didn't talk to Corinne after that, and Corinne couldn't blame her—she'd told Corinne her biggest secret, and Corinne had given her a *pamphlet.*) (Corinne's mom was so proud of her.)

Corinne didn't talk to people at school about church or God unless they asked her a direct question about it. Sometimes they asked her why she didn't swear. Or why she didn't date. A few times, worldly boys had asked for her number, and she'd told them that she wasn't allowed to talk to boys outside of church. (She hadn't wanted to talk to those boys anyway, so it didn't really count as being virtuous.)

Enoch Miller didn't seem to be talking to any worldly girls. Why should he? He had his pick of the congregation.

He was just another boy at this school. Nothing special.

He looked like he probably carried Bible tracts in his backpack.

Chapter Six

Nobody went roller-skating in high school.

Nobody but people from Corinne's church.

They went in big groups. Their parents took turns chaperoning. Corinne had gone along a few times, not very often. Her mom couldn't really afford it, and anyway Corinne was a terrible skater. You had to go all the time to be good at it.

Shannon Frank went all the time. She had her own skates. White with glittery pink laces. Enoch had his own skates, too. Black ones. They were old and blocky, but they were his. He didn't have to use the rentals—bruised tan leather with fraying red laces.

Bonnie said that Corinne and her siblings should go roller-skating with her boys tonight. She'd gotten out her pocketbook to give them money for admission and skates, and an extra two dollars each to buy a hot dog and a Coke. Enoch was going to drive them in Bonnie's station wagon.

"Let Corinne sit up front," Bonnie said, when they were all getting in the car. "She's the oldest."

"Don't make me nervous," Enoch said, when he was backing out of the driveway.

"Why would I make you nervous?"

"I'm serious, Corinne. I'm driving."

He drove five miles below the speed limit and braked for every red light when he was still blocks away. Corinne waited for him to get on the interstate to whisper, "Don't kill us all, Enoch. Our mothers have been through enough."

He clenched his jaw and ignored her.

Once they got to Skate City, Enoch left Corinne with the younger kids at the rental counter and went ahead to find Shannon.

Everything at Skate City was covered in carpet. The walls and the counters and the round, mushroom-shaped benches. Shannon Frank already had her skates on. She was sitting with her best friend, Juanita, a Black girl with perfectly curled bangs, on one of the carpeted mushrooms. They were whispering. Shannon looked over at Corinne and then said something so funny, Juanita looked like she'd probably be giggling for three weeks. Enoch sat on Shannon's other side, lacing up his skates and not frowning for once. Practically smiling, even.

He stood up, steady on his feet, and put his shoes and his puffy coat into one of the family-sized lockers. Then he stood there, holding the locker door open, frowning at Corinne.

Corinne was dragging her siblings over from the rental counter.

"Give me your stuff," he said.

"Go ahead," she said. "I'll take care of it."

"If I let the door go, it'll lock."

"Fine." Corinne kicked off her shoes and knocked Noah onto the bench, pulling his shoes off without untying them. Holly and Shawn left their coats and shoes in a heap. Enoch helped Corinne shove everything into the locker. Then he let it swing shut and skated away. Shannon and Juanita were waiting for him at the edge of the rink.

Corinne's sister had already found her friends from the congregation and eased her way onto the rink. Shawn was clomping around with another boy his age. (Not Japheth. Japheth Miller couldn't stand the sight of any of them.)

Corinne was stuck with Noah, who couldn't stay on his feet for more than a few steps but was determined to run anyway. Corinne skated with him up and down the row of lockers, holding his hand so tight, she was worried about dislocating his elbow. At least when he fell, which was a lot, it was onto the carpet.

Enoch and the other teenagers stayed on the rink for every song.

Friday was Oldies Night, so you didn't have to worry about cursing or sexual content. Enoch and Shannon held hands during couples' skates. Sometimes she'd shift in front of him, skating backwards, still holding his hand. Sometimes Shannon would hold Enoch's arm up, then twirl underneath it, and he'd practically laugh. She had glossy, chestnut-colored hair that fell to the middle of her back. Tonight it was pulled back on the sides with white combs. She was beautiful, you had to give her that. Enoch obviously thought she was beautiful. He watched her. He held her waist when she was skating backwards—but only for a few seconds, it was borderline against the rules. He'd hold her waist, his big hands spread over her ribs, and she'd hold his shoulders, and then they'd drift apart and hold hands again. They were going to get married after graduation. Bonnie had told Corinne's mom. Corinne would get invited to the wedding reception in the church basement—or maybe at a park pavilion, if the weather was nice. Bonnie would make the cake and the mints. There'd be music, but no dancing. If Enoch's dad had lived, he would have said the blessing. Enoch and Shannon were holding hands out on the rink. There had been three couples' skates so far. The song this time around was "My Cherie Amour."

Noah had given up on skating. Corinne had gone around the rink with him once, hugging the wall the whole time. It had taken them all of "Great Balls of Fire" and "Lollipop" to make the full circuit—he'd pulled them both down three times—and then, thank God, he'd let Corinne talk him into getting a hot dog.

They ate their hot dogs at sticky tables (the only things not covered with carpet), and after that, Corinne let Noah pretend to play some video game with a big shotgun attached to it. Hopefully the Miller kids wouldn't tell Corinne's mom. She was crazy strict about guns.

"Hey," Enoch Miller said in a voice so deep, Corinne didn't know how he expected anyone to understand him. (He sounded like an airplane that was flying too low. He sounded like the bass line in a Rush song.)

"It's the ladies' skate," he said.

Corinne said something like, "Huh?"

"You should go skate. I'll watch Noah."

"That's all right."

Enoch rolled his eyes and started to argue.

"Fine," Corinne said. She nudged Noah—"Listen to Enoch"—and then tried not to clomp toward the rink. The deejay was playing "Chantilly Lace." It was easier to keep upright without Noah, but Corinne still stayed close to the wall. She skated like someone who was penguin-walking across ice. She almost never coasted. Or glided. Sometimes she moved her legs furiously and still didn't make any progress, like someone running in place.

Shannon and Juanita passed her, holding hands. (Girls and women were allowed to hold hands at Skate City, but boys over twelve weren't.) They wound their way through the other skaters like a ribbon, going twice as fast as everyone else but hardly moving at all. They both came skating every Friday night, they'd been coming since they were kids. Corinne watched them. And she watched Enoch and Noah, even though Enoch didn't seem like a child molester or anything. And she watched her feet, her rented brown skates. *"Chantilly lace, and a pretty face, and a ponytail, hanging down."* Corinne didn't know how to stop. So when the song was over, she aimed for the low concrete wall on the lobby side of the rink and pulled herself onto the carpet.

Enoch had moved Noah over to a *Pac-Man* machine. Noah had taken his skates off. He was standing on a chair in his socks, holding the joystick with both hands.

Corinne looked at Enoch and mouthed, *"Is he actually playing?"*

"He was," Enoch rumbled. "You can skate another song. I don't mind."

"That's okay, you go. I suck at skating—" She looked up at him, worried. "Suck" wasn't a curse word, but it for sure wasn't a church word, and you might as well be at church around any of the Millers. "I'm not very good at it," she tacked on.

"You just need practice," he said. "It's not Olympic-level archery."

Corinne surprised herself by laughing. "Olympic-level archery?"

"Have you ever watched archery? It takes technique, athleticism, focus."

"Yeah, okay, I believe you."

"I'm done skating," he said. "You may as well go."

"I'm done, too," Corinne said. "So . . . there."

Enoch rolled his eyes. There was a pinball machine next to the *Pac-Man*. He scooted over to it and got out a quarter.

Corinne watched Noah not-play *Pac-Man*. She watched Enoch play pinball. He was just okay at it; he wasn't going to break any hearts back in 1974 or whatever. With his skates on, he was too tall for the machine. He had to hunch over it. In his crisp white shirt. Enoch had changed his clothes after school, from a polo and plain dark jeans to a white Oxford with a button-down collar and nicer, stonewashed jeans. This probably counted as a date for him and Shannon. Enoch really *wasn't* all that great at pinball—he held two long fingers over each flipper button, and when the ball rolled down the middle, he hit the machine with his too-high hips. The ball sank anyway.

"You wanna play?" he asked.

"I don't want to waste your quarter."

"I'll just waste it myself. I suck at pinball."

Corinne looked up at his face. He was frowning and feeding two quarters into the machine.

"You're player one," he said, pushing himself away.

Corinne wasn't any good at pinball either, but she could keep a ball alive sometimes, if she sort of forgot she was playing. She had good timing—she could catch the ball and let it roll back on the flipper—but she could never hit the ball far enough to get any bonuses. So she just bounced it at the bottom of the machine until it went down the middle.

"You're not hitting it hard enough," Enoch said, on Corinne's second turn, when she just barely pulled the plunger hard enough to get the ball into the game.

"I don't want it to tilt."

"It won't tilt."

"Don't give me advice. You suck at pinball."

"You suck harder," Enoch Miller actually said out loud. Corinne could get him publicly disciplined for saying that. She almost missed the ball.

But she didn't—she caught it on the right flipper, hugged it back, then let it roll to the tip. Enoch laid two fingers over hers and flicked his wrist at the exact moment Corinne pushed. The ball shot up into the upper bumpers and got caught in them, setting off flashing lights and whistling noises. Then it landed in the extra-ball trap. Another silver ball popped out and bounced around. Corinne could see herself smiling in the surface of the glass. There were red lights in her eyes. Enoch's hand dropped away. It had only been there for a second.

"I told you," he said.

She ignored him. She lost the extra ball almost immediately. Then she tilted the machine trying to hit the other one.

It was Enoch's turn. Shannon and Juanita skated up to the machine. "Last skate," Shannon said.

Enoch pointed at the pinball game. PLAYER TWO was flashing on the little display.

"Come on," Shannon said, pulling on his arm. "The deejay said he'd play Amy Grant."

Enoch glanced at Corinne on his way back to the skating floor. "Free ball for you."

"They were all free," she said.

He didn't hear her.

⌒

Enoch drove like less of an old lady on the way home. Corinne didn't say anything. They listened to the radio. The golden oldies station.

The next Friday night, when Bonnie offered to pay for their skates again, Corinne said she had homework. Holly was at a friend's house, and the boys had both fallen too much to have fun—they weren't interested. Bonnie looked relieved. The Millers weren't poor, but they had a lot less money since her husband died, and Bonnie was already feeding five extra people. Enoch looked relieved, too.

The Friday night after that, nobody mentioned it. Enoch changed into a button-down shirt and put on Polo aftershave and left with Japheth before dinner.

Chapter Seven

Weirdly, Corinne had spent more time in the Millers' living room before she moved in with them.

When they used to come visit the Millers, Corinne and her siblings always hung out in the living room and watched TV or played board games. If they had to go to the bathroom, they'd use the one upstairs, the one with all the Millers' toothbrushes in a cup by the sink.

They never used to go down to the basement—that would have been weird.

Now they never crossed over the boundary between the kitchen and the dining room. They never, ever went all the way into the living room. They could see it from the kitchen table . . .

The dusty-blue carpet, the pink couch. A grandfather clock that kept them up the first few nights they were here. And in the corner, an oak entertainment center with a newer TV and a VCR, and tucked onto one of the shelves—a Nintendo.

At first they thought they'd be able to play it when the Millers weren't home. (The Millers went out for family outings sometimes, like to visit their grandparents or for birthday dinners.) But Corinne's mom was even stricter when they had the house to themselves. They weren't allowed to use the bathroom upstairs, even if somebody was taking a shower in the basement. Corinne's mom and Bonnie were still best friends, and her mom wanted to keep it that way.

The two of them seemed closer than ever. They hung out together all day. They went grocery shopping and volunteered at church. They made dinner together. Bonnie had helped Corinne's mom sign up for welfare and food stamps. She was on a waiting list for rent assistance.

Sometimes after the kids were in bed, Corinne's mom would go upstairs, and she and Bonnie would stay up, drinking tea and talking. They both cried a lot. Corinne could hear their tearful conversations from the basement. Could Enoch and Japheth hear them from the second floor?

Corinne didn't think her mom and Bonnie ever would have been friends outside of church. Bonnie was a middle-class housewife. She was raised in the church. She got married young. Her husband was an electrician.

Corinne's mom had grown up poor and turned out wild. She didn't get married until after she found God. Corinne was already eight years old by then. (Corinne's dad wasn't her dad, but he'd been around as long as she could remember.)

Bonnie met Corinne's mom exactly the way you were supposed to meet a worldly person—by spreading the Good Word. It was probably one of the scenarios she'd practiced on a Thursday night.

And now she was invested in Corinne's mom, in Corinne's whole family.

Like, Bonnie definitely cared about them—she was a kind and generous person—but she also got *credit* for them. They were five souls she'd saved. Some people went their whole lives and never brought a new person into the Lord's flock; Bonnie had brought in a whole family. She wanted it to stick. She wasn't going to let them slip through the cracks.

Corinne worried that her mom wouldn't find a place for their family to live by summer. What if they were still with the Millers when school got out? They'd have to spend all day, every day down in the basement, avoiding them.

Weekends were already pretty terrible, especially if Corinne's family couldn't find some reason to leave. Sometimes they'd get invited to someone's house for dinner. Sometimes they walked to the park or to the library. Holly was lucky—she went to a friend's house every Friday night and didn't come back 'til after church on Sunday. Corinne and her brothers didn't have those sorts of friends.

Today was Saturday, and Corinne hadn't been out of the basement all day. Her mom had gone upstairs at lunchtime to make sandwiches, but they'd eaten them downstairs. They'd probably eat dinner in the basement, too. The Millers had their family Bible study on Saturday nights, in the living room, and Corinne's mom didn't like to disturb them.

Sometimes she pretended they were hiding down here—from the Nazis or the secret police. Or that the Russians had dropped the bomb, and they were staying in the basement until the fallout had dissipated. Or that she had a strange disease that made her allergic to sunlight.

It was almost dinnertime. Corinne was sitting on an old exercise bicycle and trying to read a *Reader's Digest*—the Millers had stacks of them—but she wasn't really pedaling, and she wasn't really reading. Shawn and Noah were watching basketball. They looked bored and lethargic. It had been too cold to go outside today, and they were tired of playing with the Millers' old toys. (All the good toys were upstairs.)

There was a knock at the basement door. The Millers only knocked when they needed to come down to use the washing machine. Usually it was Bonnie, but sometimes she sent Enoch or Japheth. Corinne sat up taller on the exercise bike.

It was Bonnie. She was smiling.

Bonnie was a tall, thickly built woman. She always wore dresses. You didn't have to wear dresses all the time, that wasn't a church rule, but it was for sure extra credit if you did. Her hair was deep red, and she wore it pulled back into a tight, shockingly thick bun. Her hair must come to her knees. None of the women at church cut their hair. Girls could wear it down, but once you were married—or too old for anyone to marry—you started wearing it in a bun or a tight braid down your back. Sometimes Corinne's mother wore hers in a very loose braid with a lot of hanging tendrils, but she was a convert and married to an unbeliever, so people didn't really expect any better from her.

"Is the TV up too loud?" Corinne's mom asked. She was sitting on the couch, folding clothes. She always meant for them to use this time to have a family study of their own, but they never did.

"Oh, no," Bonnie said. "No, I never hear it . . . Carolyn, I've been thinking. We're so happy to have you as part of our family—you should be part of our family study. We can all read the Bible together, and then afterwards, the kids can play games. Like they used to."

"Bonnie, no, you all need a night for yourselves."

"We have that. Every other night. You're not here as tenants." (*Tenants pay rent*, Corinne thought.) "You're part of our household. And First Timothy tells us to provide for our household. That means spiritual provision, too."

Corinne's mom was tearing up. Shawn was eyeing the stairs like a cat trying to escape from the house.

"Come on upstairs," Bonnie said. "We'll have dinner and make a night of it."

"Are you sure about this?"

"I'm certain."

Corinne's mom wiped her eyes. "Give us a minute. We'll get our Bibles." As soon as Bonnie was upstairs, Corinne's mom turned to them. "Do you all want to go upstairs?"

The boys nodded. Corinne nodded, too. She couldn't help it, she *really* wanted it—the Millers ordered pizza on Saturday nights.

"Then I am asking you to be on your best behavior. Or Bonnie will never invite us again."

This seemed like an empty threat to Corinne. Everyone knew that Noah wasn't capable of best-level behavior.

When they got upstairs, Japheth was in the living room, playing with Legos. (There were no Legos in the basement. Only old Matchbox cars and stuffed animals.) Enoch was still at Shannon Frank's house. He spent every Saturday at Shannon's house. He sat in on the Franks' family study, then he came home for his own family's study. Did anyone get more Bible in their diet than Enoch Miller? If you cut him open, proverbs would spill out, and letters to the Galatians.

(Corinne liked the books of the Bible that were written as letters. She liked that they actually sounded like letters. Like, the first verse would be *"Dear Galatia."* And she liked that Paul—who wrote most of them—was so mean. *"Dear Galatia, how are you? No wait, don't tell me. I already know: You suck."* Paul really put the piss in the epistles.)

They ate pizza without Enoch, but they waited for him before they started the study. They all sat in the living room with their Bibles in their laps. Noah was staring at the grandfather clock, fascinated by the swinging pendulum. Shawn was staring at the entertainment center. The sliding cabinet door was half open, and you could just see the edge of the Nintendo box. Corinne was sitting on the floor, trying to keep her corduroy skirt tucked over her knees. She was only allowed to wear skirts that covered her knees, but this one hiked up when she sat down. It was fine; she was wearing tights. And socks over her tights, to hide the holes in the toes.

Japheth sat on the couch in what was probably his usual spot. He'd been pouting ever since Corinne's family had come upstairs—he hated having them there. Corinne couldn't really blame him. She wouldn't have wanted the Millers to move into their house. When they had one.

They all heard Enoch come home. (The garage door. The station wagon engine.) He walked into the living room with a piece of pizza in his hand and his Bible tucked under his arm. "Sorry, Mom, I—" He looked around the room. He looked at Corinne.

"The Callahans are joining us for family study tonight," his mom said, making eye contact with him. "We're coming together as a household, like we talked about."

Enoch nodded. Solemnly. He was wearing that white button-down shirt again. And jeans. And white socks.

He led the Bible study. You could tell that he was embarrassed with them all there. With his mom and Corinne's mom treating him like the man of the house. His dad must have led the study back when he was alive. Did Enoch take over right away? When he was sixteen? His older brother was already a missionary in Africa by then.

Enoch did all right, leading the study. There was nothing cocky about him. Not like some of the brothers at church, who you could tell just *lived* for the chance to boss people around and have a captive audience.

Why didn't more men stay in the church? It seemed like a pretty sweet life to Corinne . . . You got automatic seniority over women and children. And all but the very least able men got to lead services. There were only two men in Corinne's congregation who weren't elders or deacons: One of them was mentally disabled, and the other one had a nervous breakdown a long time ago—now he'd sneak out before the last hymn, so he didn't have to talk to anybody.

Some of the brothers just loved to lord it over you, that they were in charge. The ones who pulled you aside at church to remind you what the Bible says about modesty or to tell you to honor your mother.

There were a thousand scriptures telling people to take care of "widows and fatherless children," so it was open season on Corinne's family, 24–7.

The Millers were "widows and fatherless children" now. How would that feel, to be a normal person one Sunday, and then somebody who everybody felt sorry for on the next? Did Enoch Miller feel fatherless?

Enoch asked good questions during their study. He asked the younger boys questions they could answer. He asked Corinne to read out loud—girls were allowed to read out loud during a meeting in their own homes. (This counted as Corinne's home.) Enoch sat on the couch, with his legs kicked out. Corinne sat on the floor, with her Bible on her lap and her skirt mostly covering her knees. Bonnie covered her head with a silk scarf to say closing prayer.

None of them were sure what to do after that. Bonnie turned to Enoch. "Why don't you all play some board games? You used to have so much fun . . ."

Enoch nodded. Bonnie and Corinne's mom went into the kitchen. Probably to drink tea and crochet. Bonnie made blankets for everyone in the congregation who had a baby. Corinne's mom was helping.

Enoch got up and walked over to their game closet. It was an entire closet stacked with board games, floor to ceiling. Corinne loved that closet. She would live in that closet. (If she were allowed in the living room without an invitation.)

"What do you want to play?" He looked over his shoulder at Corinne.

She shrugged. "I don't care."

"Could we play Nintendo?" Shawn asked. Like he couldn't spend another minute *not* asking.

"No," Japheth said. "You might break it."

Enoch frowned at his brother. "Of course we can play Nintendo," he said in his slow, low way.

"But—"

"Zip it, Japh. Do you think if Jesus had a Nintendo, He wouldn't let His guests play?"

"Jesus would play *Super Mario Brothers* with prostitutes and money-lenders," Corinne said quietly.

Enoch gave her a sharp look. Like maybe she shouldn't be talking about prostitutes. But then he said, "And lepers."

"At that point," Corinne said, almost smiling, but definitely *not* smiling, "He'd probably just give them His Nintendo."

Enoch had crouched in front of the TV. "True," he said, untangling the Nintendo controllers.

Japheth was on his feet, stamping. "Enoch, are you giving them our Nintendo?"

"No. Calm down—we're gonna take turns."

They did. It was glorious. Video games were glorious. You couldn't even feel time happening when you were playing video games, and watching other people play was almost as good.

At ten o'clock, Corinne's mom went downstairs to put Noah to bed. The four older kids had set up a tournament. Enoch made popcorn. It was like it used to be—back when they were being forced to play together, but they weren't being forced to live together.

At eleven o'clock, Bonnie came in from the kitchen, yawning. She lingered in the archway between the dining room and the living room. Corinne started picking up the popcorn from the carpet around her. That was their cue. But Bonnie said, "I haven't heard you kids laugh like this in a long time—you keep playing. In bed by midnight?"

They all nodded. "Yes, Mom," Enoch and Japheth said.

Enoch looked surprised. Maybe he was thinking the same thing Corinne was—that the two of them weren't supposed to be alone together. Not anymore, not for the last few years. Not without a chaperone.

It was a joke, really. The idea that Enoch Miller would need a chaperone—that anyone would—to keep his hands off Corinne. But it was a rule. Men and women couldn't be alone together. It was a precaution.

Two twelve-year-olds must add up to one chaperone. Or maybe Bonnie could see the truth of the situation. Of Enoch, engaged to Shannon Frank. The truth of Corinne.

They played Nintendo for another hour. Enoch and Japheth won the tournament. At midnight, Enoch shut down the TV. And Corinne and Shawn went downstairs.

Chapter Eight

It didn't really change anything. Family night.

Corinne's family still gave the Millers plenty of space every other night of the week. Enoch Miller didn't start talking to Corinne at church or at school.

But it was still good.

Pizza and Nintendo every week. That was really good. Even Bible study wasn't so bad. Corinne might not mind church so much if Enoch were the one preaching. He would be someday. In suits that fit. Shannon Frank, sitting next to him in the front row.

Japheth got *The Legend of Zelda* for his birthday. Everyone wanted to play that Saturday night, but you had to go one at a time, and one turn went on forever.

Noah distracted himself with Legos. Shawn watched Japheth play *Zelda* like it was a TV show.

"You want to play Monopoly between turns?" Enoch asked Corinne. He was sitting on the couch. She was sitting on the floor. In a little bit, he'd make popcorn.

"Sure," Corinne said.

Enoch got Monopoly down. He could reach any game in the closet. He was wearing a blue polo shirt, and it made his shoulders look stark and square. No matter what Enoch wore, he looked like the answer to the question *"What would a large, heavy box look like wearing human clothes?"*

He sat back down on the couch and laid the game board on the cushion next to him.

"Let's play on the floor," Corinne said.

"I don't want to sit on the floor."

"You're too good to sit on the floor?"

"No, it hurts my back."

Corinne got up, but made a show of it. She sat on the sofa, on the other side of the board. "You're getting old and feeble."

"It's always hurt my back. God didn't invent chairs so we could sit on the floor."

"I guess He *was* a carpenter . . ." Corinne said.

Enoch made a sound like "hmph" in his throat. It counted as laughing. He tossed Corinne the top hat. (She was always the top hat.) "You go first."

Corinne went first. She landed on Reading Railroad. She didn't buy it.

"You're gonna lose," Enoch said.

"Joke's on you," Corinne said, "we're not gonna finish." They'd never be done by midnight.

"So what's your strategy?"

"To buy the things I like."

"So . . ." he said, "my strategy should be to keep you from buying the things you like?"

"Or your strategy could be to buy the things that *you* like."

"Don't pretend to be a communist, Corinne. I've played Monopoly with you before."

"*Hmph.*"

The thing about playing Monopoly was, it wasn't much of a game.

There was no strategy beyond *"buy everything you can and hope for lucky dice."* Your average game of Monopoly was just two to three hours of watching your luck play out.

Enoch and Corinne used to change the rules to make it more interesting. They'd start with more money. They'd play with more than one piece at a time. Once, they'd fused a game of Monopoly with a game of Parcheesi—another game that was all luck and almost no thinking. And once, they'd laid out Monopoly, Parcheesi, and Clue, and played them all at once. (When it was your turn, you'd roll the dice, then decide which piece you wanted to move, on any board.) (It was fun. They should play that again.) (They called it Monocheesue.) Their younger siblings never lasted long in these games, which was another reason to play. To get some peace.

Tonight, they played Monopoly for a couple hours. On the couch. Corinne tried not to care who won, but Enoch was right—she wasn't a communist. By the time she gave up on not caring, she was already losing. She landed on Illinois Avenue, and Enoch owned the whole red block.

"It's only a matter of time now," he said.

"You don't know that," she countered. "Anything could happen."

"I'll think you'll find that everything you have is mine."

"Let's do the thing where you can Yahtzee your way out of paying rent."

"It's too late to set house rules."

"You can do whatever you want with house rules," she said. "That's what makes them house rules."

Enoch shook his head at her. He was smiling. His teeth weren't crooked, but they were messed up somehow. They were too far apart. "You always try to cheat when you know you're losing."

"How is renegotiating the rules cheating? Cheaters *break* the rules. They don't make them."

"It's your turn to play *Zelda*, Enoch," Japheth said.

"You can skip me."

"Then it's Corinne's turn."

"You can skip Corinne."

"No way," Corinne said. "I want my turn."

"Only because you're losing."

"All right, fine—skip my turn," she said over her shoulder, without looking away from Enoch. She lifted her chin at him. "Let's start the game over. And I'll try this time, for real."

Enoch lowered his eyebrows at her.

Corinne slipped a finger under the Monopoly board, like she was going to flip it. "Ehhh?"

He rolled his eyes. "Fine."

She flipped the board closed. The top hat went flying. Enoch shot out his hand and caught it.

Corinne picked up his Monopoly money and started sorting it. She was always Banker. "New rules," she said, then laid out a ridiculously intricate plan to make the game more interesting.

Enoch agreed and added a few amendments, to which Corinne agreed. It didn't matter that they had to go to bed soon. Finishing wasn't the point.

"We're going to need more dice," Corinne said.

"I'll get Yahtzee." Enoch got up and headed toward the game closet.

His mom was walking past him, up the stairs. "Not too late," she said, patting his shoulder.

"Not too late," Enoch agreed, grabbing Yahtzee and for some reason—a reason Corinne was eager to hear—Trivial Pursuit.

Corinne chose another Monopoly game piece, the shoe—they were double-fisting it this round—and held the game board steady when Enoch sat back down on the couch. She started dealing out money. This was already more fun.

"I never see you at school," she said.

"We're in study hall together," he replied.

They were. Enoch always sat on the other end of the cafeteria. Sometimes he slept.

"You know what I mean," she said.

"I'm in the construction program in the afternoon."

"What's that?"

"It's like an internship. We work at construction sites."

"Do you get paid?"

"I get work experience. Toward my electrician's license."

"Like your dad?"

He nodded.

Lots of people in church worked in construction. It was a good way to make a living without going to college. Going to college wasn't *strictly* against the rules, but it might as well be. Going to college was a sign that you were more invested in man's world than in God's plan. Corinne hadn't actually known anyone from church who'd gone to college, but she'd heard horror stories.

Corinne's mom practically collected horror stories about good Christians who'd been lured off the narrow path. Alcohol and immoral sex were the usual culprits. But at college you could be seduced by books, too. By thinking you knew better than Jesus. *"Imagine being led off the path by your own hubris,"* her mom would say.

The thing was, Corinne *could* imagine it. Alcohol and sex seemed like they were happening on different planets from where Corinne was currently operating. But books and arrogance . . . Corinne could be seduced by that. Corinne might enjoy being seduced like that.

"What are you going to do?" Enoch asked.

"It's not even my turn."

"No—when you graduate."

"Oh." That didn't seem like a fair question. What *could* Corinne do? What did girls do? Girls like Shannon Frank would get married. And then pregnant. Girls like Corinne could go to missionary school . . . But the church preferred married missionaries; they were more useful. And anyway Corinne would make a terrible missionary. She didn't like talking to people about Jesus, which was pretty much the whole job. Maybe there was such a thing as inbound missionary work. Like inbound telemarketing. Corinne could answer phone calls about Jesus. "Get a job, I guess," she said.

"What kind?"

"I was thinking about being an electrician, but my counselor told me I'm too intelligent and charming."

"That's half right."

Corinne looked up at him. Was that a compliment? Enoch was moving his game piece. He always picked the horse and rider. And then the race car. "Shut up," she said, "I know you have to be smart to be an electrician."

"I like how you knew I wasn't calling you charming."

"Ha ha," Corinne said.

"Ha ha," Enoch echoed.

Monopoly was more fun when it was hardly Monopoly at all. The game wasn't over by midnight, not by the rules they'd laid out, but Enoch didn't want to quit—he was winning. Japheth was still playing *Zelda;* Shawn was hypnotized by it. Corinne and Enoch agreed to go into sudden-death mode, and finally finished at 12:28, right before the grandfather clock struck the half hour. (It went off twice an hour, all night long.)

Enoch was grinning because he'd won. Corinne was grinning because it was fun. Because this was what counted as fun in her life. Being let out of the basement to play board games with Enoch Miller.

⌒

The next day was church. Enoch's family left in the station wagon. Bonnie was driving. Corinne's family waited outside for the Merediths' minivan.

When they got to the service, there weren't enough seats for their whole family in the back of the room, so Corinne had to go halfway up, by herself. Which meant she had to walk past half the congregation later when she got up to go to the bathroom. In her long gray skirt and her black sweater with the frayed wrists. (She folded the cuffs under so no one could see.) Enoch was in the aisle counting people. Frowning so you could tell he was serious. Or just frowning because that was his natural state.

He didn't raise an eyebrow when Corinne passed him, but a muscle just below his eye twitched. And Corinne knew it was for her, and that he was thinking about beating her at Monopoly. She lowered her eyebrows at him like he was making a scene.

He kept walking. Counting. Doing the Lord's work.

Corinne hid in the basement for fifteen minutes. Everyone she walked past on the way back to her seat would think she had colitis.

Enoch was onstage, reading, when she got back up.

Corinne didn't go the bathroom again. It wasn't worth it.

Chapter Nine

There wasn't space on the couch for Monopoly and Clue and Operation, plus some game from the fifties called Hūsker Dū. They'd commandeered the coffee table in the middle of the room, but Enoch complained about sitting on the floor. He dragged the table over to the couch, so he'd at least have something to lean against.

"*I can't sit on the floor,*" Corinne said in a dopey voice. "*I'm the man of the house.*"

"It's uncomfortable. I'm not built for this."

"*My legs are too long,*" she said. "*And my feet are too big, and my head is too heavy.*"

"Shut up."

"Enoch," Bonnie said reproachfully from the kitchen. None of them were supposed to say "shut up."

Corinne caught his eyes over the coffee table and made a shocked face, mouthing his name. "*Enoch.*"

He rolled his eyes at her.

They were setting up the game and agreeing on the terms for the night. They both wanted it to be as complicated as possible. Corinne wanted to include Mouse Trap, a 3-D game with plastic obstacles and a marble.

"Mouse Trap never works the way it's supposed to," Enoch argued.

"We'll factor that in," she said.

Enoch was still dressed up, from his Bible study at Shannon's house. He still smelled like aftershave. His hair was short, but longer than most men wore it at church. Like he was trying to balance out his off-kilter face. His big nose. His wide mouth, too big for his teeth. His tiny little brown eyes. (Actually his eyes were probably normal-sized; they just got lost in all the clatter.)

Corinne sat across the table from him, wearing jeans, which he shouldn't judge her for, because girls didn't actually *have* to wear dresses outside of church. Even though Corinne's mom had taken to wearing a dress or a skirt every day since they'd moved in with the Millers. And Corinne's sister always wore them now. Holly was trying to move up in the world. Her best friend, Jill, was from a good family, and she and Holly shared clothes—which just meant that Holly borrowed Jill's clothes, because Holly didn't have anything of her own worth lending. Sometimes Holly sat with Jill's family during church, her back straighter than usual, looking up all the scriptures and following along with the preacher.

Anyway. Corinne was wearing jeans tonight, with the same black sweater she always wore to church.

This sweater was the source of much consternation for some of the older brothers and sisters, the type who got all worked up over other people's church clothes. They'd give Corinne dirty looks and pull her aside to share 1 Timothy 2:9—but all that scripture really says is *women should be modest*. And Corinne's shapeless skirts and stretched-out sweaters were certainly that. She was like a big, baggy blob with a head attached. Like the blueberry girl in *Willy Wonka*. Nothing about Corinne was ever immodest or on display; that's not what bothered the church busybodies. What bothered them was that she wasn't *pretty*. That she wasn't even *trying* to be pretty.

"Fine," Enoch said, "go get Mouse Trap."

Their little brothers were already playing Nintendo. Enoch and Corinne had relinquished their rights to all future turns. This was more interesting. This thing they were building. There were game boards all over the coffee table and on an adjacent footstool. Corinne was the top hat, and Enoch was the horse and rider, and the rules were so elaborate that Enoch had to write them down. In his cramped handwriting. With his giant hands. There were freckles across his knuckles, but not on his cheeks. He wasn't really a redhead. He was just a brunette with red-haired tendencies. His hair was the color of watered-down Cherry Coke.

The game they'd worked out was basically Monopoly, with a dozen trapdoors into and out of other games. Corinne answered a trivia question correctly, then purchased Connecticut Avenue. Enoch successfully removed the funny bone, and then bought the Water Works.

It went on for hours because they'd designed it to be interesting, not to end. And they kept making it more complicated because they both thought it was funny to make it more complicated. And fun. It was so much fun. Corinne wasn't used to having fun. Her life wasn't designed to be fun. It was designed to be . . .

Godly, she supposed. That was the point of going to church three times a week, and studying for church all the other days—so that you didn't have time and space for anything else.

Enoch didn't say much while they were playing, but he'd never really been much of a talker. Even when they were kids.

Corinne wondered what he talked to his friends about. To Shannon Frank and the other teenagers in their literal circle, when they stood in the lobby after Sunday services.

People at school talked about TV and music and movies. But people at church weren't allowed to listen to much secular music, and most of what was on TV was off-limits, too. All there was to talk about was each other. Is that what Enoch's friends did in their circle, gossip?

Corinne's mom and Bonnie were gossiping in the kitchen right now—mostly about other people's kids. Adolescence was a spectator sport for the whole congregation. Who looked like they were stumbling? Who looked like they were falling away? Who might be cast out?

You *could* get cast out. For breaking the rules. For sinning and not being sorry enough. You could get cast out, and the elders would decide when you were allowed back. And nobody was allowed to talk to you in the meantime.

In some other kitchen, some other mothers were gossiping about

Corinne. With her ratty sweaters. And her nail polish. And her fifteen-minute bathroom breaks. (And they didn't even know about all the things Corinne said in her head. All the things she wasn't sure she believed in.)

No one, nowhere was gossiping about Enoch Miller.

He wasn't giving anyone anything interesting enough to gossip about—and besides, they were all rooting for him to cross the finish line.

Enoch Miller would make a fine elder someday. Kind, like his father. And smart. And with a real love for the Lord, you could tell.

He wouldn't be the sort of elder who'd make the Sunday service go a half hour long just to show that he could. He wouldn't corner other people's daughters and make them read 1 Timothy. Enoch Miller, sitting up front with his beautiful wife and a row of kids with cherry-flavored hair. Enoch Miller, watching out for the widows and the fatherless children.

"It's your turn, Corinne." Enoch was frowning. Because he always frowned. Because he always looked serious. Even playing the most ridiculous game of Monopoly known to God or man. Even when he was having fun.

Corinne moved her top hat around the board. She answered more trivia questions. She was foiled by Mouse Trap. (It never worked, but imagine how fun it would be if it did.)

Their moms went to bed, and their brothers played video games, and Corinne found herself humming along with the *Legend of Zelda* theme song. When it wasn't her turn, she lay back on the floor.

"Are you tired?" Enoch asked.

"No," she said from the floor. "Is it my turn?"

"No, but I need you for my turn. It's trivia."

She sat up, groaning.

"Does your *back* hurt?" Enoch sounded like he might laugh.

"I've been sitting on the floor for three hours!"

Enoch laughed. With his lips pressed together. With only his eyebrows and his chest moving. Like he'd get a ticket if someone caught him enjoying himself.

He scooted over. "Come lean on the couch. And stop making fun of me."

"Never," Corinne said. She crawled to the other side of the table. She had to squeeze to get behind it. She was fatter than he was.

"Careful," Enoch said, holding the table steady, so that the boards weren't upset.

Corinne settled down next to him and leaned back against the couch. It was such a relief.

Enoch pressed his lips together, and his chest shook.

Now that they were sitting next to each other, the game boards seemed like a control panel. Like they were sitting next to each other in a cockpit. Enoch's voice dropped even quieter, even deeper. So low. Like the sound of electricity running in a building. That hum you hear when you hold your breath.

Their game was still going at midnight. Corinne couldn't even tell who was winning. The grandfather clock went off, and the other kids kept playing Nintendo—they'd keep playing until Enoch told them to stop. Corinne was also going to keep playing until Enoch told her to stop.

At twelve fifteen, he sighed. "Find a save point, Japh."

Corinne looked at the table. "Should we call this a draw?"

"And start over next week?"

"If you want."

"It took forever to set up . . ." Enoch was frowning down at it all. "Let's just leave it, until next weekend."

"What if your mom needs her coffee table back?"

"Nobody needs a coffee table."

"It's kind of a mess . . ."

"My mom won't care. My dad was the one who needed everything to be perfect."

"Oh, wow, do you remember—" Corinne shook her head. "You probably wouldn't remember."

"The Jell-O?" Enoch was already laughing. With his eyebrows. And his lungs.

"No one told me!"

It had happened ten years ago, one of the first times Corinne had been to the Millers' house. They'd served Jell-O for dessert, and Corinne sat down on the couch with her bowl . . .

"How old were you?" Enoch asked.

"I was eight!"

Brother Miller saw Corinne sitting on the couch, and his kind face went *cold*. *"Corinne,"* he'd snapped, *"we don't eat Jell-O on the couch."*

"You just dropped it," Enoch said, laughing with his cheeks and even a little bit with the corners of his mouth. "An entire bowl of Jell-O."

"He told me I couldn't have it on the couch!"

"I don't think he meant for you to drop it."

"I know, but I was scared!"

"And then you started to cry . . ."

"Don't laugh at that," Corinne said, elbowing him. "That part's not funny."

"The whole thing's pretty funny now—it was pretty funny then, too. He was so mad at you . . . and then he felt so *bad*. He said you cried all the way home."

"You remember him saying that? It was so long ago . . ."

"He told the story a lot. As a lesson in controlling your temper. And sometimes as a lesson in perfectionism. And perspective. What's more important, keeping your new couch clean? Or making a new person feel welcome in God's family?"

Corinne was still mortified, ten years later, just thinking about that night. "Well, I'm glad I could be instructional."

"Don't be offended—Dad always made himself out to be the bad guy."

"He wasn't the bad guy." Corinne liked Enoch's dad. "He was just a man with standards and a very deep, scary voice."

Enoch nodded, agreeing. "He did have that. When I was really little, I thought he was the voice of Darth Vader."

Corinne laughed. "Why would you think that? Were you even allowed to watch *Star Wars*?"

"No! I still haven't seen it."

Corinne laughed even harder.

"But I remember hearing my dad say that the person who played Darth Vader wasn't the same person who voiced him. And my head kind of turned that into my dad being the one who voiced him."

"You thought your dad was James Earl Jones? Didn't you wonder why you weren't allowed to watch the movie?"

"I was four."

"When did you figure it out?"

"I don't even know, eventually . . . Before I told anyone, thank the Lord."

Corinne was still giggling.

Enoch tilted his head and looked over at her. "Have *you* seen *Star Wars?*"

She stopped giggling. *Star Wars* wasn't *officially* against the rules. But it was broadly *understood* to be against the rules. If Corinne said she'd seen it, it would be a black mark on her reputation. A gray mark, at the very least. But lying was probably worse . . .

"Yeah," she said. "All three movies. With my dad."

"Were they good?"

"I mean, obviously," Corinne said.

"Did they bother your conscience?"

That was the real question, that was the test. If something wasn't explicitly bad and against the rules, you had to trust your conscience to guide you. But what if your conscience *itself* was bad? Corinne's mom said that if you did sort-of bad things all the time, your con-science would acclimate. It would stop shouting at you to be careful.

So, if you watched *Star Wars,* and your conscience didn't bother you, maybe that meant the movie was okay—or maybe that meant you were corrupted beyond reckoning. Maybe you didn't feel any shame because you were *shameless.*

Star Wars didn't make Corinne feel bad. It made her feel great. She loved it.

"There's a lot of magic," she said.

Enoch was back to frowning. He nodded. He carefully pushed the coffee table away from himself, so he could stand up.

Then he held out his hand to Corinne.

She wasn't going to let him haul her up like a two-hundred-pound sack of potatoes. She got up on her own two feet.

"Save your game," Enoch said to Japheth, "and don't touch this stuff."

Corinne took Shawn down to the basement while Enoch was still waiting for Japheth to shut down the Nintendo.

The next morning, when she walked through the kitchen to the side door, their game was still set up in the living room. And it was still there on Monday afternoon, when Corinne came home from school. It stayed there all week. And when Saturday night came around, they had their family Bible study with the game boards taking up space in the middle of the room.

Other things happened that week, but nothing worth talking about. Nothing new. Corinne went to school and to church. She slept on the floor in a sleeping bag. She ate lunch with two worldly girls who talked about songs Corinne didn't know. Her mom got a call from her dad. (She took it in the basement, and Corinne and her siblings sat upstairs and had dinner with the Millers, so their mom could have some privacy. When she got off the phone, she looked like she'd been crying, and she stayed up late that night, talking to Bonnie.)

Other things happened that week and the next, and none of them mattered. Saturday nights were the only nights worth mentioning. Those were the only hours Corinne felt awake. Saturday nights with Enoch Miller across the table. And sometimes with Enoch Miller sitting next to her, leaning against the couch. Wearing aftershave he put on for somebody else. His voice like the noise the walls make when you're lying in bed, listening.

"You guys are really having fun," Corinne's mom said one Saturday night. She'd wandered into the living room to check on them. Corinne and Enoch were deep into a new version of their game, even more complicated than the last one. They'd incorporated Simon and Battleship. "Maybe all of you kids should play this," her mom said. "It looks a lot more interesting than those video games."

Corinne and Enoch looked up at her blankly. Shawn looked ready to cry. Japheth ignored her.

"Maybe next week," Corinne said. "We'd have to start over."

Her mom watched them play for a few more minutes, and Corinne honestly couldn't tell whether she was trying to give Corinne some sort of coded warning or whether she was trying to show a sincere interest. Every once in a while, her mom and Bonnie seemed to be deciding whether this was safe: the two of them, Corinne and Enoch, getting along so well. But hadn't their mothers been telling them to get along for ten years? And weren't they all family? And wasn't this nice? Wasn't it easier? It *was* nice, it was easy.

Don't ruin this, Corinne wanted to say. *It won't last forever, and it's all that I've got. And I know. I know, I know. Who I am. Who he is. The score.*

Her mom lingered over them, smiling, weighing, trying to show a sincere interest. But the game was impenetrable to outsiders, and eventually she wandered away.

Chapter Ten

Tonight during family study, Noah was messing with the Monopoly board, and Corinne's mom was letting him, and Enoch actually interrupted one of the scriptures to say, "Noah, please don't touch that." And the way that he said it was very *"We don't eat Jell-O on the couch."* And Noah started crying, and Bonnie frowned and said, "Enoch," like Enoch was just a kid and not the man of the house. And Enoch said, "I'm sorry, Mom. I'm sorry, Carolyn. Noah . . ." And Bonnie said, "You can hardly blame the child," and for a minute, Corinne thought that Bonnie was going to draw a line. A reasonable line. The games had taken over the room. Laid out in a way that only made sense to Enoch and Corinne. They'd taped a few of the boards together. They'd glued the Mouse Trap pieces, so they wouldn't fall apart—Enoch did it on a weeknight. And he'd brought down his dad's cribbage board. It was all a huge mess. It was like that scene in *Close Encounters* with the mashed potatoes, but with board games. Right in the middle of their Bible study. Corinne could tell it drove Bonnie crazy.

But Enoch did everything Bonnie asked him to. He was her rock. Especially since her husband died. Since he lost his father. And if he wanted to do this one thing—this strange thing that wasn't against any rules, that was made of only wholesome parts and pieces—she wasn't going to tell him no.

So she didn't.

After the Bible study, Corinne sat on one side of the coffee table, and Enoch sat on the other. And their moms sat in the kitchen drinking tea and eating popcorn, and their brothers played *Legend of Zelda*, and Enoch's older brother was in Arkansas starting a new church, and Corinne's little sister was across town, pretending to be someone else. And her dad was in California, and when he called, he didn't even ask to talk to her.

Corinne was winning, according to the score Enoch kept. She'd won the game once so far, and Enoch had won it once. But the game kept changing, and they hadn't discussed whether they were playing best of three or best of five, or just until they got bored. Or until Corinne moved out. Or Enoch married Shannon Frank.

Their moms went to bed at the usual time, and Bonnie didn't even mention wrapping up by midnight. A half hour after they left, Corinne did a few twists and stretches, like her back hurt. Her back might actually hurt, if she thought about it. Enoch pushed the coffee table out, carefully, so Corinne could sit next to him against the couch. She didn't say anything, and he didn't say anything, then she didn't say anything. She just sat down next to him and reached for the dice; they rolled them six at a time in Yahtzee cups.

"You got called out of study hall," Enoch said in his sitting-right-next-to-Corinne voice.

"Yeah."

He turned his head, just enough to give her a look—a *Don't make me ask another question, I was born with a limited number of questions, and when I get to heaven, St. Peter is going to judge me if I go over* look.

"It was nothing," Corinne said. "My counselor wanted to talk to me."

"Are you in trouble?"

"No."

He gave her another look. This one was a warning: *Don't make me give you another look.* But Corinne liked his looks. She liked it when he turned his head. She liked seeing both of his tiny brown eyes and both of his stern eyebrows; the entirety of his nose. She liked his whole messy face, which should have made her special. But it didn't. (That wasn't fair, was it, that Enoch could be ugly, and she couldn't. And also, additionally, that he could be ugly, and she could *like* it, and that it wouldn't mean anything to him . . . Because Enoch Miller could look any old way and still have anyone he wanted. He could have anyone.)

"Seriously, Corinne, are you in trouble?"

"No, why would I be in trouble?"

"I don't know," he said.

"My counselor wanted to talk to me."

"Why?"

"Because"—was she going to tell Enoch the truth? he would judge her for it, it was another black mark, a dark gray mark—"I took the ACT at my old school, and she wanted to talk to me about scholarships."

"You took the ACT?"

"Yeah."

His head was turned toward her. She could see both his eyes. Both his ears, peeking out from his wine-brown hair. "Why?"

"Because my counselor at my old school wanted me to." Guidance counselors cared a lot about convincing you to go to college. It was half their job, at least.

Enoch didn't say "Yeah, but"—but Corinne heard it anyway. *Yeah, but why would you take a college entrance exam if you're not going to college?*

"I didn't have to pay for it," she said, like that was an answer. She shook the cup of dice out onto a Candy Land board. "I just wanted to see how I'd do."

She moved her top hat, and two green Parcheesi pieces, and a little plastic car full of plastic pegs, from the Game of Life. She had to lean into Enoch's space to manage it.

Enoch was still turned her way. "So your counselor wanted to talk to you about scholarships?"

This had surely been a scenario during Thursday-night services. There was an ongoing series on Youth Needs:

> *Should I drink alcohol?*
> *Are violent video games dangerous?*
> *Will going to college affect my relationship with Jesus?*

Corinne knew what she was supposed to say next in this scenario, so she said it. And it wasn't hard, because it was true: "Yeah, but I told her that I wasn't going to college."

"What did she say to that?"

"She said, 'Are you sure?' And I said, 'Yes.'"

Enoch nodded. There wasn't anything more to say now. There was no corrective required—he didn't need to share a scripture with her. The scene could end.

"How'd you do?" he asked.

"Fine, I think. She didn't really push me on it."

"No, I mean—on the test."

"Oh." Corinne looked up, into his eyes. "Well," she whispered. "I did well."

Enoch twisted his mouth to one side. His lips were thicker and pinker than cute boys ever got away with. His face looked like one of those caricatures you could get done at Worlds of Fun. He was smiling at her. "I'm not surprised."

Corinne nodded. Then shook her head. "It doesn't matter."

"It's still nice to know," he said.

"It's your turn."

They played. Corinne leaned into Enoch's space to move her pieces. Enoch didn't have to lean into Corinne's space, his arms were so long. He was very good at Operation. Big, steady hands. She was very good at Simon. Good short-term memory. He thought it was funny when the blinking lights eventually got too fast for her to keep up. He laughed without ever opening his mouth. He laughed with his eyes, mostly. They both hummed along to *The Legend of Zelda*. It had kind of creepy music—they were working on lyrics. *"Zelda, my name is Zelda, I am a princess."* It drove Japheth crazy. Everything drove Japheth crazy, what a twerp. Corinne tried to remind herself that he'd lost his dad, but she wanted to remind *him* that he still had his own room and a Nintendo. (That wouldn't be kind, that wouldn't be loving.) It got late. It always got late. It always went too fast. Saturday night. Dinner at five thirty, and Bible study at six, and now it was almost midnight. And Corinne would keep playing 'til Enoch said they were done. Enoch so close to her, their elbows brushed. Their shoulders bumped. He laid his hand over Corinne's under the table.

Corinne stopped.

Everything.

The *Legend of Zelda* music was playing, and under that, the lights were buzzing, and under that, she wasn't breathing.

Enoch was looking at Candy Land.

His left hand was definitely still on top of Corinne's. His big hand. His sweaty palm. Corinne's palm was pressed into the carpet.

She looked down at Clue.

She could pull her hand away. It wasn't pinned. She wasn't pinned. He wasn't pinning her.

She could pull her hand away.

She lifted up two fingers.

Through his.

He didn't move. He didn't say anything. She didn't say anything. And then she didn't say anything.

Her smallest finger wrapped around one of his. And he didn't move. Their hands were under the table. No one could see. Corinne couldn't see.

Enoch picked up the Yahtzee cup with his right hand and rolled the dice.

It was almost midnight. They played until twelve fifteen.

Chapter Eleven

Corinne couldn't sleep.

She lay in the sleeping bag, with her head on one of the Millers' extra pillows. Was Corinne's pillow in Brother Fiala's garage? Had it made the cut? Were the rest of her clothes there? Her mom hadn't grabbed them all, to bring to the Millers'. She hadn't grabbed any of their books or toys or games. Maybe Brother Fiala had loaded that stuff up in the back of his truck. Probably he hadn't.

If Corinne was quiet, she could hear her mom snoring and Noah breathing, and Shawn sleeping on the other side of the room. If she drilled a hole through the ceiling, she'd be in the kitchen, and if she kept going, where would she be? She couldn't remember the layout of the bedrooms upstairs. She couldn't get a fix on where Enoch was. Was he asleep?

⁓

The next day was Sunday. Their game was still spread out in the living room. Corinne liked that. Liked seeing it there all week long. Proof that Saturday nights happened. A promise that Saturday night would happen again. The Millers drove to church in their station wagon, and Corinne's family got a ride with someone else.

Corinne sat in the very last row of the church. Enoch sat up front.

But he hardly sat. He had to walk up and down the aisles, taking attendance. He didn't look at Corinne, even when he was counting her. Up and down the aisle in his brown suit. And then onstage to do the Bible reading. In his low, musical voice. Like a song with only low notes. Corinne didn't get up to go to the bathroom even once.

After services, she didn't stand in the lobby with everyone else. With Enoch's circle. She stood outside on the porch and pretended it was her job to watch the parking lot.

Chapter Twelve

The next week passed, and it was even less worth mentioning than usual.

Corinne went to church, she went to school. She saw Enoch during study hall, in the cafeteria. Enoch used the time to do his homework. Because that's what you were supposed to do during study hall. Corinne used it to watch Enoch. She watched him hunch over his books, his hair falling into his eyes. Watched his wide shoulders. Watched for hints of his spine in the back of his polo shirt, signs of his shoulder blades moving. Watched the back of his neck. From a distance. From an angle. She could only see one ear. She held her own hands under the table.

And then, finally, Saturday came, and Corinne came up from the basement. Enoch was still at Shannon Frank's house. They ate pizza without him. They waited for him in the living room, and nobody touched the game boards. And then Enoch came in, still wearing his wool church coat. He was holding his Bible.

Corinne felt like there had been a thousand rubber bands wrapped too tight around her core, around whatever there was inside of her—her soul, maybe, and all her organs—and then Enoch walked in, and all of them snapped. All at once and one by one. He sat down, and Corinne was sure everyone in the room could hear her coming alive.

Rubber bands snapping. Ice cracking. She was wearing jeans and a ratty black sweater, and all her blood was in her cheeks.

Enoch led their Bible study. He let Corinne read. He asked all the boys questions they could answer. Shawn was staring at the Nintendo. Corinne wouldn't let herself look at the coffee table. Bonnie said closing prayer with a cloth napkin on her head, and then she and Corinne's mom went into the kitchen.

Corinne knelt on one side of the coffee table, and Enoch sat on the other, against the couch. He smelled like aftershave. Corinne's cheeks were flushed, she couldn't help it. She was alive. For now, for a few hours, even if he didn't touch her. Even if he never touched her again.

They focused on the game. It wasn't Monopoly with trapdoors anymore. It was a hero's journey through the game closet. Enoch conquered Mastermind, and Corinne kept Simon going for so long, she practically went into a trance. When she finally missed a color and looked up, Enoch was laughing so hard, his eyes had disappeared.

"Don't laugh at me," she said. "That was amazing."

"You looked like you were being possessed."

"Have you ever seen anyone last that long at Simon?"

"I've only played Simon with you, Corinne."

"I'm some sort of Simon savant."

"Like an idiot savant?"

"No, like . . ."

"A virtuoso."

"Yeah, I'm a Simon virtuoso."

"It's sad really."

"It's not sad. It's amazing."

"Of all the things to be good at."

"You're just jealous."

"It could have been piano . . ."

"So jealous."

". . . but it's Simon."

"All right, rein it in."

"'She's the best there is at Simon,' no one will say. Because no one plays Simon anymore."

"My hands are tingling," Corinne said.

"Because you were beating on it. I'm surprised you didn't break it."

"I can't control myself, I get lost in the pattern."

Enoch didn't stop smiling after that. With his eyes. With his lips pressed together, like he was trying not to.

Their moms went to bed. "Midnight," Bonnie said on the way upstairs.

And then Enoch pushed the coffee table out, carefully, and said, "Take a load off, Sally."

Corinne sat next to him.

There were a thousand rubber bands. Tightening. Snapping. All at once. One by one.

They kept playing.

She left her right hand on the carpet between them, her palm pressed into the carpet. She played with her left. And maybe he wouldn't touch her again, maybe he never would. This was still good. This was still the best part of every week. His face, his voice, this game that they'd built together for no reason other than it was fun and funny. (And it was.)

It was ten thirty, it was eleven. Japheth was playing *Zelda*. Shawn was watching him play. Corinne wasn't moving her arm. Not to roll or spin or move her top hat. It was eleven fifteen, and Enoch was stuck playing Mouse Trap, and it wasn't going well, and it was all Corinne's fault, she was the one who wanted it. "It never works how it's supposed to," he said, and laid his hand on top of hers.

He laid his hand on top of hers, and Corinne closed her eyes, she couldn't help it.

She turned her palm up and caught his fingers, and his hand closed like a vise around hers. His big hand. His sweaty palm. Corinne pressed her lips together, but it wasn't a smile.

Did they play after that? Who could say, Corinne was lost. The grandfather clock chimed. Enoch let go of her hand. Everyone went to bed.

Chapter Thirteen

Did she think about it? She thought about it once. That Enoch had spent that Saturday afternoon at Shannon Frank's house, and could have broken up with her then, if he wanted to. (God, even the thought was ridiculous.) He could have broken up with Shannon. After he touched Corinne. And before he touched Corinne again. He *could* have. (But it didn't bear considering. Because he didn't, he wouldn't. And Corinne knew it. She absolutely knew it. This was folly. This wouldn't take her anywhere good.) He could have, but he wouldn't, and Corinne didn't think about it again.

Chapter Fourteen

Shannon Frank was wearing a dress with pink roses at church on Sunday. And her shoes with pink bows. And a hat, because it was spring.

Who even wore hats? Girls in teen fashion magazines and girls at Corinne's church.

Shannon had dark brown hair and eyes that sparkled. She used to have braces, but they were off now. She and Juanita sat together, away from their parents, because they were practically grown.

Corinne watched the backs of their heads, from twenty rows behind them.

Chapter Fifteen

Another week, and none of it mattered.

Saturday night. Pepperoni pizza with black olives. Enoch Miller, walking in late, wearing date clothes. Galatians, Ephesians. Closing prayer. Ice cracking. The neighbors could probably hear it, how alive Corinne was.

She sat on one side of the coffee table, and Enoch sat on the other, and their knees bumped. His legs were so long that they stuck way out under the table. His white socks. His big, square feet.

"Zelda. My name is Zelda. I am a princess."

"Shut up, Enoch."

"Japheth!" from the other room.

"You rolled a twenty-two, Corinne."

"I rolled a twenty-four."

"Don't cheat."

"Is cheating even possible?"

The clock chimed ten, their moms were still drinking tea and crocheting.

The clock chimed eleven, and they were still deep in conversation in the kitchen. Noah was asleep on Corinne's mom's lap.

Corinne couldn't focus. Enoch rolled the dice without saying anything.

The clock chimed eleven thirty, which was excessive. It was excessive to chime forty-eight times a day.

"It's so late," Bonnie finally said. "I never stay up this late. We may as well all call it a night. Come on, boys."

Enoch didn't look at Corinne, and Corinne didn't look at Enoch, but she was screaming inside—*no, no, no!*—and she thought he might be screaming, too. She thought she might hear him screaming all night, two floors above her.

Chapter Sixteen

Saturday night.

Ten o'clock. Bonnie and Corinne's mom were already yawning.

Corinne was chewing on the neck of her sweater. Even though that was gross. Even though Enoch Miller was right there and would see.

He wasn't looking at her. He was looking at the game. Furiously. His jaw was so tight, the muscles kept jumping in his cheeks.

"Wrap up by midnight," Bonnie said, on her way to bed.

Enoch waited for his mom's last creaking footstep on the staircase.

Corinne listened to her own mother padding down the basement steps.

Then Enoch pushed the coffee table away, carefully, and Corinne dropped to the floor next to him, and he was already holding her hand. He was holding it so tight. Like two weeks was too long to go without touching her. (It was too long. It was eternal.) Enoch held her hand, and he pressed his face into her hair. Into her falling ponytail. And Corinne squeezed his thick fingers. Like she'd almost lost him. She *had* lost him. She'd lost a week of this, and her weeks were already numbered. His face was in her hair. Something was touching her ear, maybe his chin—but just for a second. And then he was looking down at Candy Land again. His cheeks were red. He held her hand under the table; he held her hand so tight, it actually hurt. It hurt.

Chapter Seventeen

The weeks passed, and the days mattered less than ever.

On Saturday nights, Enoch touched her.

He held her hand. Under the table. While their brothers looked the other way, and their mothers slept above and below.

They didn't look at each other.

They didn't say anything about it.

They kept playing.

They held hands. Tightly at first. And then less so, once they didn't have to be scared of the other person letting go. He circled her wrist with his long fingers. He stroked the inside of it, where her skin was thin. He laid his hand on her thigh. Once. For an hour. Corinne leaned against him. Against his square shoulders. His thick arms. Enoch Miller. *Enoch, Enoch, Enoch.* She was drunk on him. She'd never been drunk, but this must be how it felt. Like all the oxygen in her blood had been replaced with Enoch Miller. Like only Enoch Miller was available to her brain.

What did he get out of this?

It wasn't worth thinking about. It didn't matter. She'd take it. She took it. Every second of it.

Corinne had read that adrenaline makes time expand. That basketball players and fighter pilots experience time differently when they're under the gun. Like their brains start recording more frames per second. That's how hours holding Enoch's hand turned into days, into lifetimes. Like she walked into the fairy world with him and came back an hour later, an old woman.

That was all right. She'd waste her life like that. She'd throw it away. For an hour on the floor next to him. Clinging to him.

Japheth was about to beat *Legend of Zelda*. He and Shawn were constantly talking to the screen. "That was close." "There you go." "That wasn't fair!" They couldn't care less about Corinne and Enoch.

Enoch had pushed his left arm behind her back. His hand was on her waist. It was still under the table. No one could see. He was squeezing her. Petting her. It was getting harder to pretend it wasn't happening. Too many of her parts were in motion. She tried to roll the dice, but her body was moving, moving with him, and a few of the dice went clattering off the side of the table. Corinne decided to pretend it hadn't happened. She wasn't going to pull away from him. Who even cared. About dice. She clenched her hand on his thigh.

"Corinne," Enoch said, so low that only Corinne and possibly a seismograph could hear him.

When she turned her head, he kissed her.

Enoch Miller kissed her. With his fat lips. And his arm around her waist. Corinne couldn't even tell whether it felt good; she just wanted it. She wanted it. She'd throw everything away for it. She'd do it until he stopped—even though she didn't know what to do. Corinne hadn't even *seen* people kiss, she wasn't allowed to watch TV shows with kissing. (That ruled out almost everything. *Happy Days. Mork & Mindy. The Love Boat.*) Enoch pushed his mouth against hers, and it felt like he was eating her, so she ate him back. His lips were salty, hers were chapped. It stung.

"Yes!" Japheth hissed, and Enoch recoiled from her. He pulled his hand away so fast, his cuff got caught in her sweater. His face was bright red.

Japheth was still playing. Shawn was still watching the TV screen. Enoch and Corinne stared down at their game boards. Corinne couldn't remember whose turn it was. She couldn't remember what they were doing. Her hair had gone gray. She'd lived a lifetime, raised an army, been crowned a queen.

Chapter Eighteen

Corinne's mom talked about your conscience like it was something that would get stretched out if you used it too much. Like something you could ruin with wear.

Corinne waited for that to happen . . .

For it to stop feeling so bad, the knowledge of what she was doing with Enoch Miller. What she'd done.

Because she knew she wasn't going to *stop* touching him.

As bad as it felt, it still felt more good.

It *couldn't* feel more bad than it felt good—it wasn't possible. That's how good touching Enoch felt.

Chapter Nineteen

It was Saturday night, and he hadn't kissed her again. He probably never would. That had been a stupid risk.

Corinne still sat next to him.

He still held her hand.

That should be enough. It had been more than enough, before. Almost more than she could process. But now she knew about his mouth. (Did he kiss Shannon Frank with that mouth? Corinne didn't actually care. What did that say about her?) (About Corinne, not Shannon.)

At eleven forty-five, Enoch let go of her hand.

"Find a save point," he said.

"We've still got fifteen minutes!" Japheth argued.

Corinne wanted to say the same thing.

Enoch was already standing up. "We're going to clean up the kitchen, so Mom doesn't have to do it in the morning."

Japheth moaned. He was *such* a twerp.

"I'll give you a choice," Enoch said. "You can help me, or you can go to bed."

Japheth threw down the controller and stomped upstairs.

"I'll help," Corinne said.

"Does that mean I have to?" Shawn asked. He was only half a twerp.

"No," she said.

He disappeared down the steps. Corinne rounded up the popcorn bowls and the water glasses. Enoch washed them in the sink, without filling it up. Corinne dried.

When they were done, he took hold of her wrist and pulled her into a corner of the kitchen that you couldn't see from the living room. He reached one long arm out to turn off the lights.

Time expanded. Corinne stood there a year, at least, just knowing he was going to kiss her. He did. It was different, leaning against the wall. He was so much taller than her, he had to hunch over. His big hands were on her sides. She put her arms around his neck. It was dark and quiet. The refrigerator was whirring. Enoch was breathing hard through his nose. Because of her. No matter what else was happening, she was making it hard for Enoch Miller to breathe. She'd take it, she'd take whatever he gave her. It felt so good, even though it was all just pushing, really. Pushing felt good. Corinne didn't hold back, why should she. She was going to push right through him. The clock struck midnight, and they ignored it. Enoch kissed her so hard, her head pressed back into the wall. It hurt, and she didn't care. Her shoulder knocked a coupon envelope onto the floor. Enoch pushed his whole body against her. It didn't fit. She was wider, but he was taller. There wasn't enough of Corinne to take him, but she tried. She pulled on his neck and his shoulders. He smelled like aftershave and popcorn seasoning and like his deodorant had stopped working. His hair was smoother than she was expecting. It wasn't like hers. He wasn't like her. She didn't understand how he worked. She didn't care—she'd take it.

The clock didn't chime again, but Enoch stepped away from her as if it had. Corinne was glad it was dark. She felt wrecked, worse than usual. Ruined. She was panting like a wild-eyed dog.

Enoch rubbed the back of his hand against his mouth. He was panting, too. The porch light was on, and it shined in his eyes. He took another step back. He left Corinne in the kitchen.

She didn't stay. She went downstairs.

Chapter Twenty

It was almost impressive, the way Enoch didn't look at her.

As much as Corinne needed to look at him, that's how much he needed to look away. At church, at school. He never turned. He never lingered. He must not know her, the way she knew him.

Corinne *studied* him. Nothing about him wasn't interesting. Wasn't exciting. Wasn't something to pack away in the base of her throat and the pit of her stomach. That's where he lived. That's where she thought of him. Enoch must not know her as well. The back of her neck, the set of her hips. The way she moved and leaned and yawned. He couldn't know her. Like she knew him. He didn't look at her when he was touching her, and he didn't look at her in between.

He probably felt guilty.

Corinne felt guilty, too.

But she felt everything else more.

Chapter Twenty-one

It was Wednesday afternoon. Which only distinguished itself by being closer to the next Saturday than it was to the last one. Corinne used to love Wednesdays, because Wednesday was one of the only days with no built-in church. But now that meant less built-in Enoch. She'd exhausted herself today, staring at him during study hall. Watching him so hard, she felt a little sick from it. Like he was a glass of water she drank too fast.

Corinne was walking out of school with a friend. Not a real friend—a school friend. Lisa. The worldly girl who she walked partway home with, most days. But when Corinne walked out today, Enoch was waiting for her by the flagpole. Watching for her. He met her eyes, from across the courtyard. Time slowed down. It stopped.

"I'm getting a ride home," Corinne said, and the other girl waved and walked away.

Enoch Miller was waiting for Corinne. He probably wanted to talk to her—she knew what he was going to say, she'd been waiting for it, since the first time he touched her. He was going to tell her why they had to stop. He didn't even have to say it. Corinne already knew. All the reasons, every one. She didn't need the corrective, the scriptures. There were so many scriptures. They'd be here all day, with their Bibles open, if they were going to cover *resisting temptation* and *keeping yourself clean for the Lord.*

How could Corinne skip this next part? Maybe she could just shout at him. *First Corinthians six-eighteen! Matthew five-twenty-eight! I know! I knew all along, and I don't regret it!* She could shout that from here. *I don't regret it! But I know, and you don't have to say it. Don't say it, Enoch.*

She met him under the flag.

"We got back from Construction early," Enoch said. "I thought I'd wait for you."

Corinne nodded.

He looked over her head. "You normally walk home with Lisa?"

"Yeah. Do you know her?"

"Not really. We've been in school together since kindergarten. But . . . you know."

"She's all right," Corinne said. "It's better than walking alone." *Romans, chapter thirteen,* she thought, *verses thirteen and fourteen. I know.*

Enoch started walking, his backpack over one shoulder, his hands deep in his jeans pockets. His jeans were the wrong color of blue. He looked like his mom shopped for him, she probably did, and he didn't seem to care.

"Do you get graded for Construction?" Corinne asked.

"It's more of a pass-fail situation."

"And you're building a house?"

"Yeah, for a charity."

"I don't think I'd want to live in a house built by high school students . . ."

"We have supervision."

"Yeah but you're doing the wiring? I wouldn't want a high school guy doing my wiring . . . All jacked up on whip-its and listening to Mötley Crüe. That's a fire hazard."

Enoch was frowning. "I only get to do the preliminary stuff. It's a lot of running around, carrying equipment for the licensed electricians . . ."

"I guess that makes it a little more reassuring."

". . . but you're already living in a house wired by a high school student. My dad let me hook up most of the basement when we redid it."

"That doesn't seem legal."

He rolled his eyes. "File a complaint."

Corinne looked up at him. It felt safe to look up at him, if he was never going to look back. "Do you have to go to more school? To be an electrician?"

"No. It's all work experience. I've already got a job—with Brother Williams—when I graduate."

"That's nice," Corinne said. It was nice. For Enoch. To have everything all lined up.

He turned at the corner. They were supposed to go straight. Corinne followed him. They were walking between two hills. In the low point. There was a little park here. Hardly a park—a clearing, tucked into some trees. With a merry-go-round. And some broken swings. A tornado slide.

Enoch took her hand.

He pulled her into the park, across it, over to the slide. He started climbing the metal stairs.

"You're too big for that," she said.

"Come up," Enoch said in his *I'm sitting right next to you* voice. But he wasn't sitting next to her. He was up at the top of the slide. She followed him. There was a platform at the top, with metal walls to keep kids from falling off while they were climbing into the tunnel. Enoch sat backwards on the platform. There wasn't really room for Corinne anywhere. Maybe beside him. Maybe standing on the steps between his thighs. She got to the top, and he pulled her down, half on the platform next to him, half in his lap. "Corinne," he said, and kissed her.

It was awkward. She felt like she was crushing him. And like she was going to fall. Enoch held her waist even tighter than usual. She held on to his neck like he was carrying her. He kissed her, and she still wasn't sure whether it felt good (it was just pushing), but she wanted it. She hugged him so tight, the back of her T-shirt pulled up. His arms touched her back, and he groaned. He spread out his hands. He was touching her skin, and she wanted it. His big, square hands. His thick fingers. She leaned into him, and he fell back against the tornado part of the slide. His head hit the roof. He groaned again, but it was because of her, not the pain; she knew it. He touched her back. Her bra strap. She pushed into his mouth, nodding her head yes. She knew she wasn't good at this, she knew she didn't know how to do it—but she'd let him have what he wanted. She'd take it, she'd take it, she wanted it.

Enoch broke their kiss to breathe hard on her neck. To kiss her there. She held on to him. He rubbed his face in her shoulder, like he'd just realized he could. He could. He was rocking her against him, against the metal wall. The slide creaked. Her legs slid out of his lap, and he caught them. "Corinne." He kept kissing her, and catching her, and keeping them both from falling too far forward or too far back.

Then there were kids there.

The elementary schools got out forty-five minutes later than the high schools.

There were kids shouting and making noises on the swings.

Enoch pulled his head away and let it rest back, against the roof of the slide. There were patches of red on his cheeks. His mouth looked more swollen than ever. His hair hung in his eyes. Corinne soaked it in. She packed it away.

"Do you want to go down the slide?" he asked. Quietly.

"No," Corinne whispered. "I'll get stuck."

"You won't get stuck."

She sat up and used the wall to climb off of him. She reached one leg down to the steps. Enoch held her steady. She walked down backwards. There were kids on the merry-go-round and the swings. Shawn would never come to this park—he'd go straight home.

"Are you coming?" she called up to Enoch.

"You go ahead."

Corinne nodded. He was already looking away from her. He'd hardly looked at her, this whole time. Did Enoch even know what she looked like?

It was just as well . . . Corinne was a mess. Her ponytail was hanging, tangled, at the bottom of her neck. She felt flushed and sweaty, and her underwear were slick. There were scriptures about this. About being defiled. Letting yourself be defiled. About letting the fire burn in you and feeding it. Apostle Paul had a lot to say about it. He'd put it in all of his letters. *"Do you not know that your bodies are members of Christ?"* Corinne knew, she knew.

She got home before Enoch. She went down to the basement and stayed there. She slept in his brother's sleeping bag and listened to the electricity humming in the walls, and knew that Enoch had put it there.

Chapter Twenty-two

They were running out of Saturday nights.

The semester was almost over. Corinne's mom had found a house in their old neighborhood, with three bedrooms. The girls would share a room, and the boys would share a room. Brother Fiala still had their beds in his garage. They just had to wait a month, and then they could move in. Then they could move out.

"You don't have to help me with the dishes," Enoch told Japheth. "You can go to bed."

"I'll help," Corinne said.

He kissed her against the wall. Against the refrigerator. The magnets got caught in her hair. His hands were wet from the sink. Wet on her back. On her stomach. One palm, damp over her breast, while he pressed her head into the wall and groaned into her mouth. *Enoch, Enoch, Enoch.* His pale skin and mahogany hair. His big nose in her cheek. In her neck. In her ear. The clock chimed, and he pushed his body into hers, and she tried to make room for it, to be enough for it, every square inch of him. He was built like a wall. Out of bricks. He was big and heavy and stronger than she was, and she wanted it.

Enoch was always the first one to pull away. To leave her in the kitchen.

She kept hoping that he'd find her other places. That he'd show up at the flagpole again. That he'd stop her on the stairs to the church basement. Not even to kiss. Just to be alone. *"What are you doing down here, Corinne?"* She'd linger there, waiting for him, bouncing on her toes on the edge of a step. He didn't come.

It was Saturday evening, and Corinne's blood was singing. She was ready, she was already holding her Bible and sitting on the stairs, waiting for the rest of her family.

"I wish you'd make an effort with yourself," her mom said.

"What do you mean?" Corinne had brushed her hair and redone her ponytail and glossed her lips with Carmex.

"The Millers all dress nice for Bible study." She was right, they did. Bonnie wore a dress (Bonnie always wore a dress), and the boys wore cotton pants or their nicest jeans, with collared shirts. "It's a way of showing respect."

Corinne was wearing threadbare jeans and her black sweater. She'd chewed a hole at the neck. "I can change if you want," she said.

"Put on a skirt," her mom said. "It doesn't have to be fancy."

Corinne didn't own anything fancy. She put on a long gray skirt and didn't bother with tights. She put her black flats on without socks. There was a mirror in the laundry room, and Corinne looked at herself. Her clothes hung on her, they hid her. Her skirt came to her ankles. You couldn't say she wasn't modest. She tightened her ponytail. There was nothing she could do about her body, nothing she could do about her face. She hadn't worn nail polish since they'd moved into the Millers' house. She didn't have any.

She walked out of the bathroom. "Better?"

Her mom smiled at her. "Thank you. Jesus notices." Jesus noticed everything. He was always watching, and when He couldn't, He had His angels watching. There was probably an angel assigned to every one of us, her mom said. *"You're never alone."* If God kept track of the little sparrows, He wasn't going to lose track of Corinne. Especially when she was flouting Him so boldly.

When they went upstairs, the pizzas were already there. Enoch had stopped to pick them up. He was home. Early. Corinne wasn't used to seeing him at dinner, to watching him eat. His big hands. His fat lips. His tongue. He was wearing a new shirt. Dark green, long sleeves, button-down collar. It looked like it came from JCPenney. He looked cheap. His jeans were too dark, his waist was too thick. That green shirt made his hair look like a campfire, like every shade of red and brown. It made his skin glow pink. Corinne drank it in. She made herself sick off him. Her belly felt too full. He was rising up the back of her throat. *Enoch Miller. Enoch Miller. Enoch Miller.*

They had their Bible study. They played their game. Enoch had stopped keeping score—there was no way to win. They rolled the dice and asked each other questions. They made each other jump through hoops. They teased each other. They laughed with their mouths closed and open. At ten thirty, Corinne moved over to Enoch's side of the table. He rubbed her thigh through her skirt. She leaned against him, she knew she was allowed to—she knew he wanted to touch her now. That's what Saturday nights meant, what they were for. "It's time to find a save point," Enoch said, and Japheth grumbled, and Shawn slipped downstairs, and Enoch turned off the lights. But he didn't pull her into the kitchen—he pulled her onto the couch instead. "Corinne," he said, so low she almost didn't hear him.

They'd never kissed somewhere this easy. Somewhere made for kissing. Everywhere Enoch pushed her, it was soft. She held on to the back of his head. She held his ears. She was allowed to do it. He wanted it, and she wanted it. He couldn't stop touching her skirt, sliding the fabric against her thighs. The couch was against the wall, directly across from the staircase. There was a light built into the grandfather clock. It wasn't dark, they weren't hidden. Corinne could imagine how they would look from the stairs. Or from the kitchen. But she didn't stop, she never would. Enoch pushed her skirt up her legs. He was leaning on her, flattening her against the arm of the sofa. It wasn't comfortable, but she wanted it. She kissed him the way she always did. Like someone trying to eat him. Like someone saying yes. He slid his hand up her skirt, and she loved it. She loved it. She hadn't shaved her legs in four months. She didn't have a razor. Enoch didn't seem to care, he didn't seem to notice. He was squeezing her thigh. His other hand was grinding into her chest. It was all just pushing, it was always pushing. He pushed her thigh up, so he could squeeze the back of it. He sank between her legs. She rocked underneath him, she couldn't help it—and she might as well, the couch didn't creak. They'd stopped kissing, they'd forgotten how, they'd never known. "Corinne," Enoch whispered in her hair. "Can I?"

Corinne nodded. He could. Whatever it was, he could. (She knew what it was, and she wanted it.) He pressed his face into her shoulder, and leveraged his hips up, reaching down to do something that Corinne couldn't see. She pulled one leg out of her underwear. It wasn't pretty. She was still wearing shoes. Enoch fell on top of her, jammed his mouth onto hers. Corinne didn't know what her job was, what her part was in this. She tried to make room, to be open. She wanted it. She ached for it. For something. All she could imagine was making a fist and rocking into it. She couldn't picture Enoch . . . there. She'd never seen him, never seen any man. And his body was too big, too blocky; she couldn't see past his shoulders. She could feel his pants open between her legs. She could feel something warm. That must be it. Or maybe that was his hand. Time must be slowing down now. There were more frames per second. Something went into her. It was easy, she was wet. She waited for it to change her. To change everything. Enoch was in her. Something was. It pinched for a second, and then it felt full. And then it really didn't feel like much of anything. She'd wanted him so much, was this what she wanted? Was this what the ache was for? It didn't feel like anything, but she still wanted it. It didn't feel like anything, but she didn't want him to stop. It didn't feel like anything, and she didn't regret it. Enoch was whispering her name. His eyes were closed, his eyebrows were high. He was making a face she'd never seen before, like he was drunk on her. Like she was in his blood instead of oxygen. *"Corinne."*

It was over.

She thought it was over.

Enoch's eyes were closed in the regular way. He was catching his breath. He sat up, off of her, and fastened his pants before she could see. He held his hand out to her, and she took it. She let him pull her up. Enoch wiped his hands on his knees. He was staring at his lap. Corinne closed her legs. The grandfather clock chimed, it was only midnight.

"We should . . ." Enoch said.
He stood up.
He went upstairs.
Without doing the dishes.

Chapter Twenty-three

Corinne couldn't take a shower, not at midnight.

She sat on the toilet, and let him run out of her. She wiped herself mostly dry. It smelled so strong . . . Her mom would smell it. She washed her hands and her face. She rinsed the spots out of her skirt.

Chapter Twenty-four

The next day was Sunday. Corinne sat in the last row of the church. Enoch Miller stood onstage in his gray suit and read the Bible into the microphone. Letters to the Thessalonians. Corinne had always loved the word "Thessalonians." Enoch Miller said it like a little song.

When he wasn't reading, he looked out into the audience, and Corinne felt like he was looking right at her—but she knew that he wasn't, because he never did.

Corinne sat in the back row. She was different now. She was something new. Something she hadn't been last week. Marked in gray and black. She knew things she couldn't un-know, and it didn't seem fair, because she still didn't know anything at all.

Chapter Twenty-five

On Monday morning, Corinne walked through the Millers' kitchen on her way to the back door. She glanced into the living room.

Their game was gone.

Every board.

Someone had put them away.

~

On Monday morning, Enoch wasn't in study hall.

~

On Monday afternoon, Corinne detached from the world. From the ground. From time. She was a dead thing. A dead thing floating. There wouldn't be another Saturday night, and none of the other days mattered. None of the other hours. She'd crossed into the fairy world too many times, and she'd lost the hang of this one. She couldn't breathe this air. Or maybe she didn't want to. The air on the other side was golden. The hours there were decades. Corinne had lived a dozen lifetimes by Enoch Miller's side.

And now she was something different. A dead thing. A dead thing floating.

～

On Monday afternoon, Corinne's mother was waiting for her by the flagpole. "I've got a ride home," Corinne told Lisa. She walked over to her mother and stood in front of her.

Her mother slapped her.

Corinne took it.

2005

Chapter Twenty-six

Corinne stirred the gravy. She wasn't good at it. But it helped to have a job—when everyone was packed into her mom's kitchen, and the rest of them were so easy there. So at ease. Corinne's mom finishing the mashed potatoes, and Holly fussing with her lemon bars, and Holly's kids chasing the dog in and out, and her husband, Isaac, yelling at them from the living room. Noah at the kitchen table, eating black olives. His wife, Mercy, rubbing her pregnant belly. All of the wives, all of the husbands. Corinne's stepdad and his kids. All of their kids. They all belonged here, were allowed here, in a way that Corinne wasn't.

Corinne was here conditionally—and even that was a recent development. She'd been back in Kansas for almost a year now, but she still wasn't a regular at these Sunday dinners. She was easing back in, letting them get used to her.

The first time her mom had invited Corinne back for Christmas, Holly had been so offended by the idea, she and her family had refused to attend. But Corinne had come home anyway—she'd flown in from Boston—and it had been fine. Nobody's crosses had started burning. She hadn't tricked anyone into drinking alcohol or watching R-rated movies. She hadn't talked about anything that might upset them. Nothing from her worldly life. It wasn't hard. Corinne's life wasn't that sinful. It wasn't hard to act like one of them, because she'd *been* one of them for so long. She could pin up her hair and put on a dress—it was worth it, all of these small things, to be near them. She missed them. She wanted to know them. And it was okay if they didn't really want to know her. This was progress. This: Corinne in the kitchen, standing next to her mom. Corinne's nephews opening gifts she'd brought for them. *"Thank you, Aunt Corinne."*

"Aunt Corinne" was progress. She was grateful for it, she'd take it.

Her mom was telling a story about Holly's son giving his first presentation at church, and Corinne was smiling and stirring the gravy with a fork. Her sister kept interrupting with corrections. Holly was fully transformed now: She was exactly who she'd wanted to be at fourteen. Corinne was impressed. In awe, really. Corinne hadn't known at fourteen who she wanted to be, but it surely wasn't this, who Corinne was now, at thirty-one. Holly was a Christian wife and a Christian mother. She'd won the prize, and Corinne was happy for her. That was weird, but it was also true—Corinne was happy for her.

Holly was *not* happy for Corinne. She still couldn't quite look at Corinne, and she wouldn't speak to her directly. Corinne was still cast out of the church. Officially. It wasn't the sort of thing that expired. Their mom had chosen to speak to Corinne—she said it was a conscience matter—but Holly had a conscience like a steel trap.

That was okay. Corinne understood. It was Corinne's job to understand. To accept it all. If she wanted to be here. Holly wasn't talking to Corinne now, but their mom was telling Corinne a story, and Holly was correcting it, and that was *so close* to talking. That was progress.

The front door opened.

Corinne didn't hear it, but she felt the draft roll in from the living room. Then she heard her brother Shawn's voice. And all the men in the living room greeting him. A second later, Shawn's wife, Alicia, was gliding into the kitchen, still wearing her church clothes and holding a cake pan. Corinne loved Alicia—she *loved* her. Alicia grew up three hours away, she hadn't known Corinne before. She just treated Corinne like another person. Alicia grinned when she saw Corinne standing at the stove. "Hey, you! We didn't know you were coming! This is the best surprise!" She was already hugging Corinne, and Corinne was hugging her back. With one hand. Stirring the gravy with the other.

"That looks good," Corinne said. "What'd you make?"

"It's Snickers cake," Alicia said. "Have you had it?"

Corinne shook her head.

"It's so good. And so easy—you could make it. It's just boxed cake and Snickers bars and chopped apples and whipped topping, not whipped cream. Shawn and I are doing Atkins, but we're cheating. We cheat on weekends"—she giggled—"which is probably why I haven't lost any weight."

Corinne could hear Shawn laughing in the living room. Shawn had welcomed her back into the family right away. At worst, he seemed to feel really sorry for Corinne, like he pitied her—but he was never judgmental or cold. She appreciated it. Shawn was out there talking about the football game. With Corinne's stepdad. And someone else. Someone whose voice was too deep to make out.

Time stopped a little bit. It slowed down.

That happened sometimes, still. False alarms. Flashbacks. It was worse when she was around her family. Too many memories. Too much context. Too much of her own context. It would be all right. It would pass.

The man in the living room rumbled.

Corinne's stomach hurt; she wanted this to pass. "Did someone else come in with you?" she asked Alicia.

"Oh, Enoch Miller," Alicia said. "Do you remember him from the congregation?" She leaned in close to Corinne and dropped her voice: "Shawn's taken him under his wing. He's had such a hard time since his divorce."

Corinne's mom had stopped mashing the potatoes.

Holly was staring at Corinne, not saying anything.

Shawn came into the kitchen, and his eyes lit up when he saw Corinne—but then his face fell.

Enoch Miller was right behind him. In Corinne's mother's kitchen. Ducking a little bit to get through the doorway. Enoch Miller, looking just like himself, but more so. Had anyone ever been so thick and so square, anyone ever? Enoch Miller. With his big nose and his Cherry Coke hair. In her mother's kitchen. Corinne drank it in for a second. Stashed it in her throat and her stomach. Enoch wore eyeglasses now. And clothes that fit. Jeans that were just the right shade of blue.

He was smiling a little, still looking serious, but smiling like he was happy to be there, like he was allowed, he was welcome.

He stopped when he saw Corinne.

His smile stopped. Time stopped.

He didn't say anything. And she didn't say anything. And then she didn't say anything.

She'd never practiced for this scenario.

"Corinne!" her mom said, grabbing the fork. The gravy was bubbling—it was smoking, it would taste scorched.

"I—" She looked at her mom, who was frantically trying to save the gravy. "I'm sorry. I was just, um—"

Corinne smiled at Alicia and stepped away from the stove, toward the door, toward Enoch, who was standing in front of it. He staggered back, and she passed him. She didn't look at him. Her purse was by the front door. Her jacket was in the bedroom, she didn't need it.

"Aunt Corinne, are you leaving?"

"I'm just—I forgot something." She opened the door. She was careful not to let the dog out. She'd just—

She hurried down the steps, down the sidewalk. There were so many cars parked in the driveway. Hers was on the street. She'd just—

"Corinne!"

It was Enoch's voice, and it hit her in the back like a gunshot. She imagined her body staggering with the blow.

"Wait!" He was closer now.

Corinne was at her car. Enoch Miller was walking toward her.

"I'm sorry," he said. "I didn't know you'd be here."

She shook her head. She unlocked her car.

"You don't have to go," he said. "I'm leaving."

"You don't have to leave, Enoch."

"It's your family, I'll go. I'm sorry. I didn't know—"

Corinne just nodded, looking at herself in her car window. She was making a face like a cartoon dog. With her bottom lip pushed up and her mouth turned down, and her chin trembling.

"I'm going," Enoch Miller said.

"Okay," she said.

"I'm really sorry."

"It's fine."

She heard him walking away then, and turned to watch. Because she'd never been strong. Never once. Enoch was parked on the street, too. He had a big pickup truck, they all did. He was walking away from her. He was walking away—

He stopped in the middle of the street and turned around. "Corinne?"

He took a step back toward her.

Corinne tried to close her car door. Even though she was standing inside of it. She closed it over herself like a shield.

"Could we talk?" Enoch asked.

"Now?"

"No, I mean . . ." He shook his head. "No. Just, sometime?"

"Why?"

Enoch shook his head again, like he didn't know. Like it hurt him to think about. "I guess I . . . I'd just like to talk to you."

"You don't owe me anything, Enoch." *Enoch, Enoch, Enoch.*

He was standing in the middle of the street. Like a wall. An even bigger wall than before. Like someone had built a wall right there, right in the street. "I don't think that's true," he said.

"I say it's true."

"Corinne . . . please? Could we talk sometime?"

"No," she said. "I don't think so."

He started walking again. Toward her. She crushed her hips in the door. He was reaching into his pocket, taking out a leather wallet. He held a card out to her. A business card. Enoch Miller was handing her a business card. "You can throw this away." He swallowed. "But maybe . . ."

She didn't take it.

He set the card on the roof of her car.

Corinne didn't look up again until he was walking away. She watched him get into his truck. Watched him leave.

She could leave, too. It would be easier than going back in and facing them all. All of them looking at her and thinking about what she'd done. (Not tonight. Before.) But Corinne had come so far . . . She'd worked so hard, just to be here.

"Corinne?" Her mother was standing on the porch. "Dinner's ready!"

Corinne took the card from the roof of her car and went back into her mother's house.

Chapter Twenty-seven

Miller Electric.

It was what his dad's business had been called. It was the same logo, with the little lightning bolt. It used to be painted on the side of Brother Miller's truck.

Miller Electric. Enoch Miller.

Corinne set the card on her bedside table.

She'd gotten through dinner at her mom's house.

When she'd gone back inside, all the men in the living room had acted very interested in the television. Alicia was crying in the kitchen. Holly was patting her back. When Corinne walked in, Alicia ran to her. "I'm so sorry, I didn't know."

It's okay, Corinne thought, *you aren't the one who slept with him.*

"It isn't your fault," Holly told Alicia, obviously thinking the same thing.

"It's all right," Corinne lied. "It's not a big deal."

Later, Shawn caught her in the hallway and apologized. "I'm so sorry, Corinne. I didn't know you were coming."

"I didn't know you were friends with him," Corinne said. She didn't think that any of the Millers spoke to anyone in her family.

"He changed congregations after his wife left him," Shawn said, like he was defending himself. "He's had a real rough time."

"Alicia said."

"He had to give up his place as an elder."

"Shawn, it's okay. I'm not mad at you for being friends."

Shawn looked down. "Well. Maybe you should be."

Corinne stayed until after dinner. She listened to their stories, she laughed at their jokes. Then she went back to her apartment. She took a shower, she got into bed. She held the card in both hands. *Miller Electric. Enoch Miller.*

Enoch Miller had had a real rough time.

Well.

So what.

So had Corinne.

Chapter Twenty-eight

The last time that Corinne had seen Enoch Miller was at her elders' meeting. Their elders' meetings had been scheduled back-to-back. (That was convenient. For the elders.) Enoch was coming up the church basement steps with his mother. Corinne was waiting in the lobby with hers.

None of them spoke to each other. Bonnie was crying. Enoch looked beaten. He must have apologized so much and so well. He must have humbled himself. The elders must have looked in his eyes and seen true repentance.

Corinne apologized in her meeting, too. She said she was sorry and meant it. She *was* sorry. She knew what she'd done was wrong. A sin. And beyond a sin, a mistake. But they'd looked in her eyes, and they'd seen the truth: that she'd do it again. That she didn't regret it.

Once Corinne was cast out, she didn't want to do the work of crawling back in. There was nothing for her out in the world, but there was even less for her in the congregation.

She went to college instead.

The last time Corinne had seen Enoch Miller, he was walking past her, looking beaten, and he hadn't looked up. He'd told everyone what they'd done together. He'd confessed it. Without warning her. He'd laid himself low and told them everything. Maybe he got a plea bargain, for turning witness for the state.

The last time Corinne had seen him was the worst she'd ever felt. Ever, in that whole terrible year.

His business card sat on her table.

"You don't owe me anything," Corinne had said. But what she meant was, *I don't owe you anything.*

She didn't owe him this.

Chapter Twenty-nine

"Miller Electric, this is Enoch."

"It's Corinne."

"Corinne?"

"Yeah."

"Hey. Just a second. Just a second, okay?"

"Yeah."

It was loud behind him. Corinne imagined him building a house with high school students. She heard a door open and close.

"Corinne? You still there?"

"Yeah, I'm here."

"Hey. You called."

"Well, you said you wanted to talk."

"Yeah . . . yeah, I do. Do *you* want to talk?"

Did she want to talk? "I guess . . . I want to hear what you have to say."

"I'm not very good on the phone."

"Enoch, you asked me to call you."

"No, I mean—could we talk in person?"

"Um . . ." Jesus. Jesus *Christ*. "Sure. If that's what you want. Do you want that?"

"I could meet after work. Do you work?"

"I do. Where do you want to meet?"

"Oh, um . . . I guess I don't know, um . . ."

This might be the end of it. There was nowhere Enoch Miller could meet with her that would be appropriate. Men and women didn't meet without chaperones. And Christian men didn't meet with women who had been cast out, not for any reason. Never mind their history. Never mind it; Corinne tried not to.

This was stupid. It was ridiculous.

Corinne didn't want to talk to someone who considered talking to her a sin. (Not someone outside of her immediate family.)

Enoch Miller was short-circuiting on the other side of the phone line . . . He'd probably have to have an elders' meeting just to confess to giving Corinne his card.

Corinne wouldn't have to go this time.

They couldn't throw her out twice.

Corinne talked to men. Regularly. She met them for lunch and for drinks. Usually for work. She could talk to a man without confessing. Without praying over it. Without laying herself low.

"Do you like Village Inn?" Enoch asked.

"Do I *like* it?"

"Do you know where it is?"

"Yeah . . ."

"I could meet you there by six," he said.

"Okay," Corinne said. "I'll see you then."

Chapter Thirty

Corinne spent the rest of the day looking in the mirror.

At her round face and her dishwater more-brown-than-blond-now hair.

What did she want Enoch Miller to think of her? That she was pretty? That hadn't mattered, before.

She could try to show him what he'd lost, but that seemed foolish. He'd never really had her. Or wanted her. This was probably going to be an apology. Enoch Miller was going to apologize to her at a Village Inn for taking her virginity—and for pushing her out of God's warm embrace.

Maybe he needed her to forgive him. His wife had left him, and he'd been dishonored again in the eyes of the congregation. Maybe he wanted to clear his conscience.

Or maybe he blamed Corinne—did he blame her? That would make this easier. If he revealed himself to be cruel and stupid.

Corinne looked at herself in her bathroom mirror.

Maybe Enoch was just doing what he'd done before—blindly reaching out to her just because she was there and would probably say yes. He was down on his luck. And he saw her as a bad-luck girl.

She wasn't.

It had taken her a while to figure that out, but she mostly believed it.

Corinne didn't need to look pretty for any of these scenarios. She put on wide-legged jeans and a baggy, green and pink argyle cardigan. She pulled her hair up in a messy bun. She still wasn't good at makeup, but she put on mascara.

What she really wanted was to look okay. She wanted Enoch Miller to look at her and see that she was okay. The Bible says that someone who turns away from the Lord is like a dog returning to its own vomit. Corinne wanted to look like a dog who wouldn't eat its vomit.

If Enoch looked at her at all.

When had he ever?

She got to the Village Inn early, and he was already there, sitting at a table. This was such a stupid place to meet—people from church fucking loved Village Inn—and he was sitting right by a window. Enoch Miller had never had an affair, that was for sure.

He stood up when she walked over. All six-feet-something of him. His hair was damp, like he'd just showered. And he smelled like Polo aftershave. That almost did Corinne in—she rocked back on her feet, and her head tipped back—but she got through it. The waitress came by with laminated menus. And Corinne sat down. And Enoch sat down.

He looked so much like himself, it shouldn't be allowed.

His hair was a bit shorter, like he'd given up on hiding his face. All the men at church wore their hair short, and they couldn't have beards or mustaches. It made them look boyish. It made Enoch look clean and earnest. She wasn't used to seeing him with glasses—gold wire-frames that made his brown eyes look even smaller.

He looked the same.

He looked older. Thicker. Bigger. His hands were meatier on the menu.

"It's good to see you," he said, and she almost lost it again. This wasn't going well, on Corinne's side of the table.

"It's good to see you, too," she said, because she still tried not to lie.

"You look well," Enoch said. Which wasn't the same as "good," and she was grateful for it.

"Thank you," she said. "I am."

She could have gotten up then, and left, because that's all she'd wanted him to see.

Enoch was nodding, like he wasn't sure what to say next. Corinne didn't help him out; he was the one who wanted this.

"I heard you moved back to town," he said.

"I did, last year. To be closer to my mom."

"Alicia said you have a good job."

"I love Alicia," Corinne said. "She's a wonderful person."

Enoch smiled with one side of his mouth. He was still looking at Corinne. "She is. She and Shawn have been really good to me—your whole family is pretty great."

Corinne tilted her head and made a face like *That's debatable,* but really, she was just trying not to cry. This was a mistake. Enoch wasn't going to think she was well and good and okay if she broke into tears.

The waitress was back for their orders, Village Inn didn't mess around. Enoch ordered breakfast, and Corinne ordered a club sandwich.

"So, um, what do you do?" Enoch asked when they were alone again.

"I'm a freelance planner."

"A planner."

"Yeah, it's like . . . research and strategy. For advertising agencies. Or companies. I look into a problem they're having, and then I make a communications plan. For how they can address it."

"Did you study that in school?"

"No, I studied something else, but I ended up here. And I'm glad." *I'm fine,* Corinne was saying. *I'm actually doing quite well.*

"That sounds really interesting."

"It is," she agreed.

"And really difficult."

"It's for sure a specialized skill."

"You're freelance?"

"I went freelance when I moved back here. After my mom's heart attack."

"I was sorry to hear about that," he said. "Is she doing all right?"

"You probably know better than I do."

"I doubt that."

"She's doing pretty well, I think," Corinne said. "It was a small one." And then she made herself say, "How's your mom?"

Enoch could see that she was making herself say it.

How did that work: that Enoch Miller could take her virginity (he didn't *take* it) on his couch when he was practically engaged to some-one else, and now he was welcome in her mother's kitchen—but Corinne was scared to mention his mother at all?

"She's good," he said. "She stays busy. She moved to Arkansas to be closer to my brother's kids."

"Oh," Corinne said. "You have a lot of nieces and nephews?"

"Seven," he said, smiling.

"You don't—I mean, do you—"

"We didn't have any kids," Enoch said.

"Right, I didn't think . . . I, um, me neither, obviously."

Enoch nodded. So Corinne nodded. They didn't have any kids. (She'd worried that first month. Enoch must have worried, too. And Bonnie. There was no such thing as abortion. They might have forced him to marry her. What a joke. What a disaster.) (But it was fine, she was fine. Look at her.)

Enoch was trying to change the subject. Corinne could tell by the lines in his forehead, the way he was twisting his full lips—still too full to be handsome in any conventional way. Enoch wasn't hand-some in any conventional way. It hadn't mattered thirteen years ago. It mattered less now.

"I always knew you'd do something interesting," he said.

Corinne laughed. "That's a lie."

"It isn't."

She couldn't let it stand. "How could you know that? *I* didn't know that."

"Maybe you weren't paying as much attention."

"Maybe I . . . ?" She shook her head. When Enoch Miller had known Corinne, she wasn't heading anywhere interesting. She wasn't headed anywhere at all. She was like something slowly cir-cling a drain. And nobody was paying any attention—certainly not Enoch Miller.

His mouth was still twisted. One of his eyebrows was cocked down, like he was showing how well he could pay attention when he tried.

"I always knew you would be an electrician," she said, deflecting.

"Ha," he said. "You should be a fortune-teller."

"Divination is a sin. It's all over Leviticus."

"Mind like a trap on this one."

"Do you like being an electrician?"

"It's all right."

"That's not an answer."

"It's fine. It's what I wanted. Something steady. That would support a family." He colored. He'd always blushed easily. "I suppose you heard, about me and Shannon."

"Just that you weren't together," Corinne said gently.

"That's right." Enoch was nodding and rubbing his temple. "Not for three years."

"I'm sorry."

He laughed out loud, and it sounded like Corinne felt, like he might fall over. "Okay, well. Thanks."

"I am," Corinne said. "I never wanted—" She didn't know how she was going to finish that sentence. It was headed for a lie.

Enoch cut her off. "No, I know. Thanks. I mean—It's—Thanks."

The waitress was back with their dinners. With Corinne's dinner and Enoch's breakfast, some kind of skillet.

"Do you work by yourself?" she asked.

"With Japheth."

"Wow, Japheth. In my head, he's still twelve years old and doesn't want to share his Nintendo."

"He's mellowed out."

"He'd have to've."

Enoch laughed. With his lips pressed together this time. With his lungs and shoulders. "Don't get me wrong, he's still a pain in my neck."

"Do you work with Shawn a lot?" Shawn was a carpenter. He'd gotten a job with a brother from church after high school.

"Yeah. You know how it is . . ."

Corinne did.

Enoch looked up at her, his face earnest and pained again. Like he was about to make himself say something: "Your family has more cause to judge me than anyone. But when Shannon left, and people gossiped . . . Well, I had to step down, you know, because my own household wasn't in order. And a lot of people in the congregation treated me different. But your family was kinder than ever. They showed me true mercy."

"That's good to hear," Corinne said. (It wasn't really. She'd work out later why not.) "I guess they were returning the favor," she said. "Your mom was very kind to us. She took us in."

Enoch's face fell.

Because, of course, then his mother had kicked them out. But the first kindness still counted. It counted for Corinne. She was grateful.

"Is that what you wanted to tell me?" she asked. "That my family has been kind to you? It's fine with me that you're all friends. It's not even my business, really."

"What? No. That's not—"

"Then *what*?" That last word came out desperate. It came out honest.

"It wasn't anything specific," Enoch said.

"It wasn't?"

"No, I just—I guess I wanted to catch up."

"To catch up." Corinne was just going to keep repeating what he said until he said something that made sense to her.

Enoch swallowed. "I've missed you, Corinne."

"You . . ." Her mouth was hanging open. She could hardly pronounce consonants. ". . . *missed* me?"

He rolled his eyes. He huffed softly. "I mean, yeah. We were thick as thieves for so long."

"I—Enoch, you never even talked to me."

"You were one of the *only* people I talked to."

"I wasn't in your circle. It was a literal circle." She spun her finger around. "Every Sunday, after services. And I wasn't part of it."

"You didn't *want* to be part of it—you made that abundantly clear— and anyway, that wasn't real talking. Some of my best memories are you and me, in the back of my mom's station wagon. Do you remember the time we drove to Mount Rushmore?"

She did. They'd played Twenty Questions and Name That Tune, and everyone else got sick of playing, but Enoch and Corinne never did. Not for ten hours. They were thirteen. They were the same height.

"Yeah," Corinne said. "I got on your nerves."

"Yeah," Enoch agreed. "You did."

"So you didn't ask me here to apologize?"

He looked down at his breakfast skillet. The front of his hair slid forward. She remembered how it felt. Smoother than hers. Like it didn't know how to tangle.

"It doesn't matter," Corinne said in a very quiet voice. She was throwing him a bone. A rope. He didn't deserve it. "I'm glad I got to see you again." He didn't deserve it, but it was true.

Enoch lifted his head. He didn't say anything right away.

Neither did Corinne.

Chapter Thirty-one

Corinne worked from home. On the internet and conference calls. Occasionally, she flew other places to conduct interviews and surveys. Or to present to clients. Most of her projects were with the same two or three companies and the ad agency where she used to work. Her job was problem-solving. A hamburger place might say, "People hated our chicken sandwiches, so we changed the recipe, but now we can't get people to try them again." And Corinne would talk to people for hours about how they felt about chicken sandwiches. Then she'd research lifestyle trends. And shopping trends. Commuting trends. And she'd write a new plan for how to talk about chicken sandwiches. *People crave simple pleasures. People are comforted by abundance. What if a chicken sandwich could provide you with a moment of respite?*

It was not important work.

It was maybe embarrassingly not important. Corinne had studied history and political science. And now she was helping people sell fast food.

But she genuinely found it interesting. She found most things interesting; it's what made her good at her job. And she liked solving situational problems in a mathematical way. She liked emotional math. Behavioral logic.

Sometimes when she first met people, she'd joke that she got paid to think. It wasn't really a joke. Corinne spent a lot of time staring

into space, trying to make connections. She worked at her kitchen
table these days, with a laptop and a mug of tea, and Enoch Miller's business card at her right hand. She tapped it on the table and
rubbed the corners. The type was raised. Thermographic ink.

They hadn't lingered over their dinner that night. They'd finished
eating, and then Enoch had asked for the check. They'd stood outside the Village Inn, with their hands in their pockets, both of them
looking out at the parking lot.

"Thank you," he finally said. "For meeting me."

"Thank you for dinner," Corinne said.

He'd nodded. So had she. Neither of them said, *"We'll do this again
soon,"* or *"Well, I'll see you."*

Enoch had walked to his truck.

And Corinne had walked to her car.

And she'd spent the next week thinking about it. Thinking about
him. About what he'd said. *"Thick as thieves."* She supposed he was
right. They'd been thrown together, for all those years when their
mothers were friends, but they'd *chosen* to talk and play and argue.
When Corinne got thrown in with other church kids—when she was
stuck at their houses or at congregation gatherings—she'd sat mostly
quiet. If she could get away with it, she brought a book. But she
never brought a book to Enoch's house. *"Thick as thieves,"* he'd said,
and *"Some of my best memories."* Was it all one long stretch for Enoch
Miller? Corinne in the back seat, Corinne in the basement, Corinne
on the couch?

What had those years been like for Corinne? She didn't think
about them often. It hurt to look back. To see herself, as she was.

Corinne tapped his business card on the table.

She stared into space.

She jumped when the phone rang.

"Hello?"

"Corinne?"

"Yes."

"It's Enoch."

"I know."

"Oh, um, hello."

"Hello."

"How are you?"

"I'm fine," she said. "How are you?"

"Fine, fine. Did I catch you working?"

"You caught me thinking, so I guess so."

"Sorry about that."

"It's fine."

"Well, I won't keep you long . . ."

"Okay."

"I was just, um, I was wondering if you wanted to get together again."

"Again?"

"Yeah. If you wanted?"

If this were a normal situation, if Enoch were a normal person, he'd be asking Corinne on a date. But he couldn't ask her on a date— that was against the rules. So this must be something else.

"Did you have something more you needed to say?" she asked. Enoch still hadn't apologized.

"Um, no. Not exactly . . ."

"Oh."

"We don't have to—" he said. "You don't have to. Obviously. But, um . . ."

"All right," she said.

"All right, we can get together?"

"Yeah, if you want."

"We could go for a walk," he said. "Tomorrow. If you don't have to work."

"I work for myself," Corinne said.

"Yeah, me, too."

"It's supposed to be cold—"

"Oh, I guess I hadn't thought—"

"I don't mind. If you don't."

"I don't mind," Enoch said. "I could meet you at the river, by the pedestrian bridge. At two?"

"All right," she said. "I'll see you there."

Corinne was early again—but again, Enoch was earlier. Standing near the benches, wearing that heavy, tan canvas coat that all tradesmen wore, with a dark green hooded sweatshirt underneath. He was wearing thick white pants and industrial boots. He must have come straight from work. His hands were in his pockets, and he watched her walk from her car. Corinne still hadn't made any effort to look pretty. She'd put on comfortable jeans and a soft, flowered T-shirt-type thing, and then a long, plaid cardigan that was warm enough to wear as a coat.

Enoch was smiling at her with one side of his mouth. "Corinne."

"Hello," she said.

"Is it too cold for you?" he asked. The wind was ruffling his hair. His cheeks were flushed.

"It won't be, once we start walking. I like it."

"Me, too. It's my favorite time. Which way? East or west?"

She shrugged, and he started walking. She followed him.

"Was the weather different in Boston?"

"Not really," she said. "A little colder. In the winters."

"Do you miss it?"

"Boston?"

"Yeah."

"Yes."

"What do you miss?"

She took a second to think it over. "My friends, mostly. I worked in an office, and I'd been there for years, with the same people. Now I work from home. So I don't really meet anyone . . ."

"Do you have friends here from before you left?"

Corinne laughed and looked at him like he was being dense. "No."

Enoch looked embarrassed. Because, obviously, anyone she knew from church wasn't allowed to talk to her now. And who would want to, anyway? "I thought maybe you had people from school . . ." he said.

"No," Corinne said. "I mean, there are a few people from college. But they're all . . . You know, they have kids. I guess I'll have to join a book club or something. Or just be a hermit, which wouldn't be so terrible."

"Your mom says you travel a lot."

She turned her head. "Does my mom actually talk to you about me? Because I've got to say, that's weird."

"She doesn't," he said quickly. "She just talks. To people. And I put things together. I'm probably just listening extra hard for it."

Corinne nodded, as if that wasn't just as weird. She walked beside him. It was brisk—Enoch's nose was red—but it already felt good. To be out and moving. She spent too much time inside. Sitting. She looked like someone who spent all her time inside and sitting. She was still fat, she'd always be fat. She could afford better clothes now, so at least it wasn't constant misery.

"I do travel," she said. "Especially now. All my clients are other places. Do you travel?"

"Me? No."

"You don't go on vacation?"

"I mean . . ." he said. "No. I did. Some. With Shannon. I've been to Mexico a few times. Have you been to Mexico?"

"No."

"We usually— We did a lot of camping. Do you ever go camping?"

"No. Do you still?"

"Uh, I guess not, now that you mention it. It feels strange to go anywhere by myself, after all those years of— I guess I went to Iowa City this year. With your brother. For a football game. I must seem so boring to you, compared to the people you know."

"No," Corinne said sincerely. "It's not like people in big cities are inherently more interesting. Everyone watches football games and hangs out in bars, no matter where you go."

"Is that what you did in Boston?"

"Me? No. I was sort of a hermit there, too . . . I'd go out to eat. And to concerts sometimes."

He looked up. "I go to concerts." He sounded excited to have something in common with her.

"You do?" Corinne was surprised.

"Yeah. All the time. Well, not all the time, but . . ."

"You're allowed to go to concerts?"

"It's a conscience matter," Enoch said.

She shook her head. "I definitely didn't know anyone at church who went to concerts."

"You and I grew up in a really strict congregation . . ."

"So the one you're in now is less strict?"

"Oh yeah. People are way more laid-back. We don't have Sister Walters taking notes on everyone's hemlines . . ."

Corinne wrinkled her nose. "*God*. Sister Walters—I haven't thought about her in years. What a terror! She talked to the elders when I got my ears pierced!"

Enoch laughed with his lips pressed together.

"My mom was so embarrassed, she made me take out the studs! The holes closed right up—for a long time, I had scars, but I couldn't wear earrings."

"Not now?"

She pushed her hair back behind her ears. She was wearing gold hoops. "No, look, I got them re-pierced."

Enoch laughed. "Jezebel."

Corinne laughed, too, but it hurt a little bit. (She'd unpack why later.)

"There are lots of women in my congregation with pierced ears," he said.

What a strange brag.

"So, in your new laid-back congregation, are you allowed to take unchaperoned walks with women?" Corinne looked at Enoch's face when she asked him this. It fell. He lowered his eyebrows and twisted his mouth down and hunched his shoulders. And all of that was okay with Corinne. Because she didn't *owe* him anything. She didn't owe him this walk. She didn't owe him . . . plausible deniability.

They walked in silence for a minute or two. The river was gray and empty beside them.

"I think that would still be frowned upon," Enoch finally replied.

"I suspected," she said.

They walked through more silence.

"Corinne . . . do you want to turn back?"

"Are you suggesting or asking?"

"I'm asking," he said, "if you'd rather not walk with me."

"I work for myself, Enoch."

More silence. Enoch's heavy boots on the pavement. His hands in his pockets. His hunched shoulders.

"Do *you* want to turn back?" she asked.

"No."

Silence. Enoch's heavy boots. Corinne's heart beating. The river. The trees.

She cleared her throat. "What was the last show you went to?"

Enoch seemed confused. "The last show?"

"The last concert."

"Oh." He swallowed. "Um, Ben Folds."

"I love Ben Folds," Corinne said.

He looked down at her. "You do?"

"I really, honestly do. I saw Ben Folds Five, in Boston. They were fantastic."

"Yeah?"

She nodded. "Who do you go to concerts with?"

"I go by myself. Usually."

"I wish I could go to concerts by myself. I feel too vulnerable."

"Sometimes it's good to be a large man."

"I'll bet it's good to be a large man almost always."

Enoch was smiling again. "Do you want to hear something really weird?"

"Almost always."

"I go to concerts with Shannon sometimes."

Corinne was genuinely surprised now. "You do? You still get along?"

"Yeah." He was looking down at her. He looked worried.

"I'm not going to tell on you, Enoch. About anything."

"No, I didn't think—I didn't think that. Did, um, did Shawn tell you why Shannon left?"

"No."

"Huh . . . I thought he'd tell you. Or that Alicia would. It's the sort of thing people like to tell . . . It packs a punch."

"I didn't even know you and Shawn were friends."

"Shannon left— Well, she didn't want to be married anymore." Enoch's face was flushed. "Because she didn't want to be married to a man."

"Oh," Corinne said, not sure she was getting it. "So Shannon Frank . . . is *gay?*"

His forehead was furrowed. "She wasn't sure at first. But, yeah, probably. I mean, definitely now."

Holy shit. That really did pack a punch. Shannon Frank was a lesbian? A few of the brothers in their congregation had thought that Corinne was a lesbian. Because of her ugly clothes and her terrible attitude. Not Shannon Frank. Shannon was everything a Godly young woman was supposed to be. *Holy shit.* "Was that why she was such a bitch?"

Enoch looked shocked. "What? No. I don't think so."

"God," Corinne said. "Poor Shannon."

He was squinting, wincing maybe.

"I mean," she said, "poor you, too. I'm so sorry. What a mess. How long were you married?"

"Almost ten years."

"Jesus, Enoch."

He kicked a pinecone on the pavement in front of him.

"So you two, you still go to concerts together?"

"Sometimes. Less now. More at first. Neither of us was used to being alone."

"That makes sense . . ."

"Yeah. It was nice to be somewhere where we wouldn't see anyone from church who might wonder why we were together."

"Who did you see? In concert."

"Oh, um." He started laughing. "Ani DiFranco."

Corinne giggled. "Okay. Well. Good choice. I like Ani DiFranco."

"And the Indigo Girls."

Corinne giggled. Enoch giggled, too. Still flushed.

"I mean . . ." Corinne said. "Another great choice. I also love the Indigo Girls."

Enoch was laughing. "Great. Good. I'm glad to hear it. I like them, too."

"Enoch, did you go cruising for girls with your ex-wife?"

"She was still my wife. We were separated."

"The question stands."

"She was having a rough time . . ."

"Sounds like there was a lot of that going around."

Enoch's shoulders were shaking, he was shaking his head. There were tears in his eyes.

Corinne touched his arm. For just a second. To comfort him. To remind him she was there. And that she wasn't judging him. Was that why he was telling her all this? Who could Enoch Miller talk to, who wouldn't judge him?

"I don't remember you being this . . . forthcoming," Corinne said.

"Yeah, well . . . That was probably to both of our detriment."

Corinne didn't know what to say after that. She kicked a pinecone, then Enoch kicked it. Then Corinne kicked it. After a few more passes, Enoch kicked it sailing into the river.

The path they were on wound down to the water. She followed him to the edge.

"I am sorry, Corinne."

Corinne looked out at the river. The closer you got to it, the more brown it was and the less gray. She wanted to ask him which part he was sorry for, but she wasn't sure she could stand hearing his answer.

"I think about it a lot," Enoch said.

"About being sorry?"

"Well, yeah, honestly. And, you know . . . everything."

"It wasn't just you. There by yourself."

"I'm sorry for my part of it. For . . ."

He didn't finish. She didn't ask him to. And she didn't apologize.

"Do you want to turn back?" she asked. They were at the end of the path.

"Sure," Enoch said.

They had less to say to each other on the way back. When they got to the parking lot, Corinne wasn't sure how to say good-bye. There was nothing to thank him for this time.

She balanced on the edge of the curb.

Enoch took one hand out of his pocket and scratched the back of his neck. "Would you want to go to a concert?"

"What concert?"

"I don't know," he said. "Just a concert sometime? With me?"

A concert sometime. With him.

"Sure," Corinne said.

Enoch nodded.

"Only lesbian folksingers though," she added. "That's all I'm interested in."

He closed one eye, looking down at her. "Ani DiFranco is bisexual."

That shocked a laugh out of Corinne. "The truth is," she said, "I would love to see Ani DiFranco in concert."

"She was pretty amazing, she had a whole horn section . . ." Enoch smiled, like he knew how absurd it all was. How ridiculous. "Thank you," he said. "For walking with me."

Corinne nodded. "I'll see you," she said. Because she knew she would.

"Yeah. See you, Corinne."

Chapter Thirty-two

Corinne's mom invited her over for lunch on Sunday. Everyone else came straight from church. Corinne wore a very modest skirt. Like she'd come straight from church, too.

She didn't mention Enoch Miller.

Chapter Thirty-three

"Hello?"

"Hey, Corinne?"

"Enoch?"

"Yeah."

It had been a week since their walk. She'd thought maybe he was done calling her. Done with this . . . game. Or whatever it was. This experiment. It was against the rules. And Enoch Miller apparently cared less about the rules than he used to—but he was still Enoch Miller. He was still the kind of person who kept a Bible on his dashboard, Corinne had seen it.

He might step off the path for Corinne—he'd pull her off of it, pull her to the top of a tornado slide—but he'd always go back.

She'd known that when she was eighteen, and she'd gone along with him anyway. She'd taken what she could get.

She was thirty-one now. She was still taking his calls. She was still saying yes. But she also still knew where this was headed, she knew who she was dealing with.

"Hi, Enoch."

"Hi. Hey, I was going to wait until there was a concert you might want to see. To call you. But your choices are Toby Keith and Big & Rich. At least for the next few weeks."

Corinne laughed.

"Do you think we could go for another walk?"

"Yeah," she said. "No offense to Big & Rich."

"None taken, I'm sure. Have you been to the creek trail, up north?"

"No."

"It's good."

"Okay, let's do it."

"Do you want to meet me there? Tomorrow, around three?"

Tomorrow was Tuesday, Corinne had a meeting, she'd move it. "Yeah. See you then."

⁓

Corinne got to the trail early. Enoch was already there. It was a Tuesday afternoon, but he'd changed out of his work clothes into jeans and the sort of big gray sweater a fisherman might wear. All of Enoch's clothes looked like they were made for someone to work in.

Corinne had tried to look pretty today. Who knew whether she'd succeeded. Or whether Enoch would notice. Or whether he was susceptible to that sort of thing. But she was wearing rose-colored lipstick.

"I like your sweater," she said.

He looked down. "Thanks. I didn't pick it out."

"Have you ever purchased clothing for yourself?"

He smiled at her. "Do work clothes count? I've bought pants at Menards."

She laughed. Menards was a big-box hardware store.

"Eventually I'll run through the clothes that Shannon bought me," he went on, "and I'll have to go to the Gap or something. Is that where people shop?"

"You should just buy all your clothes from Menards."

"That's fine with me. They have these coveralls with a million pockets . . . Bright orange."

He'd started walking, following the path into the trees, and Corinne was walking beside him. The path was narrow. (Just like the path to heaven, Corinne thought.) Their arms kept bumping. Enoch smelled like aftershave. Corinne was better able to bear it this time. To bear the sense memories. Of Enoch, coming into the living room, holding a piece of pizza and the Bible. Of waiting for the moment when she could slide behind the coffee table next to him. She'd never gotten to smell his aftershave when it was this fresh from the bottle. He'd never put it on for her.

It was sunnier today, a bit warmer. Corinne hadn't worn a jacket. Just a big, purple sweater with dolman sleeves. And bootcut jeans.

"Do you remember that black sweater you used to wear?" Enoch was smiling down at her.

"Yes."

"You loved that sweater . . ."

"I mean, I only had two sweaters—but I did love it."

"It was coming apart at every seam. It drove my mom crazy."

"Your mom bought me a pink twinset. When we were staying with you guys . . ."

"That sounds like her."

". . . but it was too tight across the front, and my mom wouldn't let me wear it. I had to give it to Holly."

He huffed a laugh through his nose. "Damned if you do, damned if you don't."

"Title of my memoir."

Enoch laughed out loud, a rare treat. Corinne smiled up at him. He looked handsome in that sweater. Shannon Frank always did have good taste.

"Do you miss being married?" Corinne asked. Before she could think better of it.

Enoch raised his eyebrows. "That's a . . . question."

"You don't have to answer it," she rushed out.

"No, that's all right. I may as well. Now that I'm, what'd you call it . . . forthright?"

"Forthcoming."

"There you go." He looked thoughtful. "Yeah, I miss it. That's pathetic, huh? That I miss being married to someone who didn't . . . Well."

"I don't think it's pathetic," Corinne said. They were both concentrating on the trail. It made talking a little easier. Even talking about this.

"I always got along with Shannon," he said.

"Yeah," Corinne said. She remembered.

"I know you didn't like her."

"Oh, I was just jealous."

Enoch glanced over at her, surprised.

"Well, I was," Corinne said. "She had everything. She was perfect. Do you remember those hats she used to wear, with the silk flowers and the ribbons?"

Enoch didn't answer. Corinne guessed that he probably did remember. Instead he said, "You never would have worn a hat like that."

"What would I have worn it with? My holey black sweater? That floor-length gray skirt that Sister Walters made for me? She made me all those drab skirts with elastic waists—I dressed like an angry nun."

Enoch laughed again. His silent, shaky Enoch laugh. "Shannon and I got along," he repeated. "I think that's why we stayed married as long as we did. She wasn't happy, but what we had was pretty easy. For both of us."

"Were you happy?"

"I thought I was. If you'd asked me then, I would have said yes."

"But now?"

"Oh, I don't know . . ."

Corinne let him keep thinking. She'd never been to this park. It felt removed from town. The path kept forking. They'd already taken so many turns, she wasn't sure of the way back.

"Shannon says I'm too good at making the best of things," Enoch said. "She said I never really expected to be happy."

"Well, that just seems practical," Corinne said.

"Yeah," he laughed, "maybe." He glanced down at her, then back at the trail. "Did you ever want to get married?"

She waved her hand and made a dismissive noise that could have meant *yes* or *no* or *don't be silly.*

"No one would describe you as forthcoming, Corinne."

"Oh, I'm sure there was plenty of gossip about how forthcoming I was with you."

"Geez." He shook his head. "The things you say sometimes."

"Sorry."

"I didn't mean that you should stop. I just mean . . ." He frowned at her. "You don't seem to want to talk about . . . what happened. With us. But then you sort of throw it in my face."

That was exactly what Corinne was doing. It was all that she could really manage. "I'm sorry about that," she said. "Genuinely."

"It's all right. I'm glad to hear what you're thinking . . ."

They'd come to a creek, and the path had transitioned into a raised boardwalk. Their feet sounded like drums beneath them. Corinne's heart was beating fast in her chest. "It's different for me," she said. Certainly. "It's different in the world. Marriage is."

"You've never considered it?"

"No, I have. I was engaged for a while."

"You were?" Enoch looked hurt. Which was so unfair, Corinne wanted to slap him.

"My mom didn't tell you?"

"She wouldn't—"

"I'm kidding," she said. "My mom doesn't know. It was before . . . Before."

"What happened?" he asked. "I mean, did something happen— you're not still . . ."

"Engaged? No. We just . . ."

Corinne almost said that they'd drifted apart. But that wasn't true at all. It had been bloody and terrible. She and Marc kept getting back together, then breaking up for the same reasons: He was a liar. And a narcissist. And probably an alcoholic.

She shook her head. Her ponytail swung. "I don't really want to talk about this, Enoch, I'm sorry. You were right—I'm not forthcoming. I'm forthgoing, is that a thing? Forthwrong?"

"It's okay, you don't have to talk about it."

"I know I don't. And also, thank you."

They kept walking. Drumming. The path turned into dirt again.

"Did you live together?" he asked.

"Um . . . yeah. We did." She was frowning. "But I *really* don't—"

"I miss having breakfast," Enoch said. Forthrightly. "With some- one else. On the weekends."

Corinne sighed. She was the one who'd started this. "Did Shan- non make breakfast?"

"We both did."

They'd come to an incline—railroad ties set into the dirt like a staircase. Enoch's breathing picked up. Even his breath had a low hum to it.

When they got to the top, Corinne stopped for a second to get her bearings. Enoch stopped with her.

"I miss some general things," she said, looking up at him. He was looking down at her. His glasses were smudged. "Like breakfast," she said. "But not breakfast. You know—the companionship. And then I miss specific things. About him. And those are harder to talk about."

Enoch nodded.

"But it was a long time ago. Years ago."

There was a crease between his eyebrows. "Are you seeing some- one now, Corinne?"

Jesus, Enoch—am I?

"I told you," she said, "I never leave my apartment."

⁓

They followed the trail as it looped around itself. Along one stretch, the hedge apple trees arched over their heads like a tunnel. They stopped talking as they walked beneath them. The leaves were yellow-green turning greenish yellow. Enoch had to duck.

They got to a postcard-ready fishing pond and decided to take a break, sitting down on a low stone bench by the water. Enoch grunted a little when he settled.

"How's your back?" Corinne asked.

"My back is garbage," he said.

She laughed gently. "I'm sorry to hear that. You should have been born with two spines. For extra support."

"Are you calling me fat?"

"God, no. I'm calling you . . . a sequoia."

He laughed and shook his head.

⁓

The walk back was faster. And easier. Every minute with Enoch was easier. More natural. Corinne had to remind herself how absurd this was. That she was here with him at all.

At the end of the trail, she slid on a loose patch of gravel. Enoch caught her elbow, but he let go as soon as she'd regained her balance. When they got to their cars—to her car and his truck—neither of them seemed to know what to do. They stood there awkwardly for a minute. The sun was just starting to dip. "Are you hungry?" Corinne asked.

Enoch checked his watch. "I should probably get home . . ."

She nodded. "Big Tuesday-night plans?"

"Just the usual."

"Oh"—she looked up at him—"duh. You have church tonight."

"Yeah, you want to come with?"

"Is that a joke?"

He shook his head, like he was shaking sense into himself. "Yeah . . . probably. Unless?"

"I'll pass, thanks."

"Right. Sorry."

They kept standing there. Awkwardly. Absurdly.

"I'll be hungry tomorrow," Enoch said. "We could have lunch. If you want."

"Okay," Corinne said. "I'll probably be hungry, too."

Chapter Thirty-four

Corinne tried to get her bearings.

She'd gone thirteen years without seeing Enoch Miller. Without *expecting* to see him. Enoch was a fork in her road. A long-ago fork. A turning point.

Enoch Miller was *the past*.

He was Corinne's past.

He was the thing she carried around in an old-fashioned suitcase. One with a broken handle and no wheels.

Enoch Miller. Fucking Enoch. *Enoch*.

Corinne didn't even talk about him—she left him out—when people were talking about their first loves, their first times.

Enoch Miller was too heavy to share.

He was too big to contemplate.

She'd gone thirteen years without seeing him, without expecting to see him again. And now he was back, in her present, and it was too much. *"I'll be hungry tomorrow"* was too much.

Corinne couldn't find her bearings.

Chapter Thirty-five

They had lunch the next day. They met at a park, a different park, and sat at a picnic table. Enoch brought soup. And when they said good-bye, they made plans to meet again. Like they were two normal people who were allowed this sort of thing. Like they ever had been.

What was happening?

What had Corinne allowed to happen?

She couldn't explain it to herself. Sitting in her car after she saw him. Staring at the rearview mirror, her cheeks still flushed from the wind. She couldn't make sense of it.

Enoch didn't wait a week to call her the next time. Or the next. They were constantly touching base and making plans now.

They met for walks. They met at the river. Sometimes Enoch brought coffee. Once he brought a picnic. Nothing fancy—bread and cheese and cold Polish sausage, shoved in his work bag. They ate it by the postcard pond, sitting on the low stone bench, then left when Enoch's back couldn't take it anymore.

When it was cold, Enoch wore his green sweatshirt and tan coat. When it was warm, he wore sweaters that Shannon Frank had picked out. When it was very warm, he wore T-shirts that said MILLER ELECTRIC in red script. He was completely familiar to Corinne. Every time she heard his voice, it was a shock.

October was sunny and bright. October was unseasonably cold. Corinne had never spent this much time outdoors in her life.

She knew *why*. She wasn't stupid. Or naive. She knew the game Enoch was playing. The line he was walking. She knew why they always took separate cars. Why they met in daylight, in public places—but not too public. Corinne knew. She was complicit, really. Corinne didn't have any rules of her own to worry about, but she was afraid of Enoch's rules. She was afraid, so she didn't push him.

Enoch called in the mornings. They met in the afternoons.

He always beat her wherever they were going. She got used to seeing him standing outside of his truck, waiting for her. (She'd never get used to it.)

Enoch called in the mornings, and Corinne said yes to whatever he suggested. They made time for each other. Corinne pushed off work, she moved meetings. Once, when they'd gone two days without seeing each other, they squeezed in a walk before Enoch went to church. Corinne met him at the river. He was wearing a navy-blue suit, and his hair was gelled back. She saw him standing there, and she could see him standing at the pulpit. She could hear him reading Letters to the Thessalonians, books 1 and 2. (Apostle Paul couldn't leave the Thessalonians alone . . .) (*What was happening? What had Corinne allowed to happen?*)

They met in daylight. In public. They drove separately.

It wasn't good. What they were doing. But it wasn't strictly against the rules. Enoch's rules. There was still nothing for him to confess—he'd hardly touched Corinne. He didn't even call her after sunset.

Enoch had called this morning and asked Corinne if she wanted to have lunch. She said yes. She said she'd meet him at a park, another park. He said he'd pick up sandwiches.

(Maybe Corinne should be the one to pick up sandwiches sometimes. She could at least get coffee. But she still didn't *owe* Enoch anything. She was meeting him, almost every day, and she didn't have to, and that felt like more than enough.)

Enoch was waiting outside his truck when she got there. It was too cold today to sit down, the wind blew right through them. So they kept moving, eating while they walked. Enoch's nose got so red, and Corinne's ears were numb—but neither of them suggested that they go inside or sit in one of their cars. They just suffered through it and said good-bye a little earlier than usual. He said he'd call her in the morning.

Chapter Thirty-six

Enoch couldn't see Corinne this weekend. He had a wedding on Friday night. On Saturday, he had work and some social obligation he couldn't get out of. Then on Sunday, he had church and he'd promised to help someone move.

But that's three days, Corinne almost said.

She held her tongue. She could go three days without seeing Enoch Miller—she could go thirteen years. (She'd have to go more eventually. Inevitably. *Soon,* right? Weren't they almost done doing this? Weren't they about to turn the corner?)

Enoch said he'd call her on Sunday, and Corinne said okay, but that really, he shouldn't worry about it—she had so much work to catch up on. It was true, she hadn't been able to focus for weeks.

She didn't get anything done on Friday.

On Saturday, she stayed in bed 'til two, then lay on her couch, drinking tea and eating canned soup with saltine crackers. Finally she dragged herself up and out. She drove to SuperTarget. Just to feel less lonely and like she had her own agenda.

She bought ingredients to make Alicia's Snickers cake. Corinne should do something nice for Alicia; Alicia always sent her cards and remembered her birthday . . . On impulse, Corinne bought a big bunch of sunflowers. She'd drop them off on the way home.

Shawn and Alicia had a very cute house in an older part of town. They were doing just fine. All of Corinne's siblings were doing just fine. They'd changed congregations after—well, after Corinne had ruined the old one for them. And it had been a good change. The brothers and sisters in the new congregation looked out for them. They helped the boys find work. They helped Holly find her husband.

Maybe Corinne's family did so well because Corinne hadn't been around to make them look bad. To drag them down. In her worrisome sweaters and her grim skirts. Looking like either a lesbian or the sort of girl who would open her legs for the first person who asked, nobody was sure which. (Until she showed them.)

Corinne never went to the new church. Just Holly, in her wannabe dresses and Corinne's pink twinset. And Shawn, who just wanted to be good, and who was a boy, which made him worth some effort. And Noah, who was born into the church. He was a little wild. He got in trouble with a girl (not the worst trouble), but he married her. And now they were both in good standing and expecting a baby, and nobody seemed to hold a grudge.

Corinne's mother was doing just fine, too. After her parents had finally separated for good, Corinne's mom had married a widower in the congregation. A retired plumber, almost twenty years her senior. He was fine. He didn't seem to care one way or another about Corinne—which was lucky. He was the head of the house; he could have decided Corinne wasn't welcome there.

Corinne parked in Shawn and Alicia's driveway and grabbed the bouquet of sunflowers. She thought about leaving them in the door, but it was supposed to freeze tonight. Corinne rang the doorbell, then heard someone calling, "I'll get it!" And then Enoch Miller opened the door.

Corinne was standing there with sunflowers.

"Corinne . . ." he said. Stunned.

Corinne was stunned, too. Too stunned to say his name.

"Who is it?" Alicia called from the kitchen.

"It's . . ." Enoch said.

"Hey, Alicia!" Corinne called. "It's just me!"

Alicia came up behind Enoch, and he backed away from the door. "Corinne," Alicia said, alarmed. Like she was in real pickle. Like she'd messed up again somehow.

"Sorry," Corinne said, "I should have called. I just wanted to drop these off for you. I, um—" She held out the flowers.

"For me?"

"Yeah."

"Oh my goodness, I never get flowers!" Alicia took the bouquet and started fussing with it. "Come in and say hi to Shawn. Shawn! Corinne brought me flowers! No one ever brings me flowers."

"I should head home," Corinne said.

"That's not even true." Shawn walked out of the kitchen, drying his hands on a towel. "I bring you flowers."

Alicia was holding the front door open, standing back from it to make room for Corinne. Corinne felt like she had to step in. She promised herself that she'd step right out. The house was warm, it smelled like something savory. "I didn't mean to interrupt your dinner . . ."

"Family can't interrupt," Alicia said. "And we were just sitting down." She took Corinne's arm and squeezed it. "Stay for dinner, Corinne. I mean—I don't want to make you uncomfortable, but we'd love to have you." She looked back at Shawn. And at Enoch, who was standing behind him. "Wouldn't we?"

Corinne looked at her brother—he was concerned, worried, embarrassed, sorry—and she looked at Enoch, expecting to see the same panic she was feeling. She didn't see it. Enoch wanted her to stay.

Alicia squeezed her arm again. "Stay, Corinne. I made a taco ring."

"Okay," Corinne said. "I'll stay. Thank you."

～

The taco ring was made with canned crescent rolls and taco fixings. It was terrible and delicious, and Alicia was certain that Corinne could make it herself, it was just so simple.

Shawn and Alicia made sure that Corinne and Enoch didn't have to sit next to each other at the table, which left them sitting across from each other, which was worse. It was familiar and worse. Corinne felt like she was waiting for Shawn and Alicia to go to bed, so she could slide over to the other side of the table.

Enoch and Corinne didn't talk to each other directly. What could they say that wouldn't betray how well they knew each other? How reacquainted they were? What could they say out loud that was true?

Shawn was silent and on edge, like someone presiding over a nuclear disaster. Like he knew this had been a bad decision, but he didn't know how to get out of it. He wouldn't challenge Alicia. He never did. Shawn was the head of the house, but Alicia was the brains of the operation. Shawn trusted her to run things, and she rarely steered him wrong. What was Alicia doing tonight? What was she up to? It was almost like she *wanted* Enoch and Corinne to connect. She didn't understand what a bad idea that was. Alicia grew up in Missouri—she didn't know that Corinne was *fundamentally* a bad idea for Enoch Miller. A dead end. A dead end with consequences. A road that went right off a cliff.

"We should play cards!" Alicia said, while they were still eating their dessert. (Banana-split brownies. She made them with a brownie mix; it was so much easier than it looked.)

"Cards?" Corinne repeated, surprised.

"Alicia grew up in a congregation that allowed cards," Shawn explained.

"But not dice," Alicia said. "Isn't that funny?"

"So you never played Monopoly?" Enoch asked.

"We played with a spinner."

"How'd you get out of jail?" Corinne wondered.

"I can't remember—oh! We should play spades! We never have the right number of people for spades. Corinne, do you know how?" Alicia was up and rummaging through a basket on the sideboard.

"No . . ." Corinne wasn't even allowed to play Go Fish after her mom joined the church. She looked at Shawn and glanced at Enoch. "Are *you guys* allowed to play cards?"

Shawn shrugged. "The church doesn't really get hung up on stuff like that anymore . . ."

"Huh," Corinne said.

Alicia was back with a deck. "Clear the table, Shawn. Corinne, it's so easy. Do you know how, Enoch?"

"No," he said. His voice was so deep.

"I should probably . . ." Corinne started to say. She stole a look at Enoch. (Every time she'd ever looked at him, it was stealing.) He was watching her. Signaling to her with his big open face. *Stay, stay, stay.*

"You're doing me such a favor," Alicia said. "I haven't played spades in ages—Holly still thinks it's a sin, and your mom can't focus enough to learn the rules."

Corinne picked up the cards as they were dealt to her.

"You'll be my partner," Alicia said. "Trade chairs with me, Enoch. Shawn, you've got Enoch."

Shawn was standing in the kitchen doorway. Corinne met his gaze. He was signaling to her, too. *I'm sorry, you don't have to do this, you can go.*

Corinne shook her head. She pressed her lips together, like, *It's okay.* (Could you lie with your face?)

Alicia explained the rules, and Corinne sort of forgot how mortifying the situation was because she was concentrating so hard on figuring out the game. She had it down after a couple hands. Enoch had it down, too. She was sitting at his right hand. She half expected him to touch her leg under the table. He didn't, of course. He hadn't in years.

"You guys are quick," Alicia said.

"They're the worst," Shawn said. "My mom used to make them play with me, and they only wanted to play board games, and *only* if they could make them harder. They used to play Clue with two murders."

Corinne and Enoch both smiled at him.

"I forgot that you used to play with us," Corinne said.

"You never let me win. I was just a little kid—you're supposed to let little kids win."

"I'm not letting you win tonight either," she said.

Alicia hooted. "That's what I'm talking about!"

"We'd try to play Monopoly with you," Enoch remembered, "and you'd get bored after a half hour and give away all your money."

"Monopoly is the worst," Shawn said.

"That's true," Corinne agreed.

Enoch was smiling at her. Because it wasn't the worst the way they'd played it. (He should stop smiling at her. Someone would see.)

"Shawn's just like your mom," Alicia said. "No head for games."

⁓

Corinne didn't leave when she should have. She didn't leave any of the times she should have. They kept playing spades. They switched partners, and Corinne played with Shawn, and they lost because he was bored and only playing because Alicia wanted him to. After a couple hours, Alicia heated up the leftover taco ring. Corinne drank three Diet Cokes.

She didn't look at Enoch anymore, but she felt him beaming. He was laughing breathily at everyone's jokes, especially Corinne's. He snorted twice. He complimented Alicia's taco ring. He gently mocked Shawn's playing. He didn't speak to Corinne, and she didn't speak to him, but she was aware of his every move, and she was aware of him being aware of her.

They left at the same time, but Corinne got herself out the door first, with Alicia saying how much fun it had been and how they needed to do this again. "We could play Hand and Foot! Do y'all know Hand and Foot?" Corinne made it to her car before Enoch left the house.

⁓

She noticed on the way home that Enoch was driving behind her. She saw his truck in her rearview mirror at a red light.

When Corinne pulled into the parking lot behind her building, he pulled in beside her. They both got out of their cars. Enoch walked over to her and stood there, scratching the back of his head, looking down at Corinne out of the top of his eyes.

Corinne looked up at him. She wasn't sure what to say. She felt like she should apologize, but she wasn't going to let herself do that.

She wanted to say, *Well, that was weird,* but what it had really been was *nice.* And she didn't think she should say that either. She didn't want to deal with any of this—how guilty she felt for misleading Shawn and Alicia, how afraid she was of getting caught. She hated that she was in a situation where getting caught was an *issue.*

Enoch was still scratching the back of his head, looking sheepish. Eventually, he said, "Can I still call you tomorrow?"

That was it, that was all he said.

Corinne exhaled. "Yeah."

"Maybe we can squeeze in a walk?"

"That sounds good."

He nodded. "Walk you to your door?"

"Okay. I have groceries."

He stepped back so she could open her trunk. Her milk was probably half frozen. There were just a few plastic bags. Enoch picked them up and followed Corinne to her building.

She unlocked the outer door and then stood there with it open, holding out her hands. "I've got it."

Enoch gave her the groceries. "Good night, Corinne."

"Good night."

Chapter Thirty-seven

"Hello?"

"Corinne!"

"Hey, Enoch. Don't you have church right now?" It was Sunday. The next Sunday. Not quite noon. Corinne was still in bed.

"I just got out. Do you like Wilco?"

"The band?"

"Yeah."

"What I know of them."

"They're one of my favorites," he said. "Do you want to go see them live?"

"Sure, when?"

"Tonight."

"They're in town tonight?"

"Close. Kansas City."

"Kansas City?"

"I'll drive," he said.

"It'll be late coming back."

"I don't mind if you don't mind."

"I don't mind," she said.

Corinne was waiting outside for him when he pulled up. She didn't care about looking eager—Enoch knew she wanted to see him, and she knew he wanted to see her. That was clear, at least. They'd met up every day since playing cards last weekend.

He hopped out to get the door for her. He was grinning.

Corinne climbed into his truck. It smelled like vanilla air freshener, and there wasn't so much as a gum wrapper on the floor. "Your truck is so clean," she said, when he was sliding behind the wheel.

"I vacuumed it for you."

"I'm touched." She was.

Enoch smiled out of the corner of his eyes at her. He was already starting the engine. "Do you like living here? In these apartments?"

"It's fine. I like having secured entry. There are a bunch of old people in my building, and they'll yell at you if you prop open the door." If he'd been anyone else, she would have said, *"I'll invite you in next time."*

It was cold tonight, and Enoch was dressed somewhere between his work clothes and his church clothes. He was wearing a navy-blue peacoat that Corinne had never seen before. With jeans. And slightly-less-industrial-than-usual work boots. The cab of the truck was massive, and Enoch was massive inside of it, and Corinne already liked being able to look at him when he couldn't look back.

"I should have driven," she said. "This must eat gas."

"It's fine," he said. "I like driving."

"You could have driven my car."

"Thank you for coming on such short notice."

"I never mind short notice."

Neither of them mentioned it, but they both relaxed once they were out of town. Enoch sat back in his leather seat, and Corinne turned toward him a bit. He'd brought Wilco CDs, so she could listen to them before the concert, if she wanted. He guided her through his favorite songs. It was weird to think of Enoch Miller having CDs and favorite songs.

"When did you start listening to secular music?" Corinne asked.

"After I got married. Shannon's family was never as strict about music, and she liked to listen to the radio in the car. I realized that there was a lot of music that didn't challenge Christian values . . ."

He glanced over at Corinne. "Do you remember how our moms used to say, '*Would you do*'—whatever it was we were doing—'*if Jesus was here?*' Like, would you play that song or watch that movie?"

"I remember."

"Well, I kept thinking about it. When I was listening to music. And a lot of the time, I'd think 'Jesus would probably like this.' Do you know John Prine?"

"No."

"Well, I think Jesus would really love John Prine."

"So basically you have the same standard as your mom; you just imagine that Jesus enjoys more things."

Enoch barked out a laugh. "I guess that's right." He shifted in his seat, getting more comfortable. "When did you start listening to secular music?"

"When my whole life became secular, I suppose." Corinne shook her head, thinking back to her first year of college. Living in the dormitory. Watching MTV with her roommate. "I was like someone from another country. I never got any pop culture references." She affected a Russian accent: "I like your American blue jeans. I like your Coca-Cola and your rock 'n' roll."

"Has your whole life been secular?"

She tilted her head at him. "That's a weird question, what are you really asking?"

He glanced over at her. "You never tried a different church?"

"Like, a different denomination?"

"Yeah."

"God, no. My mom would have never talked to me then. The wrong church is worse than no church."

"But you didn't . . ." Enoch was still trying get to the heart of his question. "You didn't want that for yourself? Spirituality? Community?"

Corinne stared up at his pale cheeks and his too-short hair. At his serious brown eyes, focused on the road. "No," she said. "I don't think I ever would have gone to church if left to my own devices. Would you? If you hadn't been born into it?"

"I don't know," he said. "That's hard to imagine. I *hope* I would've . . ."

Corinne hummed thoughtfully. She listened to the music for a minute. It was good music for talking and driving. Twangy guitars, rumbly vocals. Then she said: "I told my mom once, when I was in high school, that I never would have accepted a Bible tract from a stranger—that I would have run the other way. And she said, 'Jesus knew that, and He made sure that *I* accepted that tract from Sister Miller. So that I could bring you into His flock with me.'"

"Did you think she was crazy?" Enoch asked.

"At the time? Not really . . . I still wanted to believe that I was on the right track—that we were God's people, and that I was good enough to *be* one of God's people. That maybe Jesus would have made a very special effort for me."

Enoch glanced over at her again. "And now?"

Now . . . Now Corinne wondered whether her mom had accepted that tract so that Corinne could find Enoch, not Jesus. Even if she only got to have him for a little while. (She'd only had Jesus for a little while, too.) "I don't know," she said.

They stopped and got tacos, and smiled at each other more than usual. Corinne didn't worry about who was watching or what they might see in her eyes when she looked at him.

They got to the concert just as the opening act was starting. The venue was an old-school social hall. There were no chairs. Enoch and Corinne found a place to stand up front, toward the wall. "Normally I stand at the back," he said, "so people don't throw beer cans at my head."

It was nice to be at a concert with someone who wasn't drinking. Someone who wouldn't hang an arm holding a scotch and soda over Corinne's shoulder. And it was nice to be with someone so big that people just naturally gave him space—because they didn't want to be standing behind him. And it was nice to be with Enoch. That was the main thing. It was almost always nice to be with him. There had been a few terrible moments, but the rest had been nice, all of them, even when she'd been sitting in the back row of the church, and he'd been up onstage; it'd been nice to see him there. It was nicer now. It was better now. Here, in another city, in a dark room, colored lights catching on his gold-rimmed eyeglasses. He bought her a Coke. The music was mellow, the crowd was high. Enoch was happy to be here.

He bobbed his head in time. He held his hands over his head to clap. Corinne never knew what to do with herself at concerts. She'd spent too many years without music, too many years being forbidden to dance. She usually folded her arms. Sometimes she swayed. Tonight she watched Enoch. He bent over to talk to her. "You doing okay?" he shouted.

"I'm fine!"

"What?"

Corinne stood on tiptoe to reach his ear. "I'm good."

Enoch bent farther to find Corinne's ear. He rested his fingertips on her shoulder. "We can leave whenever you want."

"I don't want to leave. I'm glad we're here."

He smiled at her. He nodded.

When Corinne had to go to the bathroom, Enoch walked with her to the back of the room. He guided her through the crowd with his hand on her back, and waited for her outside the door, then led her back to the middle of the room, by the wall.

"Do you want to be closer?" In her ear.

"This is fine." On tiptoe.

"I want you to be able to see." Fingertips on her shoulder.

"Don't worry about me." In his ear, breathing his aftershave. "I'm having a great time."

"Me, too." Arm settling around her. Staying there. Staying there. Standing in a dark room with Enoch Miller. Red lights bouncing off his glasses. His arm around her, like they'd come here together. They had. His arm around her like she belonged to him. She did, she always had. For as long as he wanted her. His mouth at her ear, "I love this song." His arm around her for everyone to see, as long they didn't recognize them. Corinne would take it. She'd take this. This night. This song. Every time they got to the chorus, all the instruments cut out. *"I am trying to break your heart,"* the singer sang. Enoch tightened his arm around Corinne's shoulders. Corinne let her head rest against his chest. *"I am trying to break your heart."*

After the concert, Enoch bought himself a T-shirt. And he bought Corinne one, too. It was a little like being at the circus with your parents and getting a souvenir. He paid for everything one-handed, like, if he took his arm off Corinne, it wouldn't be allowed back. They walked to his truck like that. His hand stayed on her shoulder until she was in her seat and he was closing the truck door. "Are you good to drive?" she asked when he climbed up beside her. "Are you tired?"

"No," Enoch said, "I'm full of adrenaline. That was great. Did you like it?" He'd already asked her three times.

"I did," she said. "I loved it."

His face was still flushed. He was happy. They both wanted to listen to something different on the way home. Corinne turned the radio to the oldies station. Enoch rested his arm on the center console. Corinne wished he had a less expensive truck, something with a bench seat. Now that they'd touched, she didn't want to spend another minute together not touching him. She laid her hand on his forearm, and Enoch immediately shifted to take her hand. Immediately. Like he'd been waiting for it. Enoch Miller's big square hand. His long, blunt fingers. Remember when she'd had this every week?

We're holding hands, Corinne almost said out loud.

We're holding hands, and I don't want to pretend that we're not.

I can do this under the table, if that's what you need, but I can't pretend that it isn't happening. Not when it's just you and me. I don't want to. I don't want to cut myself in half, the half that touches you and the half that talks to you and looks in your eyes. I can't answer trivia questions and roll dice while you touch me.

"Do you want to play Name That Tune?" Enoch asked.

"Sure," Corinne said.

He squeezed her hand. They played Name That Tune. They already had their own rules: You had to start with the chorus. And it had to be a song you thought the other person would know. Corinne was really good at guessing with just a few notes, but sometimes she let Enoch get through the whole song anyway just because she liked his low, rumbling hum.

She remembered playing this with him on the way to Mount Rushmore. She remembered how much fun it was to play games with Enoch, because he never made you feel stupid or immature for wanting to play. Other people got tired of games. Enoch never did.

He didn't let go of her hand until he pulled up in front of her apartment building.

"Don't get out," Corinne said. "It's cold."

"Will you blink your lights when you get in? So I know you're okay?"

"I'll call you," she said. Enoch had a fancy flip phone.

"All right."

"Thank you," Corinne said. "For everything."

"Thank you," he said. "Can we do this again?"

"Yeah." She nodded. "Yes."

Enoch didn't try to kiss her or anything, and Corinne didn't try to kiss him. A kiss would be something else.

She called him from her apartment. She stood by the window and looked down at the truck.

"Hey," he answered.

"I made it in," she said. "I'm waving at you."

"Oh, you are? Let me look. There you are. I'm waving back."

"Thanks again."

"Hey, Corinne, you still want to go for a walk tomorrow? After work?"

They were supposed to meet at a park with a walking trail.

"Yeah," she said. "Of course."

"All right, see you then. Good night."

"Good night, Enoch."

Chapter Thirty-eight

It was bitterly cold when Corinne woke up the next morning, but she didn't check the weather forecast. And she didn't call Enoch to see if he wanted to cancel their walk.

He didn't call her either.

Around three, it started to sleet. Corinne didn't call him. And he didn't call her. They were supposed to meet at four.

Corinne wore her warmest coat, a sunshine-yellow down jacket that came almost to her knees. Plus a hat and a scarf. The streets were treacherous. She left early and got to the park late. Enoch's truck was the only car in the lot. As she eased in next to him, he hopped out of the cab; he left the engine running.

It was too cold for this, it was absurd. Maybe it was finally all too absurd. Maybe it had hit Enoch last night. When the adrenaline from the concert wore off. How ridiculous this was. Where they were headed. What waited for them there.

Corinne rolled down her window. Enoch was wearing his gold-tan coat and a gray stocking cap. He took off his glasses and smiled at her, like he was acknowledging how ridiculous everything was. "Hey, Corinne . . ."

"Hey, Enoch," she said quickly, "do you want to try for some other day?" She wasn't ready to hear him say it—that this was senseless. Pointless. Doomed.

"I was thinking . . ." He licked his bottom lip. "Do you want to just come over to my house? I'll make dinner."

Corinne's mouth hung open for a second. "You don't have to do that."

"I want to."

"It'll be warmer tomorrow."

"Corinne . . ." The sleet was already collecting in his hat. "I don't want to wait 'til spring to see you again."

"But . . ." *I don't want you to regret this. I don't want you to do anything you'll regret. There's a line, and when we cross it, it's all over. I'm not in any hurry. I could go on like this forever. I'll take it, Enoch. I'll take it.* ". . . you weren't expecting company."

"It's fine. I've already got something in the crockpot."

"You have a crockpot?"

"Corinne?" There was ice in his eyelashes. "Will you come?"

"Yes," she said, because how could she say no? When had she ever?

"Follow me?"

"Go slow," she said.

"I will."

"I'll follow you."

〜

The sky was dark, the roads were slick, and Enoch lived in the opposite direction as Corinne's apartment; she should just go home. She followed him from a safe distance.

When they got to his house, he opened his garage door remotely and motioned for her to pull in ahead of him.

Oh, Corinne thought. *Right.*

Enoch parked behind her in the driveway and met her in the garage. He hit the button to close the door, and took off his hat. "That was nasty. Are you okay?"

Corinne closed her car door. "It's been years since I drove through something like that."

"Doesn't it snow in Boston?"

"I didn't have a car there."

He was opening the door to his house. "Come on, come in, get warm."

The house was already warm. Corinne had never dated someone with a house. It smelled like dinner. Enoch took off his work boots, so Corinne took off her shoes. He held her steady while she did it, then took her coat. They were in his kitchen. It didn't look like a single man's kitchen—it wasn't, she realized. He'd lived here with Shannon. Shannon had been the one to leave, not Enoch.

"Sit down," he said, motioning toward a breakfast nook. "Do you mind talking to me while I finish up?"

"Can I help?"

"I'm literally just scooping it out of the crockpot. I'm so lazy— everything I make is a bowl of mush."

"I don't make anything," Corinne said.

"What do you eat?"

"Cheese," she said. "Crackers. Hummus."

"You like hummus?"

"Not really. But it's easy."

"Well, then never mind, this will be the best meal you've had in weeks."

"I don't doubt it."

Enoch's auburn hair was still sticking up from his hat. His glasses were fogged up. He wiped them on his flannel shirt. He washed his hands, hunched over the sink. He glanced at Corinne over his shoulder and caught her watching him. He smiled with his eyes. "What do you want to drink?"

"What do you usually have to drink?"

"Water," he said. "I have root beer though. And Orange Crush."

"Your house is like a small-town gas station in 1978. Do you also have pickled eggs and pork rinds and Richie Rich comics?"

"I have . . . one of those things."

"Pickled eggs?"

"Pork rinds."

"I'll have an Orange Crush."

"It's in the fridge."

Corinne got up and opened the refrigerator. There were magnets on the door from places Enoch had probably gone with Shannon . . .

Branson, Missouri. Cabo San Lucas. Tucked behind the magnets were the usual business cards and pizza coupons. Plus a photo of Enoch with Corinne's brother. Alicia had probably taken that. Alicia always ordered prints and sent you the doubles.

"Do you want to eat in here?" Enoch asked. "Or in the living room? We could watch a movie."

"Let's do that. Let me help."

"You can carry these out." He was ladling his mush into two bowls.

Corinne washed her hands over the sink. "What kind of mush are we having?"

"Chicken and rice." He handed her the bowls. "The living room's right through that door. You can't miss it."

Corinne took the bowls and walked through a small dining room, into the living room. The whole house was compact. One story, she was pretty sure. The rooms were painted fashionable colors, creams and golds and shades of olive green. There was a widescreen TV hanging over the fireplace and a big brown leather couch sitting on an expensive-looking braided rug. The walls were lined with shelves—an entire library of CDs and DVDs. Corinne set their dinner on the glass coffee table. Enoch came in behind her with their drinks, spoons, and napkins.

"Your house is so nice," Corinne said.

"Thanks. Shannon picked everything out."

"I was referring to the abundance of three-prong outlets."

He snorted a laugh. "I did rewire the whole thing."

"I had a feeling."

"What do you want to watch?"

"Something we've both seen," she said, "so we can talk. Have you watched all these movies?"

"Yeah."

"Making up for lost time, huh?"

"I guess so."

Corinne walked over to a shelf. The movies were organized alphabetically. "Didn't Shannon take anything with her?"

"Not much. I think she wanted a fresh start."

"Didn't you?"

"I mean . . . no."

Corinne turned her head. Enoch was standing behind her, awkward in his own living room.

"I definitely didn't need a fresh start from, like, the couch," he said. "Your brother tried to talk me into moving, but—why should I lose everything? I like this house. I like my kitchen. I like my bed—is that weird?"

"I don't know," Corinne said. "It doesn't sound weird, when you say it like that. You don't feel, I don't know, haunted? Like Shannon's still here?"

He laughed, just a breath. "No. It definitely feels like she's gone."

Corinne picked a movie. *Raising Arizona.* Enoch put it in the DVD player.

"Do you want a fire?" he asked.

"Always. I wish I had a fireplace."

Enoch knelt in front of it. "Don't wait for me to eat."

"I don't mind waiting."

He looked even bigger when he was kneeling. Or hunching. Anytime he tried to make himself small. Corinne took in his broad back, the back of his wine-dark head, the flannel shirt tucked into his jeans. She sat on the couch and sipped her Orange Crush. "Have you dated anyone? Since your divorce?" Anyone else, she meant. It was a dangerous question. The sight of him made her reckless.

"No."

"It's been three years?"

"Since Shannon left. A year since it was final."

"Why haven't you dated?"

Enoch shrugged.

Corinne leaned on the arm of the sofa, her chin on her hand, watching. "Have things changed since I've been gone—is it two brothers for every sister now? Are the odds against you?"

He laughed again, with his shoulders. He didn't turn to look at her. "No. I suppose the odds are still in my favor."

The fire was catching. He pumped air into it.

"Why then?" Corinne pushed.

Enoch fed the fire. "I guess I didn't want to make the same mistake twice."

"There can't be that many lesbians . . ."

He stood up. His knees cracked. He smiled at her with one side of his mouth. "I'm going to wash my hands. Don't wait for me. Your mush will get cold."

"It's still too hot anyway," she said.

When he got back to the living room, he sat down right next to her and started the movie.

Corinne took a bite of her chicken and rice. "This is really good." She sounded more surprised than she meant to.

"There's plenty more. I like to have leftovers."

The opening sequence started. Corinne loved this part. "This movie has swearing, is that all right?"

Enoch smiled. "My ears won't bleed."

"You don't pick it up?"

"No."

"I do," she said with her mouth full. "I swear all the time."

"I've never heard you swear, Corinne."

"I'm good at turning it off." She swallowed. "This is really delicious, I mean it."

"Thank you. I literally just put the ingredients in a crockpot, then leave it all day."

"Maybe I should get a crockpot . . ."

"Maybe you should just let me cook for you."

Corinne laughed. To cover up how strange and sad she felt all of a sudden.

They ate their chicken and rice. Enoch got them both seconds. He finished first, and set his empty bowl on the table—and when he leaned back, he put his arm around Corinne's shoulders. It felt so good. It felt so good that time got stuck again. For a minute. Maybe longer. (It's hard to measure time when it isn't moving.) Enoch's arm. His hand. His side when she let herself relax against him. The saddle-brown couch. The fire. The movie she'd seen a thousand times before. Corinne finished her dinner, and he took her bowl and set it aside. Jesus. Jesus Christ, this was good. Enoch pressed a kiss into her hair. Time got stuck, but the movie kept playing, it was already almost over. Neither of them moved. They didn't move when it ended. Corinne's head was on Enoch's chest. His voice humming right below her ear. "Corinne?"

"Yeah."

"I'm so happy right now."

"Me, too," she whispered. Corinne's mother used to say that God was always watching, and when He wasn't, His angels were. They were always with you. In the room with you. But the demons were there, too. They were battling it out for your soul. And so you should never speak your fears out loud—because then you'd be giving them something to use against you. But you shouldn't say your hopes out loud either, for the same reason. "*Me, too*," Corinne whispered, and she wondered who would use it against her, the angels or the demons.

Enoch didn't move. "Last night was perfect," he said.

She nodded.

He ran his fingertips down her spine, between her shoulders. "And last weekend. With Shawn and Alicia . . . It felt like . . . Well, it felt like how it was supposed to be. With us. Like, we could have that . . . We could be a couple. Who has dinner and plays cards. Like, maybe that's how it was supposed to be for us."

Corinne swallowed.

"Corinne . . . what's wrong?"

She'd pulled away from him. The left side of her body was already cold. She swallowed again and tucked loose hairs behind her ears.

"I'm sorry," he said. "What did I say?"

Corinne shook her head. She was upset. *Why was she so upset? This was good, they were happy.* "You felt like that was how it was supposed to be for us?"

Enoch looked confused. Scared. On the hook. "You didn't feel that way?"

"How it was supposed to be," Corinne said again. "For us." Her bottom lip was trembling—but she wasn't crying, or even about to cry. This was something worse.

"Corinne?"

"You're the one who didn't want that," she said. "You didn't want that."

"What do you mean?"

"It *could* have been me, Enoch. I could have . . . We . . . But you didn't want that with me."

His eyes were wide. "That's not true."

"It is true. It *is*." She pushed her hair behind her ears. "I can pretend a lot. I can forgive . . . everything, really. But I can't . . ." Her lips were shaking. Her chin. Her hands. "You didn't want that with me."

"It wasn't an option, Corinne."

"Yes, it *was*." Corinne raised her voice. "Don't. Don't try to . . . You made this choice. You're the only one who made a choice."

"I didn't *have* a choice," Enoch said. He was defending himself. It was pathetic. It was outrageous. "I was engaged to Shannon."

"You didn't have to stay engaged."

"I wanted to have a life in the church."

"You could have had that life with *me*, Enoch."

"No, I couldn't—you were already halfway out the door!" He was angry now.

So was Corinne. "So you thought you'd help me out?"

"What? No!"

"I wasn't halfway anywhere!" She moved back, farther away from him, to the end of the couch.

"You were checked out, Corinne. Everyone knew it. You came to church dressed like you were in a goth rock band." He was leaning his big body toward her.

She leaned toward him and pointed. "Are you really going to talk about my *clothes*? Are you Sister Walters now? Do you think Jesus cared about my nail polish?"

"You were going to college!" His voice broke. "You took the ACT!"

"I went to college because I got kicked out of the church!"

"You could have come back!"

"For what?"

"For yourself, for God!"

"Can you hear yourself?" Corinne was shouting. "How does any of this make what you did better? You knew I wasn't a good Christian, so that made it okay to fuck me?"

"Corinne. That's not—"

"I was halfway out the door, so you may as well take what was on offer?"

His face was flushed. "No!"

"And then you could still marry your perfect girlfriend, she was still waiting for you. She'd forgive you . . . Everyone would forgive you."

"That's *not*—"

Corinne was standing. She was shouting. "Everyone *did* forgive you!"

"It wasn't like that!"

"It was exactly like that! That's how it happened, Enoch! You got what you wanted from me, and you never looked back!"

Enoch was standing taller. He was shouting louder. "I never got what I wanted from you!"

"How can you say that?!"

"I loved you, Corinne! I was in love with you!"

Corinne took a step back. Away. Enoch's voice was so low that when he shouted, it was like standing next to a speaker and feeling the bass in your stomach and the bottom of your feet. Corinne was crying now. She was still shaking. She hated him. (She'd always kind of hated him, hadn't she?)

"If that's true," she whispered, "it makes it all worse . . ."

Enoch was crying, too. He looked furious. "How does that make it *worse?*"

"To do what you did. To someone you loved."

Enoch closed his eyes. He held his head. His voice dropped very low: "I'm sorry for pushing you. That night."

"You didn't push me."

He opened his eyes. "I'm so sorry. If I could take it back—"

"That's not—that night wasn't even the bad part, Enoch. Do you really think it was the bad part?"

He didn't say anything.

"You *turned* on me!" she cried. "You turned me in! You never even talked to me about it—and you're going to do it again!"

"Corinne, I'm *not.*"

"You are! Could you just stop lying? And pretending? I don't want to pretend anymore! I know what we're doing here—don't you? We're going to keep moving closer until you can't stand the guilt, and then you're going to cut me off again."

"That's not—"

"*Stop. Lying.*"

"Corinne . . ."

"I'm going home." She was walking through the dining room, into the kitchen.

Enoch was following her. "You can't go home."

"Yes, I can."

"You can't drive in this."

"You don't have any say in what I do."

"Don't kill yourself just because you're mad at me!"

"I'll drive slow."

"Let me drive you, I've got four-wheel drive."

"No!" She was putting on her shoes.

"Then let me call Shawn. He'll come get you."

"I'm not calling my brother to your house, where I'm alone with you, at night. You'll have to have an elders' meeting."

"I'm going to have to have one anyway!"

"Jesus *Christ*, Enoch!"

"What?!"

"Jesus Christ." Corinne was sobbing. She had one shoe on.

"Corinne. Just sit down. I'll leave you alone. I'll go to bed."

She sobbed.

"Promise me you won't drive home," he said.

"Fine."

"You promise?"

"Yes! Fuck!"

Enoch left her alone in the kitchen. Corinne leaned against the door to the garage. Eventually she took her shoe off and went to the living room. She sat down. She cried some more. She stared into the fire. What was left of it.

This was always going to happen.

She hadn't thought it would happen *tonight*.

Enoch Miller just said that he was in love with her. No—he said that he *had* been. That he was in love with Corinne thirteen years ago. On the living room floor. With his hand on her leg and their little brothers looking the other way.

Had he felt that way at the time? When he was spending every Saturday afternoon at Shannon Frank's house? Or had he decided retroactively that it was true? It was prettier to think that he'd loved

Corinne all along, and not the beautiful girl who never really wanted him.

Enoch didn't love Corinne. Then. When he was calling her to the top of the tornado slide. When he put himself inside of her and then left her sitting on the couch. When he told his mother. And cleared away their game. When he walked past her in the church lobby without lifting his head.

That wasn't love.

That wasn't how love behaved.

"Love suffers long and is kind.

Love does not envy. Does not parade itself, isn't puffed up.

Love does not behave rudely, does not seek its own, is not provoked.

It thinks no evil—it does not rejoice in iniquity, but rejoices in the truth.

Love bears all things, believes all things, hopes all things.

Endures all things."

Corinne stood by Enoch's front window and held back tasteful curtains purchased by Shannon Frank. It was snowing hard outside. Gray, icy snow. Corinne couldn't drive home in this. She wouldn't let Enoch drive her. And she wouldn't let him call her brother. Corinne had something to lose here, too. She'd worked so hard to get back to her family. To be back in the fold. Conditionally. She didn't want to be cast out, again, for ruining Enoch Miller. Again.

She sat on his couch and stared at the fireplace. Eventually she had to pee.

She went looking for a bathroom . . . There was one right down the hall. It was very cute. Shannon had painted it mint green and hung vintage prints of mermaids frolicking. Very homoerotic mermaids, if Corinne was being honest. She peed and washed her face and cried some more. She felt trapped.

When she got back out to the living room, there were blankets, sheets, and a pillow stacked on the couch. Enoch had set out a glass of water for her. And a toothbrush, still in its package. It was preposterous.

Corinne laid out one of the blankets. She could get through this. One last night. And then she'd be back to normal. Back to not worrying about Enoch Miller or his rules. (To not worrying about them very often.) The pain of this would fade—it had faded before, even if it never quite went away. Corinne would never be over him, but that was all right. She was used to that. This last month, these last six weeks—last night—hadn't changed anything. Or altered her. Enoch Miller was already the person in her life who loomed largest. He had been, all along.

She sat on his couch. She pulled the other blanket over her and reached for the pillow. It smelled like Enoch. Not like his aftershave, but like his laundry detergent. Like his house. Like his mom's house, really. That clean, kind-of-sweet Miller smell. Corinne laid her head down on it. She didn't have to sleep; she just had to get through this night. She cried some more. She started the movie again, the volume turned low. She heard tires squealing outside, like someone on the street couldn't stop.

～

It was late when Enoch came back to the living room. He still hadn't changed out of his work clothes. His voice was low, low, low. "You still awake?"

"Yes," Corinne said.

"Can we talk?"

"I can't imagine that there's anything more to say."

"Please."

Corinne sat up. She pulled the wool blanket up around her. Enoch sat in a leather chair on the other side of the coffee table.

"I don't want to argue with you." He sounded hoarse.

"Good."

"But I want to tell you how it was for me."

"I don't want to feel sorry for you," Corinne said.

"I don't want you to feel sorry for me, either. I just—we never really talked back then. And we should have. I think things would have been different if we'd talked."

"I'm sure that's *why* we didn't talk."

"Maybe you're right . . ." He took his glasses off to clean them on his shirt, then put them back on and looked up at her. "At the time, I felt like . . . if we acknowledged what was happening, it would stop. Like, a dream where you're flying—but then you remember that you can't fly, and that's when you fall."

"If we had acknowledged what we were doing," Corinne said quietly, "we would have had to admit we were breaking the rules—and then decide either to stop or to keep breaking them."

He nodded. "You're right."

"I would have kept breaking them," she said. "And you wouldn't have."

Enoch didn't nod. But he didn't argue with her. After a second, he said, "I felt like I had to be the person my mom wanted me to be, that my dad wanted me to be before he died."

"I know."

"Sometimes I'd lie in my bed and try to imagine dating you. Sitting with you at church. Getting married and raising kids . . . I couldn't picture it. I couldn't picture you wanting that." He lowered his eyebrows. "*Did* you want that?"

Corinne clenched her fists in the blanket. "I never even considered that it might be possible." She really hadn't. She used to fantasize about him sitting with someone else.

"Why not?"

"Because you were you." She waved a hand at him. "You were going to be an elder. I wasn't elder's wife material."

"Why is it terrible when I say that, but not when you say it?"

"*Because*," Corinne said. "Because you're agreeing that you were too good for me."

"That's not what I'm saying."

"Oh, come on. Stop. We're both adults now. We both know how it was—my family was trash. We were on the fringe. We were charity cases."

"That's not true."

Corinne rolled her eyes. "Enoch."

"It's not as true as you *think*. Look at your family now—they're all paragons in the congregation. Shawn is going to be head elder someday. Meanwhile, they won't even let me adjust the mics."

She was quiet. Maybe Enoch was right. Maybe it was just Corinne who was trash, not the rest of them.

"I didn't think you wanted what I wanted," he said.

"I wanted you," she said. It came out more sad than angry.

Enoch's square shoulders slumped. "And you would have signed on for the rest? For a life in the church?"

Corinne thought about it. About how she'd felt at eighteen. What she'd wanted then. "Yeah . . . I think so."

Enoch was quiet. Corinne pulled his blanket tighter around her.

"I didn't know that," he said, his voice very low.

"You didn't ask."

"I'm sorry, Corinne."

"What was your plan?" she asked. "Back then. When we were . . . doing what we did."

"I didn't let myself plan. What was your plan?"

"To be with you. While I could."

Enoch rubbed his face with both big hands, pushing his glasses up his forehead. He exhaled for a long time. Like his lungs were twice as full as most people's. Then he said, "I thought I could walk a line. I didn't think of it from your side. I was young and selfish, and you're right—I thought you were leaving the church anyway, so you didn't have as much to lose as I did."

"I was a virgin," she whispered. "I'd never even kissed anyone."

"Jesus, Corinne." His shoulders were shaking, his face was hidden. "I'm so sorry."

"I don't regret anything we did," she said. Tearful. "I just—Why didn't you tell me you were going to confess? We could have done it together, Enoch. Or you could have warned me."

He took off his glasses and wiped his eyes on his sleeve. "I was afraid I'd lose my nerve, that I'd look at you and slip back into . . . whatever it was with us. I felt like I had to turn myself in to the elders while I was racked with guilt, or it would just keep getting worse. It was like my feelings for you were unraveling my whole world . . . Church. My mom. Shannon." He looked up at her. "As soon you walked into the room, you were all I could think about—*and you were always in the room*. I thought I was losing my mind. I prayed constantly. It didn't help."

"You make me sound like an ordeal"—Corinne's voice was wobbly—"like I was something sent to tempt you. I was just a kid."

"I know, I was so selfish."

"What are you now?"

He didn't answer. And Corinne didn't push him. And the fire had died out a long time ago—hours. It was cold. The wind was coming down through the chimney. The snow was still falling.

Enoch looked in her eyes. "I'm in love with you, Corinne."

He should stop saying that. Corinne couldn't think when he said that. She couldn't defend herself. She couldn't experience time—and she needed time, to think.

"I'm in love with you," he said, not stopping. "And I want to be with you."

"What does that even mean, Enoch?" Corinne sounded very small.

"We'll decide together."

She started crying again. She hadn't known she could cry this much.

"Can I come sit with you?" he asked.

"No."

"All right."

She cried by herself. She tried to gather her senses.

"I want it to be different this time," he said.

She looked up at him. "How *can* it be? You're still walking the same line—I'm still something you're hiding."

"It doesn't have to be that way."

"What other way could it be? Are we going to get married, Enoch? Do you think I'm coming back to the church?"

"I don't know, we've never talked about it."

"Oh my God!" She leaned toward him as far as she could without falling off the couch. "I'm telling you now, that's not happening!"

"All right!"

"So are we done talking?"

Jaw locked. "No."

"Then what's our plan B?" she asked. "We keep inching closer to each other until we end up on the couch, and then you go to the elders the next morning?"

He sighed harshly.

"I know you're already planning your confession," she said. "That you craft our every interaction so that you don't have to feel guilty about it later."

"You can't blame me for that! You know what the rules are for me."

"I do. And I jump through every stupid hoop—I parked in your fucking garage tonight!"

"I thought you said you could turn off the swearing, Corinne."

"I can!" she shouted. "I don't want to! I'm tired of making you feel comfortable!"

He'd moved to the edge of his chair. He was leaning over his knees. "Don't you want *this*? What we have? Don't you want to see me?"

"Of course I want to see you—I *always* want to see you. I always say yes to you."

"Then why are you *fighting* this?"

"Because it isn't fair, Enoch." She was spreading her fingers so wide, it hurt her knuckles. "It's always about *you*. Your rules. Your relationship with Jesus, your standing in the congregation. Your guilt."

"I care about your guilt, too."

"Well, I don't feel guilty!" she yelled.

"I can't help that!" he yelled back.

"Neither can I!" Corinne threw off the blanket. "I only feel guilty because *you* feel guilty. And I'm afraid of your guilt, because I know that when it piles up high enough, you'll cut me off. You'll confess and repent. And you know it, too—you just said so."

"I didn't say I'd cut you off. I just said I'd have to talk to the elders."

"So you're already planning to confess, but—what? You want to keep going until you have something good to apologize for?"

"I'm not planning on being immoral."

"Were you planning it last time?"

"What I mean is"—his face was red—"I don't want to do that to you again."

"I *liked* it, Enoch."

He winced. "Geez, Corinne."

"So, what *are* you planning?" she demanded.

"I don't know—help me out here, help me find an answer for us."

"I don't think there is one. I think we both just take what we can get until you decide you've had enough. That's the best-case scenario."

He huffed. "That's a terrible scenario."

"Well, you're the one who makes the rules."

Enoch's elbows were on his knees. His glasses were hanging from his hand. He was looking up at her, pleading. "Let's set new ones together."

Corinne didn't know what to say to that. She frowned at him. "What does that mean?"

"Make a rule," he said. "And we'll both agree to it."

"You won't."

"Try me."

"All right . . ." She thought about what she wanted. About what she could stand. He'd never go along with any of it. "I don't want you to go to the elders," she said. "I don't want you to confess what happens with us."

Enoch frowned. He couldn't agree to that. "What if I said that me going to the elders would be about my own accountability and not about our relationship?"

"You're talking in circles."

"I'm not; I'm saying—I don't want to live a lie, but also I don't want to live without you."

She blew out an angry breath. "So, in this scenario . . . we have a relationship, and then you get punished for it? You get cast out?"

"I hope not. I don't know what will happen—I'm suggesting that you and I move forward, and that my standing in the church isn't what decides anything for us."

"You'll still feel guilty."

"Maybe."

"And it will ruin everything."

"You don't know that. Make another rule."

Corinne folded her arms. "Okay, here's one: You have to talk to me. Before you confess anything. Before you break it off."

"We'll both talk," he agreed. "But I'm not going to break this off."

"You did the first time."

"Yeah, and it was the worst mistake of my life."

"Worse than marrying a lesbian?" Even though Corinne had basically made this same joke a few hours ago, it came out really mean this time. She regretted it.

Enoch still answered her seriously: "It was all part of the same mistake, and it's the mistake Shannon made, too—to settle for something easy, something that other people want for you, instead of going after the hard thing you really want."

"I'm supposed to be the hard thing you really want?"

"Yes. Always. My whole life. Make another rule."

Corinne shook her head. "What do we have so far?"

"My relationship to the church is separate from my relationship with you. And we're going to talk about everything. What's next?"

Corinne looked at him. At his honest shoulders and his earnest expression. At his fists clenched between his knees.

"I'm not a sin," she said softly. "I'm a person."

Enoch didn't reply.

"I know you think of what we did as a sin and a mistake," she said. "And maybe we'll do other things that'll feel like sin to you. But *I'm* not a sin. I'm not a temptation. I'm a person. And if you love me, you'll treat me that way. You'll treat me like a blessing."

Corinne's voice was breaking . . .

"Like I'm more precious than rubies. Like I do you good, not harm."

It was broken.

"Like I bring you wool and flax, and work with willing hands."

There were tears rolling down Enoch Miller's cheeks. His lower jaw was swung out to the side, he was biting his bottom lip. He nodded his head. "I will."

Corinne nodded, too.

"Make another rule," he whispered.

"I'm done," she whispered back. "But I reserve the right to make amendments."

"All right," he said.

"Do you have any rules?"

"I like your rules, Corinne."

"All right," she said.

"Can I come sit with you now?"

She thought about it for a second . . . "Yes."

Enoch came around to Corinne's side of the table. He sat with her on the couch. He wrapped both arms around her, and she sank into his chest. She was shaking again. Enoch held her. He pressed a kiss into her hair. It was still snowing. The fire was long dead. Cold air whistled down the chimney and rustled Shannon Frank's curtains.

They didn't talk any more—Corinne had already talked herself hollow. She drifted in and out of sleep. Enoch's head fell back against the couch. He snored.

It was very, very late when he finally stood up. He helped Corinne spread a blanket over the couch, and after she lay down, he pulled the other blanket up over her.

"Good night, Corinne."

"Good night, Enoch."

Chapter Thirty-nine

Corinne had missed the last two weeks of high school. She couldn't go back to Enoch Miller's school. She couldn't face him—her mother wouldn't let her.

On the last day of school, Corinne called her guidance counselor to see if it was still possible for her to graduate somehow. The guidance counselor was happy to help. Guidance counselors have hero complexes, and there weren't many fucked-up, practically homeless kids at that high school; Corinne presented a unique opportunity.

She went in over the summer to take her finals. Her dad drove her. (He'd come back to town as soon as Corinne's mom was settled in a new house with subsidized rent. And Corinne's mom took him back, because they were still married, and marriage is a sacrament.)

Her family started at the new church that summer. A new congregation, but the same denomination. Corinne would still be cast out. She'd have to meet with the elders in the new congregation and tell them what she'd done. She'd have to apologize again. And make a plan to repent. To earn back God's favor. To earn the forgiveness of a bunch of people she'd never met before. Corinne's mother begged her to do it—

Corinne didn't.

Corinne wouldn't.

Corinne wasn't sorry, not about the right things.

She stayed home on Thursday nights and watched television with her dad. *The Cosby Show* wasn't on anymore.

The guidance counselor kept calling to talk to Corinne about college. *She must get a recruitment bonus,* Corinne thought. Corinne's test scores were high, and her grades were fine, and the counselor said she'd be eligible for financial aid. Corinne was all ready to explain that she wouldn't be going to college for religious and family reasons—but those reasons were gone now. She'd left them on Enoch Miller's couch.

The counselor helped Corinne apply to a state school. She pulled some strings for late admission. Corinne's dad signed the financial aid paperwork. (He wasn't her real dad, but it was still legal.) Her mother cried and asked her to reconsider. *"God loves you, He misses you."* But how could God miss Corinne? Wasn't He watching her all the time? Even now? Didn't He watch over the little sparrow? Her dad drove her to campus, smoking cigarettes and blowing the smoke out his window.

Corinne did well in college. She was good at reading and writing and following rules. She stayed on campus over the summers. She started dating another political science major. She slept with him one night when her roommate was back home doing laundry. (Was God watching? Were the angels and the demons there? Were they still fighting over Corinne's soul—or had they lost interest at the same time that Enoch Miller did?)

Corinne dated that boy, Jeremy, for almost four years. He was fine. He was Catholic, but not in any ways that you'd notice. She liked how easy he was. How little he worried about anything. He thought it was funny that Corinne was so sheltered. He joked about corrupting her. They went to see Quentin Tarantino movies and had sex in their dorm rooms, and most of the time, Corinne didn't look back. (She was like Lot's wife in reverse. Heading confidently into sin.) (Corinne had always felt so bad for Lot's wife. What if she'd just been worried about her neighbors? Or her house? Or maybe she was just gawking. Who wouldn't turn around and watch a city burn?) (Corinne had felt sorry for almost everyone who was punished in the Bible. Lot's wife and Jezebel and Joseph's brothers. That was probably a bad sign.)

Corinne got a master's degree in communication. She took a job at an ad agency in Boston. She broke up with Jeremy when she realized that she didn't miss him.

She fell in love with Marc not long after. He was an art director who'd never been to church, and Corinne was so acclimated to the world by then, Marc didn't even notice that she needed corrupting. Corinne had seen a hundred Rated-R movies. She said "fuck" and "ass" and occasionally, if she thought it would get a laugh, "cunt." Marc didn't ask why Corinne never went home for Christmas— almost no one went home for Christmas. She and Marc had Christmas together. Corinne was in love with him. She loved his wavy black hair and his dimples. She loved watching him work. When he asked her to marry him, she said yes. It didn't last, there was never a ring. Corinne broke up with him once for cheating on her. And once for lying. And once for getting drunk when he promised he wouldn't. Really, all of their breakups were about Marc getting drunk.

She didn't date much after that. She never met anyone outside of work, and Corinne's friends said she put off *Leave me alone* vibes. That was probably true. Jeremy was bad at reading facial expressions, and Marc was drunk the first time he made a pass at her; neither of them would have noticed.

Corinne didn't especially want to be alone, but she couldn't really see any other practicable options. She wasn't lonely enough to do anything desperate, or even anything foolish. And she wasn't sure she wanted to fall in love again. Falling in love hadn't led to any of her finest moments. Historically.

Corinne was doing fine, as she was. She was good at her job. She was the sort of person who people liked better once they'd worked with her. She was smart and responsible, and she got shit done.

And over the years, she'd made a lot of progress with her mom. It started with phone calls. Corinne reached out first, but her mom was open to it. Responsive. Then Corinne started going home for Christmas.

When her mom had a heart attack, Corinne decided to move back home to Kansas. She didn't know how much more time they'd have to repair things, and she could do her job from anywhere—and there wasn't anyone in Boston that she couldn't leave behind.

Marc had tried to get her to go out, the night before she left, but it was easy for Corinne to say no. She was tired, and he didn't have any hold on her.

Chapter Forty

"Come in," Corinne said.

Enoch Miller was filling up her entire doorway. In his contractor coat and his gray stocking cap. "I didn't have time to change," he said, leaning over to untie his boots.

"I don't care, I like your work clothes." She opened the door and stepped out of his way. "Welcome to my extremely boring apartment."

Enoch shrugged off his coat and shoved his hat in the sleeve. "How long have you been here?"

Corinne looked at her empty living room—at the couch and the table and the stack of taped-up moving boxes in the corner. "Almost a year?" She took his coat. "I should probably throw all these boxes out. I can't even remember what's in them."

The best thing about Corinne's apartment was the exposed-brick walls. Enoch was frowning at the stacks of framed photos and artwork that she'd propped against one wall instead of hanging them. "I tried to put those up," she explained, "but apparently you need a special drill."

"I have a special drill," he said.

She kind of loved that it wasn't a double entendre.

"Well, aren't you useful," Corinne said. "Come all the way in."

This was what came of talking about everything and solving nothing: Corinne and Enoch were going to spend time alone now.

Indoors. Where no one could see them. (Though maybe someone would see Enoch's MILLER ELECTRIC truck parked in her lot.)

"This is the living room," Corinne said, pulling his arm, "and also the dining room. The kitchen is at the end, and my bedroom is over there." She pointed to the right. "You have to walk through it to get to the bathroom."

"It smells good in here."

"Don't get your hopes up."

Enoch was smiling with one side of his mouth. "What'd you make?"

"Do you like chicken parmesan?"

"I love it."

"Me, too. I was going to make that. But I couldn't handle the raw chicken. So I panicked and called Alicia, and she told me how to make a chicken and broccoli braid. With crescent rolls. And pre-cooked chicken."

"Alicia loves a crescent roll."

"I mean, she's not wrong about them . . ." Corinne pulled him toward the kitchen. "I had to go back to the grocery store and start from scratch. Basically, this meal took six hours. Taking into consideration what I would have billed for that time, it's a twelve-hundred-dollar dinner."

"Next time I'll cook, I'm cheaper."

He was smiling down at her. She was smiling up at him. Corinne was so happy, she wasn't sure what do with it. She was running out of room inside.

"Did you tell Alicia you were cooking for someone?"

"I told I her had a date," Corinne said. "Which disappointed her. Because she's still hoping to set me up with you, I think."

"Shawn apologized to me the other day, for the night we played cards."

"He apologized to me, too," she said.

"I think I'm Team Alicia. I'm still hoping she finds a way to throw us together." Enoch was kidding and not kidding. Corinne tried not to grin at him.

"Do you want something to drink?" she offered. "I bought Orange and Grape Crush, and root beer."

"I normally only drink pop on the weekend, but—sure, Grape Crush. Lay it on me."

Enoch sat on a stool at her little breakfast bar. Corinne gave him his pop and leaned her elbows on the other side of the counter. He reached out and chucked her on the chin, the way you would a little kid. He was happy, too, clearly. They were both so happy to have this, even though it was nothing, really. They hadn't fixed anything—they were still headed for the same cliff. The only change was, now they were going to talk the whole time. They were going to narrate their demise. Enoch chucked her on the chin again and rubbed his knuckles under her jaw and up her cheek. "Thank you for having me over."

"Anytime," she said. "Honestly. I mean, I won't have dinner ready . . . ever again. But don't let that stop you."

He chucked her on the chin.

The timer went off, and Corinne pulled away from him. She took the chicken-broccoli braid out of the oven.

"That looks fancy," Enoch said.

"Freaking Alicia, right? It's supposed to rest now. So keep your voice down."

They ate dinner at Corinne's table/desk. She moved her laptop and stacks of file folders to her bed. The chicken broccoli braid was good. It was fine. Enoch acted like he liked it.

"Adding the ham was my idea," Corinne said.

"You improvised your first time making this?"

"I had a gut feeling about it."

"Did you make Alicia's banana-split brownies for dessert?"

"She gave me the recipe, but I bought ice cream instead."

"I can see why they pay you the big bucks: good instincts, able to make decisions on the fly."

Corinne laughed. "That *is* actually why they pay me the big bucks."

"I never doubted it." He was smiling at her with his lips pressed together, and his eyes were bright. He was cleaning his glasses. He had a habit of cleaning his glasses when Corinne made him laugh. He'd take them off, rub them with his shirt, and beam his brown eyes at her.

"When did you start wearing glasses?" she asked.

"About a year ago, though I probably needed them earlier. Hey—I did pick these out by myself." He put them back on his face. "Are they terrible?

"Not terrible at all. Kind of old-fashioned. They remind me of Radar O'Reilly."

"Noted sex symbol Radar O'Reilly." Enoch rubbed the side of his long nose. "They leave dents on my nose. I feel like an old man."

"Aw, you're the youngest-looking thirty-two-year-old I've ever seen. I wouldn't sell you a lottery ticket."

Enoch laughed again, quietly. "It's all the clean living," he said. Then he looked up at Corinne and laughed some more—because clean living was sort of their problem, wasn't it?

Corinne reached over the table and took his wrist. She squeezed it. "Sit with me?"

"Yeah," Enoch said. "All right."

He let her lead him toward the couch, then he sat down with one arm spread wide, ready for Corinne to sit inside of it. She did. She couldn't wait. "I like your couch," he said, hugging her.

The couch was pink velvet and probably fifty years old. Corinne had found it at an estate sale, it was her prized possession. "You know," she said, "this is only the third time we've sat on a couch together, and the previous two times were kind of disastrous."

"I thought you said you liked the first time."

Corinne laughed so abruptly, it came out, "Ha!" She leaned against him. "I guess I did say that . . ."

Enoch rubbed her shoulder. "I know you were only saying it to shock me."

She tried to catch his eyes. "I wasn't. I *did* like it."

Enoch looked down at his lap. He scratched his jeans with his free hand. "I shouldn't have brought it up. I was trying to do that thing you do; you bring it up when I'm least expecting it."

She reached for his hand and held it. "I did like it. That night. On the couch."

Enoch looked in her eyes and lowered an eyebrow, like he was trying to figure her out. "It was rushed and furtive and reckless."

"It was exciting," Corinne said. "It was you."

He turned his head away again, ashamed. "Stop."

"I'm not *lying* to you, Enoch—when have I ever lied to you?"

He looked back into her eyes, his mouth twisted to the side.

"I felt close to you," she said. "I felt like you wanted me."

"I did want you. All I could think about was what I wanted."

"I'm not saying you were a generous lover . . ." Corinne said.

Enoch groaned and pulled his hand away to rub his forehead.

". . . but I *wanted* to be wanted like that." She touched his chest. "I wanted to be close to you."

"I'm so sorry, Corinne."

"Why? Was it traumatic for you?"

"For me?" he said. "No. I mean, not in the moment. It was like all of my fantasies coming true. I was obsessed with you—sorry, that doesn't sound great. But I thought about you all the time. I wanted to bend you over every piece of furniture in the house. I was lust-crazed."

Corinne smiled. She wrinkled her nose. "I still like that," she said quietly. "Even knowing how it all turned out."

Enoch laughed hard. Helplessly. His chest shook, even though he hardly made any noise. He took off his glasses.

"Here," she said, reaching for them. She set his glasses on the coffee table, then rubbed the side of his nose with her index finger. "Can you still see me?"

His eyes were shining. "I can see you."

She rested her hand over his heart. "Did Shannon forgive you right away?"

"She did . . ." His smile mellowed into something rueful. "I think now that she needed me to cover for her as much as I needed her to cover for me."

"Oh," Corinne said. "Sure . . . Oh my God."

Enoch frowned at her. "What?"

"Were Shannon and Juanita . . ."

"Juanita's happily married."

"So were you."

He closed one eye, like he was thinking about it. "Nah . . . I don't think so. I don't think Shannon really figured herself out until later."

"You don't have to talk about this," Corinne said. "I'm sorry I brought it up. I keep bringing it up."

He shrugged. "I don't mind. I can't really talk about my life without talking about Shannon. And it's kind of a relief—I can't talk to anyone in the congregation about my divorce. The word 'divorce' gives them hives. And they act like she's a monster."

"You don't think she's a monster?"

"I know better than anyone that she isn't."

"At least you guys didn't have kids."

Enoch pulled his chin back. He sat up straighter. He looked away from her. "Yeah, I guess so."

Corinne clenched her fist in the front of his flannel shirt. "That was insensitive, I'm sorry."

"You aren't the first person to say it."

"That's, like, proof that it was insensitive. Enoch, I'm sorry."

"I thought we'd have kids right away," he said. "Most people do. You know, in the congregation."

"I know," she said. "Did you try?"

"Shannon wanted to wait. And then . . . I don't know, she kept wanting to wait. And then she told me she didn't want to have them at all."

Corinne rubbed his chest the way you'd rub someone's back if they were crying.

"I just rolled with it—I wasn't going to force her. If she didn't want kids . . . I adjusted my expectations."

Corinne kept listening. She could feel her own eyebrows pull low and sympathetic.

"Anyway," Enoch said, "then . . . the rest of it."

"I'm sorry."

"Alicia tried to set me up right away, with a sister in the congregation. A single mom with two kids under five . . ."

"Sounds promising."

Enoch laughed. "Yeah."

"You didn't think so?"

"I don't know." He picked at his jeans some more. "I liked her kids." He looked out the corner of his eyes at Corinne. "Tell me something personal and devastating, Corinne; even the score. Did you ever want kids?"

She rubbed her hand over his heart. "I was never in a relationship where kids seemed possible. I'm pretty good at not getting ahead of myself."

"Weren't you engaged?"

She nodded. She felt very careful. "I was."

"He couldn't have kids?"

"Biologically? Probably. Constitutionally? No. He was kind of permanently the center of his own attention."

"How long were you together?"

Careful, careful. "Four years."

"Why'd you break up?"

Corinne sighed. "I don't want to tell you. I don't want to tell you things that will make you like me less."

"Why would it make me like you less?"

"*I* like me less, knowing the facts of that relationship. That's why we broke up, actually, because I disliked myself so much when I was with him."

"You make it sound like you were robbing banks together or something."

Corinne shook her head. "I just don't like that I spent so much time with someone who wasn't good for me."

"Were you in love with him?"

Carrrrefullllll. "Yes."

"Was he in love with you?"

"Yeah . . . Yes. For all the good it did me."

Enoch was quiet. So was Corinne.

Then he said, "I don't think Shannon and I were ever in love. I know we weren't. I guess that's for the best. It would have been even worse if I felt that way." He looked miserable.

"My fiancé was an alcoholic," Corinne said. Offered. So that he wouldn't think he was the only fool.

"Oh," Enoch looked surprised. And concerned.

"And he cheated on me."

"Oh geez, Corinne. I'm sorry."

"I think he only cheated on me because he was an alcoholic."

"Was that a comfort?"

"Sort of. Yeah."

Enoch nodded. He looked hurt. Hurt on Corinne's behalf. "When did you break up?"

"Three years ago."

"Do you miss him?"

"No. I don't."

Enoch was looking at his lap. His plummy pink mouth was twisted to one side. Like he'd thought he wanted to know all this, but he really, really didn't.

Enoch was a failure. His wife hadn't loved him.

And Corinne was a failure. She'd lived an unclean life. She'd loved someone who wasn't any good, and now she was over him.

None of it was pretty. None of it was romantic.

Corinne clenched her fist in Enoch's shirt again. "Ask if I missed you."

His head jerked up. "What?"

"Ask me if I missed you. Three years later. Five years later. Ask me if I still thought about you."

Enoch listened, he looked careful. "Did you miss me, Corinne?" His voice was so low.

Corinne was already nodding. She sucked her lips into her mouth and bit them. "I missed you," she whispered. "I never stopped missing you."

Enoch brought his hands up to her face. Corinne fisted her hand in his shirt. He pressed his forehead against hers. "Corinne."

"It's you," she said. "And it'll still be you, even if this doesn't work out. It's always you, Enoch."

Enoch clenched his teeth, his cheeks pulsed. His eyes were closed. Corinne closed her eyes, too. "Corinne," he whispered.

                               ~

Enoch didn't kiss her. Corinne guessed that was still a line in the sand.

She'd given him nothing to confess to tonight. What would he tell the elders? *"I ate her chicken-broccoli braid. I sat for hours on her velvet couch with my arm around her shoulder. She told me that she'd never get over me."* There was no sin in that. Apostle Paul hadn't mentioned anything like that in his letters.

"This was our best couch experience ever," Corinne said at eleven o'clock.

"Mmm," Enoch said. "Top three maybe."

Corinne laughed.

He stretched his long arms over his head, then picked up his glasses. "Can I make dinner for you Friday night?"

"You can make dinner for me anytime. I'm serious—I'm never cooking again. I have deadlines."

"I can live with that. You'll come over, then?"

"Will you build a fire?"

"I will."

"Then I'll be there."

Enoch stood, so she stood with him. She walked him to the door.

"We didn't eat the ice cream," she said.

"Bring it Friday." He slid his boots on and leaned over to tie them. Corinne rested her hand on his back. When he stood up, she was still touching him. He looked in her eyes. "Did you hide my coat?"

"Oh, sorry—" His coat was in the kitchen. Corinne went and got it.

He pulled the hat out of his sleeve and put the coat on. Then he held his arms out to her. He held his arms out, like he wasn't sure Corinne would come to him. Of course she did. She wound her arms around his neck and let him hug her tight.

It was like being hugged by a wall. By a big, mostly soft wall. By a bear made out of bricks. He was hunching over to hold her. Corinne soaked it in. He sighed—his mouth was close to her ear—and she let it go straight to her head.

"It's you," Enoch rumbled. "It'll always be you."

Chapter Forty-one

Enoch had church on Tuesday nights; Tuesdays were inconsequential.

Thursdays, too—though he did surprise her once, on a Thursday night. He stopped by her apartment on his way home from church with a coconut cream pie.

Sundays were all right. Corinne could work in the morning while Enoch was at church. She could see him in the afternoon, even if she had dinner with her family that night.

But Mondays, Wednesdays, Fridays, and Saturdays . . . Those were the days worth living.

Enoch would cook dinner for Corinne at his house. (Mostly delicious mush.) Or he'd pick up dinner on the way to her apartment. They'd racked up so many good couch nights, it was hard to rank them.

Corinne had to leave town for a presentation in mid-November. Enoch dropped her off at the airport, and was there waiting for her when she landed. He carried her suitcase and hugged the living daylights out of her once they got to the parking garage.

A few days after that, Enoch was supposed to fly to Arkansas to spend Thanksgiving with his mom. It was just for the long weekend, it would be fine, but he'd warned her that he probably wouldn't be able to call much.

Corinne was sitting in his bedroom watching him pack. She'd never been in Enoch's bedroom before. He'd brought in a chair from the kitchen, so she wouldn't have to sit on his bed—as if she'd be more comfortable in a chair, and not like it would be dangerous for her to touch his flowered bedspread.

"You look worried," he said.

"I'm not worried."

"It's only four days, and then I'll come straight to see you."

"I can pick you up at the airport." She watched him pack his navy-blue suit. She watched him walk to his closet, where his ties were hanging in a rack inside the door. He picked out a gray one. "Did Shannon buy that?" Corinne asked.

"Undoubtedly."

"Huh."

Enoch was arranging his suit in the garment bag. He glanced over at her. "Why does that bother you?"

"It doesn't."

"That kind of stuff never bothers you. Usually."

"Usually I'm not in Shannon's bedroom."

He stopped fussing with his suit. "This isn't Shannon's bedroom."

"Right," Corinne said. "Sorry." She stood up. "You know what? I'm gonna wait for you in the living room."

Enoch caught her by the waist. "What's wrong?"

"Ummm, well . . ." Corinne sounded angrier than she meant to. Angrier than she felt. "You're going to see your mom."

"Yeah?"

"And you're going to feel guilty." She wasn't leaning into him the way she usually would, the way she wanted to. "And I won't be there to remind you that what's happening between us is worth it—or, not even that it's worth it, that it's hard to give up."

"I won't forget, Corinne."

Corinne tilted her head. "Mmm. You might." He had before.

He touched her chin. "Hey. I won't forget."

She squeezed her eyes closed. Tears ran out the sides anyway. She felt Enoch's lips on her cheek.

"I'm not going to forget you," he said.

Corinne opened her eyes.

Enoch's eyes were right there waiting for her. "Do you want me to stop wearing clothes that Shannon bought for me?"

Corinne let out a frustrated breath. "Do I want you to wander the streets naked? Only sort of."

He laughed with his mouth closed. Through his nose. "I can get new clothes."

"I don't really care," Corinne said, giving up and relaxing into his grip. "I'm just overwhelmed. And neckties seem . . . personal. They seem possessive or something."

Enoch backed away from her. He picked the tie up off the bed and walked over to his closet. Corinne watched. He scooped all the ties off the rack and then tossed them out of the bedroom. She laughed. "Oh, wait . . ." Enoch said. He walked out to the hall and came back with one red-and-blue-striped tie. "I've had this one since high school." Corinne laughed again. He came back to her and draped the JCPenney tie around her neck. "Okay?"

She nodded. "Okay."

⁓

She got up early to take Enoch to the airport. She didn't kiss him good-bye.

She tried to keep busy while he was gone. With work. With Thanksgiving. She made green bean casserole. It was the only thing her family would trust her with.

And she went tie shopping for Enoch—because she'd seen a romantic comedy or two, and she wasn't a complete idiot. But she'd forgotten about Black Friday. The mall was a mess. Corinne left without buying anything, and when she got home, she'd missed a call from Enoch. There was a message on her answering machine:

"Corinne? It's me. I missed your voice, so I borrowed my brother's car and went for a drive. Did you have a good Thanksgiving? Ours was good. I missed you. I miss you. Call me if you get this message in the next hour or so . . ."

Corinne went back to the mall the next day. She bought him an emerald-green necktie and signed up for a fucking cell phone.

⁓

Corinne was waiting at the airport to pick up Enoch on Sunday night, and started bouncing on her toes when she saw him walking toward security; you couldn't wait at the gate, since 9/11. Corinne waved at him. He didn't see her. She bounced some more. He saw her. She waved again. He started pushing through the crowd. Some lady gave him a sour face. Enoch kept rushing ahead. He ran past the checkpoint and swept Corinne off the ground. She wrapped her arms around his neck.

"Corinne," he said.

"Enoch." *Enoch, Enoch, Enoch.*

He set her down, he kissed her head. "I missed you."

"I missed you," she whispered. "I missed you so much."

"I tried to call."

"I got a cell phone."

"You did?"

"Yeah," she said, "but you're the only one allowed to call me."

He growled and lifted her off the ground again. "I missed you."

Corinne was so unaccustomed to being in public with him, she couldn't stop thinking about how they looked together. Enoch was big and handsome—maybe not conventionally handsome, but men didn't have to be. He was tall and strong and friendly, and he worked with his hands. People liked that in a man. Universally. He was the sort of person Republicans liked to imagine voting for them.

Corinne still looked exactly how she'd looked in high school—like a fat girl with a mildly unpleasant disposition. Her sweaters had gotten nicer. But otherwise, she was the same. She was the same.

Anyone who looked at them would wonder what he was doing with her. Somebody like Enoch could land the sort of girl who kept it tight. Someone who went to Jazzercise. Someone who was simply luckier than Corinne had ever been. In the face and body department. And in comportment. The comportment department.

Fortunately, it wasn't her job to tell him he could do better. When he set her down, she smiled up at him. "Are you hungry?"

"I'm hungry, and I need a shower. I've been on a plane or in an airport for nine hours."

"I can take you home," she said, "and we could order pizza."

"I thought maybe you were about to surprise me with dinner . . ."

She smiled, she hadn't stopped smiling since she laid eyes on him. "I told you, I'm never doing that again."

"Your chicken broccoli braid was delicious, Corinne."

"I'm retiring while I'm on top. Like Barry Sanders."

He kissed the top of her head again. "I missed you," he said into her hair. And he really must have, because he held her hand all the way to the car, in front of God and everyone, even though it meant carrying his duffel and garment bags on the same arm.

Corinne drove Enoch to his house, smiling at the road when she couldn't smile at him directly. He kept one hand on her shoulder. He told her about his nieces and nephews, and how his brother had him working on the church wiring as soon as he landed.

"Was your mom happy to see you?"

"She was, yeah." He sounded cautious.

"Yeah?"

"Yeah . . ." Enoch sighed. "She wants me to move to Arkansas. She wouldn't let go of it."

"*What*, why?"

"She's just worried about me. I'm her only kid who isn't settled."

Corinne laid her cheek on Enoch's hand, the one on her shoulder. He huffed a laugh, and she glanced over at him—"What's funny?"

He laughed again. "You make this face when you feel sorry for me . . ."

"What kind of face?"

"It's the same face a sad cartoon character would make." His voice was still laughing. "Like this—look."

"I can't look, I'm driving."

"It's like your mouth is an actual half circle. Like Charlie Brown's sad face. Look now."

She was at a red light. She glanced over. Enoch was making an exaggerated frowny face, with his thick lips pulled down at the corners, like a clown's. She slapped his thigh. "I don't look like that."

"You do so. I should know, I see that face a lot—you feel sorry for me constantly." He was laughing, and Corinne was laughing with him.

"Well, I'm sorry your mom's worried about you," she said. "I feel like it's my fault."

"Okay, Narcissus."

Corinne smacked his leg again.

He leaned over and kissed her cheek. "This time it has nothing to do with you—she's just upset about my divorce. She's upset that I'm not an elder. She's pretty sure none of this would have happened if she hadn't moved to Arkansas, and she's certain she could fix it if *I* would move to Arkansas."

"I don't want you to move to Arkansas."

"Me neither. Motion fails. What's next on the agenda?"

Corinne smiled. "Pizza, I guess."

~

Enoch took a shower, and Corinne ordered a pizza. She used one of the coupons from the refrigerator.

He came out of the bathroom in jeans and a company T-shirt, with wet hair. He'd slicked it back with his fingers. No glasses. Corinne was sitting on his leather sofa. He practically fell on top of her. "I missed you," he said into her shoulder, then he dragged himself upright and picked up her hand. "How was your Thanksgiving?"

"Fine. Good. I heard all about the new book of hymns."

"Very controversial."

"Oh, I know. And . . . I got to hold my new niece. Which was excellent."

"Mercy had her baby?"

"She did."

"How come nobody told me?"

"I'm telling you now."

"It's a girl? What's her name?"

"Ruth."

"That's a steadfast name," Enoch said. "Does she look steadfast?"

"The steadfastest."

"And you got to hold her?"

"For almost an hour. And then Holly actually had to speak directly to me because she wanted a turn."

"Ha. Your sister is a Christian soldier."

"She's something, all right."

"You like holding babies?"

Corinne narrowed her eyes. "Is this like in *Blade Runner*? Are you trying to figure out if I'm a replicant?"

He was rubbing her hand. "I just didn't know you were a baby person."

"I'm not a baby person. Necessarily. I'll hold a baby from time to time . . ."

Enoch was giving her a smile that was about ten percent mouth and ninety percent eyes.

"Stop smiling at my ovaries," she said.

He laughed. Which just meant that his chest hitched. Corinne was a fool for him.

"I missed you," she said.

Enoch put his other arm around her. "I almost called you Thursday night, after everyone went to bed. Hiding under the covers . . ."

"Why didn't you?"

"Because the reception in my nephew's bedroom is terrible."

"You slept in your nephew's room?"

"Bottom bunk. Japheth took the top."

"I didn't know that Japheth went, too."

Enoch nodded. Corinne's hair was in a ponytail. He pulled it. "Have you ever cut your hair?"

"I get it trimmed sometimes."

"Hmm . . ."

She shook her head. "It's still weird for me to see sisters with short hair . . . I was shocked when I met Alicia."

He wound the end of her ponytail around his fingers. "Our congregation was so strict, growing up. Competitively strict. Especially the women. It came up a lot when I was an elder; I spent half my time listening to grievances."

"Like what?"

"Like . . . *'I'm just really worried about Sister So-and-So. I've heard that she let her kids read Harry Potter, and now I can't sleep, I'm so worried about their eternal souls.'*"

Corinne giggled. "I love Harry Potter."

"Me, too," Enoch whispered.

She squeezed his hand. "Don't tell me that. Now I'll be up all night, worrying about your soul."

His chest hitched. He tugged on her ponytail. "That hair thing is only loosely biblical. It was never supposed to be a hard-and-fast rule. A few years ago, we got a few new families in our congregation from out of state, and all the girls had short hair. The old guard freaked out, and I ended up having to give a sermon about it. About how we should look at our brothers and sisters with love, not judgment."

"*'And why do you look at the speck in your brother's eye,'*" Corinne quoted, "*'but do not consider the plank in your own eye?'*"

"Exactly. Shannon was so proud of me. She got her hair cut the next week." After he said that, he rolled his eyes at himself. He did that a lot when he was talking about Shannon.

Corinne smiled. "Is her hair really short now?"

"So short," he said ruefully. "Shorter than mine."

Corinne laughed. "When's the last time you saw her?"

Enoch tilted his head and closed one eye. "Is this going to be weird?"

"I promise it won't be."

"I have lunch with her twice a month."

"You *do*?" Corinne was surprised.

"We were married almost a decade," he said softly, "and we didn't really fight or have a falling-out. And she was so alone at first . . ."

"She was cast out?"

Enoch nodded. "Excessively, I thought. She wasn't coming back. And it's not like she was contagious."

"She was a little contagious," Corinne said. "Freedom is."

Enoch was still holding the end of her ponytail. He tapped it on her shoulder, like he wasn't sure what to say next.

"Does Shannon know about me?" she asked.

He bit his bottom lip and shook his head.

Corinne was quiet for a minute. Then she said, "I always thought you'd make a great elder."

Enoch lowered his eyebrows. "Is that a veiled insult?"

"It's an unveiled compliment. You were great at leading our family Bible studies—you always made it interesting, you made everyone feel involved . . ."

He watched her face for a second to make sure there wasn't a joke coming, then said, "Thank you. I was an okay elder, I think."

"Do you miss it?"

He sighed and blew out his cheeks. "Yeah . . . My life got so small overnight."

"What do you mean?"

"Well . . ." He tapped her hair on her shoulder. "I had a wife. And I had a role in the congregation. Responsibilities, sermons. Secrets. Ongoing concerns. And then . . . that all went away, and all I had left was work. And I don't have a job like yours, you know? It doesn't fill up my life."

"Why'd you have to step down? As an elder. You didn't do anything wrong."

"I couldn't keep my own household in order; how was I supposed to manage God's household?"

"That's silly. You didn't make Shannon gay."

Enoch closed one eye again and twisted his lips to the side. "I think you'd find some disagreement about that, among the congregation."

"That isn't fair."

He smiled at her. Ninety percent eyes again. "That's an incredibly you response."

Corinne poked his belly. "You think you've got me all figured out tonight, don't you?"

He shook his head, laughing. "I don't have anything figured out . . ." He pulled at her ponytail. "Why didn't you ever cut your hair? You didn't have to worry about the rules anymore. Or gossip."

She shrugged and shook her head. Enoch kept hold of her hair. "I guess I was just used to it like this. Used to seeing myself with it. Back at church, I hated having the same hair as everyone else. But out in the world, it's unusual. It makes me feel different."

Enoch let go of her ponytail—only to reach higher and hook a finger under her hair tie. He was looking in her eyes, waiting for her to tell him no, if she wanted to. She sat very still. He pulled the elastic down. If Corinne had hair like his, it would have slid out without a snag. But her hair was thick and unruly. He went slow. After a few seconds, her hair fell against her cheeks, bushy and tangled. Enoch's eyes got wide. Wider. Avid. He was looking at Corinne's face. At her hair. He reached around her neck and swept the ends forward. It fell down onto her sweater, over her chest. "I . . ." he said.

Corinne swallowed. Her breath had picked up.

Enoch ran the back of his knuckles over her hair, from her forehead to her cheek. "I've been wanting to do that for a very long time."

"You could have," she said. *I'm yours,* she meant.

"I . . ." He ran his knuckles down to her shoulder.

She let him touch her. Even though she wasn't allowed to touch him. (Only Enoch got to draw lines and cross them. They both knew that Corinne wouldn't draw any at all.)

"Corinne," Enoch said, sliding his hand up between her hair and her jaw. His eyes were still wide and roving from her face to her shoulders. He cradled her chin in his palm.

"I'm so in love with you," he said. He said it like he was observing it. Like he was witnessing it from across the room. *"Look at that guy, he's so in love with her."*

He hunched his shoulders to get closer. Corinne didn't move.

"I'm so in love with you," he said again, and kissed her.

Enoch, Enoch, Enoch Miller. His plush mouth. His wide hand on her jaw, his square thumb on her chin. Corinne grabbed his T-shirt with both fists. *Enoch, Enoch.* Why was this so good? Was it just biology? What did her DNA see in Enoch Miller that it had never seen in anyone else? He kissed her. And it was different from before. When they were eighteen and inexperienced and hiding in the dark. They used to kiss like contestants on *Supermarket Sweep,* like they had ninety seconds to fill their carts with all the best stuff. It was different now. No one was going to walk in on them or turn on the lights. Their mothers were miles away. It was different. It was different.

It was exactly the same. His big hands on her face. Her heart in her throat. Corinne nodded and nodded and nodded. Enoch groaned low, and she swallowed it. It was the same. They were still kissing like they were sweeping laundry detergent and baby formula into their carts. They were still kissing like someone might take this away.

The doorbell rang, and Enoch jumped back—Corinne was already pushing him away from her.

His eyes were wild. Corinne was panting.

"It's the pizza," she said, the second she realized it.

Enoch nodded. "Right."

Corinne nodded.

"I'll get it," he said. He got up off the couch. His knees cracked. He wasn't wearing socks. Corinne had never seen Enoch's feet before, it was embarrassing.

She remembered about the coupon but didn't mention it. She found her hair tie on the floor and pulled her hair up into a finger-combed bun. She straightened her sweater, even though it didn't need straightening. She'd be normal when he came back. She wouldn't make this awkward. She'd let him off the hook. Because she liked him. Because he'd spent his whole life on the hook, and he didn't need Corinne making it worse for him. (A kiss wasn't strictly *good*, from Jesus's perspective, but it wasn't explicitly *bad*. Kissing wasn't the sin; it was just the on-ramp.)

Enoch came back into the living room holding the pizza. He looked at Corinne, his eyebrows knit and worried, his damp hair falling over his forehead. She took a very careful, hopefully not very noticeable, deep breath. It was fine. They'd be fine. They could retreat and retrench.

Enoch dropped the pizza box on the floor and stepped over it to get to her.

He climbed onto the couch on his knees and took Corinne's face in his hands. His back was bent over her. He kissed her. He kissed her like someone was going to take her away. Corinne whimpered in relief. She wrapped her arms around him, and it felt so good. He felt so good. His thick, square waist. His strong back. He was bigger— *denser* somehow—than he'd been at eighteen. A larger tank. A thicker wall. Corinne felt like he made all her electrons spin faster. Like she must be shimmering. He tongued her mouth open, and it tasted so familiar, she could cry. She did. She was. Crying. Enoch pulled the elastic out of her hair.

⌒

Corinne didn't know how to stop kissing Enoch Miller. Not in a normal way. All their other kisses had ended because they were afraid of getting caught. The last time she'd kissed him, it had ended with her skirt up. It had ended everything. She didn't know how to stop kissing him without panicking or starting a fire.

Enoch pulled away. Eventually.

He rested his forehead on her shoulder. He was petting her hair with one hand—he hadn't stopped. Corinne was gently rubbing the shallow slope of his lower back. She knew he was always sore there.

He lifted his head to look at her, and Corinne was so relieved—*he was smiling.*

Enoch was smiling. He'd kissed her. And kissed her. And now he was smiling. His lips were fatter, and pink. His eyes were light and full.

Corinne smiled, too.

He kissed her on the cheek, then stood up. She watched him. He picked up the pizza box and opened it, grabbing a piece and eating it right there. Standing over Corinne, holding the box. "I'll get plates," he said. "Water? Root beer?"

"Orange Crush."

Enoch set the box on the table and walked into the kitchen. Corinne sat back against the couch, rubbing her bottom lip with her thumb.

He came back with plates and napkins and two cans of pop, and sat down next to her. Close. Corinne shifted up onto her knees and took hold of his face. She kissed him firmly on the mouth, and then pulled away, looking in his eyes. Searching. "Okay?" she whispered.

Enoch put his hands on her waist and kissed her again. Firmly. Briefly. He looked in her eyes. "Okay," he said softly.

She didn't believe him. "You're sure?"

He squeezed her waist. "I'm sure."

"We're okay?" she said. She barely said.

"Yeah, honey, come here." He pulled her into his lap. She crawled onto him. He kissed her mouth. And her chin. He tasted like tomato sauce. "We're okay," he said. "We're good."

"I just . . ."

"I know, I'm sorry. Kiss me."

"I didn't mean . . ."

"Kiss me, Corinne."

She kissed him. He kissed her back. He held her tight. She held on to his cheeks. His ears. "I don't know what the rules are," she whispered against his lips.

"I don't always know either."

"We said we'd talk about it."

"We're talking now."

"Don't take this away," she said. Barely.

He kissed her. "I won't." He kissed her. "I need it, too."

"Enoch."

He groaned. She got to see him groan. Got to watch his eyelids dip. He kissed her urgently. Hungrily. His arms around her, his hands in her hair.

Corinne pulled away. This time. Eventually. She tucked her face against the side of his head, over his ear. Enoch hugged her so tight, her back popped. He held on to her while he leaned forward, and then back again. He was eating another piece of pizza. Corinne smiled at him. He held the pizza up to her, and she took a bite. His other arm was still locked around her. She was in his lap. She was sitting in Enoch Miller's lap, and he was feeding her pizza.

"Here," he said, handing her the slice. She took it, and he picked up the stereo remote from the table next to the couch. He turned on the radio—Enoch liked to have the radio on. He listened to the oldies station while he made dinner. Stevie Wonder was playing now. "My Cherie Amour." Corinne was holding the piece of pizza. Enoch craned his head and took a bite.

La la laaa-la la la
La la laaa-la la la

⌒

Corinne drove home before it got too late. Enoch walked her to his front door to kiss her good-bye. Then he walked her to her car. He patted the hood as she was pulling out. She called him when she got home.

⌒

Enoch called her the next morning. On his way to work. He almost never called her this early. Corinne always slept in.

"Hello?" She was half asleep.

"Good morning," he said.

"Enoch . . ."

"I just wanted to call and tell you that I'm happy."

"Good." Corinne rubbed her eyes. She woke up a little bit. "I'm happy, too."

"So we're good," he said. "Yeah?"

"Yeah," Corinne said.

Chapter Forty-two

Corinne was at T.J. Maxx with Alicia, looking at discount-price pots and pans.

"I think you'd cook more for yourself if you had nice cookware . . ." Alicia said, pushing their cart slowly down the aisle. She picked up a clay slab. "I can't believe you don't have a pizza stone."

"I never make pizza."

"You can make anything on a pizza stone, Corinne. And they're a breeze to clean."

"I had no idea."

Alicia put the pizza stone back on the shelf. "What are you doing this Friday?"

"Nothing that involves cookware," Corinne said.

Alicia slapped her arm. "Silly. I want you to play cards with us again. I bought more decks, so we can play Hand and Foot. Enoch's coming over, and I'm going to make nachos."

Corinne made a face and pulled her chin into her neck. "Alicia . . ."

Alicia stopped pushing the cart. "Corinne, I know the two of you have history, but—"

"That's not—"

"Just *listen*." Alicia looked very sincere. "Whatever Enoch was like as a teenager . . . he's been through a lot since then. He's one of the kindest brothers I've ever met."

"He was always kind," Corinne conceded.

"And he truly loves God," Alicia said. Like that was a selling point. (Maybe it was.) "He isn't just phoning it in every Sunday morning."

"Alicia . . ."

"And he *likes* you, Corinne, I could tell. I've never heard him laugh like he did that night."

"Does Shawn know you're planning this?"

"Shawn will come around."

He wouldn't. He shouldn't. This was against the rules. Corinne wasn't just *metaphorically* cast out—Alicia probably shouldn't even be walking around T.J. Maxx with her. "Alicia . . . you know I'm not in good standing with the church."

"You're in good standing with Jesus Christ."

"*Am* I?"

"He still loves you, Corinne. He's already forgiven you." She meant Jesus, not Enoch. Probably. "Please come." She was pouting. She was wearing very shiny pink lipstick. Corinne wondered if she wore it to church.

"I—I just can't," Corinne said. "I'm sorry."

Alicia sighed and pouted for a second. "Oh, don't apologize, I knew it was a long shot. Shawn told me you'd say no." She started pushing the cart again. "It's just that—somebody's going to snap up Enoch Miller. Any day now. Every single sister in town has her cap set on him. I don't want him to end up with some dumb twenty-year-old who won't play cards with me. He deserves better." She stopped the cart. "You know what? I'm buying you that pizza stone, and you're not going to argue. At least give me that."

"You're too good to me. Thank you."

Chapter Forty-three

"You're too good to me," Corinne said.

Enoch had gotten off work early and brought groceries to Corinne's apartment. (He said he was going to make something other than mush, just to prove that he could.) He'd kissed her from the front door to the kitchen. Kissed her over his bag of groceries. And now Corinne was leaning against the counter, watching him wrangle a raw chicken.

"I'm aiming for 'exactly good enough,'" Enoch said. "Where are your knives?"

"I don't have knives."

"How can you not have *knives*?"

"I told you that I didn't have anything."

"Yeah, but I thought you still had knives. Everybody has knives."

"You sound like Alicia. She bought me a pizza stone today. Can you butcher that chicken with a pizza stone?"

"Oh—" Enoch looked up at her. "Alicia's going to invite you over to play cards Friday night."

"She already did. I let her down easy."

Enoch lowered his eyebrows. "Why'd you do that?"

"Because one of us had to."

"I don't see why."

Corinne cocked her head at him. "Are you serious?"

"Yeah." He was serious. "I thought you had fun last time. We both did."

"I did, but—Well, that was a fluke. We can't do that again."

"Why not?"

"Enoch."

"Corinne."

"We can't go on *double dates* with my brother."

He shrugged his big shoulders. "It's just cards."

"It *isn't*. Alicia's trying to fix us up!" Corinne's voice was strained. "She thinks you're still in love with me."

"Well, I am!"

"Well . . ." Corinne tried not to let that distract her. "How are Shawn and Alicia going to feel if they find out we're secretly together?" Her voice was getting higher.

So was his. "I think they'll be happy for us!"

"No, they won't," Corinne squeaked. "No one is going to be happy for us—are you kidding?"

"No. I'm not kidding." He was still holding the raw chicken. "I sincerely believe that your family wants you to be happy. I think they want me to be happy, too, God bless them."

"They want me to be in the *church*, Enoch."

"Only because they love you."

"No, I know. I know that." Corinne sounded pained. She felt pained. "But it's not happening. You're not my path back to . . . *the path*. If anything, I'm luring you away from it."

"You're a person, not a temptation."

"Oh, you know what I mean!"

"Corinne—" He dropped the chicken onto a pan and shook his hands over it. They were covered in slime. "I don't understand why you're fighting this so hard. Your family loves you. I love you. Jesus loves you."

She held up her palms between them. "Whoa-whoa-whoa with the Jesus."

Enoch rolled his eyes. "Don't call Him 'The Jesus.'"

"Why are we even *talking* about Jesus?"

"Because I don't understand why you're so allergic to the entire concept of church!"

"I'm not *allergic*. I was kicked out, remember?"

"You're allowed to come back! Everyone would be *thrilled* if you came back."

"Not *me*. I don't want to come back. I've already told you this—"

"I know, but—"

"But what, Enoch?"

"Well, I don't get it!" He rubbed his forehead with the back of his wrist. "How would your life change if you came back, except for the better? It's not like you'd have to quit smoking and watching porn. You don't even drink."

"That's not—"

"Your family would take you back with open arms." Enoch turned toward her completely. He was still holding his hands up. "And I'd be there with you. *Right there*. For Sunday dinners. And cards at your brother's house. And Christmas. We could be a family. You and me."

Corinne pressed her lips between her teeth. She wanted to scream at him. She should have known . . . that he wasn't listening, that he thought he'd be able to change her mind. *Fucking evangelicals.* Changing your mind was their whole thing! Their raison d'être! She knew this. She *knew* it. She'd lived it.

"We're never going to have that," Corinne said with as much finality as she could manage. "Your family is *never* going to be happy to see me. My family is *never* going to think I'm good for you. We don't *get* to have that."

"Why not?!" He was shouting. Enoch would shout at her if she pushed him hard enough.

Corinne raised her voice: "Because I'm not coming back to church! I'm never coming back!" She held out her palms and spread her fingers. "I was miserable there—I never belonged. Getting kicked out may have been the worst thing that happened to me, but it was also the best. I never would have gone to school otherwise. I never would have had my life."

"You don't have to give up your *life*, Corinne." Enoch sounded bitter. Fed up. He turned to the sink and knocked the water on with his wrist. "If you could just set aside your pride . . ."

"This isn't about pride."

He whipped his head in her direction; he was scrubbing his hands. "Isn't it? Isn't this about you being right?"

"No!"

"If you came back to the church, it would change everything for us. *Everything.* It would make our whole lives easier."

"If I repent, you mean."

He rolled his eyes again. "No one's going to make you repent. That was thirteen years ago." He dried his hands on his shirt. Corinne didn't have kitchen towels. "You're already living a Christian life."

"There's no Christ in my life."

"You don't do anything sinful! You're kind and honest, you pay your taxes . . ."

"It's not that simple!"

He turned to face her again. His face was plaintive. "I'd make it simple for you, Corinne. I'd make it so easy."

"You want me to come back."

"Yes."

"You want me to marry you."

He didn't hesitate. "*Yes.*"

"And we'd go to church together three times a week. And sit next to each other in the front row."

"We could sit wherever you want."

"Brother and Sister Miller," she said.

He took a step forward. "I promise you wouldn't regret it."

Corinne bit her lip.

Enoch Miller was standing in her kitchen. All six-foot-whatever of him. With his big nose and his big mouth and his barrel chest. With his cherry cola hair falling onto his forehead. Enoch Miller, such a promising young brother. Such a kind young man. As devout as Timothy. He'd make a good elder someday. And a good husband.

"I would," she said. "I'd regret it."

She walked out of the kitchen.

Chapter Forty-four

Corinne sat in the living room. On her pink couch. Her prized possession.

She waited for Enoch to leave.

He didn't. He stayed in the kitchen, being right. Corinne knew he was right—it *would* change everything if she went back to church. And it wouldn't be that difficult . . . She could sit there three times a week and let her mind wander. She could reread all the biblical lists and letters. And Enoch would be there. Holding her hand. She'd get to see him onstage. In his suits. In ties she'd picked out for him. Enoch wanted to *marry* her.

He wanted to marry her because he had to. Because that was the way, the path. Because he couldn't touch her unless he did, and he wanted to touch her. He wanted to marry her because it would make everything easy.

(Why was that so offensive to Corinne? Why did she have to make everything so *hard*?)

Enoch didn't leave.

He was still in Corinne's kitchen. He was moving around. Running water. Opening cabinets. Starting the stove. *Click, click, click.*

Eventually he came out to the living room and sat next to Corinne on the couch. He was wearing white pants, like painters wear, with lots of pockets and loops. He scratched at one knee.

Corinne wiped her eyes with the neck of her shirt. "I would never ask you to leave the church," she said.

Enoch didn't say anything.

She kept going: "Because I know what a sacrifice that would be for you. To give up the only life you've ever known, the only people. I *know*," she said, and her voice cracked.

Enoch put his forearms on his knees and hung forward over his lap.

"I wouldn't ask you to leave," Corinne said. "Even though it would make everything easier—even though it would change *everything* for us."

"Corinne . . ." He sounded distressed.

"You're doing it again, Enoch. Acting like you have more to lose than I do."

He sat up and looked at her. He looked sad and angry. Confused. At the end of his rope. "The last time we talked about this, you said that you would have stayed. For me. That I could have picked you, and we would have had a life in the church together."

"Staying in is different than coming back," she said.

Enoch made a frustrated noise in his throat. Like she'd punched him there. "How?"

"Because now I know another way to be!" Corinne waved an arm around her apartment. It wasn't much. But it was more than she'd ever thought she'd have, on her own. And she'd chosen it. This place, this job. This stupid couch. "I felt so worthless at church"—she glanced over at him—"and please don't say all the things we were trained to say . . . That God loves me. That I'm precious to Him."

"I believe those things."

"I know you do. But it's how my family talks to me, and it's like— it's like having a conversation with an automated phone menu."

Enoch looked up at the ceiling. He pushed a hand back through his hair. "I don't understand why you felt worthless."

"Because I was a girl. And not the right kind . . ."

He slid his jaw to one side and shook his head, but he didn't argue.

"Not the marrying kind," she went on, "that's for sure. I was never going to be anyone's first-round draft pick. Was I supposed to wait around for someone to be interested in me? Maybe some older brother whose wife died of cancer, who needed someone to take care of his kids . . ."

Enoch shook his head harder. "For Pete's *sake,* Corinne."

"*No,*" she said, leaning toward him and pointing. "*You* don't get to act like I'm being ridiculous or shocking. You didn't marry me— who else was going to? Meshach Kittle? That little toad? Or one of the Janousek twins? How many boys in the greater metropolitan area were available to me? Fifty? Was I supposed to become a missionary to have access to a bigger pool?"

"I don't understand this argument—you didn't marry some worldly guy, either."

"Because I didn't *have* to—there are other things for me out here. I have value apart from my suitability as a wife."

Enoch took off his glasses and dropped them on the table. He rubbed his eyes with both hands. "You were valuable to—"

"Don't say Jesus."

"Jesus is relevant."

"Jesus wasn't *there*! When I was a kid—" She stopped. She wiped her eyes again, with the joint of her thumb and the heel of her hand. "I felt like the only thing I had to offer the congregation was my shame. Like it was the only thing anyone really expected of me. Like . . ."

Enoch had turned his head toward her to listen. He was watching her with his brows drawn low. His eyes were shining. He was miserable. He was listening.

"Like there were good people and bad people," Corinne said. "And the bad people sustained the good people, in a way. Fed them. With shame and guilt and salaciousness. They gave the good people something to talk about. A way to orient themselves. To know they were good, in comparison."

"You were never a bad person," Enoch whispered.

"I know that," she said. "Now."

"No one will see you that way. If you come back."

"Only because of you."

He didn't say anything.

Corinne had more to say. About sex and sin. About not wanting to be there, sitting in the front row with him, when some other teenager was cast out. About how she didn't want to be at some kitchen table, placing bets on who would be next.

She didn't say any of it.

Instead she said:

"I'm never coming back, Enoch. Do you understand that?"

He licked his bottom lip. There were tears on his cheeks. He nodded.

Then he stood up from the couch.

He walked away from her.

He stood in front of her window without looking out.

He walked over to the brick wall, where he'd hung up all her pictures and prints with a special drill. A masonry bit. He leaned forward into the wall, burying his face in his arms. His shoulders were rising and falling, rising and falling.

Corinne watched.

She waited.

"What does that leave us?" he finally asked. His voice was muffled.

Corinne didn't answer.

Enoch lifted his head. He pushed away from the wall. "What do we get to have? If you stay out. And I stay in."

"'Do not be unequally yoked together with unbelievers,'" Corinne quoted. "'For what fellowship has righteousness with lawlessness? And what communion has light with darkness?'"

Enoch pressed his tongue into his cheek. "You know, sometimes your memory isn't cute."

"I wasn't trying to be cute."

He rubbed his forehead. "I'm *in love* with you. I want to *be* with you."

"You act like that's some sort of promissory note—like it entitles you to a happy ending!"

He let his hand drop. "I know darn well that it doesn't!"

"What do you *want* from me, Enoch?"

"I want you to want this, too! I want you to help me figure it out! To act like you're invested in what we have!"

She leaned forward. "How can you even say that? I already threw my whole life away for you!"

"Come on, Corinne—that's not fair."

"You're right, it wasn't."

Enoch walked away from her again. To the window. The curtains were drawn. His shoulders were rising and falling.

She waited.

And waited.

"Can you live with it?" he asked. He didn't turn around.

"With what?"

"With being unequally yoked. Being in different worlds, but still being together. Knowing what you know. Will it feel like half a life?"

She stared at his wide back. His legs like pillars. The back of his russet-brown head. Any life with him would be bigger and brighter and longer than any life without him. (She knew how desperate that sounded; it was still true.)

"Can *you* live with it?" she asked.

"I . . ." He turned around. He had one hand on his hip and one in the front of his hair. "I need some time to think."

"Okay," she whispered.

"I'm not saying I want to . . . make any decisions. I just—I need some time to think."

"Okay. That's okay." Corinne was crying again. Harder. She wiped her face with her T-shirt. She picked Enoch's glasses up off the table and brought them over to him.

He took them. He sighed. "I don't want to keep yelling at you just because I'm scared and confused."

"It's okay. I want you to have time to think."

His shoulders slumped. "I love you." It was an apology.

"Don't say that again until it feels good."

Enoch was looking at the floor. He nodded like his head weighed ten thousand pounds. It might.

Corinne watched him put on his boots. She handed him his coat. She stood apart from him, so he'd know she wasn't expecting anything. So he'd know he was free to leave. And think.

"I'll call," he said to his feet.

"All right," she said.

"Or you can call me."

She wouldn't.

Enoch left.

Corinne closed the door and locked it. She sat back down on her couch and curled her legs up. She made herself as small as she could. (Not very small.) She thought. But not helpfully or productively. She thought about how they had always been headed here, to this dead end. And Corinne had *known* that—she'd told Enoch flat out what would happen.

He'd promised her something new. New rules. New possibilities . . .

But that was foolish, she'd known all along it was foolish. She was the same, and he was the same. And this was always going to happen.

The oven timer went off.

Corinne didn't recognize the sound at first. She thought it was the smoke alarm. She went into the kitchen. She opened the oven and tried to take the pan out with her bare hand. *"Fuck."* She pulled her sweater sleeves down over her hands and tried again.

It was chicken baked with asparagus. There were lemon slices on top. It smelled like garlic.

Corinne set it on the counter.

She went to bed.

~

Corinne got up at midnight and stood over the counter, eating baked chicken out of the pan. It was cold. And delicious.

Chapter Forty-five

Days passed.

Corinne worked.

She went to visit her new niece. Noah's wife, Mercy, had been slow to warm to Corinne. She came from a strict Christian family. She knew Corinne had been cast out and shamed, and she was wary of her. But she was also exhausted, and Corinne had offered to come hold the baby while she took a nap.

Corinne sat in their living room and rocked little Ruth. She sang her songs—hymns. (She didn't want Mercy to come in and catch her singing Led Zeppelin.) Mercy slept for three hours, and thanked Corinne profusely when she woke up. Corinne's sweater smelled like the baby for the rest of the night.

Corinne worked.

She turned thirty-two, and her best friend, Kyle, called to say happy birthday. Kyle had been her boss at the ad agency. He tried to talk her into moving back to Boston.

"Not yet," she told him.

"You always say 'not yet'—what's the 'yet'? Is there a goal here? Are you on a specific quest?"

"I want to be closer to my family for a while. We've been through this."

"Yeah, I know," he sighed. "I'm just used to you being more transparently strategic about things."

"My strategy is: Spend time with my family."

"To what *end,* Corinne?" Kyle could be very dramatic when he wasn't getting what he wanted. She promised him she'd come back to Boston soon for a visit. Maybe as soon as New Year's.

Corinne worked.

She went to the grocery store.

She went to T.J. Maxx and bought knives.

Enoch didn't call her. And Corinne didn't call him. What would she even say? Nothing had changed. Nothing was going to.

Chapter Forty-six

Days passed. A week. And he didn't call. And she didn't call. Why would she?

Chapter Forty-seven

"Hello?"

"Corinne?"

"Enoch?" Obviously it was Enoch. His unmistakable voice. That low thrum. Like an engine idling.

"Yeah. It's me."

"It's late," she said. It was almost midnight. Enoch never called at night unless it was to tell her that he got home safe.

"I know, I'm sorry—were you asleep?"

"No," she said, "not really."

"Corinne . . ." He sounded relieved. "It's good to hear your voice."

"It's good to hear yours, Enoch."

They both let the moment hang for a few beats. Corinne didn't want to move on. Enoch was there, and he was happy to hear her voice. That felt like respite.

"I'm sorry I haven't called . . ." he said. Eventually. "I felt like I should wait until I had some clarity, but . . ." He blew out a breath. "I guess I'm not really there yet. And I just . . . Would it be okay if we talked for a few minutes?"

"Yeah." She closed her eyes. Maybe he needed respite, too. "That would be okay."

"Good, I mean—thank you. Did you, um, did you have a good day?"

"I haven't had any good days lately," Corinne said softly. "How about you?"

Enoch hummed a laugh. "Pretty terrible, actually."

She could picture his face. He'd look abashed. Self-deprecating. Slightly cracked open. She wished she could *see* him—it felt like it had been months since she'd seen him. "When we were living with you guys . . ." she started to say. Then stopped.

"What?" Enoch's voice was breathy. Slow.

"Have you been drinking?" she asked.

"No, I don't even—No. I'm just tired and, um, pretty depressed, I think. Do I seem drunk?"

"Not drunk, necessarily. Just . . . slower than usual. Quieter."

"It's exhaustion, probably. I'm usually asleep by now. Are you sure I didn't wake you?"

"I stay up late."

"What were you going to say? Before?"

"I was remembering . . . Those last few months when we lived with you guys, I used to judge the days by how much I got to see you."

"Yeah?"

"Yeah. Like . . . Mondays were a wash—I'd see you in study hall, but you never looked at me. Tuesdays were a little better—study hall plus church. And Saturdays were like . . . Every Saturday was Thanksgiving plus Christmas."

He hummed again. "When you guys first moved in, I thought you hated me. I thought I'd done something to tick you off."

"You had," Corinne said. "You'd grown up and become incredibly attractive."

"Objectively untrue," he said.

"Incredibly attractive *to me*."

"Now you're just trying to cheer me up."

"Objectively untrue," she said.

He laughed something closer to a laugh. An Enoch laugh. A hard breath out his nose. "I wish I would have talked to you at school," he said.

"Why didn't you?"

"Because I thought . . . Oh, it doesn't matter, I was an idiot."

"It matters to me. Tell me."

He sighed. He sounded sad and exhausted again. "I had all these rules for myself, about how I was going to keep the situation from getting out of hand . . . I'm still an idiot, aren't I?"

Corinne didn't answer.

"Can I ask you something, Corinne?"

"I guess."

"Do you think less of me? For staying in the church?"

She thought about it for a minute. "No," she said, and mostly meant it.

"But the church chewed you up and spat you out. And Shannon . . . It was worse for Shannon. It attacked her at the root, you know?"

"I know."

"And I still want to be a part of it—I still feel like it's the best place for me, the path that leads me closest to God. What does that say about me?"

"I think . . ." She shrugged, even though he couldn't see her. "There are probably multiple paths. For different people. Maybe this really is the one that's right for you."

"That's a very diplomatic answer, Corinne."

"I don't want to hurt you, Enoch."

"I don't want to hurt you, either."

Corinne didn't say anything.

"Too late, right?" he whispered. "That's what you're thinking."

"No," she said. "That's not what I was thinking."

Enoch didn't say anything.

"Enoch?"

"Yeah . . ."

"This phone call makes today the best day I've had in a long time."

"It's technically tomorrow," he said.

"Well then, tomorrow's off to a great start."

Enoch stayed quiet. Corinne listened to him breathe. She wanted to *see* him—she hoped that she'd see him. (Did that mean she was rooting for clarity? Or would clarity mean they were done?)

"When we were kids . . ." he said. "Not kids—when we were teenagers, I used to volunteer to take attendance at church, so I could go looking for you."

"No, you didn't."

"I did. It gave me an excuse to follow you."

Corinne didn't know what to say.

"I should let you sleep," Enoch said.

She wanted to argue—she didn't need to sleep, she needed to see him. "You should try to get some rest," she said.

"Yeah . . . Can we talk again soon?"

"I haven't gone anywhere," Corinne said.

Chapter Forty-eight

He didn't call again.

Corinne waited. She stayed up late every night, hoping he might be having trouble sleeping. He didn't call. Maybe he'd found some clarity. Maybe he'd never tell her either way.

Days went by, none of them worth a damn.

Corinne's mom invited her over one Sunday after church; there was a football game on, so they were eating earlier than usual. Corinne offered to bring a vegetable. Her mom told her to bring rice. Corinne had never made rice before—it was a mess. First, it was all wet, and then it stuck together. Corinne threw it away and threw on a skirt, and stopped to buy a few loaves of bread on the way to her mom's house. Everyone else was already there, she had to park halfway down the block. They were probably already eating.

When Corinne walked in, some of the guys were in the living room, watching the game. They *were* already eating. "I brought bread," Corinne said. "If you need some." Her stepdad lifted a hand to acknowledge her.

Corinne took the bread into the kitchen. Maybe she could heat it up or something. "Well, I'm not surprised," Holly was saying. All the women in the family were standing around the island. Alicia was crying; Corinne's mom was trying to comfort her. Shawn was standing there, too, with his hands on his hips, frustrated. Holly looked angry.

Mercy was patting baby Ruth's back, like she was trying to calm her down—but the baby seemed fine. Mercy looked like she needed someone to pat *her* back.

"What happened?" Corinne asked.

Everyone looked up at her, stricken. Mercy patted the baby's back harder. The baby started to cry.

"Nothing," Corinne's mom said. Then: "We lost someone at church today. We're all just grieving a little bit."

"I'm sorry to hear that," Corinne said. "Was it someone I know?"

Holly huffed and walked into the living room.

"Let's talk about happier things," her mom said. "Did you bring the rice?"

Corinne held out her bread. "I brought a differently delicious carb."

"That's okay," her mom said. "I had Mercy bring rice, too. Make yourself a plate, Corinne. You, too, Alicia. The chicken's getting cold."

Corinne's mother had made a big pan of chicken in paprika sour-cream sauce. The smell of it took Corinne back to being a kid. It had been her dad's favorite dish. You ate it over rice.

Shawn was comforting Alicia now, while Corinne's mom took care of the bread.

"You okay?" Corinne asked Alicia.

Alicia covered her mouth and nodded. Shawn looked like he'd like to cry, too. Ruth was fussing. Corinne reached for her. "Make yourself a plate, Mercy. I'll walk with her."

Mercy nodded. "Thanks, Corinne."

Corinne took the baby and held her against her chest, cupping the back of her head. She walked with her into the living room, bouncing her gently, and pretended to pay attention to the football game. Eventually everyone else came out, too, to the living room or the dining room, and started acting mostly normal. Ruth sucked on her fist and crabbed quietly. Corinne bounced her. She kissed the back of her head.

Mercy ate quickly, even though she didn't have to, then came for the baby. "Thanks, Corinne. It's nice to have a meal to myself."

"I think she's hungry, too," Corinne said.

"It's about that time. I'll take her upstairs and feed her. Let me get my bag."

"I'll follow you."

Corinne followed Mercy up the stairs to the spare bedroom and waited for her to get situated in an easy chair before she handed Ruth down to her.

"Thanks," Mercy said.

"Anytime. She's like a little bundle of serotonin."

"I must be immune. I still feel so anxious all the time."

"You're doing fine," Corinne said, watching Mercy get the baby attached to her breast. It took a second, and Ruth cried, but then it was all right. "Look at that. You guys are so good together."

Mercy looked up at Corinne. She looked sad. "It was Enoch Miller," she whispered. "He fell away."

Corinne felt her heart leave her chest and flutter to the ground. "Enoch?"

Mercy nodded.

"Wait, what does that mean—is he all right?"

"He asked to be marked as bad association."

"I've never heard of that," Corinne said.

"Shawn said it almost never happens."

"Is it like being cast out?"

"I guess it's like casting yourself out."

Corinne just stared at her.

"I'm sorry, Corinne, I know you were old friends."

Corinne shook her head. "Thank you for telling me."

Mercy nodded.

"Do you need some water?" Corinne asked.

"I've got some. We're fine."

Corinne nodded. She headed back downstairs. Alicia was waiting for her in the stairwell. She looked up at Corinne's face. "Did Mercy tell you?" she whispered.

Corinne nodded again.

Alicia started to cry some more. "It's just so awful, Corinne."

Corinne put her hand on Alicia's back.

"He'd been doing so well," Alicia sobbed. "We thought he was back on his feet."

"I'm sorry," Corinne said.

"Why would he ask to be *marked*? Shawn won't tell me what happened in the elders' meeting, but why would Enoch *do* that? If he made a mistake, he could ask for forgiveness. Everyone would forgive him."

"I don't know," Corinne said.

"Oh, Corinne, I'm sorry. You know I wanted something better for you both."

"I should get something to eat, Alicia. I'm feeling a little . . ."

"Of course," Alicia said, wiping her eyes. "I'm glad Mercy told you. Your mom doesn't want you to know—she thinks if you hear Enoch Miller's name, you're going to turn to stone."

Corinne broke away from Alicia and went to the kitchen to make herself a plate of chicken with sour-cream gravy. Whenever anyone looked at her, she took a bite. She swallowed it without chewing. When her mom looked at her, she smiled. When anyone talked to her, she nodded. Her hands were cold.

She was standing in her mother's kitchen, it was Sunday afternoon.

She was walking across the church lobby, and Enoch Miller was walking the other way, and he wouldn't look at her.

She was sitting in her elders' meeting, and they were asking her if she understood the scope of her sins. Did she see how repulsive she'd been before the eyes of the Lord? How she'd saddened and disgusted Him? Yes, Corinne had said, thinking of Enoch Miller, and the way he wouldn't look at her. The way he hadn't talked to her. She thought of the games safely put away in the closet.

"Aunt Corinne, will you play Candy Land with us?"

Corinne nodded. She sat at the kitchen table. She helped her nephews get ice cream cones for dessert.

It was Sunday afternoon, and she was at her mother's house, and she was *allowed* here, she'd take it. She was sitting at the kitchen table. She was sitting at the kitchen table.

She was walking across the church lobby.

She was sitting at the top of a tornado slide.

She was hiding in the church basement, hoping he would find her.

"Aunt Corinne? Can we play again?"

Corinne nodded. Holly walked through the kitchen to make sure everything was okay. To make sure Corinne wasn't corrupting her boys. Corinne was eating ice cream and explaining to them what peanut brittle was. Corinne knew her place. She knew where the lines were, every one of them. Corinne smiled at Holly. Corinne's hands were cold. She was eating ice cream. She was sitting in her mother's kitchen.

She was sitting.

She was hiding.

She was touching Enoch Miller under the table.

She was meeting him in parks.

She was never coming back.

Corinne was never coming back.

Chapter Forty-nine

"Heading home already?" Corinne's mom asked.

Corinne had stayed for hours. The sun was setting. "I have some work to do tonight."

"I thought working for yourself meant setting your own hours."

"It does most days," Corinne said. "Thank you for dinner."

Her mom hugged her. "We're glad you're here," she said, and she meant it. Corinne knew that she meant it. That she'd missed Corinne for all those years. That her mom wouldn't cross any lines for Corinne—but she'd walk this one.

"Me, too," Corinne said. She meant it, too.

Corinne drove to her apartment. She could hardly feel her hands on the steering wheel. Her mom had sent her home with a plastic container of chicken paprika, and the whole car smelled like it. Corinne wasn't blinking as much as she should. Her eyes were watering.

She was driving home. She was driving to her apartment.

She was in the front seat of the Merediths' minivan. Her mom had borrowed it to take Corinne to her elders' meeting. They weren't speaking. There was too much to say. Sister Miller had asked Corinne's mom to move out the same Monday morning that Enoch confessed. Bonnie had come down to the basement and helped pack their things while all the kids but Enoch were at school.

Corinne's family never went back to the Millers' house. They never went back to their old congregation—except for Holly, who stayed with her best friend through the summer.

And Corinne's mom and Enoch's mom weren't friends anymore. Bonnie couldn't forgive her. (Which wasn't fair, Corinne always thought. Because *both* of them had left Corinne and Enoch alone at night. It was Enoch's mom who invited her family up out of the basement.) (What Sister Miller really couldn't forgive her mom for was *giving birth to Corinne*. For creating and raising the perfect trap for her son.) (That's what Corinne was, a trap that Enoch Miller kept falling into.) (That's what Satan and his demons did: They watched you, they walked with you. They got to know you. And then they presented you with tailor-made temptations. Satan was God's most beautiful angel, he was the father of temptation. The mother of it.) (Maybe that's why Corinne was brought into the church. Maybe it had nothing to do with her soul. Or her mother's. Maybe it was always about Enoch Miller. He was the one who mattered. He was the Job. The Joseph. The David. And Corinne was brought into the congregation just to tempt him. All of the demons were watching and all of the angels, just like in the Children's Bible illustrations. All of the giant men made of air, watching from above. Watching Enoch Miller, the only solid thing on the page. *What would he do? What would he choose? Would he stay on the path, though it be narrow and winding?* Corinne wouldn't make it into the illustration. [Would anyone have ever painted Corinne? Maybe during the Renaissance. As an excuse for some perverted oil painter to depict a woman's bare breast. *The Temptation of Enoch.*])

Corinne was driving herself home. She was wearing a modest skirt. Her car smelled like her dad's favorite food.

She was in her dad's truck, and he was driving her to college. And her mom had cried in the driveway. Had begged Corinne not to go. *"I can't talk to you, once you're out of my household. You aren't considered a child anymore. You know the rules, Corinne. You're cast out."* And her dad had gotten involved—*"This has gone too far, Carol"*—but that just made it worse. Because her dad was allowed to abandon her mom (and probably cheat on her), but he wasn't allowed to criticize the church, and they both knew it. They all knew it. That was the line. There were so many lines. Corinne was going to college. She was done with them all.

(What had changed between now and then? Why was Corinne allowed at Sunday dinner? Had she served her sentence? Had her punishment timed out?)

Corinne was driving home. To her apartment. She couldn't feel her hands; they belonged to someone else.

She was in her car, it was cold. She was driving home. She parked on the street and grabbed her leftovers—including two loaves of bread that no one had touched—and ventured out into the wind. She was careful, she was always careful, walking to her building by herself, after dark.

There was a man sitting outside the front door. Folded over himself on the steps.

Enoch Miller.

Chapter Fifty

"Enoch?"

He looked up at her. He was sitting on the concrete, leaning against the iron railing. Wearing his dress coat and no hat. He looked terrible. He looked frozen through.

Corinne bent over him. She shifted the leftovers to one arm, so she could touch his cheeks. Cold. His ears. So cold. "How long have you been here?"

"I don't know," he rumbled. "A while."

She pulled his collar up to protect his ears. "Come inside." She helped him get to his feet. His knees cracked. He swayed. "Jesus," she said, and took too long to open the door.

Corinne lived on the second floor. She shepherded Enoch up the steps and into her apartment, cranking up the thermostat as soon as they were inside. She got him to the couch, and he sat down, too limp and loose, like a marionette. Corinne unbuttoned his coat, it was freezing. "Jesus," she said again, pushing it off his shoulders. Enoch just watched, without helping. "You're chilled through," Corinne said. "What were you thinking?" He was wearing leather gloves, at least. Corinne took them off and held his fingers against the warmest part of her neck. Enoch watched. His head wavered, his eyelids drooped. He looked almost languid. "Say something," Corinne said, chafing her palms against his cheeks. She knelt on the couch beside him. "You're scaring me."

Enoch looked up into her eyes. And his face crumpled.

He fell forward onto Corinne, his head on her shoulder, his nose so cold on her neck. His shoulders started heaving. He was sobbing. When Corinne cried this hard, her noises were high-pitched and childlike. Enoch didn't have any high noises in him. He cried like an injured animal. A wounded cello. It made Corinne feel sick. "All right," she said. "It's all right." She rubbed his back and shoulders. He was wearing a dark brown suit. Did he come straight from church? She kissed the side of his head. She held her mouth over his ear, and exhaled as hotly as she could. "It's all right," she whispered.

Enoch cried. He cried and cried.

Corinne wondered if he'd cried like this the first time. If he'd fallen on his mother's shoulder and let her tell him it was going to be all right.

Corinne was bitter.

She was angry.

She was worried about his ears and his fingertips and his toes. She was worried about his eternal soul, even though she didn't even really believe in an eternal soul. She didn't believe in her own. She didn't believe in eternity.

She stroked his shiny, silky hair. She kissed his head compulsively, thoughtlessly, like she was stanching some wound. "You're all right," she said. "I've got you."

Enoch cried himself out. He was a dead weight, pinning Corinne to the couch.

She cupped the back of his neck. "Did you come here straight from church?"

He nodded.

"Were you sitting outside the whole time?"

"I was mostly in my truck." His voice was full of gravel.

"I didn't see your truck."

"I parked behind the building."

"Have you eaten anything?"

He shook his head.

"Let me get you something hot."

His arms tightened around her shoulders. "Corinne . . ." he said, and the tears were back. "I . . ."

"I know," she whispered. "I already know."

She let him cry some more. She closed her eyes and pressed her face into the side of his head. His ears were still red, but they weren't cold. When he wore himself out again, she pushed on his shoulder. "Let me get some food into you, okay? You're still scaring me."

"I'm fine."

"You seem fine," she said. "You seem great."

Enoch snorted miserably and let her push him off. He sat back against the couch, still limp and listless. His face was a thousand miles long. Corinne stood up. She picked up his hand to reassure herself that his fingers were warm. They were. "I'll be right back."

She took the leftovers into the kitchen and put them in the microwave. She filled the teakettle and turned on the stove. She checked on Enoch. He was still a big lump on her couch. She dumped the chicken and rice into a bowl and made tea in her biggest mug. She brought it all out to the coffee table and sat next to Enoch, who was staring vacantly into some middle distance.

"You okay?"

Enoch nodded and sat up, pulling himself a little bit together. He smoothed down his hair. (Corinne had already smoothed it plenty.)

"Where are your glasses?" she asked.

He felt in his jacket pockets and pulled his glasses out, putting them on.

"Here," Corinne said. "Let's . . ." She moved his suit jacket off his shoulders, and he shifted forward, pulling out his arms; that was an improvement, he was moving. She laid the jacket aside and checked him over. His chest was warm. His neck was warm. His eyes were empty. Corinne tried to loosen his necktie—she didn't know how to untie it, she'd never dated anyone who wore a tie. Enoch didn't say anything or help, just let her maneuver him. "Have some tea," Corinne said, sitting back and giving up.

Enoch did as he was told. He sipped at the tea, wincing.

"Is it too hot?" Corinne asked.

He looked down at it. "Uh . . ."

He really *wasn't* okay. Corinne wrapped her hands around his on the mug and blew on the tea. He took a few more sips. He didn't wince. Corinne picked up the bowl of chicken and traded him for it. "Eat something," she said.

He did. Mechanically. After a few bites, he seemed to realize how hungry he was. He took bigger bites, he chewed more quickly. Corinne rubbed his shoulder, his biceps, still trying to soothe and smooth him.

"This is good," he said. "Did you make it?"

"Of course not. I had dinner with my family."

"Oh," Enoch said, swallowing. And then, "Oh." He looked over at her, his face threatening to fall again. "Corinne . . ."

"Hey," she said, taking his cheeks in both hands. "It's all right. You're going to be all right." (She wasn't sure that he was. He'd un- plugged himself. Taken himself off life support. And what did he have to plug into—Corinne? Was that the plan? Was there a plan?) "Eat something."

"I feel sick."

"You're hungry."

"No."

"You're in shock, I think."

He took another bite. He closed his eyes to chew. A tear ran down his cheeks. He swallowed. "This is *really* good."

Corinne laughed and kissed his cheek, just relieved to hear him say something normal. He caught her with one arm and held her tight. He set the bowl down and wound that arm around her, too. "Corinne . . ." he said.

She hugged him back. He felt better. Warmer. More alive. Like his arms were connected to his body.

"Did they tell you?" he whispered.

"Yes, but I don't understand."

Enoch didn't explain. He held her. He leaned on her. She let him. She inched back to the arm of the couch, for support. She couldn't get her arms around much of him like this, so she cradled his head and rubbed his back. (She pushed all of her bitterness and anger to the far side of the room, knowing it would still be there for her later.)

Corinne held Enoch for a long time. His breath evened out; she thought he might be dozing—but when she checked, his eyes were open. He was still staring off into the distance. Enoch noticed her checking on him and hid his face in her shoulder. "I know I was supposed to talk to you," he said, his voice all bass notes.

"Why didn't you?"

"I didn't want you to change my mind."

"That's a troubling pattern."

"I know."

She cupped his head. She rubbed his back. (Her bitterness was still waiting for her on the other side of the room. She could see it from here.) She thought Enoch might have fallen asleep. This time, she didn't check.

She startled when he lifted himself off of her. "I have to . . . Could I use your bathroom?" Of course he could use her bathroom.

Corinne felt cold without him. She watched him lumber into her bedroom. She picked up his coat and gloves, his jacket, and made a nicer place for them. She went into the kitchen and heated up more water.

Enoch found her there. He was wearing brown dress pants, a white shirt, and the green tie she'd given him. And wing tips. Normally he took his shoes off at the door. He looked like he'd washed his face. His eyelashes were wet.

"I'm making you fresh tea," Corinne said.

"Thanks," Enoch said. "Thank you for . . . this."

"Do you feel any better?"

"I don't feel great, but . . . yeah."

Corinne watched the kettle. Enoch leaned against the counter by her side.

"I still don't understand," she said.

"I . . ." His voice trailed off.

She looked up at him.

"I just . . ." he said. "I got tired of thinking about how I was going to confess. I got tired of revising my confession in my head."

"So you pre-confessed?"

"No. I just told them the truth—that I'm in a relationship with a worldly person, and I want to stay in it."

"But that's not sinful," Corinne said. "We weren't sinning." She knew she was being pedantic, but the whole *system* was pedantic.

"No, I know, I just . . ."

"You said you didn't want to be immoral. I wasn't going to push you."

"I know, but I want—" He looked up at her, helplessly. "I want to be with you. And I'm going to be with you, if you'll let me. However you'll let me. I understand that you can't—that we can't do this my way, their way, whatever. But I still want to *do* this, Corinne. And I don't want to spend every moment with you wondering if *this* is the moment that's going to get me cast out."

"So you cast yourself out?"

"I mean . . ." He shrugged, flapping both palms in the air.

The kettle whistled. Corinne busied herself with the tea. "You told them you were in a relationship?"

"Yeah."

"With me?"

"No."

"They're going to figure it out."

"Not necessarily," he said. "Not right away."

She looked up at him. "Did you even consider that you'd be marking me, too? Casting me out again?" The anger had crept in from the living room when she wasn't looking. She'd meant to give him the whole night to recover.

Enoch looked confused.

Corinne tried not to shout. "It's taken me *years* to get close to my family. Do you think they're going to forgive me *twice* for ruining you?"

"You didn't do this."

"That's not how they'll see it—this just proves that I can't be trusted, that they shouldn't have let me close again." She pressed her fingertips into her temples. "We reconnected under my mother's roof, Enoch!"

"Corinne, I'm sorry, I didn't know—"

"Because you didn't *talk* to me."

"I'm sorry, I really am. I felt like I didn't have any good options."

"We could have talked through the bad options together."

"I didn't want you to talk me out of it!"

"You didn't want me to tell you that we should break up!"

"You're right, I didn't!" He jerked his palms into the air again. "But you still can!"

Corinne threw her palms into the air, too. "Oh right, I'm supposed to break up with you, after you threw yourself on your sword for me?"

Enoch shook his head. He looked tearful. (How could he have any tears left?) "Do you *want* to break up with me?"

No. "I don't know!"

"Well . . ." Enoch rubbed his eyes. "I knew you'd be mad at me for not talking to you. But I thought you'd be happy, too. Partly. That I'd chosen you."

"Over Jesus?"

"*No.* Just. In general. I took a stand—" He looked up at her. "I'm taking a stand. I want to be with you. If you'll have me."

"Maybe you should have run that past me before you destroyed your life." Corinne's hands were shaking. She clenched them in fists. "What's the return policy for confessions?"

"Corinne, what are you saying?"

"I'm saying, you shouldn't have *done* this. It's too much, Enoch. Losing your friends and family . . . Your whole community, your way of life. I can't compensate for all of that. It's not a fair trade."

"That's not for you to decide. And that's not—That's not what's happening."

"Isn't it?"

"I'm not leaving the church, I'm just stepping away."

"Temporarily?"

"Yes."

"Until this wears off?"

"*No.* I thought we could use some space, you and me."

"For what?"

"To see what we have."

"And then you'll go back to church?"

"I'm still *going* to church."

Corinne shook her head. "You're gonna keep going, even though no one there will talk to you?"

"Jesus will still talk to me."

"Oh, God, oh, Enoch." Corinne could feel her lips pull down at the corners. She was crying. "You're always kind of a walking Johnny Cash song, but this really takes the trick."

Enoch twisted one side of his mouth up, like he wasn't sure whether that was a compliment or whether he was allowed to smile.

Something terrible dawned on Corinne. "You were there today, weren't you, when they announced it?"

He looked at her, his brows low, his tongue touching his upper lip. He nodded.

Corinne coughed up a sob. She lifted an arm and hid her face in the inside of her elbow. "*Oh, Enoch.*" Corinne cried into her arm. She made high, childlike noises as she tried to catch her breath. She felt Enoch's big hands on her hips.

"Do you want me to leave?" His voice was close.

"I never *want* you to leave."

He squeezed her hips. "I'll leave anyway, if you tell me to."

She didn't say anything.

"Can I hold you?"

She didn't say anything, but she leaned against him. She hid her face in her arms and rested her arms on his chest. He put his arms around her. He laid his head on top of hers.

"Corinne . . ." It was a never a question when Enoch said her name. And it was almost never to get her attention. He said her name like he was saying it to himself. Corinne couldn't decide whether she resented that—that he was saying her name for himself, and not for her. But it still sent a shiver right up her spine. He held her tighter. "I kept thinking," he whispered, "about what you said . . . that you didn't regret what happened back in high school. Between us. And I realized . . . the thing I regret most is losing you. I don't regret anything that's happened these last few months. Any of it. I'm not sorry about it. I'm not repentant."

Corinne moved her arms so she could bury her face in his shirt.

He whispered in her ear. "I'm not sorry."

After a few seconds, Corinne lifted up her head. "I'm not sorry either."

Enoch looked in her eyes. His glasses were a little fogged up. "I'm not sorry," he whispered, and kissed her. It was a short kiss. Not very forceful.

"I'm not sorry," she whispered, and kissed him. A little longer. A little more forceful.

"I'm not sorry," Enoch said against her mouth, and kissed her.

Corinne shook her head. "Not sorry," she said without pulling her mouth away.

Enoch held her even tighter. He shook his head while he kissed her.

Corinne opened her mouth. He lifted her off the ground. She held the back of his head.

She wasn't sorry, she would never be sorry. And she'd never ask him to leave. Even when he deserved it. He'd given them some space, some time, to figure this out. And Corinne resented that it was all his to give. But she'd take it. God knows, she'd take it.

Chapter Fifty-one

Enoch pulled away.

Corinne sucked in a breath.

"Just a second . . ." he said, letting go of her. He stood up straight and pulled his arms up, arching his back. It made a painful crunching noise.

"You should try to fall in love with someone taller," Corinne said.

Enoch smiled. "I'll add that to the list." He rolled his shoulders. He took off his glasses and looked down at his shirt—then reached for the end of Corinne's soft cotton top to clean them. "You should try to find someone with more years left in him," he said. "You missed my young and limber days."

"You were never limber."

He laughed a breath through his nose.

Corinne brushed his hair out of his face. He looked tired. He put his glasses back on.

"Could I have a glass of water?"

"Yeah," she said. "I never gave you your tea. Do you want me to make you a new cup?"

"I'd like that."

He leaned against the counter while Corinne got him water and put the kettle back on.

"I don't want to fight in your kitchen anymore," Enoch said.

"You want to fight in my living room instead?"

"I don't want to fight at all . . ."

"I thought you said you wanted to be with me." She dumped out the cold mug of tea.

Enoch rested a hand on the small of her back. "Does that mean fighting?"

Corinne tipped her head up at him. "Everybody fights. Even people who have it easy. And we . . . Well, we're never going to have it easy."

"But we can work some things out, right?"

"Agree on house rules, you mean?"

He smiled and rubbed her back. "Yeah . . ."

"We *did* agree on house rules, Enoch, and you immediately broke them."

He winced. *Too bad.*

"What kind of tea do you want?" Corinne asked.

"Something with caffeine. I need to get it together before I drive home."

Corinne opened up her cabinet. A box of tea fell out.

Enoch looked up. The whole cabinet was crammed with tea boxes. "Do you go to the grocery store and only buy tea?"

"Sometimes." Corinne made him another mug of tea. Earl Grey. And one for herself. "Do you want milk and sugar?"

"Yeah."

She added milk and sugar to both cups and walked into the living room. Enoch followed her and sat on the couch. He drank some tea. He picked up the bowl of chicken, cold now, and started to eat what was left.

Corinne watched him. "I missed you," she said, so soft she could barely hear herself.

He smiled at her. "I missed you, too."

"Don't do that again."

He stopped chewing. "I won't."

"I mean, if you need space, I guess you should take it. But it was so painful, not knowing whether you were going to call me—or whether you were going to come to your senses."

"I thought I made it pretty clear that I wasn't coming to my senses anytime soon."

"I don't even know what I'm asking," Corinne babbled. "I know I can't ask you to stay no matter what."

Enoch set down the bowl. It was basically empty. He took Corinne's hand. "You could ask me that . . ."

"Well . . ." Her chin was twitching. She didn't want to cry any more. "I'm not asking that."

"All right."

"But don't do that again."

"I won't," Enoch said.

"You look really tired," she said.

"I am really tired."

"You should get some sleep."

"I'd like to hold you some more first," he said seriously. Enoch Miller, grave as the grave. "Is that all right?"

Corinne nodded. She was crying, despite her best efforts. Enoch held her. He drank his tea. Corinne didn't know what was going to happen now. They'd never been here before, standing on the same side of the line.

When he finished his tea, he kissed the top of Corinne's head. He stood up and stretched. His back cracked.

"I'll get your jacket," Corinne said, standing up. "You look nice. In your suit." She touched his tie. "And this." She went for his jacket—and his coat. His gloves. When she brought them back over, he was looking a little lost again. "It's going to be all right," she said.

Enoch lifted one side of his full lips and nodded. "Can I make you dinner tomorrow?"

"Yeah," Corinne said.

"I still owe you a real dinner."

"Your chicken with asparagus was delicious."

"Was it?"

"Yeah."

Enoch kissed her.

"Drive safe," she said. "Stay awake."

"I will. Good night, Corinne."

"Good night."

Chapter Fifty-two

Enoch Miller had left the church for her.

Well—

He hadn't really left. He'd stepped away. Stepped out. Gone out to check the parking lot. He was going to go back. So what was this, a detour? He'd left the path to do whatever this was with Corinne, but then he was going to find it again.

And then, what? Would they keep walking along together, Enoch on the path, Corinne in the weeds? Enoch going to church three times a week, and everyone looking at him with pity . . . *"Poor Brother Miller, he got himself unequally yoked. It's so brave of him to come to church by himself. He's very brave."*

They would let Enoch back in. He'd repent, and they'd let him back in, unless the Day of Judgment came first, in the intervening time, which would be very bad timing for Enoch Miller. To take a break from church at the exact moment that Jesus finally returned for the final reckoning.

Corinne didn't really believe in a final reckoning. But she didn't explicitly *not* believe in it—it had been banged into her too deep. She still imagined it sometimes: Jesus would come back. He'd descend from the sky, larger than life, carrying a sword and wearing sandals. And He'd say, *"Corinne, I offered you My love, and you turned away from Me."* And Corinne wouldn't argue with Him. She'd take whatever punishment was on offer. (Hopefully just oblivion.) Maybe she'd tell Him that it wasn't personal, that she'd usually been doing the best she could in the moment.

Corinne didn't believe in a final reckoning, but Enoch surely did. So she hoped for his sake that it didn't come now. While he was lost in the weeds with her.

Enoch.

Enoch Miller had left the church. For Corinne.

Well—

For himself, really.

Because he wanted her. She couldn't decide if that was selfish. Was it selfish of him? Was there any other way to fall in love?

Maybe what she really resented was the way her feelings for him never seemed to change anything. Corinne wasn't choosing her own adventure, she was waiting for Enoch to choose his.

"You did *choose your own adventure,"* she told herself. *"You just did it so long ago that it doesn't feel like a choice anymore. You chose Enoch. You choose him every time he's presented to you—you choose him even when he isn't an option. You write him in. It's not his fault that you're easy."*

"Enoch would never call you easy," another part of her said.

"Yeah, why do you make it so hard for him?"

None of the voices in Corinne's head particularly liked her. But they all liked Enoch.

Enoch Miller, that wall of a boy, that fortress of a man. Enoch Miller, who was going to make someone a good husband someday. Who had made someone a good husband already. Enoch Miller, sturdy and upright. *"He shall be like a tree planted by the rivers of water, that brings forth its fruit in its season, whose leaf also shall not wither, and whatever he does shall prosper."* He'd left the church. For Corinne.

She would have told him not to.

Chapter Fifty-three

Enoch's truck was parked on the street outside his house. He'd left the garage door open for her. Corinne pulled her car in and closed the door behind her. They were still hiding. It was a new variety of hiding, more for her sake than his.

Corinne knocked on the door between the garage and the kitchen. When Enoch didn't answer, she cracked the door and leaned in. "Enoch?"

He didn't answer.

Corinne stepped in. The kitchen didn't smell like anything. "Enoch?"

She walked through the kitchen and peeked into the living room. Enoch was walking down the hall from his bedroom. "Corinne, hey. Sorry." He was still in his work clothes, his white pants and his MILLER ELECTRIC T-shirt. His face was long—he looked nearly as lost as he had last night.

"What's wrong?" she asked.

"Nothing," he said. "I mean . . ." He rubbed his face. "Same thing. I probably shouldn't have expected myself to be in great shape tonight, I'm sorry."

"It's all right. Do you want me to leave?"

He reached for her hand. "No." His eyes were plaintive. "No. But . . . maybe you should anyway. I'm not good company."

"I don't need good company," Corinne said, squeezing his hand.

"I haven't started dinner," he said. "I haven't even showered."

She let go of his hand. "You shower. I'll take care of dinner."

He twisted his mouth down, like he wasn't sure she could manage it.

"Take a shower," she said, pushing his arm. "Then come out and be miserable near me."

"It's good to see you," he said. A little less lost.

She stood on tiptoe to kiss his cheek. "It's always good to see you, Enoch." (She could be easy sometimes. When he needed it.)

He smiled with his eyes, and she pushed him again, and he walked away.

Corinne went back to Enoch's kitchen to see what she could rustle up. His fridge was mostly full of ingredients—raw meat, milk, butter—which Corinne couldn't really work with. But she found cheese and summer sausage. And there were crackers in the cupboard. Oh, and microwave popcorn. Corinne knew how to make popcorn. She found a jar of olives. And some oranges. She spent most of the time that Enoch was in the shower trying to arrange it all artfully.

She was putting the popcorn into a bowl when Enoch came into the kitchen. In jeans and a flannel shirt. Barefoot. Corinne still couldn't look at his feet. He started laughing, with his chest and through his nose. "You made popcorn."

"You like popcorn, I've seen you eat it."

"I do—but it's like I'm dating Charlie Brown."

"It was actually Snoopy who made the popcorn."

"Come here, Snoopy." He took Corinne by her upper arm and kissed her. (She was never going to get used to this. The easy kisses. The fact that this was allowed. That Enoch was allowing it.)

"There's also an antipasto plate," she said.

"Show me the way."

They sat together on the couch, eating cheese and crackers. Corinne liked the way Enoch ate. Like he was hungry and unapologetic about it. Even for a man.

"I've never really dated before," he said, eating an orange wedge.

"You dated. You went roller-skating every Friday night. While I stayed home and washed my hair."

He rolled his eyes. "You were invited—which is kind of the point. Do you know, Shannon and I weren't ever alone until our wedding night?"

"Jesus," Corinne said.

"Saves," Enoch added, reaching for some crackers.

"Even when you proposed?"

"Her parents were in the next room. The day that I apologized to her for, well, everything, was the closest we ever came to being alone—we were sitting on her front porch. But her parents were just inside."

"Did you ever . . . kiss?"

"We kissed a lot. When we said good-bye. But her parents were always keeping an eye on us."

"That's so weird," Corinne said.

Enoch shrugged.

"Don't you think it would have been different if you could have spent time alone together? And touched?"

"I don't think she would have told me she was gay," he said with a mouth full of crackers. "She didn't even know."

"No, but you might have realized that you weren't supposed to get married."

He swallowed. "The fact that I was in love with you probably should have been enough of a red flag."

Corinne laughed. Helplessly. (Sometimes the ridiculousness of it all was overwhelming.) Enoch quirked up one side of his mouth. He reached for her. She was right there already. He put his arms around her waist and laid his forehead on her shoulder. "This was a nice dinner, thank you. Is this how you cook for yourself?"

"I never have olives in my cupboards. Or oranges."

He shook his head. He rubbed his nose into Corinne's sky-blue cardigan.

"Rough day?" she asked.

"Yeah." His voice was muffled.

"Do you want to talk about it?"

Enoch groaned and pulled away from her. He leaned back against the couch, covering his face with his forearms. Corinne touched his chest. She rubbed his flannel shirt between the buttons.

"I argued with Japheth."

"About . . ." Corinne didn't want to say it.

She didn't have to. "Yeah," Enoch said. "I told him a few days ago, before they announced it at church, and he was upset then—but now he says he can't work with me anymore. Because I'm not good Christian association."

"Is that a rule? That you can't work with someone who's been cast out?"

Enoch's arms dropped to his sides. "You can work with someone. You're just supposed to keep it professional. Nothing personal or spiritual."

"Okay . . ."

"But Japheth says he doesn't want to just stick to the letter of the law. That owning a business together is already too intimate."

"You own the business together?"

"I started it. I mean, I restarted it, after my dad died. And Japheth joined when he got his license."

"Then he can't fire you."

"He doesn't want to fire me. He wants—" Enoch growled and rubbed his face, pushing up his glasses. "I don't know what he wants. He says all the brothers we work with are going to be uncomfortable. That when you work with brothers, it's an extension of the congregation."

"Do you agree?"

"I think I can keep my head down and focus on the wiring, but it's not really my place to tell people how they feel around me. If it bothers their conscience to have me around, I can't exactly argue with them."

"Pfft," Corinne said.

He turned to her. "You think I should argue?"

"No. I just don't believe that it"—she made air quotes with her fingers—"'bothers their conscience' to be civil to someone they already know and love."

Corinne normally wouldn't talk this way in front of Enoch. She wouldn't be disrespectful toward the church. She wouldn't be honest. But they were in some liminal space together now, someplace where the rules were blurry. Plus, she was pissed.

"Like," she went on, "what sort of thing *actually* bothers your conscience? When you've hurt someone, right? Or cheated. Or maybe when you've done something that you truly believe God hates. But God is mostly reasonable—the Ten Commandments hold water. This . . . This is just performative nonsense. *'I couldn't sleep last night because I spoke to a sinner.'* Jesus sat down with sinners. He hung out with them."

"Only to lead them out of sin," Enoch countered.

"My point is—this isn't real. Jesus isn't going to get mad at them for being polite to another one of His children, no matter how fallen."

Enoch laid his hand on her knee. He didn't say anything to agree with her, but he seemed happy to have her on his side.

"What did you say to Japheth?" Corinne asked.

"I told him that I'd leave our usual jobs to him, and I'd bid jobs for worldly contractors."

"Have you done that before?"

"I've never really had to."

"Does it worry you?"

"It's just . . . different. I wasn't expecting this part of my life to change, too."

"I'm sorry," Corinne said.

Enoch reached up and thumbed the corner of her frown. "I can tell. It's all right—I'll get through it."

"Japheth is a little twerp."

"Huh," Enoch laughed. "Not so little anymore. He's as big as me."

"No one's as big as you," Corinne said with conviction.

Enoch looked up at her. Something had shifted in his eyes. From lost to fond—to wanting. He spread his hand along her jaw, and she leaned into him. She kissed him. His mouth was warm and wet, and he tasted like olives, but she didn't care. She kissed him hungrily. Generously. She couldn't make up for all he'd lost; she wasn't a fair trade. But she wanted him to know that he had her. For what it was worth. For what she was.

Enoch held her neck. He stroked her cheek with his thumb. He held her against him with his other arm around her waist. "I still can't believe that you're here."

"I'm here," Corinne said.

He opened his mouth to catch hers. Corinne licked his fat tongue, his gappy teeth. She was here. He had her. He always had.

They were still new to this. Kissing each other.

And so far they'd been more careful than their teenage selves. Once or twice, they'd started to get carried away, and Enoch had stopped them. Redirected them. Reached for pizza or taken a breath to stretch. As soon as they pulled up to the gates of Carried Away, he'd backed off.

But this kiss had *started* at those gates—and then it kept going. Corinne felt Enoch's hand pulling at her waist. She remembered all the other times he'd pulled on her. She felt eighteen again. Urgent and wanton.

She'd never kissed anyone else like this. Like she might lose him before it was done. She'd never liked anyone else's mouth this much. It took two kisses for Corinne to cover Enoch's lips. She had to kiss him in double time to keep up.

She held his cheeks, his chin.

"Corinne," he said. She inhaled it.

Enoch ended the kiss—a mile past the gates—by pulling her even closer. By burrowing his face between her neck and her shoulder. By groaning so low and loud that she felt it in her kidneys. She wound all ten fingers in his hair.

Then a familiar clock chimed, and Corinne jumped away from Enoch so abruptly, she hung in the air like Michael Jordan.

"What?" Enoch said. He was still panting.

Corinne was kneeling next to him on the couch. Her hands were over her heart. "Is that—"

"What?"

The clock was still chiming.

"Is that your mom's clock?"

"Oh." Enoch's mouth was flushed berry red. "Yeah."

"Where did it come from?"

"The hallway? It's always been there."

"I've never heard it."

"I just changed the batteries."

"Holy shit," Corinne said.

"I can take them out."

"Holy *shit*," she said.

Enoch started laughing, his lips pressed together, his shoulders shaking.

"It's not funny," Corinne said. "I was ready for your mom to come down the stairs."

"I don't have stairs," he said.

She scrubbed her face with her hands and finally let herself smile.

Enoch pulled her back against him. "We're so messed up." He sounded amused, resigned, tired, affectionate.

"I know you don't like to swear," she said, "but this is really a case for the F-word and none other."

"Are you saying we're fucked up, Corinne?"

She laughed. It was a little like hearing Mr. Rogers swear. Or the Jolly Green Giant. "I am."

Enoch hugged her. He laughed, too, and he was holding her so tight that she shook with him. "I suppose we are."

Chapter Fifty-four

Corinne came over the next night to eat dinner with Enoch before he went to church. They sat on his couch and ate bierocks, stuffed meat rolls that that you could get all over Wichita but almost nowhere else. Then Enoch went into the bathroom to shower and change. He came out in a gray suit with his green tie hanging around his neck. (She should probably buy him more ties.) He looked pale and serious. More pale and serious than usual.

"You don't have to do this," Corinne said. "You don't have to prove anything to them."

"It's not about them."

"What's it about?"

There was a mirror over the couch. (There were mirrors all over this house—proof that Shannon Frank was as vain as she looked.) Enoch was using it to tie his tie. "It's about being there, hearing the message. Taking what encouragement I can from it."

"That's very noble," Corinne said, standing up and putting on her coat.

"It's not noble."

"Well, it's something—it's admirable. I never would have done it. I didn't want to be part of a club that didn't want me."

"You didn't want to be part of the club, period. And anyway, it's not a club." His tie was knotted. He looked squared off and neatly finished. Broad and handsome.

"It's admirable," she said. "That you aren't letting your pride stand in the way. That you aren't embarrassed."

He hunched over her, touching her face, tucking wayward pieces of her ponytail behind her ears. "I'm mortified. But I'll get through it. Can I come by after? And kiss you good night?"

Corinne nodded.

Church passed much faster when you weren't there. Corinne went to the grocery store. She bought olives and oranges—and bananas, because she was already standing in the produce aisle. She bought hummus and precut celery sticks. And tea.

She imagined Enoch. Sitting alone in the back row of the church. Leaving during the closing hymn. Everyone watching him out of the sides of their faces. She thought of him sitting there, without a role or a job, without anything to do but listen.

She wondered if it would be too much for him.

She wondered if he'd change his mind.

He stopped by her apartment afterward. He looked tired, he didn't come in. He stood in the hallway and bent down to kiss her. "I want to see you tomorrow," he said. "I want to see you every day."

Because no one else will talk to you, Corinne didn't say. (Because it wasn't fair to say; Enoch had wanted to see her every day, even when he still had other options.)

"Okay," she said.

"Come over after work?"

"Okay."

"I got you something." He reached into his coat pocket. For a second, Corinne worried it was a ring. It would be just like Enoch to jump ahead and do the thing she'd told him not to.

It was a garage door opener. The kind you clip onto the sun visor in your car.

Corinne laughed. "Thanks. I hope it fits."

"Come over? Tomorrow?"

Corinne pointed the remote at his nose and pushed the button.

Chapter Fifty-five

Enoch kept on asking to see her, as if Corinne might say no. Even though she never had, so far.

"Will you have dinner with me?"

"Can I stop by after church?"

"Can I buy you lunch?"

He was lonely. He didn't have any friends out in the world, and he didn't want to make any.

"I don't mean to lean on you so hard," he'd say.

And Corinne would say, *"It's all right,"* because it was. Corinne didn't really have friends either. She should probably feel bad about that. She should probably feel bad about this whole situation. Her friends in Boston, her friends from college—they'd all say this was a dysfunctional, codependent relationship. Unsustainable, probably.

But they hadn't understood why Corinne was moving back home in the first place. To be closer to a family that only sort of welcomed her.

They didn't understand who Corinne was. What she was made of. What she needed—and what she'd do for it.

Enoch understood. He went to church and let them look on his disgrace. He let them eat his shame. He didn't resent it.

Corinne did wish, for Enoch's sake, that he'd waited to pull his ripcord until after Christmas. He already had plane tickets to Arkansas. He didn't use them. She didn't ask what his mother had said.

Corinne went to her mom's house for lunch on Christmas Day, then bailed out early to go to Enoch's. He'd never spent the holiday alone before—had never spent it apart from his family. He was used to a long table and a huge feast. Kids everywhere. His mom's oyster stuffing and his grandma's pumpkin chiffon pie. Presents.

Corinne couldn't replace that. She couldn't even try.

While Corinne was at her mom's, Enoch stayed home and cooked his first turkey. When she showed up, he was listening to Christmas carols. His table was set, and his eyes were too bright, and there was no way Corinne was *worth* this. She couldn't be worth it.

She stuck close to him. Touched him. She brought him half a dozen gifts, all individually wrapped. A sweater. CDs. Two decks of cards. He built a fire, and Corinne taught him to play a card game she'd learned in college called Nertz.

Enoch gave her a beautiful vintage lamp. Pink. Ceramic. Someone had been throwing it away at a house he was working in. He'd taken it home and rewired it. "It reminded me of your couch," he said.

"My prized possession."

Corinne stayed late and kissed him soundly. And when she left, he asked if he could see her the next day.

The answer was yes, it was always yes.

The world spun like that for a while, with just the two of them.

Chapter Fifty-six

Corinne had three jobs tonight:
    —Take the chicken breasts out of the freezer.
    —Preheat the oven.
    —If she was feeling industrious, peel the potatoes.
    Corinne was feeling industrious. She was feeling domestic. She got to Enoch's house early, just to start their evening together sooner. He was always tired now, after work. He'd started doing more commercial jobs, and every day was a little different. Different people, different problems. He didn't like it. He missed Japheth (twerp though he may be), and he missed his regular group of drywallers and plumbers and concrete guys. If he saw one of them at Menards, it put him in a funk.

Corinne was peeling potatoes when she heard him at the front door. (Enoch always used the front door now that Corinne parked in his garage.) He was home early. Corinne washed her hands, so she could go to him. So she could try to move him as quickly as possible from sad and lonely to appreciated and relieved.

"E?" someone called. A woman called.

Corinne froze in the middle of Enoch's kitchen.

Shannon Frank walked in from the living room—

Then jerked to a stop. "Oh . . ." she said. "Corinne."

Shannon Frank was as beautiful as ever. More beautiful. With her

dark hair cropped short at her neck and swooping across her forehead. She was still thin. Willowy. In straight-legged jeans and a pearl-
snapped cowboy shirt. She probably had the sparkliest eyes in the
world, Shannon Frank did. And the most elegant eyebrows. She wasn't
wearing any makeup—apparently she'd never needed it. She was fucking lovely.

She was looking at Corinne like she couldn't decide whether to
be shocked or sad. She settled on sad. "This explains a lot," she
said.

"I'm sorry." Corinne wiped her hands on her jeans. "I was just . . ."

"No," Shannon said. "I'm sorry. I didn't think anyone would be
home. Enoch said I could borrow his shop vac."

"I'm sure you can," Corinne said. "I'll just go."

"Please don't, I'll come back."

"No, I mean—No, you should take the vacuum. If you know where
it is."

"I know where it is," Shannon said.

"Just pretend I'm not here."

Shannon smiled at that. Awkwardly. Still sad. "Right. I'll just,
um . . ."

The front door opened again.

They both stood still. Enoch rushed into the kitchen like he was
there to put out a fire. He stopped when he saw them. "Shannon,"
he said.

"Hey, E."

He exhaled hard. "The shop vac."

Shannon nodded. "Yeah."

They were looking in each other's eyes. Shannon looked sad, and
Enoch looked sorry, and Corinne felt like she didn't belong there. In
their house. In their kitchen.

Then Shannon smiled at him. Rueful, Corinne thought. Loving.
Her eyes were even more sparkly than they'd been before. Shannon
shrugged. (God, she was gorgeous.) Enoch lowered his eyebrows at
her. It was the look he gave Corinne sometimes, when he was worried about her, when he didn't believe she was okay.

"I'll get it," Enoch said.

Shannon motioned at the door. "I'll just wait in my truck."

He nodded. He glanced at Corinne on his way to the garage—checking on her, eyebrows low. Corinne didn't put on a brave face; there wasn't time to find one.

When Corinne looked back at Shannon, she was giving Corinne a very effortful smile. An extremely determined-to-smile smile. "Sorry I surprised you."

"Sorry *I* surprised *you*," Corinne said. This wasn't the apology she owed Shannon Frank.

"I didn't know you'd moved back."

"Yeah, about a year ago."

"Ah." Shannon nodded. "Well. It was nice to see you." (She couldn't possibly mean it.)

"It was nice to see you, too," Corinne said. (She also didn't mean it.)

Shannon took a few steps toward the door, then turned around again. She looked torn, troubled. Corinne braced for whatever was coming: Old hurt. Righteous indignation. Run-of-the-mill bitchiness. "I really mean it, Corinne," Shannon said. "It's good to see you. Here."

She looked in Corinne's eyes. And Corinne didn't look away.

Corinne nodded. Shannon left.

Corinne heard the garage door open, and she walked to the front door to look out the window. Enoch was setting a bulky vacuum cleaner in the back of Shannon's truck. Then he stood by the cab to talk to her.

Corinne went back to the kitchen. To the potatoes. She'd been listening to music before, to the oldies station Enoch liked, and she could hear it again. Crosby, Stills, Nash & Young.

The garage door closed.

Enoch came back into the kitchen. He took off his work boots and walked over to Corinne to lean against the counter next to the sink. "I'm sorry," he said, his voice solemn and low.

"There's nothing to apologize for. I was early."

"I didn't know she was coming. I mean—I knew she was coming, but not tonight."

"It's okay. It's her house."

"It's not her house."

"I just meant—it makes sense that she'd come by sometimes. That she'd feel comfortable here."

Enoch sighed. "It didn't matter before. If she dropped in."

"It doesn't matter *now.*"

"It does, I'm sorry."

Corinne threw the potato peeler into the sink. It was a cobalt-blue basin—it must have been a special order; Corinne loved it. Shannon had definitely picked it out. "I'm not *angry,*" Corinne said harshly. She was crying a little. Enoch touched her shoulder. She pulled away from him. "I'm not angry," she said again.

"Corinne . . ."

She turned to him. "You should have seen her face, Enoch—she looked like she'd found me in her bed!"

"She was just surprised."

"That wasn't surprise—it was hurt."

"I think she was hurt that I didn't tell her about us."

"Why *didn't* you tell her?"

He held up his hands. "You didn't want me to tell *anyone.*"

"She looked so *sad.*" Corinne was crying, she was miserable. She felt racked with guilt. Ridden. "Is she still in love with you?"

"She was never in love with me. She's been pretty explicit about that." He took Corinne by the shoulders. "We've been separated for three years, Corinne. She lives with her girlfriend."

"Then why . . ." Corinne wiped her eyes. Her hands were wet. "Do you think she still hates me? Because of what happened?"

"Honestly . . ." Enoch looked so tired. "I think that I had to stop thinking of Shannon as my wife a long time ago . . . but she hasn't really had to stop thinking of me as her husband."

Corinne pressed her palms into her eyes. "God. I feel so terrible."

"You didn't do anything wrong."

Corinne dropped her hands. "I mean, I did sleep with her boyfriend."

"A million years ago," he said, "and that's on me, not you."

"It's a little on me," Corinne said. "Fuck." She looked up at Enoch. "I didn't make a habit of that, you know. Seducing other people's boyfriends. I didn't cheat with anyone else. I didn't *cheat.* I'm not . . ."

"I believe you," Enoch said.

"*Fuck,*" Corinne said.

"I didn't cheat again either," he said.

"I didn't think that you had."

"Well, I'm just saying. Point of information."

Corinne looked up at him with a cartoon frown. Her chin was trembling. "I don't want you to be anyone else's husband."

Enoch took her chin in hand. "I'm not."

"I know it's not fair . . ."

"Corinne, I'm not."

"I don't usually think about it."

"I'm yours," he said.

She moved her face out of his hand and slumped against him, crying into his work shirt.

"I'm yours," he told the top of her head.

—

Enoch made some kind of creamed chicken for dinner. Corinne didn't feel like helping. She sat on the floor in front of the leather couch and watched a Tom Hanks movie that was on cable. The one with the mob. Enoch brought out their dinner and sat behind Corinne on the couch, watching the movie with her. Corinne leaned against his leg. He played with her ponytail.

When it was over, Enoch turned off the TV. "We don't have to spend so much time here."

"I like it here," Corinne said.

"Well, I like being at your apartment."

"Yeah, but you have a nicer TV and a bigger kitchen and . . ." Corinne tried to think of what else made Enoch's house so nice. "Better lighting."

Enoch tugged on her ponytail. Corinne cranked her head around to look up at him.

"I could move," he said.

Corinne sighed. "You *could* move. Maybe we could even move in together someday. But I'm worried that it will never be as nice as this house—because I won't spend all my time making it nice. The way Shannon did. When you're not around, I just want to work. It feels stupid to make you leave your really-nice house to move into a house that will never be as good."

Enoch was grinning at her. It was Enoch, so his mouth was still closed—but he was smiling with his eyes and both sides of his cheeks. He climbed off the couch and pushed Corinne down to the rug, on her back. (The really-nice and probably expensive wool rug.)

"What are you doing?" she said. "You're never going to be able to get up."

Enoch was kissing her face and her neck. He was using his nose to push aside her shirt collar. "You're going to move in with me?"

"I said someday. It was hypothetical."

"You're going to move in with me," he said.

"Someday," Corinne said. "Maybe. Depending on a lot of factors."

He kissed her throat. It tickled. Corinne brought down her chin. "You're going to move in with me," Enoch rumbled in her ear.

Chapter Fifty-seven

After that, Corinne felt decidedly weirder about being at Enoch's house—but she still preferred it to her own apartment. And as long as Shannon wasn't actually standing in the kitchen, Corinne was mostly able to not think about her—or to think about her the appropriate amount. Because Shannon was still Enoch's ex-wife. She was probably still his best friend. She was still the person who had been with Enoch for all those years when he was becoming the person he was now. And Shannon was the reason for Enoch's crisis of faith—he was already primed for it when Corinne walked back into the picture. Corinne was never going to get rid of Shannon Frank. Shannon Miller. She probably shouldn't try.

Chapter Fifty-eight

Corinne was sitting on the chair by Enoch's bed, watching him tie his necktie in the big mirror next to the closet. Sometimes she felt jealous of all the time he spent at church. At least Thursday-night services were only an hour long. Maybe he'd stop by her apartment after.

"Is something different in here?" she asked. "Did you paint?"

"I bought new bedding."

"Oh," Corinne said. Then, "Oh."

Enoch was blushing into the mirror. He untied the tie and started over.

"What did you do with the old bedding?" she asked.

"Gave it to the Goodwill. Did you want it?"

"I mean," Corinne said. "I think it was Ralph Lauren."

Enoch started giggling. His face was still red. He leaned forward and rested his forehead against the mirror.

Corinne pointed at him, like she'd just realized something. "Did you also give away the lesbian mermaids from the bathroom?"

He snorted and lifted his head. "They're in the garage—and they're not lesbians."

Corinne's eyes got big. "Ummm . . ."

"They're just frolicking."

"Topless frolicking."

Enoch was making eye contact with her in the mirror. Laughing.

"Mermaids frolic, Corinne. And they don't have shirts available to them."

"Your male gaze is astonishing." Corinne got up and slid in front of the mirror to hug him. He hugged her back. He looked relieved to have her close. "You don't have to change everything for me," she said.

"I should probably change a few things. For me."

"But not the lesbian mermaids. I love them."

Enoch brushed Corinne's hair out of her face, his eyes roving from her forehead to her chin. "I'll put them back."

They kissed.

Corinne wanted to ask him to skip church. To stay home with her. But she thought she'd feel bad if he said yes—and worse if he said no.

"You could stay here . . ." Enoch said. "I'll only be gone an hour. Ninety minutes tops." His eyes were bright and hopeful. His hand was in the small of her back, he seemed to like it there.

Corinne felt too aware of his new sheets. Hunter green, just like his tie.

"I didn't bring my computer," she said.

Enoch looked down. Like she was saying no to something bigger, and he knew it.

"I'll bring it next time."

He nodded.

She kissed his cheek. "Will you stop by and kiss me good night?"

He lifted his head again. He kissed her sweetly. "I will."

〜

He did.

Chapter Fifty-nine

Corinne kept going to her mom's house for Sunday dinners.

She went shopping with Alicia, she bought presents for baby Ruth.

Mercy and Noah had Corinne over for dinner. Corinne didn't know Noah very well. He was only six when she was cast out. She'd missed his growing-up years entirely.

He and Mercy rented one half of a duplex in a quiet neighborhood. Corinne couldn't imagine being a parent at twenty, but they seemed to take it mostly in stride. Maybe they'd wanted it to go this way. They'd already been married two years now. Corinne hadn't been invited to their wedding. She was just starting to talk to her mom again two years ago, and besides, Mercy's family was very strict. There were no card games at Mercy and Noah's house. No secular music or occasional beers. (God, neither of them were even old enough to drink.)

Was this the life Corinne had wanted with Enoch?

It's what he'd expected to have with Shannon.

Corinne tried to imagine being twenty years old and married to Enoch Miller. Living with him, in a small house. Staying home and making dinner for him . . . Maybe he still would have been the one to make dinner. Maybe Corinne could have taken a few college courses. The elders wouldn't have liked it, but Enoch wouldn't have minded. What trouble could Corinne have gotten into, with Enoch Miller in her bed every night? What kind of trouble would have even been tempting?

Corinne stayed at her brother's house after dinner and did the dishes. She talked to Noah about his job. He was a drywaller, but he wanted to be a carpenter.

It was better, when Corinne was around her family, to avoid talking about herself. (Even before this thing with Enoch.) There was too much in her life they didn't approve of. Whenever Corinne talked about herself, they'd get very nervous—as if she was going to surprise them with something profane and immoral.

Corinne had always been considered a goody two-shoes by her friends. She didn't drink much. She tried to be scrupulously honest. She was cautious with men. But her mom couldn't even handle hearing that Corinne had gone to a Beastie Boys concert. If Corinne had dated anyone since she left home, her family didn't want to know. They didn't even want to think about it.

It made Corinne feel seasick sometimes. Like she couldn't decide whether she was a good person or a bad person. Like she was ashamed of things she'd never done, and vehemently not ashamed of what little she had.

She asked Noah and Mercy questions, and she listened, and she hoped that when she left, they'd sigh and say, *"Well, that wasn't so bad."*

Chapter Sixty

Corinne's mom was going to a wedding on Sunday, so they weren't having a family dinner, and Enoch was weirdly excited to have access to Corinne for the whole day. She was lying in her bed, talking to him on the phone while he got ready for church.

"When are you coming over?" he asked.

"I'll come over while you're at services," she said.

"Yeah?"

"Yeah."

"That'd be great," Enoch said. "I'll pick up lunch."

"*I'll* pick up lunch," Corinne said. "Just come straight home."

"Yeah?"

Corinne laughed. "*Yes.*"

⁓

It was snowing, so Corinne drove slow. She stopped and got lasagna at a place Enoch liked. DeFazio's. Every entree came with soup and bread and enough lasagna for two meals. Corinne ordered extra cheese bread because she knew he liked it. It felt good to spend money thoughtlessly on small things. When she was a kid, there wasn't enough money for big things, let alone garlic bread.

By the time she'd gotten up, gotten dressed, picked up lunch, and made it over to Enoch's house, it was almost time for him to come home. He never lingered after church anymore. Corinne felt a little guilty about feeling glad of that. She put the foil lasagna pans in the oven, and turned it on low.

She was in the bathroom fussing with her lip gloss when she heard the front door open. She smiled so genuinely, she hardly recognized herself in the mirror.

"Corinne?" Enoch called.

They met in the hallway. Enoch was still wearing his coat. There was snow in his hair. He swept her off her feet. He liked to do that, even though Corinne was seriously, no-joke heavy, and Enoch had a bad back.

"Corinne, Corinne," Enoch said, kissing her cheek and neck. He set her down, and they fell against the wall, kissing each other like it had been thirteen years, not thirteen hours. Enoch was huge in his wool peacoat. Huge and cold. Like he'd driven home before his truck had had a chance to warm up. She rubbed his cold ears. She rubbed her nose against his. He leaned over her like a question mark, grabbing at her mouth the way he did sometimes, like he was taking huge bites of her.

Corinne brought her hands to his broad shoulders, to the thick wool lapels. She tried to unbutton his coat. "You're always wrapped up like a present," she said. Enoch laughed and grabbed at her mouth again. His chin was especially smooth. Corinne wasn't used to kissing him this early in the day. She got his coat open and pushed herself inside of it. He was warm, he was good. He was pressing her into the wall. She remembered this feeling. Of wanting more surface area to push against him. Of stretching her shoulders wide and her neck long. He was hunched. His knees were bent. He grabbed with his mouth and pushed with his chest and hips. Jesus. *Jesus Christ.* Corinne nodded her head as she kissed him. All she'd ever told him in her whole fucking life was yes.

Enoch shook off his coat and took hold of Corinne's hips. His hands were big, but her hips were bigger. He braced her against the wall. She squeezed his thick, warm neck, his wide shoulders. He was still wearing at least three layers. Corinne pushed his suit jacket off his shoulders. It got stuck on his biceps; he wouldn't let go of her.

She whined and pulled her mouth up, away. He crouched lower to gobble kisses out of her neck. "Take off your jacket," Corinne exhaled.

Enoch groaned. He held her hips. He crushed her.

Corinne tugged at his jacket, frowning. "*Please . . .*"

He let go of her hips, and she yanked the jacket down as far as his elbows—then shoved him away from her, so she could see what she was doing.

Enoch's chin was up, his eyes were narrow. He was looking down at her, panting, his tongue resting on his top lip—he looked like a boxer who'd just stumbled back into his corner.

Corinne got his jacket off, then pulled hard on the knot of his necktie. He fell back on her, kissing her. She really didn't know how to get the tie off, they always came off so easily in movies . . .

Enoch got his hand between them, over hers, and moved the knot back and forth, working it loose. Corinne nodded her head more quickly. *Yes, yes, yes.* She touched his neck. His Adam's apple. She unbuttoned his top button and curled her fingers inside his T-shirt, against his throat.

He was touching her, too. Her arms, her hips. But Corinne's brain could only be so many places at once. Her brain was on his throat. On the edge of his T-shirt. On all of these layers. On the fact that she'd never seen Enoch Miller's chest. That had never seemed fair—it wasn't fair, she'd paid so much for so little.

Enoch pushed her against the wall. He wormed his arms into the small of her back and lifted her up again, so they were almost eye-level. Probably to spare his neck. Corinne clung to the collar of his shirt and breathed roughly into his mouth.

Enoch took a step away from the wall, still holding her. "Corinne," he whispered.

"Enoch," she said.

He took another step back. She waited for him to set her down. He took another step. He was rubbing his nose against hers. He didn't set her down. Corinne put her arms around his neck to hold on. Another step. Toward his bedroom. "Okay?" he asked.

A hum caught in Corinne's throat. "You sure?"

"I'm sure, Corinne." He took another step back. "Okay?"

She nodded her nose against his. "Okay."

Enoch growled and put her down. Then he leaned over and got his arms around her thighs, swinging her over his shoulder.

"Jesus Christ!" Corinne shouted.

"Can't you just curse?" Enoch asked. Miraculously, he didn't sound strained—or paralyzed from the waist down. "Instead of taking the Lord's name?"

"Mother fuck!" she said. "What are you doing?"

Enoch already had her in his bedroom. He dropped her on the bed and crawled over her. "Corinne . . ."

"Mother *fuck*."

"You don't *have* to swear at all," he said, trying to kiss her.

"I think I do, if you're going to perform feats of strength."

Enoch laughed breathily. He was doing everything breathily. He probably *had* strained something. His bed was so big, and he had a down comforter that swallowed you up as soon as you lay on it. Corinne felt surrounded. She went back to unbuttoning his shirt—his tie was still in the way. "I've never seen you," she said. "It isn't fair."

"What isn't fair?"

"That I haven't seen you."

"I haven't seen you either."

"I know," she said, "it isn't *fair*."

Enoch sighed and dropped onto the bed, half on top of her, holding her by the back of her head. "I love you so much," he said. "Do you know it?"

Corinne looked at his smudged glasses, his flushed cheeks, his solemn expression. She knew that he *believed* he loved her. Was that the same thing? She nodded. She pulled on his tie.

"You're ruining my tie," he whispered. "And I only have two."

"Take it off," Corinne said. "Please."

Enoch looked in her eyes while he pulled the knot all the way free. Corinne took off his glasses and set them as far away as she could reach. He tried to kiss her again, but she wanted to see him. She wanted to have this—before he changed his mind about doing it and just in case they never did it again. She unbuttoned his shirt. He sat up a bit to help her, and Corinne sat up, too, pulling the tails out of his dress pants. She wanted it off. She pushed it down his arms, and the sleeves got caught on his wrists. His arms were trapped behind him. "Cuffs," he laughed.

"You wear too many clothes," Corinne said. Enoch tried to kiss her. She reached behind him to unfasten his cuffs. She was working blind, practically in his lap. He tried to kiss her. "You're like a French courtier," Corinne said. "With all these layers." The shirt was finally off. She threw it, spitefully, off the bed.

Enoch's arms came back around her. He was wearing a white T-shirt. The kind you buy to wear under nice shirts. Fruit of the fucking Loom or something. It was tight and thin, so it wouldn't interfere with his shirt and jacket. He looked broader than ever. His pecs were round. Corinne had never dated someone with such ostentatious pectoral muscles. She could see his nipples; it was embarrassing. She was embarrassing. She wanted this shirt off, too—she wanted to *see* him. "Enoch," she said, pulling at it. "*Please.*"

He seemed a little bewildered. He lifted his arms up, so Corinne could pull his shirt off. She got it off and sat back to look at him, his T-shirt still clutched in her hand.

Enoch was tremendous—she knew he'd be tremendous. She knew his shoulders were as broad as a barn door, that his arms were thick and heavy. She knew about his rib cage; she'd struggled to get her arms around it. But she didn't know about the freckles along his shoulders or the hair on his chest and his belly. She thought about how he'd felt on top of her at eighteen. So much heavier than he looked. Like he had a lead core.

Corinne was used to being wanted—by her past boyfriends. She'd been turned on by the fact that they were turned on by her. She'd liked their bodies in a sort of abstract way. As part of the larger whole. Mostly, during sex, they'd wanted to see Corinne and touch Corinne, and that was good for her. She liked that dynamic.

But Enoch had always been different. Maybe she'd imprinted on him—no, really, she thought that she probably had. That she'd wanted him so profoundly and at such a young age, he'd become the only person she'd ever properly desire. She just wanted to *look* at him. Well . . . she did want to touch him *eventually,* but for now just looking at him made her weak and floppy. Made her tongue hang forward and stick to the roof of her mouth.

She liked all his muscles. She liked all his fat. The way it looked like he was made of steel and then wrapped in something soft. She liked his preposterous shoulders—Enoch's shoulders were so wide, they made his head look small. (His head would have to be an alarming size to match those shoulders.) Corinne sucked her bottom lip between her teeth and smiled at him.

When she looked up into Enoch's eyes, he seemed embarrassed. Maybe even apologetic. He looked away.

No, Corinne thought. She leaned closer to whisper in his ear. She didn't touch him. "I've thought about you so much. Like this." Her voice broke. Enoch turned to look at her. To check on her, his eyebrows low. She evaded him, kept her mouth by his ear. "It's hard to believe this is happening when you look so *unreal.*" He shook his head, like he didn't believe her. She stayed by his ear. "I want you. Enoch, I want you. Can I have you?"

"*Corinne . . .*" He put his arms around her again. His bare arms. His bare chest. Corinne closed her eyes and bit her lip. She let her head flop forward. Enoch pushed her back on the bed. She went like a rag doll. He pulled the elastic tie out of her hair. It snagged, she didn't care.

"I've thought about you so much," Enoch said, kissing her. "Too much. Can I—"

She nodded. She was wearing a thick, flowered sweater. He was pulling on it. Pulling it the wrong way. She laughed and lifted her arms up over her head. Enoch pulled it up. She crunched her stomach to lift up her shoulders.

"Oh," Enoch said hoarsely, "oh, Corinne."

He was kissing her bare shoulders. Corinne didn't mind. She liked her shoulders. She generally liked the way she looked out of her clothes better than how she looked in them. If Enoch had wanted her in her baggy sweaters and plus-sizes, he probably wouldn't be disappointed by anything he'd find underneath. At least, she hoped he wouldn't be. He was still curled over her. One of his hands was on her stomach. Corinne liked her stomach less than she liked her shoulders, but there was no hiding it. And generally, guys were distracted by the rest of her. Enoch seemed distracted. He was dragging his lips messily over her shoulder. He was biting her bra strap and groaning.

Corinne spread her hands over his ribs. She let herself go weak again. She let herself sink into Enoch Miller's bed. Enoch. *Enoch.* Pinning her down. Pulling her bra strap down with his teeth. He wouldn't swear or say the Lord's name, so he just kept chanting Corinne's name. Into her arm. Along her clavicle. Between her breasts. Enoch. *Enoch Miller.*

She was lying on his bed. He was pinning her down.

She was lying on his couch. In his parents' house, his big hand cupping her breast over her bra.

Corinne's bras back then were white and industrial. Purchased off a rack meant for nuns and exhausted grandmothers. Enoch hadn't cared. He'd pawed at her desperately—clenched her breast in his hand, like he was afraid to do anything more dexterous. Like it would have been a worse sin if his fingertips touched her nipple.

She was lying in his bed. On his down comforter. And her bra was mint-green satin with sprays of pink lace. And Enoch was cupping her breast through the satin, like he wasn't sure what happened next. Enoch Miller's square hand. His long, blunt fingers. His smooth chin between her breasts.

Corinne brought her hands up the back of his neck, through his silky, dark hair. "Touch me," she said. "You can touch me."

He groaned.

Corinne picked up his hand. She slid it into her bra. "Touch me."

Enoch groaned again. He touched her. He lifted himself up to watch. Corinne reached up to her chest and pulled the cup of her bra down completely. Enoch rolled his brown eyes like she'd hurt him. She liked that. She liked it very much.

She couldn't decide what was better: Touching him. Being touched by him. Or watching him touch her. It was all very good. It was all the best. And she only sort of felt robbed. (Because she should have had this the first time—she should have had this all along. Enoch Miller belonged to Corinne. She'd marked him, and he'd marked her. They'd both been robbed.)

He hunched over her with his big pink shoulders. His surprising freckles. His drunk face and fat lips. He took Corinne's nipple into his mouth—and it was so perfect, she almost didn't resent the thirteen-year-wait. (Enoch Miller *belonged* to her. He belonged *with* her.) Corinne made a noise so high and wet that Enoch came back to her mouth to lick it out of her. She liked it when he got grabby. When he forgot to be scared or ashamed. She made the noise again, and he went for the front of her jeans.

Corinne held his cheeks. "I missed you," she said. "I missed you so much."

Enoch looked in her eyes. He looked overcome for a moment. "I missed you, Corinne," he said. "I missed this. Even though I never really had it."

Corinne pulled his jaw into hers. She kissed him.

Enoch got her jeans unbuttoned and unzipped. She lifted up her hips to help. She wasn't afraid of him seeing her. If he wasn't disappointed by her top half, he'd be fine with her bottom half. Corinne had wide hips and fairly giant thighs and an even more giant ass. But none of that could be too much of a surprise. He'd seen her in jeans. (He'd seen her once before, that night on the couch, with her skirt pushed up to her waist.) (Had he even looked?)

Enoch stopped kissing her, so that he could work her jeans down her legs. He kissed her thighs and her knees on the way. He said her name again. It was fine, they were fine.

Corinne was wearing plain, cotton underwear. She really hadn't expected this today. At least her underwear were clean. They were relatively clean. Enoch was kissing her hip, rubbing his nose up under the elastic. Corinne wound her fingers in his hair. It was so smooth that it immediately slipped free. She pulled at the back of his head. She wanted him closer. "Come here."

He crawled back over her. "Corinne."

She pulled his arms. "Come here."

He kissed her. She held the back of his head with both hands.

He drew away, breathless. His face was red. "I'm kind of overwhelmed," he said. "I don't know where to touch you."

"Anywhere is good."

His chest hitched. His pecs bounced. It was a laugh. "Anywhere . . ."

She kissed him. "I'm overwhelmed, too. You're tremendous."

Enoch huffed out another laugh. He kissed her. His hand settled on her waist, and he groaned.

Corinne rubbed the inside of her knee against the outside of his thigh. Against his suit pants. She wanted to see his legs, too. She wanted to *see* him. He was rocking his hips into her. Corinne rocked back. This didn't have to be perfect, she didn't need it to be perfect. She just needed it to happen. She reached down to his fly. It was some sort of clasp. His stomach was warm and solid, she'd never touched it before—it was distracting. Enoch had never had a waist, and now he had a belly. It was firmer than she was expecting. He was firm all over. Like he was built of sterner stuff than she was. Higher-quality parts. He hummed and rocked into her hip. She squeezed her other hand between them and undid the clasp and then a button, and pushed down the zipper.

Enoch was panting over her mouth. "Corinne."

"Okay?" she asked.

"Yeah."

"I want you, Enoch. I want you so bad."

"I want you. You feel—"

"I missed having you on top of me."

"*Corinne.*"

"I never got enough."

His hand was on her hip. He pulled at the waist of her underwear. He'd have to get up if he wanted to take them off. She didn't want him to move. She rubbed inside his waistband. She rubbed the top of his hip.

They were kissing sloppily.

"I'm really nervous," he said.

"Do you want to stop?"

"*No.*"

"Good. I don't want you to stop."

"You want—" He was rocking into her, kissing her.

"Yes."

"Corinne, tell me."

She wished she had better words for what she wanted. For this moment. "Fuck" wasn't right, it might never be right with him. What else was there? Why weren't there better words for something so important? "Make love to me," she said, hoping he wouldn't laugh at her. "With me."

Enoch was nodding. Kissing her. He lifted himself up onto his knees. He pulled at her underwear. She kicked her legs to help him. His face was red, his hair was hanging in his eyes. His fly was hanging open. He was tremendous. Corinne was a fool for him.

Her underwear were still hanging from one ankle when Enoch fell back on top of her. He was groaning so deep, he was practically purring.

"Wait," she said, "take off your pants."

"I will, I just—" He was touching her hip. Her side. Her ribs. "I want to come back and touch all these places. At a later date."

"Okay. Yes. Good."

Enoch lifted one of her knees up and spread it.

"Yes," she said.

"You're so beautiful," he said. "I can't get over it."

"I can't even see you. You're still dressed."

His hand ghosted between her legs, and she jumped. Enoch growled and pushed her knee wider. She wasn't going to get to see him. Not this time. Maybe next time. There better be a next time. He was lifting his body up. Strategically. She spread her legs, she wanted it. "Did you get the . . ."

He was breathless. "The what?"

There weren't good words for this either. "The, uh—the condom."

"The . . ." Enoch lifted himself higher. He rolled off Corinne, onto his back.

Corinne closed her legs. After a few seconds, she moved onto her side to look at him. His arm was up over his eyes. He was breathing heavy.

She touched his ribs. "No condom?"

"I'm so sorry."

She tapped his side, thoughtfully. "You bought new sheets. But not condoms."

He groaned. A different kind of groan. "It didn't even occur to me."

"Now I'm insulted."

Enoch breathed out a laugh.

She rubbed his bare stomach. "Did you not buy them because that would mean acknowledging that we might be immoral?"

He dropped his arm and looked at her frankly. He was blushing all the way down to his chest. "No. No, I was mentally prepared to be immoral."

Corinne smiled. "That's actually very comforting . . ."

He touched her cheek. "Good."

They looked into each other's eyes. They were both still breathing hard. Enoch's eyes were soft. Corinne knew hers were, too.

"I'm about to tell you something very embarrassing," he said.

"Okay." That worried her. She furrowed her brow.

Enoch rubbed a finger between her eyebrows. "I didn't buy condoms because . . . I've never bought condoms."

"Geez, did Shannon buy those, too?"

He closed one eye, embarrassed. "No . . ."

"Oh," Corinne said.

"She went on the pill before we even got married. To regulate her period."

"*Oh.*"

"I guess I assumed you were . . . taken care of," he said. "I'm sorry I'm so stupid."

"You're not stupid. We should have talked about it, but I . . ." Corinne trailed off.

"You what?"

"I guess *I* didn't want to acknowledge that we were probably going to be immoral."

Enoch laughed. He pressed his lips together and puffed air out his nose.

"I can't take the pill," Corinne said. "It makes me feel dead inside."

"I'll buy condoms."

"That'll be fun for you." She pulled her bra strap back up, and tugged the cup over her breast.

Enoch watched her. "You're so beautiful," he said lowly.

"So are you." She meant it. She sat up and shimmied back into her underwear.

Enoch looked away. "Aren't you supposed to say I'm handsome?"

She lay back down next to him, propping her head on her hand. "You're both. You're beautiful like this." She trailed her fingers up his chest. "You look like a centaur."

He actually laughed out loud. "Isn't the meaningful part of a centaur its horse body?"

"Oh, I don't know . . ." Corinne grinned. "They always have very powerful chests."

Enoch reached behind her neck and swept her hair forward, over her shoulder. "Well, you look like one of those mermaids from my bathroom."

She leaned over him, letting her hair fall around his face.

He lifted his face up to kiss her, then fell back onto the bed again. "You're even better than I imagined. It's overwhelming. I want to touch you everywhere at once."

"You can still touch me," Corinne said. "We don't need birth control for that."

"That's true . . ." Enoch said.

She nodded.

He very deliberately reached up to her shoulder and pulled her bra strap back down her arm.

Corinne grinned wide. She settled over him, kissing a line from his throat down his sternum. Over all the dark pink freckles that had somehow missed his cheeks . . .

Enoch was so much bigger than anyone she'd ever been with before. Marc was small. And Jeremy was regular-sized. She couldn't help but compare them. Was Enoch comparing her to Shannon? He must be. That was such an unfair comparison. Like comparing a dressmaker's dummy to a . . . Buick. Hopefully Enoch had imprinted on Corinne, too. Hopefully she was bathed in flattering nostalgia.

He was touching her shoulder with one hand and brushing her hair away from her face with the other. Everything was lighter than it had been a few minutes ago, less frantic.

"I love you," Enoch said.

Corinne shivered. She rubbed his chest. "I'm sorry I used the word 'immoral' before. I shouldn't joke about it."

"It's okay."

"I don't think of it that way," she said.

"I don't think I do either."

Corinne looked up at him. He pushed her hair out of her eyes.

"You don't?" she asked.

Enoch shrugged.

It's was glorious to see that shrug naked. She kissed both of his shoulders. "Why not?"

He shrugged again. One of his pecs twitched. (Corinne was going to be wet forever.) "You don't want to know," he said.

"Yes, I do." She looked up again. "Did you make some sort of weird deal with Jesus?"

"*No.*" Enoch looked affronted. "Well . . . maybe."

"Maybe?"

"It's like John Prine," he said.

"I still don't know who that is."

"We'll listen to him."

"Okay . . ."

He was still playing with her hair. "I just think Jesus can see things in context."

"That seems likely."

"Like, black-and-white rules are for us. Because we're human and imperfect. We need the structure."

Corinne tilted her head back and forth, like she partly agreed, but mostly just wanted him to go on.

"But God doesn't need rules. For Him, it's about goodness and honor and intention."

"So . . . you think He's okay with this?"

"No. I didn't say that."

Corinne touched Enoch's bottom lip. His very sweet mouth.

"I think He loves us," Enoch said. "And He sees us in context. He sees you, and He sees how unkind the congregation was to you. And He sees me, and He knows what you are to me. And He saw us even back when we were kids—He saw better than we did what we meant to each other."

Corinne's eyes felt very soft. She rubbed Enoch's lip with her thumb. "You always make Jesus sound really great."

Enoch laughed, with his chest and his warm breath. He wrapped his arms around her. "Well, I still don't think He's giving us a pass . . ."

"Damn." Corinne let him hug her closer. "I'd give you a pass," she whispered.

"If you were Jesus?"

"If I were in a position to hand out passes."

He kissed her.

She'd give Enoch a pass. She already had. Corinne lay on top of him. She touched his chest. His ribs. His stomach. She thought about all the angels in the room. She tried to imagine Enoch's version of them—looking on with compassion instead of fury. (Did he even think of demons? Of a holy war for his soul? Did Enoch Miller believe in a jealous god at all? Was it always First John for him? And never Exodus?) Corinne imagined the angels. She imagined the demons. She imagined herself. In color and context.

Enoch made the world seem kinder. She loved him. (She'd always loved him, hadn't she?)

"Enoch," she said, kissing him more deeply.

Enoch groaned. All of his noises were groans. All of his noises were engine noises. He was touching her back, along her bra line and the elastic edge of her briefs. Did that feel safer to him? To touch the only places left where she was still clothed?

She kissed him even deeper. Like she was sinking her heart into him through her mouth. Like there was nothing about her he couldn't have.

He groaned and slid his hand into the back of her underwear. Corinne nodded her head. He cupped his hand and squeezed. Enoch's hand. His fingers. He was craning his head up to kiss her, even though her face was right there, even though she was happy to do the hunching.

Enoch shifted her more completely on top of him, so he could get both hands on her ass. (Something *else* with no good words, with only crass or juvenile options—it was like the world never wanted them to talk about sex out loud.) He held her there, pulling her between his knees, rocking his hips into her. She loved that he couldn't seem to help that. That he never could. She was holding his head by his ears. Every muscle in his neck was straining.

"Here," she said into his mouth. She tried to pull away, but he lifted his shoulders up to keep kissing her. Corinne pushed his head down with her hands, then moved her hands to his shoulders and held him there. She was trying to get away, trying to move down his body. "Here," she said again. She kissed his breastbone. "Let me . . ."

He let go of her ass. "Sorry."

"Don't be sorry." She bit him right over his xiphoid process. (Crass or childish. Or clinical.)

Corinne knelt between his legs. She pulled his trousers down as far as she could. They got stuck over his hips—it was almost enough, but not quite. Corinne moved her knees to the outside of his legs. She kissed the bottom of his belly. There was dark red hair here, redder than the hair on his head. She bit him. She fisted the sides of his dress pants and lifted up her chin to look at his face.

Enoch was propped up on his elbows. His eyes were wide, and his mouth was open.

"Okay?" she said.

He nodded.

She muscled his pants down and crouched over his knees. Then pulled the waist of his boxer shorts down under his . . . ("Cock"? "Dick"? "Penis"? This was ridiculous.) She pulled out his cock. It wasn't as big as the rest of him—which was a little bit of a disappointment and a little bit of a relief. (It was like his head; he'd be a freak if it were in proportion. It would be an ordeal.)

Corinne got her left hand around it, she tried to be cool—she failed. She kissed the tip of it, then covered the rest in kisses. Like it was a baby. Or a puppy. She loved how soft the skin was. She loved how silly it looked. It seemed bigger now that her hand was around it. Fat and red. Leaking. (The "penis" drawer in Corinne's head really was a mess: Generally speaking, she was somewhat repulsed and largely disinterested—except for the moments when she really *wasn't*. This was one of those moments. Most moments with Enoch were those moments.) She was licking him. He tasted salty. He smelled close. He was groaning her name. She licked him. *Enoch. Enoch Miller.* Laid out below her. Rumbling. Leaking. His fingertips grazing the top of her head.

"You don't have to do that," he said.

Corinne looked up at him. She was licking his cock. "I want to," she said. She really did. Corinne wasn't good at being kittenish or coquettish in bed; she fell back on honesty. She *honestly* wanted to suck his cock. Really and sincerely.

She put it in her mouth (Corinne suspected she wasn't good at this part either—she secretly didn't believe that you *could* be good at it, that there was one magic technique that worked on everyone) and looked up at Enoch. She moved her head up and down, holding him at the base. She tried to be warm and wet and consistent. She tried to show him how *his* she was. That she'd let him do this. That she'd let him do anything, really. That it was okay if he looked at her sometimes and just saw a bunch of warm places to rut into.

His eyes were nearly closed. His lips were parted.

She moved. He watched.

"Corinne," he said, "it's too much."

She nodded. She wanted him to come while she was still drunk on him—and before her jaw started to hurt. She gagged a little. Her spit was running down her left hand. She wanted him to come while this was still deliriously good.

"*Corinne.*" He sounded scared.

She dug her face in.

One of his big hands landed on the back of her head. His shoulders lifted off the bed. His come hit the back of her throat, and she swallowed eagerly, as fast she could, before she could really taste it.

Enoch was quiet. His breath was juddering. Corinne's eyes were streaming. She didn't stop tonguing him until he pushed on her jaw. "Corinne," he said urgently. "Honey."

Corinne pulled away. She sat up on her knees and wiped her nose with the back of her arm. Her mouth was stuck open. Enoch was reaching for her, trying to pull her down. "Good Lord," he said. "Come here."

"Wait," she said. "I need . . ."

She moved her knees to the outside of his thighs and tried to think of where her hands had been. She pushed her right hand into her underwear and lifted her hips up a little, so she could reach her clit.

When she looked up at Enoch, he looked shocked. His face was red. His hair was sweaty. His eyes were wide.

"Can I?" Corinne breathed.

Enoch nodded. His mouth was stuck open, too.

Corinne touched herself. She looked down at Enoch's wide, freckled shoulders. The curve of his breasts—shit, she could call them pecs. Or muscles. *Shit.* This usually took much longer. Corinne whined and rocked her hips. She rubbed her clit hard with two fingers.

Enoch Miller's broad chest. His slack mouth. His brown eyes. Here. With Corinne. Corinne's. For all intents and purposes. For the moment. The taste of his come on the back of her tongue.

Corinne's hair was in her eyes. One of her bra straps was hanging. Her nose was still running. She leaned forward and crushed her fingers between her clit and his belly. She braced her left hand on his chest. She came saying his name. *"Enoch . . . Enoch, Enoch."*

Chapter Sixty-one

Corinne dropped onto Enoch's chest.

He didn't say anything.

And she didn't say anything.

He gathered her against him, his arms under hers, his fingers in her hair. Corinne hid her face in his neck.

"Okay?" he rumbled, after a while.

Corinne nodded. "You okay?"

His voice was low. "Yeah."

He was petting her hair. It tickled.

They'd never been here before. They'd never gotten this far. (He'd left her on the sofa. Wanting and worried.) Enoch coiled a finger in her hair and tugged. "Can I see your face?"

Corinne lifted up her head. Enoch's color had faded. His narrow eyes were wide and avid. Roving over her face. She wasn't sure what he'd see there. She felt embarrassed, sheepish, caught out in her wantonness, exposed for what she really was—an animal, a love-sick fool, a hungry cunt. Something long and well defiled. But she couldn't summon any regret. She'd do it again, if he let her.

"That . . ." Enoch pushed her hair back. Their heads were close. He shifted to whisper into her ear. ". . . was the hottest thing I've even seen or been a part of."

Corinne smiled and rested her cheek against his, relieved.

"Holy cow, Corinne."

She laughed. "It was okay?"

"It was amazing. I'm just embarrassed that my only contribution was to lie there, looking stupid."

"You looked incredible," Corinne said. "You *look* incredible. You make me crazy. I've spent half my life wanting to take your shirt off."

"Sorry you missed my prime."

"Your prime might have killed me," she said.

Enoch laughed.

She stayed close to his ear. "I mean it. I'm crazy for you. Everything about you turns me on."

He shook his head. But he held on tight.

The room felt colder now that they weren't running hot. She burrowed into his neck and chest.

"You cold?" he asked.

"And tired and hungry," she said.

He hummed. "Me, too."

She sat up a little. "I got lunch. Want me to bring it in?"

"Are you gonna get dressed?"

"Probably. It's in the oven."

"You have to get dressed to open the oven?"

"I don't want to burn myself."

He laughed and sat up, rolling her off of him. "You stay here. I'll get it."

"Can I have water, too?"

Enoch pulled his dress pants up and fastened them. "You can have whatever you want." He was watching her. She was lying on top of his green comforter. In her mint-green bra and wet underwear. His lips were pressed together and twisted to the side. It was a very big smile for Enoch. Practically a grin. He leaned over and kissed her knee, then hurried out of the room.

Corinne sat up. She caught her reflection in Shannon Frank's mirror; she looked like the whore of Babylon.

"You got lasagna!" Enoch shouted.

Corinne slid off his bed and stood in the doorway. "I think I'm gonna get dressed anyway!"

"Bad idea!"

She leaned her head out into the hall. "I'm going to wear your T-shirt!"

"Get a clean one! That one smells like BO!"

"So do I, probably!"

Enoch appeared at the other end of the hall. "Get a clean one. Top drawer."

She went back in the room and opened the drawer. It was all T-shirts. Corinne took one that said MILLER ELECTRIC. She sat on the bed to put it on. It was long on her, but not as baggy as she liked. If it were her own T-shirt, she'd stretch it over her knees.

She went to the bathroom and when she came back, Enoch was setting a tray on the bed. (*Who owned trays?*) He handed her a glass of water and watched her drink it. "What if I really wanted to watch you eat lasagna in your bra?" he asked.

"I'll save it for your birthday."

He kissed her. "I'm so happy you're here."

"Me, too," Corinne said.

She crawled onto his bed. She watched him change into jeans. She ate garlic bread. Enoch came back to bed and sat with his back against the headboard. Corinne stayed close to him—she felt a little anxious. Enoch seemed a little anxious, too. He kept looking at her with his eyebrows down. The ridge of his brow was very pronounced, and when he frowned he reminded her of a mop-topped Easter Island statue.

"You okay?" she asked.

"I feel like I didn't acquit myself well. Just now."

"You were perfect," she said.

He wrinkled his nose. "I don't really have much experience with, um. That."

"With?"

He reached up and thumbed her lip. He looked apologetic.

"Oh," she said. "It's pretty straightforward. I mean—did you like it?"

He rolled his eyes.

"It isn't against the rules," she asked. "Is it? I mean, profoundly?"

"I think it might be against the rules to even talk about it—which makes it hard to make a rule against it."

Corinne laughed. She tucked herself against his side.

"Was I supposed to hold it?" he asked.

She looked up at him. "No. I had time to pull away if I wanted. I liked it."

The side of his mouth pulled down. "It looked pretty uncomfortable. You were crying."

"That's just . . ." She was going to say *my gag reflex,* but stopped herself. ". . . what happens."

"Well. You don't have to do that for me. You don't have to anything."

"Enoch, I know. You have to believe me—I did it because I wanted to. You saw what it did to me."

"You really *like* it?" He looked a little grossed out by that, which didn't seem fair.

And also it wasn't exactly true that she liked it. Objectively speaking. "I don't like it for its own sake. Like, I wouldn't do it recreationally."

"Wasn't that recreational?"

"I mean, I like it in the context of you. And us. And that moment. Making you feel good. Being as close to you as I can."

Enoch looked dubious.

"In the moment, I liked everything about it," she insisted. "Even the uncomfortable parts."

"Are there times when you don't like it?"

"Today?"

"No, in general."

Corinne didn't want to answer that. Because there had been plenty of times in her life when she hadn't liked doing it, but even then, she hadn't *minded* it. And she couldn't really explain what made it good or bad. "I guess I'm not always in the mood to do it one hundred percent of the time. But that's true of everything."

His eyebrows were low.

"I'll tell you if I don't want to do it," she said. "Okay?"

"I'll just let you tell me when you *do* want to—*if* you do."

"All right," she said, holding out her hand to shake. "Deal."

He shook it, smiling. "This is my first oral sex agreement."

"Mine, too."

He kept hold of her hand. "I think I'm pretty messed up, Corinne."

She squeezed his hand. "What do you mean?"

He shrugged. He still wasn't wearing a shirt. It was magnificent.

"I'm kind of like a thirty-two-year-old virgin. But worse."

"Did you and Shannon not . . ."

"Oh, no. We did. Regularly."

"Oh," Corinne said.

"It was fine. I mean, obviously it *wasn't* fine. I just thought it was fine. Which is the problem, I guess. Or one of them."

Corinne kissed his shoulder.

"I really don't want to tell you all this," he said. "Sorry. I don't know why I'm saying it."

"I don't mind," she said.

"I do. It's not very sexy."

"You really have no idea how good you look without a shirt."

Enoch snorted. "Topless ex-wife talk—that's what does it for you?"

Corinne laughed. "Apparently."

He rubbed his eyes. He groaned. "I'm worried that you'll be miserable, and I won't notice. Because I'm too busy having the best orgasm of my life."

"You're worried about that today, or in general?"

"Both."

"The best in your *life?*"

"Don't pretend you didn't notice."

"You were very quiet, Enoch."

He laughed softly. His pecs twitched. "You weren't."

Corinne put her arms around his neck. "I thought you *wanted* positive reinforcement . . ."

"I do, I liked it." He pulled her close. His voice dropped very low. "I liked it."

Chapter Sixty-two

Corinne didn't stay the night at Enoch's house. Even though she could tell he wanted her to. She felt like she needed to get some outside air. To look at herself in one of her own mirrors. And she didn't want to be there when his shame kicked in. If it did.

She went home. She slept in her own bed. (Which felt flat and hard compared to Enoch's.)

She woke up heavy.

They'd crossed a line. They'd lost ground they'd never get back. If Corinne was feeling it, Enoch must be feeling it more. Would he want some more time apart, to think? Would he confess again? Even though there was no more penalty left for him, not on this side of Judgment Day . . .

Corinne lay in bed longer than she should. She kept replaying the day before—the way she'd replayed their first time, too, for the last thirteen years. She laid the two scenes over each other, like double-exposed film, and compared them. The ways Enoch was the same. The ways he was different. How much more she'd been allowed of him this time. Enoch Miller had never laughed when they were making out in the dark of his mother's kitchen. There'd been no warmth; only heat. This time . . . This time he'd smiled at her. This time he'd looked in her eyes. This time there was no denying what they'd done, and that they'd both wanted it.

Chapter Sixty-three

Corinne was too distracted and anxious to work that afternoon. She ended up back at the mall, buying Enoch a few more neckties. When her cell phone rang, she assumed it was him—but it was Mercy.

"Hey, Corinne, I'm sorry to bother you . . . I know you have to work."

"Don't be silly—is everything okay?"

"Do you think you could come over and hold Ruth for a little while? I'm just . . ."

"I'll come right now," Corinne said.

"Are you sure you don't have to work?"

"Nope. I'm on my way."

Mercy came to the door, holding Ruth. They both looked like they'd been crying for an hour.

"Hey, Corinne."

"Let me wash my hands," Corinne said, kicking off her shoes.

Mercy followed her into the kitchen. "Thanks for doing this. It's just . . . She keeps me up all night, nursing."

"That sounds exhausting."

"The doctor says I'm supposed to sleep when she sleeps. But she only sleeps for an hour at a time. And sometimes I'm just dropping off when she wakes up again."

Corinne took Ruth from her. "I don't know how you do it."

"If I could just sleep," Mercy said.

"Go take a nap. I've got this."

"I pumped a bottle for you. It's on the table. If she cries . . ."

"I'll walk with her," Corinne said. "We'll be fine."

Ruth did cry a little bit. Corinne gave her the bottle and walked with her. They ended up in the rocking chair, Corinne murmuring nonsense for about an hour before the baby finally fell asleep.

Ruth woke up—in a better mood, fortunately—before Mercy did. At five o'clock, Corinne called Enoch. They were supposed to meet for dinner. Enoch was making posole in his crockpot. (He hadn't called her to cancel, and she was trying not to *worry* about him calling to cancel.) "Hi," she said softly when he answered.

"Hey," he said, "are you all right?"

"Yeah, I'm fine."

"Why are you whispering?"

"I'm at Noah and Mercy's, watching the baby. Mercy's taking a nap."

"Ohhh," Enoch whispered. Christ, she loved him.

"I might be late for dinner."

"It'll keep; that's the beauty of the crockpot."

"You don't have to wait for me."

"I'm not going to stop now."

Corinne laughed. *Christ.* "I'll call when I leave," she said.

"All right. I love you. I'll see you soon."

"Bye."

When she put the phone down, she jumped. Mercy was standing in the archway at the edge of the room.

"Sorry," Mercy said. "I didn't want to interrupt you."

"Did you get some sleep?"

"Oh my goodness—as soon as my head the hit the pillow." She sat on the couch. "I never used to take naps because they'd keep me up at night. But now I'm up at night anyway, so I guess I may as well."

Corinne rocked Ruth. The baby's eyes were jumping around. "She hears your voice," Corinne said.

"She hears the milk truck."

Ruth started to cry.

"Here, I'll take her." Mercy held out her arms. Corinne brought the baby over. Mercy lifted up her shirt. The baby waved her fists and swung her mouth around wildly. "Calm down," Mercy said. "It's right here." Ruth latched on, and Mercy hugged her closer. "So much drama."

Corinne smiled and sat down next to them. Ruth was wearing pink, footed pajamas. She kicked while she nursed. Corinne caught one of her tiny feet and rubbed it.

"Was that your boyfriend?" Mercy asked.

Corinne looked up at her.

Mercy looked shy. Hopeful. "On the phone."

Corinne thought about lying. She thoroughly considered it. "Yeah."

Mercy smiled. "Have you been seeing each other very long?"

"No," Corinne said. "It's pretty new."

"But you like him, I can tell."

"I like him a lot."

"How'd you meet?"

"We . . . I knew him before I moved."

"So, an old friend."

"Yeah."

"Noah and I were friends before we dated."

Corinne didn't know how that was possible. Noah and Mercy got in trouble for sneaking out when she was sixteen, and they got married the next year. Mercy's parents had to sign something to give them permission.

"Tell me about him," Mercy said.

Corinne smiled like, *Are you sure?*

And Mercy smiled like, *Please, I'm stuck here all day with this baby, tell me some worldly gossip.*

"Well," Corinne said, "he's very smart."

"He'd have to be to date you."

Corinne smiled sincerely. "And he's funny. And he tries really hard to do the right thing."

"That's important," Mercy said.

Corinne nodded.

"I won't tell your mom."

"Thanks."

"But I don't think she'd mind—she worries about you being alone."

Did she? Did she really? Had she worried about it when Corinne was eighteen and completely on her own? Probably. That's how fucked up it all was. Corinne's mom had probably been miserable, and still totally sure she was doing the right thing.

"I could come over more often to help you with Ruth," Corinne said. "Once a week. For the afternoon."

"You don't have to do that."

"I don't mind."

"Oh my goodness, Corinne. *Really?* That would be a lifesaver."

———

"So you're going to go over there every Thursday?" Enoch was ladling out the soup.

"Yeah, so she can get a nap in before church. Mercy looks so wiped out. That baby is especially exhausting—you can already tell she's gonna be a pill, just like her dad."

He nodded. "Noah *was* a pill . . ."

"It took all my self-control not to tell Mercy horror stories about him. I was always stuck with that kid."

"Eat at the table?"

"Yeah," Corinne said. "You want water or milk?"

"Milk." He carried their bowls to the table. "I wish I could go with you. I never get to hold babies."

"I don't believe that. There are always at babies at church."

"No one ever hands them to grown men." He sounded so disgruntled about it, Corinne laughed.

"If I ever have a baby, you can hold it."

"Don't make jokes about that," he said. "I'm tender."

Corinne came up behind him and hugged him. "I know."

Chapter Sixty-four

The truth was, when Corinne offered to watch Ruth every week, she hadn't really expected Mercy to say yes—and then she hadn't expected her brother to go along with it. There had to be other, more suitable people in Mercy's support network. Corinne's mother would be happy to help with Ruth—her mother loved babies.

Maybe Mercy didn't want her mother-in-law to know she needed help. She didn't have to be embarrassed with Corinne. No one did.

When Corinne came to the door today, Mercy hadn't seemed at all worried about handing her baby over to a publicly disgraced sinner. "Oh, Corinne, you're a godsend. Thank you." She practically flew upstairs.

Ruth was less accepting of the situation. She'd been fussing for an hour already. She wouldn't sleep. And she didn't want her bottle. And she really, *really* didn't want Corinne to sit down.

Corinne had thought she could squeeze in a work call while Ruth was chilled out. That had been a bad plan; Ruth had no chill.

So now Corinne was pacing the living room floor, patting Ruth's back—trying to pacify both the baby *and* Kyle, who was currently acting a lot more like her boss than her best friend.

"You really need two more days? The Corinne I knew could finish a presentation like this overnight!"

Corinne sighed. She patted Ruth's back. "The Corinne you knew was young and tireless." (The Corinne he knew didn't spend every available minute with Enoch Miller.)

"You need to get out of Kansas, Dorothy. It's draining you of color."

"I'll finish the deck by Monday."

"Yeah, but I would prefer *Friday* . . ."

Corinne stopped pacing. "Friday is tomorrow."

"Indeed," Kyle said.

Ruth squalled. Corinne shifted her to her other shoulder.

"Was that a *baby*?" Kyle was alarmed. "Holy shit, do you have a baby now? Is that why you suck?"

Corinne started walking again. "I don't *suck*. I'm just working reasonable hours. *You* suck."

"Are you an unwed mother?"

"No, I'm babysitting."

"You're *baby*sitting, Corinne? You better be getting paid two hundred dollars an hour."

"Kyle, it's my niece. I have family here. I have a life. I'm sorry if that's getting in the way of your Taco Time pitch!"

"Yeah—me, too!"

"Do you want to hire someone else for this?"

Kyle was sullen. "I only want to hire *you*. I want to clone you, Corinne. The old you, who liked work more than life. I loved her."

"She loved you, too," Corinne said. Ruth crabbed. Corinne gave her a knuckle to gum at. "Maybe she'll come back someday, if my life goes to shit."

"From your lips to God's ear."

"Inevitably."

Ruth's fussing got so loud, Corinne had to let Kyle go. They weren't making any progress anyway—he could wait until Monday. Monday was Taco Time.

Corinne patted Ruth's back, trying to hum over her crying. "Your mom is trying to sleep. Can't you cut her a little bit of slack?"

Ruth crabbed.

"Is this because I used a swear word?" Corinne rubbed her back. "I'm sorry about that." She bounced her. "I'm sorry, sweetheart." She switched to slower, firmer patting. "Am I making you nervous? Let's both be less nervous. Let's both calm down."

Corinne had been telling herself all day not to be nervous.

Nothing was wrong. Everything was good.

She'd seen Enoch every night since . . . since they'd done what they did. And everything had been fine—wonderful. They hadn't done it again, or anything like it, but there'd been no hangover. No hammer hanging over their heads. Enoch was happy to see her, and Corinne was happy to see him. They'd kissed good night in the garage or at her front door. It was good.

Then, this morning, Enoch had called to ask if she wanted to stay over.

"*Sure,*" Corinne had said, as if it wasn't any big deal. As if it wouldn't be a first. Perhaps several firsts and a few seconds.

"*Come by before church? I'm making short ribs.*"

"*Sure,*" she'd said.

Sure, sure, sure.

"Shhh," Corinne whispered, patting Ruth's back. "Let's be less nervous. Shhhh."

Corinne let herself hum just *a little* bit of secular music while she patted. Enoch had sent her home with a *Best of John Prine* CD. Every song was sad, even the funny ones—but Corinne could see what Enoch meant about Jesus maybe liking them. It was definitely music you could listen to when you were sitting down with prostitutes and tax collectors. Ruth seemed to like it. Her crying turned into sleepy complaining.

Corinne kept trying to ease down onto the rocking chair, but even the motion of sitting seemed to get under Ruth's skin. She still wouldn't take the bottle. Corinne had managed about fifteen minutes of gentle rocking when Mercy came back downstairs from her nap, looking like she could use another twenty hours of sleep.

"I know someone who's going to be so happy to see you," Corinne said, standing to pass Mercy the baby. Ruth immediately started to cry. "Well, *first* she's going to be miserable, but *then* she's going to be happy."

Mercy was already lifting up her shirt. She settled onto the sofa, and Ruth latched on, still snuffling her complaints.

It was getting late—Corinne would have to rush to see Enoch before church. She got up to put on her coat.

"Do you have another date?" Mercy asked.

Corinne had her arm in one sleeve. She stopped. "Yeah. Sort of."

Mercy smiled. Happy to be in on this secret with Corinne. Still looking a fourth asleep. "Where are you going?"

"Nowhere," Corinne said. "Dinner at home."

"Oh, what're you making?"

"I'm not. He usually cooks."

Mercy sighed. "So jealous. Does he have a brother?"

"No," Corinne laughed. "But I do."

Mercy laughed, too. "I can't complain. Noah's really picked up the slack since Ruth was born. I don't know how my mom did this. She had seven kids."

"She had *seven* kids?"

Mercy nodded. She was slumping against the back of the couch, so the baby rested on her stomach. "And she made dinner every night."

"Well," Corinne said, putting on the other half of her coat, "at some point, the older kids take care of the younger ones."

"Like you took care of Noah?"

"He was attached to my hip. A few people at church thought he was mine."

"Oh no, Corinne—you must have hated that."

Corinne turned her collar the right side out. "That was the least of my problems."

"Noah remembers you playing with him," Mercy said. Her voice was hazy. "He said you used to take him to the park and to the store. And that you'd buy him Bottle Caps and Laffy Taffy."

"I was always trying to bribe him to be good—I can't believe you trust me with your daughter."

"Did you bribe her to take a nap?"

"I slipped Skittles into her bottle."

Mercy laughed and looked down at Ruth. "Maybe I should try that."

"You're doing fine," Corinne said with conviction. "It'll get easier . . . after three or four more kids."

Mercy's laugh was a careworn sigh. "Don't even *joke* about that."

Corinne had just buttoned her coat. She unbuttoned it and sat back down next to Mercy, reaching for Ruth's foot.

Noah would be home soon. Corinne could wait.

Chapter Sixty-five

"You look very handsome in your suits," Corinne said. They'd rushed through dinner—short ribs and carrots—and she was watching Enoch finish getting ready for church. She still felt like she was rushing, like she was running late, even though she was here now and staying. She was sitting on the bed, not the chair.

Enoch was tying one of his new ties. He pulled his chin into his neck, like he didn't believe her. "I look like Lurch. From *The Addams Family*."

"Both can be true."

He snorted. He finished tying the tie, then turned around and rubbed her knee. "I'll be back in an hour or so."

"I might spend that whole time in the bath." Corinne didn't have a tub at her apartment. Enoch had one of those antique ones with claw feet; Shannon had found it at an auction. Corinne had been eyeing it for a month now.

"Just don't fall asleep," he said.

"I still can't believe Shannon voluntarily left that bathtub."

"It's pretty heavy."

"Yeah, but it's so *nice*."

"She could have had the whole house," Enoch said, adjusting his jacket. "I offered to move. I think she wanted to start over in a new place. Like, she'd already made this house nice. She was bored with it."

"She should do that for a living," Corinne said.

Enoch looked up at her. "She does."

"She does? How did I not know that?"

He shrugged. "She's an interior decorator."

"How'd she get that job without going to college?"

"She worked at her dad's construction company."

"Oh . . . that makes sense. Does she still?"

"No." He was frowning. "They cut her off."

Corinne frowned, too. "This conversation took a turn."

Enoch held Corinne's face in his hands. "Take a bath. And then I'll come home, and we'll watch a movie or something. And then you're staying the night . . . Yeah?"

Corinne nodded. He knew that she was. He'd seen her overnight bag. She'd brought her toothbrush and a change of clothes and lavender bath salts. And a disposable razor. "Yes."

He kissed her. "I'll be right back."

The bathtub was extraordinary. Well done, Shannon Frank.

Enoch had hung the mermaids back up. Corinne sank into the tub and let her hair swirl around her head, pretending she was one of them.

She didn't soak as long as she wanted to—she didn't want to still be in the bath when Enoch got home. She shaved her legs more carefully than usual, feeling self-conscious. Then changed into the nightgown she'd bought especially for tonight. She felt self-conscious about that, too. Because it was all so intentional. There was a part of Corinne's brain that still felt like she had to pretend nothing was happening under the table.

The nightgown was short with long puffed sleeves. Soft black cotton, trimmed with ivory lace. The vibe was *mildly slutty Laura Ingalls.* (Which neatly summed up Corinne's sexual identity, as it happened.)

It was too short to wear in the living room. To sit casually on

Enoch's couch. So Corinne went to the bedroom and sat on his bed. She thought about how she wanted to be sitting when he walked in. Then she felt stupid and climbed under the covers. Then she wished she'd brought a book. The only book Enoch kept by his bed was his Bible. (Corinne refused.) She got up and turned on the stereo. Enoch had a big stereo out in his living room and a small one in here. With a record player. Corinne turned it to the oldies station. Diana Ross was singing "Theme from *Mahogany*." Corinne climbed back into his bed, under his covers. His new sheets were plaid. They weren't nearly as nice as the old flowered ones. She heard Enoch come through the front door, and she sat up. She still didn't know how to sit. *How did she normally sit?*

"Corinne?"

"I'm in here!"

She heard him walking down the hall. He stopped at the door when he saw her. He'd been slouching, but he stood up straight. "Oh," he said.

"We don't have to go to bed now," Corinne said. "I just, um, had my pajamas on. So."

"No, that was good thinking," he said.

"Yeah?"

Enoch nodded. "Definitely."

He looked like he was thinking about Corinne, here, and something else, somewhere else, and he hadn't decided where to land yet.

Corinne reached out her hand.

Enoch twisted the side of his mouth up and walked toward her. He sat down on the bed and took her hand.

The nightgown had a high neck and a row of shiny round plastic buttons. Corinne had already unbuttoned the top few because they made her feel like she was choking. Enoch ran his finger along the placket. "You look pretty."

"Thank you," she said.

He looked down, somberly watching himself play with her buttons.

Corinne leaned forward and kissed his neck. "Come to bed?"

Enoch looked up into her eyes, blushing. "All right."

He stood up again and took off his suit jacket. Walked to his closet and hung it up on the hanger. He had four suits, that she'd seen. He took good care of them; he wouldn't even eat in them if he could help it. He didn't want to have to dry-clean them all the time. The tie came off next. He hung it on the nearly empty tie rack.

"Hey," Corinne whispered, "let me see this part."

He looked over his shoulder at her, amused.

"I'm serious," she said.

Enoch turned back to her, his shirt already unbuttoned at the top. He still looked like he thought she was teasing. She wasn't teasing.

He unbuttoned his shirt, and she watched. He untucked it. He looked bigger with every layer he took off. Maybe because when he was all wrapped up, you assumed that some of that girth was just padding. His shirt was light blue. He hung that up, too. Then looked back at Corinne. He was a little embarrassed now.

Corinne smiled at him the way he smiled at her, ninety percent eyes. "You're so handsome," she whispered.

He went for his pants next, leaving his T-shirt on. Enoch was self-conscious about his stomach. He made jokes about being out of shape, even though he worked out in the basement when Corinne wasn't here. She wasn't sure what he expected of himself. His chest and ribs were so massive—his belly seemed like a real estate question, like his body had to put *something* there. She didn't mind it. She liked it. She wished her own belly made her look powerful.

He stepped out of his pants.

Corinne tried not to grin. "I've never seen your legs." They were long and solid. Thick at every juncture. Never mind a brick shithouse, Enoch Miller was built like a brick.

"You've seen me in shorts a thousand times," he said.

"I haven't seen your legs in fifteen years, how's that?"

He hung the pants up and closed the closet door.

Corinne scooted over on the bed. "I like them very much."

Enoch came to the edge of the bed.

She pulled back the covers for him. "I like you very much," she said.

He sat down next to her and leaned in to kiss her. Time still stuttered when he kissed her—she still wasn't used to it. To Enoch's soft mouth. To having him right here for her. She pulled him close to her. She wanted him close. She felt him relaxing, felt his mouth dropping more heavily into hers. She sighed, and she felt his lips quirk up—he was smiling at her. Corinne smiled, too. She rubbed his shoulders through his T-shirt, then tried to get a handful of it, to pull it up.

Enoch backed away from her and pulled the shirt up over his head.

"You're so much better at that than I am," she said.

"Practice," he said.

She kissed him. She was happy. So obviously happy. There was no hiding it from the angels and demons tonight. From God Himself, if He was paying attention. Corinne sank down into the bed and pulled Enoch down with her, delighting in his bare arms, his shoulders.

He was touching her thigh, playing with the hem of her nightgown. "This is nice," he said.

"Thank you."

He trailed his fingers up her leg, tentative, then pulled away from her mouth to raise an eyebrow. "No panties?"

Corinne made a face like there was a hair in her mouth. "I hate that word."

Enoch laughed. "What word would you prefer?"

"There are no good words," Corinne said. "It's a conspiracy to keep us from talking about sex."

He was petting her hip.

She kissed him. "Let's say 'underwear.'"

"'Underwear'? Really?"

"What do you want from me, Enoch? 'High-cut briefs'?"

His eyes were laughing at her. "All right . . . You're not wearing underwear."

"I'm not."

He pushed Corinne onto her back and kissed her more seriously. Touching her hip, squeezing her thigh. She felt him moving through the gates of Carried Away and past them. She loved it, she loved him. She loved being underneath him. She wrapped a leg around him. He caught it under her knee. "I bought, um . . ."

"Just say 'condoms.'"

He snorted. "I bought condoms."

"I'm proud of you."

"Should I get them?"

"You should get at least a couple."

"All right."

He kissed her and got up. He turned the light off on his way out the door.

"Did you put them in the bathroom?" Corinne called after him.

"They seemed like a toiletry!"

He came back and crawled up from the bottom of the bed, then scrambled under the covers with her. Corinne kissed his neck and his chest. He was holding the condoms in his hand. She could feel the foil scraping her thigh.

"I practiced putting them on," he said.

"That was smart." She kissed his mouth.

"Should I put one on now?"

"Yeah, if you want."

"Okay."

She kissed him. "Okay."

"You can't watch."

She laughed. "Okay." She rolled onto her back and closed her eyes. "I'm not watching."

Enoch sat up. She heard him open the packet. She heard the condommy sound. The shuffle. Corinne was indifferent to condoms. She was used to them. She'd tried going on the pill, with Marc. But it made her feel like she was too sad to cry—and pretty averse to sex, in general. *Of course* Shannon Frank could tolerate the pill . . . Though maybe Shannon Frank already felt too sad to cry.

"Dang it," Enoch said. He tore open another package.

"I can help you," Corinne said.

"I really don't want your help."

"Okay."

He huffed. She kept her eyes closed, but reached out to touch his back.

"Okay," he said, getting under the covers.

Corinne opened her eyes. Enoch's face was red. His eyebrows were pulled down.

She reached up to his chin. Gentle. "Hey."

"Hey," he said.

"Kiss me?"

He nodded. He kissed her. She slid her body against his. He kissed her harder.

Then he pulled away, growling. "I just . . ." He lay on his back. He covered his face with one arm and reached under the blanket with the other. She heard the snap of the condom coming off. "Sorry."

"Did I do something wrong?"

"No. It's me. I just. I need a minute."

"Okay."

He sat up and reached for his boxer shorts. "I need a drink."

Corinne felt her eyes widen. She pulled the comforter up over her shoulders and watched him walk out of the room.

When he came back, he was drinking a glass of milk. "I didn't ask if you wanted anything," he said, holding out a glass of water. Corinne sat up to drink it. Enoch stood there, waiting for her to finish with the glass. He set them both on his bedside table, then climbed under the covers and lay on his back. "Sorry," he said. "I don't think I can, um . . ."

"We don't have to do anything."

His palms were on his forehead. "Okay. Thank you."

"I don't have to stay tonight."

He looked over at her. "No. Please stay. I mean—unless you want to go?"

She touched his shoulder. "I want to stay."

He exhaled. "Okay, good."

"Can I touch you?"

Enoch nodded. "Yeah." They moved close again. He wrapped an arm around her waist. "Sorry."

"Stop apologizing."

He tucked his face into the top of her head.

"I'm sorry," he said after a while.

"Is everything all right?"

"Yeah . . . I just. Church was especially challenging tonight. I haven't quite shaken it off yet."

She pulled her head away. "What happened?"

Enoch's face was long and tired. "Nothing really happened . . .

I saw a sister from our old congregation. Do you remember the Greens?"

"Did they have a daughter a little older than us?"

"Yeah, Lynette." His eyes were cast down. "She came to our services tonight with her family. And I was so happy to see them—I presided over her son's baptism a couple years ago. Matthew. He's twelve or thirteen now. When I saw them in the parking lot, I called out to him. 'Matthew, my man!' I forgot . . ." He shook his head. "The kid looked completely panicked. And Lynette was there, pushing him past me. I felt . . ." He shook his head again.

Corinne's eyebrows were so low, she could practically see them. She pulled Enoch closer. She brought her hand up to stroke his hair. "I'm sorry."

He shook his head.

Corinne desperately wanted to get up and change into regular clothes. She'd been shaving her legs and thinking about seducing him—while he was being actively shunned. Shunned because of her. And then he walked into his house, and she was sitting there like actual, real-life Jezebel.

"I'm so sorry," she said.

"It's just how it works. It's supposed to be punishment."

Corinne clenched her teeth so hard, she could feel it in her gums. She didn't say anything. Enoch didn't say anything either.

She lay there for a few minutes hating the church and being angry at Jesus, and then she turned it on herself again. "I'm sorry I threw myself at you, without even asking about your night. I can't believe how insensitive that was."

He lifted his head. "Honey, no. You should definitely keep throwing yourself at me. You looked so pretty, I mostly forgot how terrible I felt."

"Mostly," Corinne said, frowning. There were tears in her eyes. "*God*. I hate this."

"No." Enoch touched her cheek. "Don't hate this."

"I hate being the reason you're in a perpetual state of being stoned."

"You're not the reason; I'm the reason."

"Enoch, don't. Don't twist this around. You know what I mean."

"I'm the one who wants to keep going to church."

"Do you think you *deserve* this? Public humiliation? Shunning? Do you think it's right?"

"It's part of being in the congregation."

"That's not what I asked."

He didn't answer her. He didn't want to argue with her. Because he wasn't going to change his mind. And she wasn't going to change hers. When the church had tried to humiliate Corinne, she'd left—she'd spared herself the mortification. She couldn't spare Enoch.

She hid her face in his neck. "How can you sit at church, being punished because of me, and then come home to me?"

His voice was low. "I don't see it that way."

"How do you see it?"

"I see this as a time to get myself untangled—"

She jerked her head up, frustrated. "Aren't we just getting *more* tangled?"

"Sometimes you have to get more tangled on the way to sorting something out."

"That sounds like a rationalization."

"I'm not giving you up, Corinne. That's not the answer here." He pressed his forehead into hers.

She pressed back.

Then another wave of shame rolled over her. She winced. "I still can't believe that I . . . leered at you while you were feeling humiliated. I'm so sorry."

"Please don't apologize. No one's ever leered at me before."

"I've never *not* leered at you, Enoch."

His chest hitched a laugh. It was a comfort. She cuddled up against him.

"It was almost fine," he said, "despite everything—it was almost great. But the, um, the condom got into my head. I was worried about doing it wrong."

"I would have helped you."

"Hey, Corinne," he said in a dumb voice, *"will you help me put this balloon on my . . ."* He shook his head instead of finishing the sentence.

"There's no good word," Corinne whispered. "But I would have helped you. I would have liked helping you."

"It feels so goofy. Like, it's already goofy-looking, and then with the—with the condom, it looks like I pressed it against a window. Or into a test tube."

"I never would have thought that."

"I was also worried about it falling off."

"You would have felt it sliding."

"Really?"

"Yeah, you just reach down and catch it."

He looked pained. "I'm sure you don't usually have to teach the men you sleep with how to use a condom."

"*The men I sleep with.*"

"Sorry. I didn't mean it that way."

"It's just something you work through with someone," she said. "It takes a little practice. It's not like . . . Olympic-level archery."

He frowned at her. "What are you quoting? Is that from a movie?"

"It's you. You were trying to get me to roller-skate."

"Your memory . . ." He shook his head.

Corinne leaned up and whispered in his ear. "I *want* to work through this with you."

Enoch started to say something, then stopped. Corinne waited. He tried again. Inhaled. Made a noise like, "Eh . . . ," then exhaled again.

"What?" she said. "What is it?"

"Can I talk about my ex-wife again?"

"I'm not sure we ever stopped."

He groaned and hid his face in the pillow.

"I'm sorry," Corinne said. "I'm just kidding—I really don't mind."

"I think you do."

"Well, I *don't mind* more than I mind."

"That's also how you feel about oral sex, right?"

"*Enoch.*" She shook his shoulder. "Talk to me."

"Talking is exhausting," he said into the pillow. "Let's go back to not talking and feeling each other up."

"Okay, but you're going to need to buy Parcheesi."

He snorted and buried his face almost completely.

"*Enoch.*" She kissed what she could see of his cheek. When he didn't reply, she poked his shoulder. "Talk to me about your ex-wife right now."

Enoch sighed and rolled onto his back, pulling Corinne in closer. She kissed his cheek again, for good measure. He caught her chin and kissed her mouth. Corinne kissed him back, relieved that he wanted it. He seemed relieved, too. Corinne tried to think hard about how much she loved him and hoped he got the message.

When he pulled away to take a breath, she nudged him. "Go on. What were you going to say?"

"It's something I've been thinking about all week . . . and even before. Before we started seeing each other again."

"I'm listening."

He looked down, past Corinne's eyes, like he was talking to her chin. "All right, so . . . Shannon told me once that it was hard for her to figure out that she was gay, because no one ever told her that women are *supposed* to enjoy sex. She was taught that *men* want sex. And that's why you can't be alone with them. Your job as a girl is to keep anyone from having sex with you until you're married, and then it's your job to submit dutifully to your husband. To not deprive him. So when she . . . well, when she felt disconnected, she figured that was probably just normal."

He sounded like he had more to say. Corinne just listened.

"I felt so terrible for her when she told me that. Like, *'Poor Shannon, she's been so confused.'* But, like—maybe I was just as confused. Because I thought that what I had with her was more righteous than what I had with you. Because it was cleaner. More controlled. Resistible. And then, after we were married, I never really expected her to want me like that. It didn't seem *strange* to me that she didn't . . ."

Enoch twisted up his face, like he was disagreeing with himself. "I don't know . . . Maybe that was the appropriate way for me to think, anyway. Like, people have different drives and desires, right? But it *really throws* me when you say that you want me. That you aren't doing me any favors here. And that's probably partly because of Shannon. But it's also just how I was taught to think about sex. That your wife does this because she loves you, she forbears you, and you should be grateful and honor her for it."

"Apostle Paul strikes again," Corinne whispered.

Enoch smiled. Rueful. "I guess."

She kissed his cheek again. "Would it be easier for you if I acted more forbearing?"

"Yeah," he said, "could you lie here and pretend not to like it?"

She shook her head against his cheek. "No," she said softly. "I don't think that I could."

Enoch hummed out a long breath and held her tight against him.

⁓

It had been years since Corinne had slept next to someone. She used to sleep with her head on Marc's chest and his arm around her. It was one of the things she missed most about him.

Enoch's chest was too thick for that. Corinne's neck got cramped almost immediately. Plus, he liked to sleep on his side. They settled like spoons with his arm around her waist.

She wondered if this was what he was used to and whether he could actually sleep like this—how he might be accommodating her.

He kissed her shoulder. "Are you comfortable?"

"Yes," she said. "You?"

He kissed her again. "Yeah. I kinda can't believe you're here . . ."

"I kinda can't believe I'm here either."

⁓

Enoch Miller's heavy arm around her. His hand on her belly. The sounds of his house. The quiet, with no one living above or below. The grandfather clock, disconnected in the hallway.

Chapter Sixty-six

There was a part of Corinne that kept waiting for her mom to show up at the flagpole.

Corinne wasn't supposed to get away with this.

Corinne wasn't supposed to have this. To have him.

When she saw her mother standing outside her apartment building, she thought for a moment that it was finally happening, that she'd come to haul Corinne away.

Her mother had never been to Corinne's apartment building before. No one in her family had. Corinne was allowed into their world, with limitations. With rules. With the understanding that their way was *the* way, and that Corinne tacitly agreed with them. But Corinne's world was *the* world.

"Do not love the world or the things in the world.

If anyone loves the world, the love of the Father is not in him."

Her mother was standing at the door, pressing Corinne's buzzer.

Corinne walked up behind her, carrying an overnight bag, looking like she'd slept on someone else's pillows. "Mom?"

Her mom turned around. "Corinne?"

They both stood there. Corinne lifted her chin.

Her mother was holding a paper bag. "I brought you kolaches," she said.

"Kolaches?"

Her mother seemed distracted. Bothered. She was looking past Corinne, to see where she'd come from. "There's a bakery, just around the corner. I went there with Marta, from church."

Corinne nodded. She could see her mother's breath.

"And I thought"—her mother was still looking past her—"Corinne used to love kolaches."

"Come inside," Corinne said. "We'll have some."

"Oh no." Her mother's face fell. "I couldn't."

Corinne moved past her to unlock the front door. She held the door open. "Mom. It's cold out. Please come in." *Come inside, there isn't a man in there. I'm obviously stumbling away from one.*

Her mother stepped into the foyer, clinging to the paper bag. "I was just going to drop these off."

Corinne headed up the stairs, and her mother followed, looking around the whole time, like something might jump out at her.

"Do you remember when we used to eat kolaches?"

"I think so," Corinne said, opening her apartment door. "From that little grocery store, right?"

"That's right." Her mom took a small step inside. "We lived right above it."

Corinne dropped her overnight bag as soon as she could. "Can I take your coat? I'll make some tea."

Her mom looked around the living room. "Oh no, I can't stay long."

"I'll just make some for myself then," Corinne said, walking toward the table.

"You don't drink coffee?"

"No, I do. I just never learned to make it."

Her mother turned to her, managing to look even more concerned. Like Corinne really was a godless heathen if she didn't have a coffee maker.

Corinne swept papers and dirty mugs off her table. Everything was the way she'd left it last night. Why did that feel as damning as an unmade bed or an extra toothbrush by her sink? "Have a seat, Mom."

Her mother sat. Still wearing her winter coat and her snowy boots. Still holding the paper bag.

Corinne went into the kitchen to turn on the kettle. "What's the bakery called? That you found with Marta?" She was just going to brave her way through this. Even if it wasn't bravery making her arms and legs move.

"It's a Czech bakery . . ."

Corinne came back to the table. She set her laptop aside.

"Is this where you work?" her mom asked.

"It is."

Her mom frowned at the table. Like she didn't want to know this. She didn't want to be here. She'd only been stopping by—which had obviously been a mistake. Look how good Corinne was at leading people off their path.

Corinne reached for the paper bag. "Do they need to be warmed up?"

Her mom looked at Corinne's hands. She held on to the bag. "No."

"I'll get a plate for them."

Corinne came back with three plates. (Corinne only had three plates. They'd come in a pack of four, and she'd broken one.) Her mother was sitting on the chair with the bag in her lap, like the situation would get worse if she relaxed even a little bit. She was wearing a printed skirt under her coat, and warm tights. She still wore her hair in a slightly immodest braid, with wavy tendrils falling around her face. That was probably what landed her her second husband. Those bohemian curls. It was the only thing Corinne had inherited from her. Her mother was small and plump, not fat, with big blue eyes and soft features. Corinne's eyes were blue, too, but less convincingly, and her features were flinty and sharp. Corinne looked like her father—she must, because she didn't look like anyone else. Maybe he was to blame for the rest of her, too.

Corinne set the plates on the table.

"Were you out having breakfast?" her mother asked. Hopefully.

Corinne didn't know what to say. She still tried not to lie. And she hadn't had a bite to eat at Enoch's house. He'd left before she even woke up. Corinne had rolled out of bed and into her car—she probably still smelled like him. Would her mother touch her? Would she recognize the smell of the Millers' dirty laundry?

"I'm still hungry," Corinne said. "Is Earl Grey okay?"

Her mother looked down, she looked sad.

When Corinne came back with the tea, her mom had laid some of the kolaches out on one of the plates. She'd set the bag on the table.

"Oh," Corinne said, looking at the round pastries, "I do remember these."

Her mom lifted up her chin. "I used to buy them two for a dollar. We'd have them for dinner sometimes. Do you remember?"

"I think so," Corinne said.

"Your favorite was the poppy-seed." She pointed at one with a black center. "The woman at the bakery counter always thought it was funny that a little girl wanted to eat something so bitter."

Corinne took it. "You have one, too. Don't make me eat alone."

Her mom chose one with red filling. Holding it gingerly. Like there was some rule about breaking bread with Corinne—there probably was a rule, but they'd already broken it. She'd already let Corinne back in. What was the boundary now? How far was Corinne allowed? She couldn't see the line. She could only feel it.

Corinne took a bite. The pastry was mild and flaky. Nothing as buttery as a croissant. But more substantial. The filling was a bittersweet paste. It was familiar. Corinne thought maybe she did remember eating these. Even though she'd only been three. She hummed, for her mother's sake.

Her mom hadn't taken a bite. "You never see kolaches anymore, and when you do, you don't see poppy-seed. When I saw they had them, I thought it must be a sign." She glanced up, nervously, at Corinne. Signs and portents were dangerous to mention. Because you never knew who was sending them. They were like luck—too close to witchcraft. "I'd been praying about you just this morning, and there they were."

She'd been praying about Corinne. She'd probably felt an ill wind. An angel probably flew directly from Enoch's bedroom to wake her mother.

"I remember that apartment," Corinne said. "Over the grocery store. My room was purple."

Her mother's shoulders dropped a little. Her eyes were cautiously eager. "That's right. I painted it for you. It was hardly bigger than a closet. It was just you and me then. I'd just met your dad." She meant Corinne's stepdad, her first stepdad.

"There was a little kitchen, right? With a fern?"

Her mom's blue eyes were bright. "Yes! I've never been able to grow a fern like that again! That one died when we moved. I grew it from a cutting our neighbor gave me. Peter. Do you remember him?" Her mother's voice dropped—"He lived with another man. Even back then, in 1977. It was shameful. But he was always very kind to us. He gave me that fern. And he taught me how to make monkey bread. I still pray for him . . . Peter." She shook her head. She looked down. Like she'd said too much. Maybe it was against the rules to even talk about bread. "Those were strange years," she said. "We were so lost, you and me."

I wasn't lost, Corinne thought. *I was where I was supposed to be. With you.*

Corinne picked up her mug, trying to remember more. "I remember watching soap operas with you . . ."

Her mother smiled. Her shoulders a dropped a little farther from her ears. "You weren't supposed to be watching those . . . If I'd known what a little sponge you were, I would have been more careful. I've never known another child with a mind like yours. You could memorize a scripture the first time you heard it. Do you remember Brother Miller, Bonnie's husband?"

Corinne nodded.

"He used to say it was a shame you were born a girl. You could have gone onstage and done the whole Bible reading by heart!"

Corinne smiled. Her mother smiled back—and then her face fell. It was too much again, too far.

She wanted Corinne to remember the good times and the good places. She wanted her to remember the years when God's light still fell on her, when she still had so much potential as one of His servants.

But there was no purely good memory. Not of Corinne. Corinne was tied to her mother's sinful years and had never managed to wash that sin away. She'd carried it with her right into the Lord's house. Right into the Millers' house. Right into her own apartment.

Corinne, who was just coming home. Whose face was unwashed. Whose mouth looked kissed.

Her mother stood up. "I should go. I was just in the neighborhood, you know, and I thought of you."

"I'm glad you stopped by."

"Next time I'll call."

"You don't have to. This was nice."

Her mother was already moving toward the door. Corinne got up to follow her.

Normally her mom would hug her good-bye—she'd always been a warm person, she'd always been loving. The other sisters at church always said that she was too soft, that there was too much slack in Corinne's leash.

Today she just squeezed Corinne's arm. She reminded her about Sunday dinner. Corinne walked her down to the front door and watched her get into her car.

When Corinne got back up to her apartment, she went to the table to put away the extra kolaches. Her mother hadn't touched hers. Corinne found a Bible tract stuck inside the paper bag. She took it out and opened it. There was an illustration of Jesus—His eyes shining, His arms outstretched. *You, Too, Are a Child of God*, it said.

⌒

She met Enoch for dinner. She brought the kolaches.

Chapter Sixty-seven

You had to think so much about food when you were with another person. You couldn't just eat celery and cream cheese all day. Or the same kind of bagel sandwich six meals in a row.

Enoch liked breakfast. He took breaks for lunch. He made dinner. Every meal was a separate event that he looked forward to and put effort into.

Corinne was starting to feel self-conscious about it. Selfish. Alicia and her pizza stones had never made Corinne feel like a child, but Enoch and his crockpot did. He took care of himself, fed himself, even when he was alone. He went grocery shopping for himself—and now for her. He planned meals.

His whole life was more structured and grounded than hers. He woke up an hour early and exercised in the basement. He owned a lawn mower. He took a multivitamin.

Corinne tended to treat herself like a head in a jar. She woke up late and worked. She stayed up late and worked. She ate whatever was easy. She exercised intermittently. She bought nice things for her house, usually when she was feeling down, but then never bothered to hang them up or arrange them.

Her life hadn't been much different with Marc . . . He was a head in a jar, too. (Rapidly pickling.) The two of them thought and worked and talked. They watched movies and read books. They came into their bodies to have sex. But not to take walks or make dinner.

Corinne felt herself shifting. Wanting to shift. Wanting to let Enoch rub off on her.

"I thought you were never making dinner again," Enoch said, when Corinne suggested that he come over to her apartment after work.

"Don't use my own words against me."

"I would never."

"I'm capable of making dinner, Enoch Miller."

"I know, I partook in the chicken broccoli braid—but you don't have to."

"You shouldn't have to cook every meal . . ."

"I would anyway."

"Yeah, if you spent the rest of your life alone. Let me carry my weight. I can make dinner every . . . so often."

He laughed a breath into the phone. "Every so often, huh? I feel lighter already."

Corinne was making pasta. (Spaghetti.) With meat sauce, because Enoch had meat with every meal. She'd bought a salad mix. And salad dressing. And bread—she was going to try to make cheese bread. As meals go, it hardly required any cooking at all, but it still took hours of time that Corinne could have spent working. How was this worth anyone's time, ever? She ran out of time to put on makeup and arrange her hair; she usually at least managed mascara. She did remember to set out the lamp Enoch had given her, on the table by the couch. It was pink ceramic with a two-tiered green shade that Enoch said was fiberglass. It was perfect.

Enoch got to her apartment earlier than she was expecting and wanted to kiss her in the doorway. "You smell like garlic," he said. "I like it."

"What do I usually smell like?"

"Deep thoughts."

Corinne laughed and pulled him in.

He took off his coat and followed her into the kitchen. He was wearing a blue plaid shirt with a button-down collar. "Can I help?"

"Everything's mostly done," Corinne said. "I just have to make the pasta."

"I can do that."

"Don't. It's the only part with actual cooking—I want to do it myself."

They ate at her table, sitting right next to each other, with Enoch's big hand resting on Corinne's thigh. He was eating and drinking with the other hand, so that he wouldn't have to move it. It reminded her of the way he used to roll the dice and move his game pieces with his right hand, so that he didn't have to stop touching Corinne with his left.

Enoch ate a huge plate of spaghetti and acted like she'd offered him something more impressive than boxed pasta with expensive grocery-store sauce. "This is so good."

"Now you're patronizing me," Corinne said.

"I'm not," he said. "Any food that I didn't have to cook myself automatically tastes more delicious."

"When did you learn to cook? Your mom never made any of you help in the kitchen . . ."

He shrugged. "My twenties. Trial and error. I got better at it when I was living alone."

Corinne nodded.

He squeezed her thigh. "How old were you when you first lived on your own?"

Corinne thought of the dorm room she'd had to herself the summer after freshman year. Did that count as living alone? "College, I guess."

"Did you have an apartment?"

"Eventually."

"You didn't have roommates?"

"I did sometimes."

"Were you on a top-secret mission for the government?"

She tilted her head toward him, trying to get the joke.

"I can't ever get you to talk about yourself," he said.

"That's not true—we talk all the time! I've never talked to anyone this much before."

Enoch laughed. He was eating a piece of cheese bread. "You make it sound like a real pleasure, Corinne."

"It is a pleasure." She couldn't not roll her eyes as she said it.

"We talk . . ." Enoch swallowed. "About me. And about life, in the moment. And you give me *reams* of sass . . . plus a smaller measure of guff . . ."

"Guff," Corinne repeated.

He shook his head. "But we don't talk about you."

"There's not much to talk about."

"There you go." Enoch winked at her. "Cagey."

She put her hands in the air. "What do you want to know? I'm an open book!"

He'd just taken another bite of bread. He laughed so abruptly, he almost spat it out.

Corinne folded her arms. "I'm an open book," she said more calmly. "Ask me anything."

"All right . . ." He chewed for a second. "When did you get your first apartment?"

"After I got my bachelor's degree. During grad school."

"Did you live by yourself?"

"No."

Enoch was watching her. His eyes were gentle. "No?"

She sighed. "No. I lived with my boyfriend."

"What was his name?"

"Why do you want to know his name?"

"For ease of reference. That's what names are for."

"Jeremy," Corinne said.

"Jeremy," Enoch repeated. "Was he nice?"

"He was fine."

"Open book." Enoch patted her thigh.

She sighed more heavily. "He was nice—I met him in class, junior year. He was in my program."

Enoch closed an eye, doing the math. "So you were together a long time. You must have been serious."

"I mean . . ." She shrugged and sighed again. She scraped her plate with her fork, moving the last bite of salad around.

"Did you like college?" he asked, changing the subject.

"It was f—"

"Fine," Enoch said along with her.

Corinne clenched one fist in her lap. Enoch moved his hand to cover it.

She bit her lips and closed her eyes. When she opened them, she said, "I still feel like I need to be careful about what I say to you."

"Careful . . . *why?* I'm not going to hold your dating history against you."

"No, I know that, actually. I just, um . . ." She wrinkled her nose. She didn't want to say any of this. "When we were kids, I got very good at being careful. Around people from church."

Enoch pulled his chin into his neck. "Is that how you see me? I'm a 'people from church'?"

"That is literally where we met."

"Yeah, twenty-five years ago. I'm not a 'people from church' now—I'm your boyfriend."

Boyfriend. What a dumb word. Corinne wrinkled her nose again. She bit her bottom lip. She went a little weak.

Enoch noticed. He leaned in to whisper it into her ear. "I'm your boyfriend . . . right?"

Corinne nodded.

Enoch kissed the skin behind her ear.

After a few more kisses, Corinne pulled away enough to get some eye contact. "I was always afraid you were going to turn me in. When we were kids."

"For what?"

"Watching bad movies. Having worldly friends."

"I was never going to turn you in."

"You might have. For my own good."

He frowned. "Well . . . I'm not going to turn you in now."

She shook her head. "It's not just that . . . I guess I don't want my worldliness to make you uncomfortable."

"That's not an issue."

"It is with my family."

"I'm not your family."

Corinne made a frustrated noise in her throat. "It *is* an issue. Sometimes. Like, you don't like it when I swear."

"I mean . . . true? Do you need to swear a lot to tell me about college?"

She frowned at him. "I'm probably not ever going to stop swearing, you know."

"I gathered as much. You dropped three F-bombs in the kitchen."

"*I burned myself.*"

"I offered to the drain that pasta for you—you're not supposed to use a plate."

"Well, I don't have one of those holey things."

"A colander."

"Yeah."

Enoch kissed her neck again. "Okay."

Corinne sighed. Again. For probably the fourth time in as many minutes. "What was the question?"

Enoch's chest hitched merrily. "Did you like college, Corinne?"

She rolled her eyes. "Yes. I liked it a lot."

"What'd you like?"

"I liked . . ." She looked over at him. He wasn't smiling, strictly speaking, but she knew his face well enough to know he was grinning. "My roommate. She grew up on a farm, and she was super into Red Hot Chili Peppers."

"What was her name?"

"Jodie."

"Jodie," he said.

"And I liked my classes. I liked that my whole job was studying. That I didn't have anything else to worry about." Corinne pushed her plate away from herself and leaned an elbow on the table, facing him.

The side of his mouth twitched up. He rubbed her thigh. "What'd you study?"

"Everything. I sort of took as much of everything as I could. In four years. I lived on campus over the summers."

"I didn't know you could do that."

"You can. It's more expensive than getting an apartment, but my scholarship covered it. I ended up with a major in political science."

"Did you go to parties?"

She rested her chin on her hand and shook her head.

"Not one?"

"Maybe one."

"I thought college was supposed to be a Bacchanalia."

"I didn't want to get raped at a frat party."

"Always thinking."

"I just really loved the game of it."

"What game?"

She lifted her legs and slid them on top of Enoch's knees. His lips twitched again, and he pulled her legs deeper into his lap, rubbing one of her calves.

"College is all a game," Corinne said. "You have to get a certain number of credits in certain areas. And each class has its own rules and requirements. None of it is all that hard, as long as you focus. And you can get rewards and bonuses. I loved it. I think you would have loved it, too."

Enoch was watching her face. He nodded. "I envied you."

"You did?"

"I still do."

They looked in each other's eyes. Enoch rubbed her calf with his thumb. Then he said, "So you kept going? After you graduated?"

"I got a master's degree in communication."

He snorted.

"Your amusement is noted," Corinne said.

"Why communication?"

"I was fascinated with advertising and propaganda. Public health messages. Recruiting. Persuasion."

"How very evangelical of you."

She laughed. "I was more interested in the why and how of it. There's this theory in communication that it's the sender's job to effectively communicate an idea . . . It's not the receiver's job to understand it."

"I don't understand."

"Like, if I'm throwing you the ball, it's my job to make sure you catch it."

"I understood. I was making a joke."

She rolled her eyes. "Oh. Well. Anyway, I really liked that idea. That if you want to be heard, you have to know your audience."

"I don't feel like you use these tactics in your everyday life."

She frowned. Genuinely. "You really think I'm a bad communicator?"

"I don't think you're manipulative."

"It's not about manipulation—or it shouldn't be. It's about making sure that you're meeting people wherever they are."

Enoch looked in her eyes. He rubbed her legs. "So," he said, finally, "you studied everything, you didn't party, you fell in love with a guy named Jeremy . . ."

She shook her head.

"You weren't in love?"

"I wanted to be," she said. "But . . . no."

"You were together a long time."

"There wasn't any reason to break up. He was a good person. We liked the same things. I remember thinking that it wouldn't be fair to break up with him, because he hadn't done anything wrong."

"Did he break up with you?"

"No. I moved to Boston. We sort of mutually agreed it wasn't working."

"Did you start a conversation with him about how you both agreed it wasn't working?"

Corinne bit her lips and laughed. "Maybe."

"Poor Jeremy."

"Oh, God, he was better off without me. He married the next girl he dated, and they had so many cute kids—a raft of them."

Enoch was still eye-smiling at her. He was rubbing her knee now.

Corinne touched his hand. "It doesn't make you feel jealous and weird? To hear about it?"

He shrugged, looking almost egregiously unbothered. "Maybe it would, if I gave it too much thought. Or if you seemed hung up on him . . . Or if I saw a picture of him, and he was really handsome."

"Says the guy who was married to Shannon Frank."

"What's that supposed to mean?"

"Just that your ex-wife is extremely beautiful. And I wish she wasn't."

Enoch laughed breathily and cocked an eyebrow. "Okay, but . . . she kind of looks like a twelve-year-old boy these days."

"Are you kidding me? She's more beautiful than ever!"

He raised both eyebrows. "Well, that *is* unsettling to hear . . ."

Corinne kicked his belly.

He caught her ankle. "Are you jealous of Shannon? Really?"

"Are you kidding me? *Yes.* I've spent my whole life jealous of her. I'll never get over it."

"But you know . . . everything."

Corinne shook her head. She kept her voice even: "I don't think you understand how much I felt for you when we were teenagers. Shannon had you, and I didn't. For those few months that we were together, and for all the years after—she had you. I don't hate her or anything, but . . . yeah, I'm jealous."

Enoch looked sad. "I feel like I'll never make this up to you."

"I don't need you to make it up to me," Corinne said.

"What do you need?"

Corinne looked in his eyes. Chocolate brown and small behind his glasses. "I need you to be mine."

Enoch leaned forward and hooked both of his bear arms around her waist. He hauled her into his lap. It was awkward. She worried about his knees. "Corinne . . ." Enoch said to himself and maybe to her. "Honey, I've always been yours."

It was both the right and the wrong thing to say, but Corinne would take it.

She'd take his kisses. His arms around her back. His teasing.

It was all she'd ever wanted, and she'd take it.

Chapter Sixty-eight

Corinne's dining room chairs weren't made for two people. Two people kissing. Corinne sat straddling Enoch's lap. He held her by the seat of her jeans. Her fingers were curled at the base of his skull, tilting his head back so she could kiss him.

The first time Enoch rocked his hips up, the chair tipped backward. He shot an arm out to the table to keep them from falling, but Corinne was already sliding off his lap. She landed in a squat on the floor, giggling.

"Come on," she said, letting him pull her to her feet. "We don't have to do this on a chair. We're not circus folk."

Enoch stood up, too. His knees cracked. His cheeks and neck were flushed, and his eyes were wide and hungry. Corinne took one of his hands and slung his arm over her shoulder, hauling him toward her bedroom. He put his other hand on her waist and followed her.

They'd never been in here together . . . Corinne's bedroom was much smaller than Enoch's. Her bed was smaller, too. A double. And she only had one pillow. (God, what an aggressively celibate statement that was.) Once they were in the room, she turned to him. His head was hanging over her like his neck had stopped working. He hunched lower and started kissing her again.

"Bed," Corinne said. "I have a bed." She sat down on it and scooted backwards, holding her hands out to him like she was calling to a dog. Whatever. It worked. He climbed over her and kissed her some more. These were her favorite kisses. The ones that were almost bites. Enoch rubbed the front of his jeans into her thigh, and Corinne bent her knee to help. He moaned. She pulled up the end of his shirt. "Let me see you."

Enoch got up on his knees to take off his long-sleeved shirt and the T-shirt underneath. "Let me see *you*," he said with his elbows in the air and his voice still muffled.

Corinne was wearing a T-shirt and a cardigan. She squirmed out of the sweater, and Enoch helped her with the shirt. She was wearing the mint-green bra again. He was going to think she only had one.

"Beautiful girl," he said, falling down next to her and wrapping one big hand around the back of her neck. Enoch Miller's thumb on her throat. His mouth over hers. His shoulders so square, his parents must have used a compass to draw them. He kissed her. Corinne spread her fingers out on his flanks and rubbed her leg up into his . . . ("Crotch"? Christ no, not even in her head.) (There should be a word, better words, for all of this, for what she was doing and how much he liked it—her knee between his legs, his hips already bucking against her.)

He let his hand drift down to cup one of her breasts, but he still seemed too timid to move his fingers. Corinne pulled her mouth away. "That feels good," she whispered.

Enoch swallowed and looked at his hand. "Like this?"

"Like that and more."

He looked confused.

Corinne took his wrist in her hand and pressed his palm into her breast.

"Like that?" he asked.

"Like . . ." Corinne arched into his hand. "I want you to take what you want from me."

He frowned. "Isn't that what I did the first time?"

She squeezed his wrist and looked in his eyes. "Is it?"

Enoch held on to her gaze. After a second, he shook his head. "No."

"I want this," she whispered. "I want you."

Enoch's head dropped back onto hers, kissing more fiercely. He clenched his fingers around her breast—his hand was nearly big enough to palm her—and she sighed, nodding her head. He went to pull her bra strap down, and Corinne lifted a hand to help him. Then he was up on his knees again, dragging both straps all the way down and off, and reaching in to scoop her breasts out of their cups. He groaned low—"*Corinne . . .*"

She arched her back again, and he touched her breasts with purpose—finally—his thick fingers stretched wide, squeezing her. His lips were parted. His face was almost pained.

"That feels so good," Corinne said, to encourage him. And because it did.

Enoch shook his head and closed his eyes. "I can hardly look at you."

She covered his hands with hers, so he wouldn't pull away. "Why?"

He looked up at her face. "You're just *more* than I expected. It's better than I imagined it could be. I wish you could see my hands on your—" He stopped short.

"Breasts," Corinne said.

"Breasts," he whispered.

She looked down at his hands. "I can see."

He squeezed her. "I wish you could see through my eyes."

Corinne whined and pushed into his hands.

Enoch squeezed and squeezed and then brought his thumbs up over her nipples. They were thick like the rest of her and already tight. It made her feel crazy; she wasn't putting him on. "Touch me," she said. "Don't stop touching me."

Enoch lay down next to her, and she rolled toward him. They took up the whole bed. (He must have a king bed at home, or some sort of extra king.) He rubbed her nipples and kissed the top of her breasts. She held his head. His neck, his ears.

"Here," Enoch said, reaching under her. Corinne lifted up, and he unhooked her bra, tossing it off the bed. "Thank you for your service."

She laughed and brushed his hair away from his eyes. Enoch drew her in close, their chests pressed together, their noses touching. Corinne shook her head. "No matter where you touch me," she said. "I don't want it to stop."

"I don't have to stop," he said, caressing her back. (Actually fucking "*caressing*" her.)

"But I want you to touch me everywhere else, too."

"I've got two hands and a fairly open schedule."

Corinne laughed again and kissed him.

"Hey, Corinne . . ." Enoch whispered. He still sounded nervous.

"Yeah."

"I feel pretty dumb saying this, but . . . I didn't bring a condom with me."

She petted his hair. "I didn't seem like a sure thing?"

"I guess I wasn't thinking, but—" He kissed her quickly. "I don't want to stop. Could we just keep going, and I can touch you? Or, really, whatever you want. Could we just keep going?"

"Yeah." She kissed him. She brought a knee up over his thigh. "Or . . ."

He kissed her. "Or?"

"Not really 'or,' but—I have, um, spermicide. I bought it today. At the grocery store."

"Spermicide?"

"It's a gel," she said.

He still looked confused.

"It goes inside. Of me."

"Does it work?"

"Not as well as condoms. But . . ."

He kissed her twice. "But?"

Corinne looked away. "You could pull out. If you want. Not if you want—but if you want to try that. It might be easier this first time than worrying about the condom."

"Corinne . . ." He rubbed his nose against hers. "Did you buy mildly effective spermicide gel because I'm condom-impaired?"

She smoothed his hair back. "Yes."

"I can't decide if that's insulting or romantic."

"I'm crazy about you," she said softly.

"I'm crazy about you, too."

"I know." She kissed him again. "And I just want to clear away as much anxiety as we can. I want to have this with you, Enoch."

"Aw, honey . . ." He brought his hand up to her chin and kissed her properly. And then he leaned closer to whisper in her ear: "I can try to pull out. It might be a real in-and-out situation though. I've been on borrowed time for an hour."

Corinne laughed and pushed closer, rubbing her chest against his. She didn't care if it was fast; at this point, she just really wanted it to happen. To prove it *could* happen. That they weren't cursed somehow. Like, they'd had sex in the worst way at eighteen and ruined their chances of ever doing it again.

And she wanted it to happen because she *wanted it to happen.* He made her *feel* eighteen again, like she'd take his cock however she could get it. It didn't make sense. Corinne wasn't obsessed with penetration. She wouldn't cross the street for it, generally speaking. But she *wanted* him, she wanted this. She wanted what they had at eighteen, the desire and the urgency and the consummation of it all. And she wanted what they had now, the love and the time and the talking—and the bed.

Enoch unbuttoned her jeans and pulled down the zip. He slid his hand into the top of her underwear. Corinne was wearing the satin bottoms that matched her bra. She should get credit for that, even if the bra was on the floor. He rubbed his big hand against the pad of her pubic bone. ("Pubic bone"; English was a failure.) Corinne hadn't shaved or done anything weird to get ready—she'd be damned if she resorted to pubic grooming, even for the love of her life. Enoch was growling into her mouth. He didn't care. Or notice. Corinne tried not to imagine Shannon Frank's no doubt impeccable vagina.

She shoved at the side of her jeans. (She really did want credit for the satin underwear.) Enoch helped her get them down under her ass and over her thighs, and Corinne kicked them off as soon as she could.

"Corinne . . ." Enoch said, rubbing her bottom.

Enoch, she thought. *Enoch, Enoch, Enoch.* She stroked his slippery hair and his thick neck; she bit his shoulder.

Enoch's hands weren't big enough to palm her ass, but he tried. "You match," he groaned.

Corinne rubbed her face into his neck, nodding.

His voice was urgent, confessional—"I'm so in love with you, Corinne."

I'm so in love with you, Enoch.

He moved one hand along the satin, over her hip and between their bodies, between her legs. She was wet through. (She wasn't usually, but it had been more than an hour of waiting.) (Technically speaking, it had been since 1992.)

"Corinne, Corinne . . ."

"Enoch . . ."

"Honey, you're so wet."

"I want you."

He worked his fingers under the fabric and inside her . . . ("Labia"? "Folds"? This is why Prince wrote "Sugar Walls.") (Before he found Jesus.) Enoch Miller's thick hand. His blunt fingers. Two of them. Inside her. (Not fully inside her. In the foyer. The sugar foyer.) He hadn't touched her like this that first time, on the couch—he hadn't touched her at all.

Corinne felt weak and wholly wanting. She whimpered against his neck. "*Enoch* . . ."

"Honey?"

She nodded.

He pushed a finger deeper. "Corinne?"

"Yeah?"

Enoch was breathing heavy. He was rubbing one finger just a little bit in and out, feeling the ring of muscle. "How effective is it?"

"Hmm?"

"The spermicide."

"Oh . . ."

In and out, in and out.

"*Oh,*" she sighed.

"Like," he pushed, "compared to condoms?"

"Mmm . . . like, seventy-five percent effective?"

Enoch pulled his finger back. "That's not very effective at all."

Corinne rocked herself (her "self," honestly) against his hand. "That's why you're going to pull out."

"I'll still leak though. I mean, I leak."

"I know," she said. "It's very sexy."

"But it's not . . . Well, it's not safe, is it?"

"I wouldn't have suggested we try this if I was fertile."

He pulled his hand away. He pulled his head back. "*Corinne.*"

"I mean, in my cycle," she said quickly. "I'm about to get my period."

He shook his head, gathering himself. "I can just touch you," he said. "I *want* to touch you."

"Okay, but Enoch—I'm not going to get pregnant the day before my period, even if you don't pull out."

"I would pull out."

"I'm not worried about it. Are you worried?"

"I just, um—" He was clearly worried. "What would we do if you got pregnant?"

"Deal with it, I guess?"

"Would you have an abortion?"

"Oh my *God.*" Corinne pulled her hips away from him. "Did you really just ask me about *abortion?*"

"I did," he groaned. "I'm sorry."

She rolled onto her back and folded her arms over her chest. "What on *earth?*"

"It just . . ." He was still propped up on his side. "It seems like something we should talk about?"

"Now?"

"Better now than . . ."

"I'm not going to have an *abortion,* why would you think that?"

He ran a hand up through his hair. "I don't know what to think—we've never talked about it. You might be pro-choice . . ."

"Yeah, I guess."

"Are you?"

Corinne closed her eyes. "Mostly. Sort of. But that doesn't mean I want to have one."

"Okay, so"—he was trying to sound reasonable—"that's good to know."

"*Is* it?"

"Corinne, I'm sorry. I guess I should have brought this up over dinner or something . . ."

She growled low in her throat. Frustrated. Irritated. Unwilling to admit that he might be right, about discussing it. Uncomfortable discussing it in nothing but mint-green underwear. "It's fine," she said, sounding very not fine. "It's just—you people are *obsessed* with abortion."

"By 'you people,' do you mean people who want to have sex with you?"

"That's not a people—that's just you. Purportedly. And I meant the church."

Enoch dropped onto his stomach next to her and hid his face in her pillow. "I'm sorry I brought it up."

"It's fine," she said again, sounding slightly more conciliatory. "You're right, we should talk about it. If I get pregnant tonight, despite staggering odds, I'll keep the baby. Just like in the Madonna song. Okay?"

"Okay," he said into the pillow.

"But we're not raising the kid in the church."

He lifted his head up. "Corinne," he said and meant, *Don't be a jerk.*

"I'm serious. No kid of mine—no miracle fruit of my loins—is growing up like that."

Enoch looked hopeful. "But 'we're' raising it?"

She scowled at him.

The corner of his mouth twitched up. "Our kid might want to go to church."

"Our kid might be gay."

"They should get to decide about church for themselves."

"At sixteen."

"Eight is the age of reason . . ."

"That's absolute bullshit," she said. "Eighteen."

"All right, eighteen, but can we reopen this conversation if we ever, actually decide to have kids?"

Corinne kept her arms tightly folded over her nipples. "Fine."

He was still smiling with one side of his mouth. His voice was gentle. "That's my first accidental-pregnancy accord."

She rolled her eyes.

Enoch shifted back onto his side and tucked one arm under his head, so he could rest on his biceps. "Do you want me to get your shirt for you?"

"Sort of."

"I'm sorry I mentioned abortion while I was touching your . . . What word do you like?"

"What word do *you* like?"

He reached down to the end of the bed, where she kept a quilt folded. He spread it out over them. "Better?"

"Yes." She pulled the quilt up over her shoulders. "Thank you."

"Come closer?"

Corinne sighed and shuffled toward him. Enoch moved his arm from under his head and offered it to her as a pillow. She took it. His biceps twitched under her cheek, it was devastating.

"I'm just trying not to screw this up," he said.

"I know," she admitted.

Corinne's hair was still in a ponytail. Enoch hooked his index finger under the rubber band and pulled it down. She reached up and held the base, so he wouldn't tear hair out of her head.

"Thank you for your service," he said, flipping the elastic off the bed.

"Are you going to personally thank all my clothes?"

"Wait 'til I get your panties off," he said soberly. "I'm going to kiss them good-bye."

She raised her shoulders up to her ears and scrunched her nose.

Enoch put his fingers in her hair, close to her scalp, to shake it loose. "You really want me to say 'underwear'?"

"Don't say anything at all. I feel like it's an avoidable concept."

He laughed. It was just a breath. "I have one more thing I want to talk about while we're not in a compromised position . . ."

"I still feel kinda compromised," Corinne whispered. Enoch was playing with her hair and it was tickling her back.

"Shouldn't we use a condom . . ." he asked. "You know, for other health reasons?"

"Three days ago, you'd never even heard of condoms—did you watch a filmstrip or something?"

He sighed. "I can't stress how much I don't want to mess this up with you."

"All right . . . Let's talk about it. Let's be grown-ups." She took a deep breath and then let it out. "I haven't had sex in a very long time,

and I've been to the gynecologist two or three times since then. So . . .
I'm definitely clear."

"Okay," he said. "Thank you for telling me."

"Have you slept with anyone other than Shannon?"

"You."

Corinne couldn't help but laugh. "Okay, well—do you think Shannon cheated on you?"

"I know she didn't."

"Enoch, I know we have a lot to worry about, but I think we can let this one go."

He nodded. "All right." He was still playing with her hair. "A very long time, huh?"

Corinne nodded.

"How come?"

She shrugged. "It wasn't a priority." He kept petting her. She shivered. "I feel like you have this image of my worldly life . . . Like I spent the last thirteen years partying and having abortions."

"I don't think that, but . . ."

"But what?"

"But I know you've been *out there,* in the world, in a way that I haven't. I got married at nineteen, Corinne."

"I *know.*"

"Well, so, I figure you've done a lot of things that I haven't. And I don't judge you for any of it."

She winced. "On the one hand, I'm grateful for your . . . magnanimity? On the other . . . it feels like I'm getting a presidential pardon for the crime of drinking a few wine coolers and being a serial monogamist."

"*Are* you a serial monogamist?"

"It's been a pretty limited series."

He snorted and pulled his fingers through a tangle in her hair. "I think you're the funniest person I've ever known . . ."

Corinne tipped her head forward and raised her eyebrows. "Enoch. *That's* what you should have said when you had your hand in my . . ." The joke fell flat because she couldn't finish the sentence.

Enoch slid his hand down to her waist, and hauled her in. "You

better tell me what word you like for that. I don't think it's an avoidable concept."

"Has been so far."

"Ba-boom-tsssssk," he said, sounding impressively like a snare
drum. He leaned closer to kiss her neck. After a few kisses, he said,
"I'm not trying to be patronizing about your life."

"I know that. I *do* know that." She touched his cheek. The curve of
his neck. The hollow at the bottom of his throat. "Some of this is my
family. The way I've learned to be with them. They don't want to hear
about my life—they're scared of it. I don't just have a scarlet letter; I
have, like, a whole scarlet letterman's jacket."

He kissed her neck some more. "I'm sorry."

"It's just . . ." Corinne felt desperate for Enoch to understand her,
to *see* her. "I came from the same place *you* did. I have most of the
same hang-ups. I'm not in the church, but I'm not . . ."

"Caligula?"

"*Caligula?*"

He lifted up his head. "I was trying to think of a famous pervert."

"I'm not a famous pervert."

"No, I know."

She could feel herself frowning. She could hear her voice coming
out too earnest—"They always taught us that people who left the
church were more debased than people who were born in the world,
that they were hungry for sin." She squeezed his shoulder. "But that
hasn't been my life. I don't drink. I've never smoked. I took some
comparative religion classes that might freak you out, but I've only
had sex with three people."

Enoch looked surprised. "Plus me?"

"No—including you."

"*Really?*"

She punched his shoulder. "Really."

"Why *not*, Corinne? You're super hot."

She laughed—half flattered, half exasperated—and punched him
again. (It was hardly a punch, and his shoulder was solid as a rock.)
"Because that's not what I wanted from life. I didn't leave the church
because I was *easy*."

He brought one hand up to her cheek. "Trust me, I never thought that . . ."

"Are you going to make a joke now about me being difficult?"

"I'm trying," he said, "but I can't quite make it work."

"Why are you smiling?"

"I'm not smiling."

"You are. This counts as a smile for you. The raised brow, the twinkly eyes."

The corner of his mouth tweaked up. "I'm really happy, I can't help it."

Corinne's voice dropped suspiciously. "Why are you so happy?"

"Because we're *talking*. We're working it out. A few minutes ago, you were making topless parenting decisions—I liked it a lot."

She huffed.

"And I guess I am relieved . . ." he said.

"That I remained sexually repressed and guided by shame, even outside of the Lord's favor?"

Enoch rested his forehead against hers. "That you haven't told me anything I can't wrap my head around."

Corinne relaxed into him. If she was being honest, she felt the same way. Gay ex-wife. Condom anxiety. Accidental-pregnancy accord. She could swallow all of it. The only thing that was still stuck in her throat was his faith. (Which was a very big thing, to be sure, but at least it wasn't a surprise.)

"I wasn't judging you," he said, "but I did think I was competing with at least twice as many guys in your memory . . ."

"It isn't a competition," she said, then begrudgingly added, "and even if it was, no one else has ever taken up so much space in my head. No one compared to you, Enoch."

He hummed, low in his throat. "I shouldn't like it so much when you say that."

"Why not?"

"I shouldn't need it."

"It's still true," she said.

Enoch kissed her. He kissed her with his jaw thrust forward, looking down at her from the very bottom of his eyes. It made her heart drop into her vaginal canal. Like a key dropping into a lock. She dug

her hands into his neck and his shoulders. She pulled herself higher
and closer to him. Enoch rubbed her lower back with the flat of his
palm and the pads of his fingers. When he pushed his hand down
into her underwear, she felt faint with relief. He got a handful of her
ass and squeezed. *Yes.* Corinne nodded her head.

He flipped her onto her back and pulled his arm out from under
her neck. Her head bounced against the mattress. He was pulling her
underwear down. Straight down. No messing around. His jaw was
set, his eyebrows low.

When Corinne's ankles were free, she bent her knees and spread
her legs; she wasn't messing around either.

Enoch tossed her underwear off the bed (silently thanking them,
no doubt) and slid the first two fingers of his right hand straight into
her. All the way to the hilt. Corinne clutched her hands in her own
hair and *whimpered.*

Enoch lay down next to her, slowly pumping his fingers in and
out, feeling her. "Corinne . . ."

"Enoch."

"Oh, honey."

She lifted her hips up off the bed then let them fall. *Enoch. Enoch
Miller.* His square palms, his long, thick fingers. His fat mouth taking
bites out of her shoulder.

He nipped at her ear. "Did you already do it?"

Did he mean, *come?* Because, wow, no.

"The spermicide . . ." he said.

"Oh." Corinne pushed herself up onto her elbows.

Enoch kept pumping into her. She fell back again. He pushed
deeper. He hovered over her, watching her face. "Is that good?"

She nodded, hard.

"Like that?"

"Yeah . . ."

"Go get the stuff, Corinne." He didn't stop touching her.

"I can't," she panted.

"You can't?"

She slapped his wrist and tried to sit up. "You're a fucking tease."

Enoch laughed out loud and slid his hand out.

Corinne rolled onto her stomach to get away from him. She rose up onto her elbows and knees. Enoch was kneeling, too. He slung his arm around her hips and pulled her back, pushing his fingers into her from behind.

Corinne gasped.

"Yeah?" Enoch breathed, fucking into her.

"Oh my God," she said.

"Yeah . . ." he said, low, dropping a kiss onto her rear. "*Corinne.*"

"Let me get it," she said.

"Go ahead."

"I can't."

"Go ahead, honey."

Her face fell onto the bed. "I can't."

"Corinne . . ."

"That feels so good."

Enoch pulled his hand away and fell back on his haunches, slapping her bottom. "Go. Hurry up."

Corinne stumbled off the bed, a little disoriented. She held her arms under her breasts, like she was holding a baby. Enoch was watching her. His eyes were dancing.

The spermicide was in her dresser. She grabbed the whole box. Enoch was standing next to her bed, taking off his jeans. There was light coming in from the living room. He glanced up at her and pushed everything off—boxers, too—then stood up straight. He was a wall. A perfect rectangle. A slab. She walked back to him on the balls of her feet, one arm curled under her breasts, one carrying the box. Enoch caught her by the waist and pulled her into him, bending over her, kissing. She'd waited her whole life for this, to be with him like this. To stand in his arms, swaying. Enoch kissed her mouth and her cheeks. He put his hand on the box. "Is this self-explanatory?"

"I'll do it," she said.

"I can do it."

"It's not attractive. It's like a hypodermic needle."

"Fine." He kissed her. "You do it. Do it."

She lingered, nuzzling against him. "This is very good," she said.

"What?"

"This whole thing you've got going on, from the floor to the ceiling."

He beamed down at her. He pulled her back onto the bed. Then up toward the headboard. Corinne opened the box and took out one of the tampon-shaped packages. "Don't watch," she said.

Enoch sighed and lay back on the pillow. His toes hung off the end of her bed. His cock was full. The spermicide came in an applicator, with a plunger. Corinne had used it before, lots. With condoms. It was fine. She shot it in and dropped the plastic pieces and the box over the side of the bed, then clambered back over to Enoch and leaned over him. "Okay . . ."

He opened his eyes, getting his arms around her shoulders. "Okay . . ." He kissed her. He tasted like . . . like he'd been *licking his fingers*. Time stopped. But not in the usual way. Corinne wanted him so bad that the rules of physics didn't apply to her anymore. Enoch was saying something. She licked his bottom lip.

"Right?" he asked.

"Huh?"

"I said, this is just the beginning for us, it doesn't have to be perfect."

Corinne took his entire lip in her mouth, sucking on it. She lay on her back, pulling him onto her.

Enoch's hand went between her legs again, his knuckles rubbing over her clit. "I need some direction . . ."

"I want you inside me."

"Will that . . ."

"That's what I want. Please, Enoch. I want you."

"Corinne . . ." He pushed his fingers down again. And in.

Corinne spread her legs. "I want you."

Enoch hunched over her. He pulled his fingers out and took hold of his cock, pushing into her. Corinne took a deep breath and reached for the top of his head.

Time didn't stop—it spun around her.

She was lying in her bed, with Enoch Miller holding himself over her. She was lying on his mother's couch. His father's couch. She felt full. She was lying in her own bed, in her own place. It was dark. She was wet. She was full. She was eighteen. Her underwear were hanging from one knee. Enoch Miller was squeezing the back of her thigh. He was holding himself over her. His hair was in his eyes. Wine dark. Cherry brown in the light from the hall. In the light from the grandfather clock. Corinne was on her back. Her legs were open. Enoch Miller was inside of her. She felt a pinch. She felt full. She didn't feel much of anything at all. She was on her back. Enoch Miller's big body on top of her. Enoch Miller's thick cock pushing into her. She was eighteen. She was thirty-two. She was a fool for him. She wanted this, she'd take it.

Enoch rocked his hips into her. "Corinne," he said, "Corinne . . ."

Enoch. Enoch Miller. *Enoch.*

"Gorgeous girl," he said, rocking. Rocking. Grounding her. This was different from before, this was better—everything about this moment was more substantial.

"Enoch," she said.

"Corinne, I love you."

She tried to wind her fingers in his hair, but it kept slipping away. Her voice kept catching in an "m" sound in the back of her throat. Enoch leaned on one elbow and reached for her leg, holding it up with his hand behind her knee. He pushed deeper. (It was still just pushing. Corinne would never know what to make of it.) Her "m"s were getting more urgent. She couldn't come like this, but she still felt frenzied. Wanton.

Enoch was right there. Watching her. Panting on her. She looked up into his eyes. She held his head. His eyelids came down, and his hips rocked harder. And then he was pushing away from her, kneeling up, pulling himself out, looking a little panicked.

For a second, she worried that he'd stop. Out of politeness. Or embarrassment.

But he looked down at her, and his lids dropped, and his hand kept pumping. He finished on Corinne's stomach, groaning her name.

Chapter Sixty-nine

Enoch took a long time in the bathroom, but when he came back, he had a hot washcloth. He must have waited for the water to heat up.

Corinne had her arms folded over her chest again, and she'd slid her legs under the quilt. Enoch wiped her belly clean—it felt good, she closed her eyes. Neither of them seemed to be ready for eye contact anyway.

"Do you want to get under the covers?" he asked.

Corinne nodded.

"Do you want your clothes?"

"No." Corinne sat up, covering her nipples with one arm. She wasn't sure why she was still doing that, but it was hard to stop. She pushed the blanket and sheet down and made room for him.

He climbed in and pulled the covers over his big shoulder, lying on his side. "Do you really only have one pillow?"

"I'm a spinster," Corinne said. She pushed it toward him. "You use it, I'll take your arm."

Enoch folded her pillow in two and propped his head on it, offering Corinne his arm again, groaning. It was a contented groan, she thought. A purr. She laid her head down and rested a hand on his chest.

Enoch ran a finger from her widow's peak to the tip of her nose. "You okay?"

"I'm good," she said. She'd already told him this. When he'd gotten his breath back and hunched over her, still on his knees, covering her face with kisses.

"Did you . . ." He tapped her nose.

Corinne lifted her head up and caught his fingertip between her teeth. She shook her head no.

"Did you want to?"

She shook her head again.

He tugged his finger away. "Why not?"

He didn't look upset; she was glad of that. Just concerned. Curious.

"I don't always want to," she said.

He pushed her hair off her forehead. "Why not?"

"Because it's a whole production."

"*Ha,*" Enoch laughed out loud, she loved it. "And that wasn't?"

"I just wanted to feel you and be with you," she said. "I didn't need the distraction."

He twisted his mouth to the side. "I feel like we could have worked it in."

"Maybe . . ." Corinne said.

He tapped her nose again. "Bust out that master's degree and give me a little more information."

"I *can* do it," she said.

"I know, I've seen it. It was spectacular."

She looked down, feeling blushy. She scratched gently between Enoch's pecs. "I felt like you would have tried to do it for me . . ."

"I would have. Is that . . . not . . . good?"

"It just wouldn't have worked."

"You don't know that."

"I *do.*" Corinne looked up at him. "I have to . . . make it happen myself."

"Yourself."

She nodded.

"You could show me how," he said. Sincerely. Doggedly. (It was already exhausting.)

"I can't show you."

"I could watch you—I'm sure I could pick it up, I'm good with my hands."

She pressed her hand into his chest. "You are *great* with your hands," she said emphatically. "I'd let you operate on me. I just . . ." She shook her head. "It wouldn't work. I'm dysfunctional."

He frowned at her, thinking hard. "But you can make yourself come."

"Always. Repeatedly."

"Does it have something to do with trust? Like, relaxing into it?"

"Ughhh," Corinne groaned. "No."

"Have you had this conversation before?"

She groaned again—"Uh-huh."

"I'm sorry." He looked sorry. "I just want you to feel good, honey."

"I *can* feel good."

Enoch kissed her nose. She tipped her head up and caught his mouth. When he pulled away, she said, "I think it's, like, I need to respond immediately to my own feedback."

"Like a closed circuit."

"I guess so."

"That doesn't sound dysfunctional," he said.

"It's fine from my perspective, but . . ." Corinne took a deep breath and blew her cheeks out on the exhale. "I know it makes me . . . disappointing, as a partner. You want to see me react, I get that."

"You *were* reacting . . . a lot."

"Because I felt *good*," she said, looking in his eyes. "Sometimes it feels better than coming."

"What does?"

"What we were doing . . . sex."

"How can sex feel better than an—an orgasm?"

"I don't know, I don't understand it. I just know what I feel."

Enoch was still thoughtful-frowning. "You should have told me this before."

"When was I supposed to disclose it, during our abortion talk?"

He brushed his thumb along her cheek. "You know I'm in love with you?" It was a question, a matter-of-fact one. "That I'm already all in?"

Corinne's eyebrows were low. She nodded. Briskly.

"I want you as you are."

"As-is."

"That's not what I meant—but yeah. I already told you how messed up I am, and this doesn't even seem that messy. Some women can't have an orgasm at all."

"Have you been reading *Cosmo*?"

"I have a television. I've watched *Oprah*."

"Does Oprah talk about orgasms? She has a book club."

"I've also watched less distinguished talk shows."

Corinne looked up at his long face. His dear nose. His precious mouth. "I can't help how I am," she said, her voice very quiet. "But I also can't help wishing I was different . . . I want to be everything you've always dreamed about."

"Honey . . ." Enoch wrapped his hand around her neck, his thumb on her throat. "You never have to worry about that."

"I want this part of us to be so easy and good," she whispered. "Because I know other parts won't be."

He frowned down at her. Concerned. Thoughtful. Somber. "Corinne . . . a minute ago, did you say, 'repeatedly'?"

She nodded.

"How repeatedly?"

She bit the side of her lip and tried to decide how forthright to be. "Until I get sore," she said, "or you get bored."

Enoch closed one eye. "I think we're good here."

Chapter Seventy

Enoch had probably called his ex-wife "honey." He probably called dogs "honey." He probably called his truck "honey" when it wouldn't start.

That's how it worked. He hadn't selected the word especially for her; his brain just supplied it.

Corinne understood that.

But she was going to pretend for a while that she didn't.

Chapter Seventy-one

Corinne woke up in the middle of the night. Enoch was pushing himself up out of bed and whispering, "*Ah, ah, ah.*"

"Are you okay?"

"It's just my back," he said.

"Is it okay?"

"I just need . . ." He slid his feet onto the floor, using his arms to do most of the work of standing. "I'm going to do some stretches."

"Okay."

"Could you . . ." He was grimacing.

"Do you need something?"

"Please don't watch."

"Oh. Of course." She lay back in bed and looked up at the ceiling. She could hear Enoch moving on the floor. He was breathing very intentionally.

"Do you need some Advil?"

"It's just a cramp."

"Does this happen very often?"

"*Corinne.*"

"Sorry." She lay still and quiet, listening.

Enoch's breath got quieter. After a few minutes, he stood up and climbed back in bed.

"Are you all right?" Corinne whispered.

"I'm fine." He was still being brusque. "It cramps up sometimes. I usually stretch before bed."

"Does it still hurt?"

"It always kind of hurts."

"Is it because you're sleeping in a different position?"

"No."

"Is it this bed?"

"Corinne."

"Sorry."

He pulled the pillow back under his head. "Do you want to lay on my arm?"

"No," she said, "just get comfortable."

He sighed. "I'm fine."

She reached a hand around and gently touched his lower back. There was no discernible curve. He was straight as a board. "Do you want me to rub your back?"

He didn't react. But he didn't say no.

"Roll over," Corinne said.

"I'll be fine."

She kissed his cheek. "I want to."

Enoch sighed and rolled over. Corinne hadn't really seen his back yet. It was immense. It was the side of a barn. It was the entire Great Plains. His shoulders were wide and sharp, and his waist was thick, and his shoulder blades stuck out like some sort of sunken heavy machinery. His shoulders were freckled on this side, too. Like someone had stood over him with a shaker of cinnamon sugar. Corinne bit him.

"That's one way to do it," Enoch said. He still sounded disgruntled.

"You're beautiful," she whispered.

He sighed, like he wasn't sure what to do with any of it.

She touched his lower back. "Here?"

"Yeah," he said. "Basically. That whole area. You don't have to—"

She pressed her thumb into the muscle along his spine. He took a sharp breath.

"Bad?" Corinne said.

"No. Good."

She did it again. Firm. Slow. She'd been to a massage therapist before. She tried to mimic that steady, focused pressure. Enoch hummed; she figured that was a good sign. She didn't know what the muscles in his back normally felt like, but at the moment, they were hard as a rock. After a while, he seemed to relax. "That's really nice," he said in his bass-note voice. "You're good at that."

"Well," she said, "I am good with my hands."

He laughed in his chest. His shoulder blades twitched, and his sides shook. It was a whole different view back here. Corinne kissed both of his shoulders. She nuzzled her face into the back of his neck. Into his thick, soft hair. "I love you," she whispered.

Enoch stopped laughing. "Corinne?"

She closed her eyes. She nodded her head in the nape of his neck. "I love you so much, Enoch."

Her hand was on his lower back. He reached for it and brought it around him. He held it to his chest.

"I love you," she said, hugging him. Hiding her face in his hair.

"I love you, Corinne."

She kept her eyes closed. If she opened them, tears would spill out. "I love you, Enoch. I'm in love with you."

Chapter Seventy-two

Electricians went to work very early. Too early. Why. It's not like they had to bake bread or make sure planes were landing safely.

It was still dark when Enoch got up and shuffled his clothes back on. Corinne watched with a sour look on her face.

He kissed her cheek. "Call me when you get up."

"That'll be six hours from now."

"Good," he said. He pushed her pillow toward her. She took it.

Chapter Seventy-three

Corinne woke up the second time in the middle of the day.

She woke up in her own bed, with her head on her pillow. She woke up with her mint-green satin bra on one side of the bed and the matching mint-green satin briefs on the other.

Her hair was down.

Her lips were chapped.

Her legs were sliding naked under the sheets.

She woke up new. She woke up changed. She woke up something else entirely.

She woke up with Enoch Miller's name swimming around her head. With every memory of his every touch dancing over her skin.

She woke up feeling like she'd finally closed her hands over something solid.

Chapter Seventy-four

Ruth and Mercy were both sleeping when Noah came home from work.

"Oh, hey, Corinne," Noah said, when he walked into the living room holding a bag of groceries.

Corinne was sitting in the rocking chair with the baby. She smiled and waved.

Noah walked over and peered down at his daughter. His voice dropped: "Knocked out, huh?"

Corinne hummed.

"Do you mind staying while I get dinner started?"

Corinne curved her hand over the baby's head and ear. "Go ahead."

She could see into the kitchen from the rocking chair. She watched Noah put away the groceries and start dinner. He looked like their dad—short and dark, with wavy, nearly black hair. She wondered if Noah ever talked to their dad. Corinne still talked to him. He was the same as he ever was. In and out. Here and there. Never really there when you needed him. He lived in California now. They talked on the phone.

Her dad blamed the church for his marriage failing—which was ironic because the church was the reason Corinne's mom had stuck it out with him for so long. At least, her mom always said that was the reason.

He also blamed the church for turning his kids against him. *"You know how they are,"* he'd say to Corinne. And then she'd feel like she had to defend them—even though she *did* know how they were. They'd cut her off, too.

Corinne could never fully take her dad's side against the church. She had too much to lose. *This,* for example. This tenuous welcome. This baby asleep in her arms. This chance to get to know her brother a little bit better.

"You're the only one who treats me like a father," her dad would say. *And you're not even my daughter,* she could hear him think.

Maybe she should be angrier with him. For all the years of recklessness and neglect. She was certain he'd cheated on her mom. Copiously. But he was laid-back and gentle, and Corinne was pretty sure there was nothing she could ever do to alienate him. She wasn't willing to lose that, either.

She watched Noah make dinner.

He wouldn't remember that Corinne used to rock him like this. That he was her responsibility more often than not. You didn't get any credit with babies.

Ruth woke up and started to fuss. Corinne let her suck on her index finger. She got up and walked the baby into the kitchen, where Noah was boiling water for spaghetti and heating up red sauce.

"Don't judge me," he said. "I can do this or sandwiches."

"You can do sandwiches?" Corinne said. "You've got me beat."

"I should probably wake up Mercy. We've got church tonight." He glanced at Corinne, sheepishly, like maybe he shouldn't have mentioned it. Like the word "church" might burn her skin like holy water.

"Go ahead," she said. "I've got half a bottle left if Ruth starts crying."

"Thanks." He turned the fire down under the sauce and under a pan of frozen broccoli.

Ruth got tired of Corinne's finger. Corinne figured she should probably change her, even though she'd rather do just about anything other than change diapers. When Noah was finally potty-trained, Corinne had sworn to herself that she wasn't changing any more diapers until and unless she had kids of her own.

"I guess you're the exception," she said to Ruth. She changed her on the living room floor, and when Mercy and Noah still didn't come down, she gave the baby the rest of her bottle.

Corinne didn't have to call Enoch; they already had plans to meet at his house after church.

Mercy and Noah were in their church clothes when they came down. Mercy looked exhausted and apologetic. She took the baby and immediately nursed her. She looked so worn out that Corinne couldn't quite leave. She picked up the living room and did some dishes that were in the sink. She helped Noah finish making dinner. Corinne ended up leaving when they did, walking out with them like they were all headed for church together.

They'd be there. And Enoch would be there. And Corinne would be at his house waiting for him.

⁓

Enoch almost always had ice cream after church. He was digging in his freezer, still wearing his navy suit and a pink tie that Corinne had given him. "I need to get groceries," he said. "All I've got is mint chip."

"Why'd you buy mint chip if you don't like it?"

"I always think I'm going to be in the mood for it . . ."

"I love it."

"There you go, apparently that's why I buy it. Cone or dish?"

Corinne was over being surprised that Enoch kept things like ice cream cones on hand. "Cone."

"I was thinking about you tonight at church," he said cheerfully, getting out a very fancy ice cream scoop. "There was a part about Timothy and his relationship with Paul—did you know Timothy was biracial? Well, sort of biracial. His dad was Greek, a nonbeliever."

"I did know that. Your dad told me."

"My dad told you?" Enoch handed her a very generous ice cream cone.

"I think he was trying to make me feel better about my situation." She covered her teeth with her lips and took a bite.

Enoch got out another cone. "I always thought that Paul let Timothy serve at such a young age because he was so faithful—that Timothy was. But tonight I was thinking that youth probably made Timothy easier to control. There's that scripture where Paul is like, *'I want you all to imitate me, that's why I sent Timothy. He's got it down.'*" Enoch finished scooping his cone and licked it, looking up at Corinne. "Oh . . ." he said, narrowing his eyes. "Is this weird?"

She shrugged.

"Do you not want me to talk to you about the Bible?"

"It's okay," Corinne said. "Probably."

"Probably?"

"Well . . . I don't want to be recruited. Or slowly seduced."

"You think I'd seduce you with Saul of Tarsus?"

Corinne smiled tightly. "You could seduce me by saying, *'Hey, Corinne, check it out—I also think Paul was a jerk. Look how freethinking and critical I can be.'* As a way to get me talking and thinking about Jesus again."

Enoch frowned and licked his ice cream. "Hmm. That's not my intention."

"Is it your hope?"

He licked his cone again. "I mean, I have hopes."

"Do you have hopes about me and Jesus?"

"I feel entitled to my hopes, Corinne. They're not an agenda. Honestly I was just telling you because it was interesting, and I like talking to you."

She supposed Enoch didn't have anyone else to talk to about the Bible.

He took hold of her wrist and licked her ice cream a few times; she'd forgotten about it, and it was melting down the side of the cone. Enoch's tongue was wide and thick and bumpier than hers. His hair slid into his face. He flicked it back and stood up straight. "I need a haircut."

"No, you don't." Corinne stood on tiptoe to kiss him while his mouth was still cold and sweet.

He caught on and licked her tongue, sharing the ice cream. Corinne leaned on his chest, still on tiptoe, and he bent his head down low, tonguing at her.

When he finally pulled away, both their ice cream cones were melting. Enoch made a disapproving sound in his throat and quickly licked Corinne's cone.

His own cone was dripping onto his hand—Corinne took his wrist and licked ice cream off the crook of his thumb and index finger.

He groaned her name and said, "You're very bad at eating ice cream."

She kept licking him. She got her tongue under his flat-topped thumb and sucked it into her mouth.

"Corinne . . ."

She looked up at him. Still holding his forearm and sucking on his thumb. There wasn't any more ice cream to lick off; she was just being filthy.

Enoch frowned at her. He was being very somber. He pushed down on her tongue with his thumb and moved it slowly out of her mouth . . . Then slowly back in . . . His ice cream cone hit her cheek.

Corinne's eyes were round. Playful. But also . . . not. She stuck her tongue out of her mouth and dragged it up his thumb. She was getting ice cream in her hair.

Enoch shook his head, like he was dismayed with her. He took a bite of her ice cream cone, then dropped it in the sink. Then he pulled his hand out of her mouth, dumped that ice cream cone, too, and pushed Corinne against the sink, kissing her sloppily. Corinne grinned. Some ice cream ran out of her mouth. Enoch licked it. With his wide tongue. Thick and bumpy.

She reached for him, but he caught her wrists. "Don't touch my suit. You're a mess."

"Then take off your suit."

He shook his head again, like she was a real piece of work. He wriggled out of his jacket, dropping it on the floor. Corinne wrapped her arms around his neck. He held on to her hips and ground himself against her. She kissed him hungrily. Because she could. Because he was right there. And he was hers. (For now.) And he liked it—he liked this. The more wanton she was, the happier he seemed.

Enoch kissed her mouth. He kissed her face. He kissed the spots of ice cream on her forehead and her cheek. "Come on," he said. "Bed."

Corinne shook her head. She brought her hands down to his waist, trying to keep them on his shirt. (The shirt was machine-washable.) She started to sink to her knees. "Here is good."

Enoch caught her under her arms and pulled her back up. "Bed."

Corinne leaned into him and reached her mouth up to his ear. "I'm still kind of . . . unavailable."

He pulled his head away and looked in her eyes. "Unavailable?"

She screwed up her face. *Damn it.* This wasn't sexy. She'd been letting herself be sexy, and it seemed like it was actually working, and now she had to say—"I started my period yesterday."

Enoch seemed impressed. "That was predictable."

Corinne raised her eyebrows, resigned. "Like clockwork."

He cocked his head and thoughtful-frowned. "And that means . . . unavailable?"

She bit her lips for a second. "*Doesn't* it?"

He shrugged one of his big shoulders. "*Does* it?"

Careful: "I mean . . . it's messy."

Enoch leaned down to her ear. "Corinne," he said softly. "I should show you the basement. I put a shower down there myself."

Corinne felt like she was being pranked. She took hold of Enoch's head with both her (still sticky) hands and made him look in her eyes. "Are you being serious? That wouldn't gross you out?"

He shrugged his one shoulder again. That must be his sheepish shoulder. "Conceptually, no." He closed one eye. "Am I grossing *you* out?"

"It doesn't gross me out," she said. "I spend a fifth of my life bleeding."

Enoch snorted. "That's a lot."

"I'm aware."

"I mean," he said, cautiously, "if you *want* to be unavailable and put out a Closed sign twenty percent of the time . . ."

"I didn't think I had another option."

One side of Enoch's mouth twitched up. "I'm all about giving you options, honey."

"There's got to be a rule about this . . ."

"Not in the New Testament . . ."

Corinne was pretty sure she was blushing. Her face was hot. "Let's see this basement of yours."

⁓

Enoch had a small, finished basement. There was a laundry station at one end and a work-out area in the other, with a rowing machine and a weight bench. There were shallow windows at the top of the walls, so it wasn't as gloomy as it could have been. And the whole thing was drywalled and painted.

"The bathroom's just here," Enoch said gently, leading her to the far side. "I redid it and added the shower last year. Your brother helped me." He opened the door and switched on the light. It was a large, clean bathroom. With cobalt-blue and white tiles. The shower was much roomier than Corinne was expecting—but that made sense, for Enoch.

"You built this?"

"Shawn helped."

"It's so nice."

"Thanks. I had a lot of time on my hands."

"Do you even use the tub upstairs?"

He made a face like he wasn't very impressed with his (objectively outstanding) bathtub and shook his head. "I've wanted a shower since we moved in."

Corinne put an arm around him. She laid her head on his chest, with her face turned down. "Are you still into this idea?" she asked softly. "Now that you've had a chance to walk it off a little bit?"

"Walk it off? We just walked down the stairs."

Corinne smiled.

"Worst-case scenario," Enoch said, "I get to take a shower with you."

"I can conceive of multiple worse-case scenarios."

"That seems to be your specialty."

She looked up at him, resting her chin on his chest. "We could still have ice cream."

"We can still have ice cream later, unless . . ." He looked down at her, his chin tucked into his neck. "You're driving, Corinne. Whatever you want."

What she wanted was Enoch Miller, all the time, however she could get him.

"Let me go in first?" she asked.

Enoch's lips were parted. He nodded and backed away from her—and then, without her asking, he stepped out of the bathroom, closing the door.

Corinne looked around . . . There was a clothes hamper. And a stack of clean blue towels. She wished the light in here wasn't so stark. She got undressed quickly, tucking her underwear, with its dirty maxi pad, into her jeans. That was gross. This was gross—wasn't it gross? Marc had always thought so. They'd had sex once when Corinne had thought her period was over, but when it turned out it wasn't, Marc had been truly disturbed—*"I felt like I was in a slasher movie."* Corinne had been embarrassed—*"It's just blood, it was on its way out, anyway."* And then Marc had said, *"I'd think you'd be happy that I'm not turned on by blood,"* and she guessed that he had a point. But she didn't like feeling unclean. She didn't like having to disclose it and watch him lose interest. It didn't seem fair—gross stuff came out of his body, too, and Corinne dealt with it.

Corinne tucked her underwear deeper into her jeans and started the shower. She'd rinse off first. Get most of the blood out of the way. Evacuate the immediate area. But it was only day two; there was no way Enoch wouldn't see *some* blood. This was so weird. This was gross—*wasn't it gross?*

"Corinne?" Enoch had cracked the door. "Can I come in?"

She opened the shower door a bit. "Could you turn off the light?"

He paused, then flicked the light off. "Now?"

"Yeah," she said.

Enoch came into the room, leaving the door partway open, to let in some light. "This okay?"

"Close it a little."

He did.

The shower wall was pebbled blue glass. Enoch was a blurry figure on the other side of it. He took off his glasses and his tie. His white shirt. His dress pants and boxer shorts. He stepped closer to the shower door and touched the glass. Corinne touched it from the other side.

"Can I come in?" he asked again.

Corinne pushed the door open. Enoch stepped inside, and she made room for him. He seemed taller and wider than ever. The water was hitting Corinne's back. She held a hand out to Enoch. When he took it, she stepped back, so the water would fall over her shoulder.

"Whoa—that's hot." He stepped away.

"Sorry." Corinne blocked the water.

Enoch reached around her to adjust it. The stream cooled. "This all right?"

She nodded. He was standing close to her. Her breasts would touch him if she took a deep breath. She shifted to let the water hit his chest for a few seconds. He slid an arm around her waist and pulled her closer. "Hi."

"Hi," Corinne whispered.

"You look . . ." His eyes were wide and dark. His voice trailed off.

She touched his chest. It was slick, the muscle there twitched. She felt herself grinning. She slid herself from side to side against him. Almost like she was dancing.

Enoch laughed, his chest shaking.

Corinne moved again to let more water between them. Enoch leaned into the stream to kiss her. Water ran down her face and between their lips. It changed the taste of the kiss. She snaked her arms up around his neck and kept nuzzling her whole body against him. He groaned deep and reached behind Corinne for something. Oh—a bar of soap. She hadn't been thinking they'd actually shower. Enoch brought the bar up to her chest. It smelled like a Christmas tree. He soaped up her breasts, then her stomach. *Oh.* Corinne slid her breasts against his. She watched herself do it. *Oh, oh, oh.* Enoch rumbled out a long groan. His cock was hard between them. Corinne thought again about getting on her knees.

"Corinne," Enoch said. His eyes were mostly closed. There was water dripping from his eyelashes and his long nose. He hugged her tight. He set the soap somewhere behind her and rubbed slick hands over her ass. "You look so good. You feel . . ." He groaned again, rubbing his cock into her hip.

Corinne used to take showers with Marc. In a converted bathtub with a rickety curtain and a window. She was young, and it was wonderful.

This was different. It was Enoch. He was taller. Thicker. The room was darker. Marc had never been this surprised by her. Or delighted by her. Marc had liked Corinne an awful lot—maybe he'd even loved her—but he'd never looked like this. Stricken. Lust-dumb. Awed.

"Honey," Enoch said, hunching over, arms on her, hands on her, trying to get as much of Corinne on as much of him as he could.

"Enoch," Corinne said, arching against him. "I love you. Everything you do turns me on."

He laughed, like she was lying. She wasn't. If he could live inside her head, he'd get sick of hearing his own name.

Corinne pushed her hands through his hair. Her hands were wet, but his hair was mostly dry. He kissed her, pressing his big nose into her cheek and her eye. "I brought a condom," he said, "but I don't know if it'll—"

"It's fine," she said.

"What is?"

"Everything." She kissed him. "I'm very not fertile at the moment, and I don't want to worry about it."

He didn't need to know how out of character this was for her. Corinne had never *not* used birth control. With Marc and Jeremy, she'd doubled up—condoms and gel—and had still been paranoid if her period was even an hour late. Now, suddenly, she was the queen of *"just pull out"* and *"it's all fine."*

(Was she being *more* or *less* rational about the odds now? Did she feel like she could be less worried because the worst-case scenario was something she might want anyway? That was irresponsible. That might even be manipulative.) (Oh, for fuck's sake, she wasn't going to get pregnant on the second day of her period. She might not even be able to get pregnant at all; she was thirty-two, and she never had.) (Enoch was thirty-two, too. Old enough to make his own decisions about risk. He had access to the internet. He watched *Oprah*.) (She wanted him to come in her.) (None of this made sense. Nothing did.)

He was kissing her neck. The water was hitting his face. She pushed his hair back. "You can pull out if you want."

He looked up at her. "Do you want me to?"

She shook her head.

Enoch growled and kissed her. Her neck bent back. Her mouth was slack. (Wanton.) He pulled his head away and pushed on her hips. "Turn around." Corinne did. The hot water hit her sternum. Enoch cupped her breasts. He rubbed his cock into her bottom. God, he was so much taller than Marc . . .

"Is this going to work?" Corinne said.

"Yep," Enoch said.

"You're so tall."

"Can you bend over?"

Corinne could. She moved her legs apart and leaned forward, pressing her palms against the shower wall. "Like this?"

"Like that," Enoch said lowly. He was holding on to her left hip. She couldn't see him. She felt his right hand moving down her ass and between her legs. He rubbed at her lips, opening her. Corinne lifted her hips to be more accessible. Enoch pushed his cock in—it felt good, immediately—then he took hold of her other hip and pushed deeper. God, it felt good. It always felt better like this. From behind. Corinne whined.

Enoch slid out, then back in—firmly. The impact pushed Corinne onto the balls of her feet. It was even better that way. "*Yes,*" Enoch groaned. He pumped into her again more smoothly, and she cried out.

"Okay?" he asked, stalling inside her.

"Good," Corinne panted. "I'm good."

"You steady?"

"Yeah."

He held her hips high. She moved her palms down on the wall. Thank God the floor in here was some sort of gritty nonslip tile. Enoch fucked into her again, and she shrieked.

"Corinne?"

"It's just really good like this," she said tightly.

"Yeah?" He kept going. In and in and in.

"Yes," Corinne said with every thrust. "Yes. Yes, Enoch. Oh my God." He was bouncing her feet off the floor. She braced her arms and moaned, she practically howled.

"Corinne!" Enoch swore.

Why was it so good like this? It was like he was tapping straight into her spinal column and shooting sparks straight up to her head. It was some sort of lizard-brain chicanery. She wanted it to keep going forever.

"I need a second," Enoch said, sliding out.

Corinne rested on her heels. She hung forward, panting, touching the floor of the shower. Enoch was saying her name and kissing her lower back and her ass. The water was running lukewarm down her spine, down her scalp, down her hair, onto the shower floor.

"You good?" Enoch asked, his voice so low.

"Uh-huh," Corinne said.

He pushed his fingers into her, and she whimpered.

"I love you," he said.

Corinne laughed. She was still hanging upside down. "I love you, too."

He shoved his cock in again, and she yelped. "Wait. Let me up."

Enoch hauled her up with his arms around her stomach, and she braced her hands against the wall. He held her hips and pushed back in. Corinne shook her head hard. The pleasure was almost unbearable. "Enoch, that's so good."

"I wish you could see yourself like this."

"I wish I could see *you*."

He was going fast. Corinne was grunting every time he landed. It felt so good, it hurt. "Enoch," she said. "Fuck. Oh my God. *Fuck*."

"Corinne," he said. "*Corinne*."

The water had gone cold. Enoch squeezed her hips and bent over her, his head falling onto her spine. Corinne panted. She held still. She felt his body go tight—he was so quiet.

After a few seconds, he started breathing again. He kissed her shoulder. Corinne relaxed into a forward fold, her hands limp on the floor, and Enoch pulled out.

"Come on, honey, come on up—let's get you out of the cold." He pulled at her waist, and Corinne crawled up the shower wall, feeling weak, all of her blood in her head. Enoch put his arms around her and turned them, so he was taking the brunt of the cold water. His chest felt hot against her back; she was freezing all of a sudden. She leaned against him, letting him have most of her weight. He reached behind himself to unhook the shower head. "Give me a little space to rinse off, okay?"

Corinne stumbled forward.

Enoch hissed. "Dang, that's cold."

"Is it a mess?" she whispered.

"Mostly my mess—you want me to rinse you off?"

"Yeah." She widened her stance.

"Brace yourself." He held the shower head between her legs.

"*Fuck.*"

Enoch laughed. He was spraying her, and sweeping the water against her with his fingers.

"Okay, okay," she said. "Enough."

He stopped and held her close again while he turned off the water. Then he opened the shower door and reached for a towel, one of those giant sheet towels they have at hotels. Corinne liked that he surrounded himself with big things. That he'd made this room for himself. "Come on," he said, "let's get you warmed up."

~

Enoch offered to build her a fire, but Corinne just wanted to go to bed. She used the bathroom upstairs. Changed her maxi pad. Put on the flannel pajamas she'd brought. Normally, Corinne would hide the used pad in her purse and throw it away at home. But she felt bold—she wrapped it up and dropped it in Enoch's bathroom trash, on top of his used dental floss and tissues.

When she walked into the bedroom, Enoch was lying on the comforter, eating mint chip ice cream out of the carton. He was wearing cotton pajama pants and his glasses. His eyes lit up when he saw her. He peeled the comforter back next to him. Corinne climbed onto his bed and got under the covers.

"You want some?" he asked. "It's almost gone."

She shook her head and laid it on his bare shoulder. Enoch kissed her forehead. "You good?"

"I'm good. Are you good?"

"Am I good?" he asked. "Look at me. I think I'm probably glowing."

Corinne laughed. She looked at him. He was kinda glowing. "So, it was okay?" she said anyway.

He pushed his lips out, concerned. "Corinne. That was amazing. Every time we're together, it's a new kind of amazing."

"But it wasn't . . . gross? You can tell me if it was."

Enoch laughed, breathily—then looked like he felt bad about laughing. He set the ice cream carton on his bedside table and took off his glasses. He put his arms around her. "I'm gonna be real honest with you, and hopefully you won't think *I'm* gross . . ."

She held her bottom lip in her mouth, waiting.

"I pretty much forgot about your period," he said. "You looked so good, bent over like that, and the sounds you were making . . . And then, when I noticed, I was so far gone, it just seemed hot. Like, dirty-hot. And I liked it."

Corinne looked up into his eyes. "You can talk to me about the Bible," she said.

Enoch barked out a laugh. "That's an interesting tit for tat."

"It's a separate thought," she said. "Sort of. Maybe it isn't. The thought is—I love you. Completely."

His smile faded. His eyes went soft and serious.

"Nothing is off-limits with you," she said. "I just don't want you to recruit me. Or, like, run scenarios on me."

"I wouldn't." Enoch shook his head. "I would never. I mean—largely because it would be the worst way to reach your heart."

"So you're being strategic?"

He looked in her eyes, thinking. "I don't think it's my job to save you, Corinne. I've prayed about it a lot. I don't think that's what my role is here."

"What's your role?"

"To love you," he said immediately. Like he was sure of it.

Corinne wanted to kiss him, right then, but she waited. "I won't try to recruit you either," she said. "Or stumble you on your path."

He touched her cheek. "Thank you."

Corinne held out her hand.

Enoch huffed a soft laugh. He shook it.

Chapter Seventy-five

Corinne worked late Thursday night.

Enoch was supposed to come by after church and stay the night. They weren't even making a pretense of spending nights apart anymore. Corinne was glad. She didn't want to lie in bed missing him just to feign autonomy.

Enoch called her when church was over. "Do you feel like Dairy Queen?"

"I think *you* probably feel like Dairy Queen . . ."

"We can make it if we hurry. I'll come get you."

"Are you sure you don't just want to pick up ice cream on the way here?"

"I don't feel like ice cream—I feel like Dairy Queen."

Corinne couldn't believe she was bundling up in her winter coat to get ice cream.

"People buy more ice cream in winter than summer," Enoch said, turning the dashboard vent to blow warm air her way.

There was a long line at the Dairy Queen, so he must be right.

They stood in line together. Enoch in his suit and his dress coat and a navy-blue woolen hat. Corinne in jeans she threw on and a slouchy T-shirt she liked to sleep in, and the bright yellow down coat Enoch said made her look like a fluffy duckling.

He stood with his arm around her. Corinne liked it. She leaned against him.

"What do you get at Dairy Queen?" she asked.

"I don't get the same thing every time, there are too many good options."

"What are you getting tonight?"

"A German chocolate Blizzard," he said, "or . . . a Peanut Buster Parfait, or . . ." He put his hands on Corinne's shoulders and rested his chin on her head, looking up at the menu. "A cherry-dipped cone."

"That seems basic."

"Their cherry dip is inimitable. What are you getting?"

"Banana-split Blizzard," Corinne said.

"Such a good choice."

"I'll share with you."

"Corinne, I love you."

She laughed.

They ordered. And waited at the other side of the counter. Enoch kept an arm around Corinne's shoulder. When Corinne's Blizzard came out first, she offered him the first bite. He grinned and opened his mouth to take it. She loved him so much, it ached. It was more lizard-brain chicanery. It made her want to shake like a dog who had just come in from the rain.

She pulled her red spoon away, smiling at him.

The bell over the door rang, and another group of people came in, letting in cold air. Corinne glanced over, without thinking.

It was Alicia. And Shawn. Alicia looked up first, looked right at them. Her face dropped. Corinne didn't look away. Shawn looked up next. He froze, right in the middle of taking off his scarf. Corinne lifted her fingers, acknowledging them. Acknowledging the whole scene. Enoch's arm slid off her shoulder.

When Corinne turned to him, he was looking at her, as solemn as the grave.

"German chocolate Blizzard," the Dairy Queen employee said, flipping the cup upside down, then holding it out.

Enoch took it, then looked at Corinne. "Ready?"

She reached for his free hand. He caught her hand and squeezed it tight. She nodded.

They had to walk past them to leave. Shawn looked away. Alicia didn't. She still looked shocked and hurt. Corinne followed Enoch to the truck.

They didn't talk on the way home. They left their Blizzards in the cupholders. Corinne looked out the window and cried.

〰

"Do you still want me to come up?"

They'd just pulled into the parking lot behind her apartment. Corinne wiped her eyes, surprised. "What?"

"If you want some space to think—"

"No," Corinne said. "I don't want space. I'm sorry I made you think I want space."

"I'm sorry," he said. "I'm so sorry."

"No," she said again. "It's not your fault. It was inevitable."

"Still . . . it didn't have to happen tonight."

"Can we go in?" Corinne asked. "It's cold."

They went in. Enoch carried their ice cream. When Corinne let him into her apartment, he took the cups into the kitchen.

"You can eat your ice cream," she called.

"I don't like to eat ice cream when I'm sad," he said. "It sets a bad precedent."

Corinne took off her coat and sat on the couch.

"Do you want tea?" Enoch called out.

"Yeah, thanks."

He came back after a few minutes with two mugs, and sat down next to her. Corinne took a few sips of tea. Sleepytime. Enoch tried to switch the lamp on, but nothing happened. "Dang. I thought I fixed this."

"It's not plugged in," Corinne said.

"Why not?"

"There's only one outlet in here."

Enoch looked at her, hangdog. "Corinne. I am literally at your service."

Corinne smiled and reached up to his cheek. She started crying again. "I love you."

"I love *you*." He took the tea from her and pulled her into his lap. "I'm sorry, I'm so sorry."

Corinne sat in his lap. She got her arms around his neck. "I'm sorry, too."

"Why are you sorry?"

"Because you're doing this for me," she said. "You disgraced yourself for me."

He looked like he wanted to argue the point, but he didn't. "This is my fault," he said. "I've actually *been* to that Dairy Queen with Shawn and Alicia."

"Enoch, really?"

"I didn't think they'd go without me—they always complained about it! Alicia always wants pie instead."

"Maybe they miss you."

He made a miserable face. "What do you think is going to happen?"

"I think they're going to tell my mom and my sister. And Noah and Mercy."

"But—how does that change things? They all already know you're in the world."

"This will give new juice to my cast-out status," Corinne said. "It's like I've returned to the scene of the crime."

"I don't want you to think of me that way," he said.

"I don't want *you* to think of *me* that way."

"I don't."

She set her forehead against his and closed her eyes. "I just hate that we have to be alone to be together. It makes me so sad. I hate that I've done to you what I did to myself."

Enoch hugged her waist. "Stop framing it that way. You're breaking the rules."

"What rules?"

"*Our* rules. You're a person, remember? Not a pitfall. And I'm a person. And we both have agency here."

She breathed out hard, pressing her forehead against his. A new sob crawled out of her. "They're going to cut me off again."

It had taken a decade to earn back their favor. A decade on her knees. Corinne had been so careful. She'd moved across the country. And she'd lost it all, she'd lost them—the same way she'd lost them the first time . . .

"I'm sorry, honey. I'm so sorry." Enoch held her tight.

. . . but it wasn't the same.

This wasn't the same.

Even if her mother showed up at school tomorrow to slap her.

Corinne was cast out. But Enoch was cast out, too. They were in this together.

"Can we go to bed?" she asked.

"Yeah, let's call it a night."

Chapter Seventy-six

Corinne was expected at her mom's house for Sunday dinner in three days.

She waited for someone to call. Would they tell her it was canceled? Would her mom call her crying? Would someone draw a new line? Who would quote Proverbs at her? *"As a dog returns to his own vomit, so a fool repeats his folly."* Corinne wasn't even the dog in this scenario. She was the vomit.

Corinne waited for the call. Enoch waited for Corinne to get the call.

They were still waiting on Sunday morning.

Corinne was lying in Enoch's bed while he got dressed for church. He got his suit on, then sat back down on the bed and held her hand. His face was bleak.

"Are you worried that Shawn talked to the elders?" she asked.

"No . . . What would he tell them? They already know I'm seeing someone. I guess he could share the gossip . . ."

"Then what are you worried about?"

He shrugged.

Corinne leaned into him.

"Just everything," he said. "Your family knowing . . . and looking at me different. Someone will tell my brother, if they haven't already. And he'll tell my mom."

Enoch hadn't talked to his mom since he called to tell her he was stepping away. She'd wept. She'd told him not to call again until he'd repented and been welcomed back into the congregation.

"At least no one will be gossiping about it in Arkansas," she said.

"That's true." He looked down at her hand, rubbing it. "You don't have to go to dinner tonight, you know. You could decide for yourself not to."

Corinne shook her head.

She'd never be the one to step away.

Chapter Seventy-seven

"You missed it, Corinne—Jonah had a big part in our services today, about young Timothy."

"It wasn't that big, Grandma."

"Well, I thought it was impressive."

"Tell me about it," Corinne said. She was peeling potatoes. Her hands were covered in slime. No one was acting like anything was amiss. Her mom was talking about church. Her stepdad was watching sports. Her sister was ignoring her. Noah and Mercy and Shawn and Alicia weren't here yet.

"Timothy is proof," Jonah said, "that God trusts young people to lead."

"From the mouths of babes," Corinne's mother agreed.

Corinne peeled potatoes and listened for the door.

The potatoes were cooked and mashed, and Corinne was stirring gravy when she finally heard the front door open. Then Shawn's voice. A few seconds later, Alicia came into the kitchen. Her eyes lit up when she saw Corinne. She made a beeline for her. "Corinne!" she said, giving Corinne an extra tight one-armed hug. (Alicia was holding a covered cake plate in the other arm.) "I was hoping you'd be here!"

"Hi," Corinne said stupidly.

Shawn came in from the living room. He just stared at Corinne for a second. Then: "Hey, Corinne."

"Hi, Shawn."

He hugged their mom. "Do you need any help?"

"Not from you," she said. "You're too late. We're ready to eat."

Alicia still had an arm around Corinne. Corinne turned to her. She didn't know what to say.

"I made Kahlúa chocolate cake," Alicia said, "but don't worry, the Kahlúa bakes right out. I use coffee in the frosting."

"That sounds delicious," Corinne said.

"You could make it," Alicia said. "It's just a devil's food cake mix with extra egg yolks."

Corinne nodded. Her eyes were stinging. Alicia squeezed her extra hard.

"Corinne!" her mom snapped, grabbing the fork out of Corinne's hand. "What do you have against my gravy!"

Corinne stepped away from the stove. "Sorry!"

Alicia set the cake plate on the counter and went into the other room.

They had roast beef and mashed potatoes and creamed corn and popovers for dinner. The gravy was ruined, and everyone blamed Corinne.

Chapter Seventy-eight

Corinne was lying on her back in her own bed. Enoch was lying next to her on a pillow he'd brought from home—and holding his right hand up, so she could play with his fingers.

They were both giddy with relief.

"I mean," Corinne said, holding her palm up to Enoch's, "I know we'll have to tell them someday. Probably soon."

"You're not going to reveal it at my funeral? When you collapse, weeping on my casket?"

She interlaced their fingers and idly moved their hands back and forth. "Tempting."

When *would* they tell her family? When Enoch had untangled his feelings? When they both knew what they wanted from each other, in an ongoing way? Enoch couldn't repent until they stopped having sex . . . Or got married. Corinne tried not to think about that. That he was waiting her out. That he might propose someday, just so that he could have his life back.

He brought her hand down and kissed it. "Well, I'm not telling them," he said. "Or my family either. It won't be hard—no one's talking to me."

"Do you think your family would ever soften?" she asked. "The way mine has?"

"You mean, if I stay cast out?"

She nodded.

"Maybe," he said. "It might take them longer—how long did you wait? Ten years? Twelve?"

"God," she said, "that's so bleak."

"Don't think about it. That's not where we are now."

"Where are we?"

"We are in your bedroom."

"Ah, yes," Corinne said. "Right."

"And we're madly in love."

"Madly, huh?"

"Some might say insanely."

She smiled. She took his hand in both of hers, and stretched out his long fingers.

"We're working through some pretty intense baggage," he said, "with remarkable aplomb."

"I've always admired your aplomb."

"We're working it out," he said softly.

She turned her face to him. He was already looking at her.

Corinne's eyebrows were low. She could feel herself frowning. "I feel like we're ignoring how hard this is going to be."

"We're not ignoring it," he said. "We're just not there yet."

She pressed her lips together, biting them.

"We're going to keep working it out, Corinne."

Corinne nodded.

Enoch tilted his chin up. He'd started doing that when he wanted her to kiss him. She liked it. She liked that he knew it would work. She turned toward him fully and kissed him.

"I like your mouth," she said.

"You like my clown lips?"

She made an affronted noise in her throat. "Who called them that?"

"Jed."

"He was just jealous."

"Was he also jealous of my nose? Because he had a lot to say about that, too."

"*Everyone* is jealous of your nose."

"And my beady eyes?"

"They're lovely," she said, cupping his chin. "You're lovely. I never get tired of your face."

Enoch rolled toward her and gave her a quick kiss. "Well, if we ever have kids, I hope they get your nose."

"Nope. If they do, I'm throwing them back."

He touched her nose. It was completely unremarkable—a little on the long side, with a small swoop at the end. Nothing about Corinne's face was remarkable. Her eyes were a normal size. A normal blue. Her eyelashes were fine. Her mouth was smallish. Her lips were even.

"It's hard for me to say why I love your face," Enoch said, like he could read Corinne's mind—like he was agreeing that it was unremarkable. "You just look so much more alive than other people."

Corinne wrinkled her nose.

He tried to smooth it out. "I remember walking down the aisle at church, counting everyone's faces. And they all seemed almost asleep. And then I'd get to the back, and there you'd be. Like a live wire. A hundred different thoughts crossing your face. I could practically hear them."

"Are you saying you like me because of my personality?"

"And your rear end," Enoch said.

Corinne threw her head back and laughed. "Rear end," she repeated, in disbelief.

He leaned in to kiss her cheek. "This is my favorite face."

She turned her head to rest it against him.

"Always has been," he said.

"You're kind of a sweet talker, Enoch Miller."

"Literally no one has ever said so."

He was kissing her neck. Corinne lifted her chin up to make her neck longer. She hummed.

"Do you like that?" Enoch asked.

"Mmm-hmm."

He kissed her harder, pushing his chin into her muscles. It made her stretch out her neck and bring up her shoulders, like she wanted him to keep going but also like she couldn't stand any more. Half a dozen wounded "m" sounds caught in her throat.

Enoch groaned and moved over her, to kiss the other side. "I like all your noises," he said. "It's like you're talking to me."

"You want me to talk to you?"

"I want to know you feel good."

"I feel good."

He sucked on her neck. It felt maddening. She bounced her palm on his shoulder. "Ah, ah, ah."

He moved his head and sucked harder. She slapped his shoulder harder. She could have been telling him to stop, she could have been begging him not to—she wasn't sure.

"You're going to leave a mark," she hissed.

"You work from home, Corinne." He opened his mouth and sucked right over the place where her neck met her shoulder. She clenched her hand in his sweatshirt and rocked her hips against him.

Enoch pulled his mouth away with a pop. He pushed up onto his knees. "Come on," he said, lifting up her sweater. Fine-knit. Deep purple.

"So bossy," she said, raising her arms over her head for him.

"Was that a complaint?" he asked, casting the sweater aside, like he didn't want to deal with it again.

Corinne was blushing. She shook her head.

Enoch looked down at her. His face somber. His eyes dancing. Corinne was wearing another satin bra—white, printed with brown and green leaves. She was still wearing a knee-length skirt from her mom's house, teal-blue denim, with magenta tights.

"I thought you were going to be one of those people who always wore black," he said.

"I only had one sweater," Corinne replied.

"You're so pretty," he said. "You look like a fairy."

"I thought I looked like a mermaid."

"Mermaids are fairies, aren't they?"

Corinne's bra fastened in the front. Enoch fiddled with it for a second with one hand, then used both hands to unclasp it. He left the cups over her breasts.

"Take down your hair," he said.

Corinne wanted to tease him again for being bossy, but she couldn't quite manage it. She reached up and pulled out the rubber band. Her bra loosened but stayed on.

Enoch took a deep breath.

Corinne watched him. He touched the base of her throat, then ran his fingertips down to her belly button. Then he pressed his other hand over the front of his jeans and closed his eyes.

Corinne brought her hands up over her breasts and whispered his name—"*Enoch.*"

When he looked at her again, she opened up her bra.

He groaned and dropped onto her, his hands on either side of her shoulders, kissing and biting her breasts. Corinne held the back of his head. *Enoch, Enoch, Enoch.* There was no history here, no slipping backwards into déjà vu. Enoch had never kissed her like this back then, never lingered over her. Some things were only theirs, only theirs now. Time felt slick and swampy, but Corinne stayed in her bed. She stayed with him here.

"Beautiful girl," Enoch said. (He hadn't said that then. When she was a girl.)

"I love you," Corinne said, stroking his hair. (She wouldn't have even thought that back then, no matter that it was true.)

"Corinne," he said, rubbing his face into her breasts, and between them. It looked silly, but it didn't feel silly. She didn't.

"I need you so bad," she said.

Enoch pushed himself up, like he was doing a push-up, and looked in her eyes. "So bad?"

Corinne bit her bottom lip. She didn't care if it looked posed. She nodded.

He got back up onto his knees. He rubbed the heel of his hand into his cock again. "Come on," he said, unbuttoning her skirt with his other hand. Corinne started to push her skirt down, but Enoch took over, impatiently pulling her skirt and her tights and her underwear down. It was sloppy. He was frowning. She pushed her tights and underwear down with her feet. Enoch threw the whole mess across the room. He looked back down at her, still frowning, impatient, his eyes dark. Corinne's knees were still bent, together. "Let me see you," Enoch said.

Her right knee dropped.

He fell down on the bed next to her, shoulder to shoulder, facing her. His right hand came to the inside of her thigh—he squeezed it. "Yes?" he asked.

"Yes," she said. "Yes."

He opened the lips of her vagina. (She was too turned on to get hung up on vocabulary.) He stroked the length of her, from her clit to the opening and around again. She was wet, it was easy. He rubbed three fingers over the hood, gently massaging.

"I—" she said.

"I know." He kissed her cheek. "I'm just getting the lay of the land."

"Okay," she whispered.

"It still feels good, right?"

"Yes." Her breath was shaky. "Yes."

He moved his mouth even closer to her ear. "It's okay if I do this for me?"

She nodded. She nodded too many times. Too quickly.

He deepened his strokes. It felt good. It felt glinting. She wondered if she could come like this if she wasn't worried about coming—but that was the same as worrying. She shook it off. She let it feel good. Enoch bumped his nose against her cheek and her temple, not even kissing, just pushing.

Corinne spread her other leg.

"What do you want?" Enoch whispered.

"Touch me," Corinne said. "Inside."

On the next stroke, he pushed into her. She pulled her hips into the mattress, arching her back.

"Like this?" he asked.

"Yeah," Corinne said. "Yes."

"You feel perfect . . ." he said, pushing two fat fingers into her. Feeling her.

Corinne nodded. She didn't know why she was nodding.

He pushed harder. "Here?"

"Yes, touch me."

"I'm touching you, honey." His voice was dark.

"Touch me . . ."

"I'm touching you, Corinne."

"Touch me like you're fucking me."

Enoch growled and pushed his face into her hair. His hand fell into a rhythm.

She liked it like this. She was tempted to say she liked it more than regular sex. But she just liked it differently. His fingers were rigid. They landed harder.

"Enoch," she said. She chanted. "*Enoch, Enoch.* Don't stop."

"I'm not stopping." He wasn't.

Corinne reached her right hand between them. "Can I?"

He inhaled. "Honey. Yes." He kissed her cheek. "Yes."

Corinne touched her clit. She was already so turned on. She was already warmed up and rocked to some edge. She just had to push herself over. "Don't stop," she said. "I need you." He didn't stop. He lifted his head up to watch her. His mouth was open. His shoulder was moving. She looked in his eyes. "Enoch," she said, and she sounded scared.

"I'm right here."

"Don't stop."

"Wild horses couldn't pull me away."

She rubbed herself. He punched into her. She felt herself falling apart. Shorting out. Her left hand shot up to his shoulder. She held her breath and clenched so hard that her shoulders lifted up.

Enoch didn't stop. "Corinne," he said. "That's my girl. Yes, honey. Yes."

She took a sharp breath and slammed her legs closed. Enoch stopped, but didn't pull away. Corinne held herself against him, hugging his shoulder. He kissed her hair. "Okay?"

She nodded. She nodded. She dropped back onto the bed and let her legs fall open, taking deep breaths.

Enoch kissed her mouth. He didn't pull his hand away. "Corinne," he said, "Corinne . . ."

"Thank you," she said.

"Don't thank me."

"Thank you," she said anyway.

He started moving his hand again, gently, in and out. "You're welcome."

Corinne arched her back. "Yes."

"More?" he said.

"*More.*"

He pushed harder, but not as hard as before. "You feel so good," he said. "You're . . . It's different now. Puffier."

Corinne laughed. She was whimpering. It was a strange combination.

Enoch pulled his hand out and quickly licked his fingers, then pushed back into her.

"Oh my God," she said, rubbing herself again.

"I like it so much . . ." he said. "Give me a word. So I can tell you how much I like it."

"There's no good word," she said. She was already close.

"What word do you use in your head?" he whispered.

"What word do *you* use in *your* head?"

He pushed his face into her hair. "Pussy," he whispered.

Corinne grunted. She was coming.

"Is that it?" Enoch panted. "Do you have a nice pussy, Corinne?"

She wasn't breathing but she was keening. Her brain stem was expanding like one of those sewing boxes that opens up into six shelves. She read once that you were supposed to breathe during orgasms. Corinne never could. She was going to die like this someday. If Enoch Miller stuck around.

"That's it," Enoch was saying, pumping her slowly. Corinne grabbed his wrist. He stopped. She sucked in a breath. "That's my girl," he said, kissing her.

Corinne started laughing. Because she was embarrassed. Because it was all genuinely funny. She kissed him with her mouth open and wet.

Enoch was smiling, too. Smiling like he almost never did, with both sides of his mouth.

"You can only say that word when I'm about to come," she whispered.

He laughed into her mouth. "I can't shake your hand right now, but it's a deal."

She wrapped her arms around his shoulders. "That felt so good."

"I could tell," he said. "I could feel." He twitched his fingers inside of her. "You're so full inside right now."

"Erectile tissue," Corinne whispered.

"Was that what I was supposed to say instead of 'pussy'?"

She hid her face in his neck. "You're already breaking the deal."

He slid his fingers slowly out and slowly back in. "Am I?"

Corinne groaned and let her legs fall back open. She looked in his eyes. "Gentle," she whispered.

"I can be gentle," he said. He could.

Corinne felt blissed out and loose. She let her head drop into the pillow and gazed up at him. He looked flushed and alive. Handsome. "Is your arm getting tired?" she asked.

"Irrelevant," Enoch said.

"Will you take off your sweatshirt?"

He laughed. He sat up and pulled his hand out of her, and pulled his sweatshirt and T-shirt over his head.

Corinne smiled at him. "Handsome," she whispered.

He shook his head, and gently put his hand back inside of her.

"You're so handsome," she said.

"I'm glad you think so."

God, it was so much better to see his bare shoulder moving. His biceps twitching.

"I love you," she said, directly into his eyes. She felt lax and slack and open. "I love you, Enoch."

"I love you," he said, kissing her.

"Is your arm tired?"

"I'm not stopping until you tell me to, and I never want you to tell me to. Are you sore?"

"Just the good kind. Tender."

He pushed a little harder. "Tender?"

She nodded. She laughed. She groaned a little. "I love you," she said, lazily.

"I love you," he growled. "I love you like this. You're all I want, Corinne."

She ran her hands up through his hair. "Enoch. My Enoch."

"Yours," he said, kissing her.

"Mine," Corinne said, her voice cracking. She let go of his head to arch her back, to push her hand between them again. He moved back to give her room.

He was right: She . . . Her . . . She was puffy and swollen. Her clit was overworked. She rubbed around it, skated over it.

"Yes," Enoch said. "Make yourself feel good."

"You make me feel good," she said. "You make me feel . . ." She shook her head. It lolled back. She looked in his eyes. "I'm a fool for you, Enoch."

"You're nobody's fool, Corinne."

"I'm yours," she said.

"Yes," he nodded. "You're mine."

She was starting to come. It was slower and thicker. She didn't have the strength left to clench every muscle. Her mind couldn't blow because it was already blown. She cried instead. "I love you," she said. "I love you."

Enoch worked his left arm under her neck and shoulders. He kissed the spot between her eyes. "Honey . . ."

Corinne whined one long, high syllable.

When she fell off the other end of it, she sobbed.

Enoch's hand stopped moving. Corinne was still crying. She pulled on his arm, trying to dislodge him. He pulled it out.

"Corinne?" He was concerned.

She burrowed against his chest.

"Are you okay?"

"I'm good," she whispered. She shivered. She was naked.

He wrapped his right arm around her. "Why are you crying?"

"It just makes me feel split open," she said. "Like I can't hide anything or . . . from anything. I love you so much, it's overwhelming." She clung to his bare chest. "I'm sorry. I know this isn't sexy."

"Incorrect," Enoch said, holding her.

She glanced up at him—like she knew he was patronizing her, but she still appreciated it.

He looked in her eyes. "You're addictive. This is all I want to do from now on."

She smiled. "Your hand would get tired."

"I keep telling you, I have two."

She laughed.

"And I'm kind of desperate to see stage four . . ." he said.

"Maybe next time," Corinne whispered.

His eyebrows twitched down. "I'm kind of desperate, in general."

She shook her head, smiling at him. Her hair tickled her shoulders. "Enoch . . . you don't have to feel desperate."

"Are you too tender for me to . . ."

"No."

"I brought a condom."

"Okay," she said.

He kissed her and sat up. His wallet was on her nightstand. He pulled out a string of condoms. "Be careful, if you've been leaking," she said.

"Do you want me to wash off?"

"No. Maybe. No. I'll use gel, too. Hang on—" Corinne rolled to edge of her bed and leaned over to get the box. She pulled out a packet of gel, and Enoch snatched it out of her hand. "No," she protested. "It's definitely not sexy."

"I like gadgets," he said.

Corinne fell back onto her bed, laughing. She was too sex-drunk to feel embarrassed. Maybe Enoch was, too.

He shot the gel into her, mumbling, "That's clever," then turned away from her to put on the condom. Corinne didn't offer any encouragement, and it seemed to go okay; they should always do this in this order. Her legs were flopped to the side. Enoch got back onto the bed and flipped them open. Corinne laughed—then sighed when he pushed into her. He held himself over her on his elbows. His eyes were closed, his hair hung on her forehead. She touched his ribs, felt his thick waist. She tried to clench around his cock, purely out of sportsmanship, but none of her major muscle groups were back online. She was so tenderized, he kept pushing little "hum"s out of her.

"Okay?" he asked.

"Good," she said, "good."

"Corinne," he said. "I just—I just—"

"I love you," she said, her brain still wet and soppy.

He opened his eyes and kissed her. "I love you." When he pulled his mouth away, he lifted up a bit and grabbed her knee. He hiked it up. Corinne laughed. Because it was familiar. She laughed because she was fucked out. She brought her other knee up, too, and held them for him.

Enoch groaned and gripped her thigh. He looked her up and down, and up and down, then rolled his eyes up and pumped into her. His pectoral muscles twitched. The cords in his neck popped. His face went red. He was so quiet. Corinne felt like giggling. She couldn't love him more. She couldn't feel any better.

When his body started to sag, she reached between them. "Pinch it."

"What?" He looked dazed.

"Hold the condom," she said, "when you pull out."

"Oh," he breathed, "right."

He held it. He moved carefully, then flopped down next to her, his eyes half closed. She kissed his nose and cheeks and pushed back his hair. He groaned and clumsily patted her shoulder. She laughed.

"What are you laughing at?" he asked.

"I'm happy," she said.

He opened one eye, and looked at her. "Come here," he said, rolling onto his side. "Oh, wait. I need to, um . . ."

"Just throw it on the floor," Corinne said.

Enoch frowned.

"Throw it on the floor, and thank it for its service."

"No," he grumbled. "Just a minute. I'll get cleaned up." He tilted his chin at her. She kissed him. He was back in a minute, wearing boxer shorts.

"Bad form," Corinne said, looking at his underwear—even though she'd covered up, too; she'd pulled up the quilt.

"Now, come here," he said, scooping her up.

Corinne relaxed in his arms. She rested her head on his chest. She kept humming for no reason at all.

"Corinne, I have to tell you two things," he said into her hair.

"Hmm."

"One . . . you have a giant hickey on your neck."

She started laughing through her nose, snorting. Enoch's chest shook.

"What's two?" she asked.

"Two is . . ." He pulled his face away. "Look at me."

"So bossy," she said, looking up at him.

His forehead was smooth, his face was soft. "I don't think I could be happier than I am right now."

Corinne looked in his eyes. She bit her bottom lip. She shook her head, just to shake off the excess nirvana gathering in her neck. "You could," she said.

He bunched up his eyebrows. "How?"

"Wait right here." She stood up—she took the quilt.

"Don't take the blanket!"

She did, she wrapped it around her. She stopped at the bathroom first to pee—and to check her neck in the mirror. (*Jesus Christ.*) Then she went to the kitchen and got their Blizzards out of the freezer. Their red plastic spoons were frozen in them, so Corinne grabbed two real spoons from the drawer. It was hard to keep the quilt tucked around her, but she worked it out.

When she came back to her bedroom, Enoch had gotten under her covers.

The quilt was sliding off her shoulder.

She held out his Blizzard.

Enoch's mouth dropped open. "*Corinne.*"

Chapter Seventy-nine

Enoch got up before the sun.

"Why do you get up so early?" Corinne whined.

He was sitting on the edge of her bed, putting his sweatshirt back on. "I have to go home and exercise before work."

"Why do you have to exercise every morning?"

"So that I can stay off antidepressants and continue to get erections."

Corinne opened her eyes. "All right. That's a good reason." She kicked him. "Go. Go do that."

He stood up and put on his jeans, then leaned over her. "Can I call you later?"

"Yes," she said. "Obviously."

He did call her.

She went to his house that night after work and stayed for three days.

Every day was good now. Mondays, Tuesdays, Wednesdays. Church nights, weekends.

Every day had Enoch Miller in it.

Chapter Eighty

"Corinne? It's Mercy."

"Hey, is everything okay?"

"Everything's fine," Mercy said. "I was just wondering, are you going to your mom's house for lunch today?"

"I am."

"Do you think you could pick Ruth and me up at church? Noah has to stay late, and Shawn and Alicia are out of town, and—"

"It's no trouble. I'll come get you."

"Thanks, Corinne. Have you been here before?"

"I know where it is."

"We get out at noon. Maybe come a few minutes early? That way, we can skip the rush."

"Sure."

⌒

This wasn't the specific church Corinne had grown up in, but it had a similar look. A wide, squat building, painted tan to fit into the neighborhood. There was a teenage boy outside with a walkie-talkie, keeping an eye on the parking lot. Maybe he'd think Corinne was up to no good and call for help. (Corinne was the sort of no good they couldn't help.)

She pulled up to the side of the front door, so Mercy would see her. Enoch might see her, too. His truck was here. He was inside.

Mercy came out with Ruth a few minutes before noon, and Corinne got out to help her with the car seat. Mercy said it would be easy to belt in, but Corinne's car wasn't really set up for it. Corinne held Ruth while Mercy wrestled with the thing.

Mercy couldn't stop thanking Corinne for picking them up. She was hoping to take a nap when they got to Corinne's mom's house, "if I can find somebody to hold the baby."

"I'll hold the baby," Corinne said, looking at Ruth. "We're old pals, aren't we, honey?"

That's when Enoch came skipping down the church steps. His head was down. He was wearing his gray suit. His hair was getting longer; Corinne kept talking him out of haircuts. It covered the top of his ears and brushed his collar.

He saw Corinne, he always saw her. He stopped on the steps. His face lit up. Corinne was holding the baby. She was wearing a flowered dress.

He moved toward her, then stopped.

Mercy was leaning into the back seat of the car.

Corinne nodded at Enoch.

Enoch nodded back.

He turned his head away from her—like someone was turning it for him—and went jerkily down the last few steps.

"There." Mercy stood up. She caught Corinne watching Enoch. Corinne smiled tightly and handed her the baby.

When they both got into her front seat, Enoch's truck was leaving the parking lot. "It's so sad," Mercy said. "He never misses a service. Why would he cast himself out like that if he wants to be here? Noah thinks he might be gay, like his wife. Or worse."

"Worse?" Corinne couldn't mask her dismay.

"Why else would he cut himself off from the congregation if he wasn't walking with some dark sin?"

"Maybe he's just confused," Corinne said.

"You don't cut off your hand because it's confused," Mercy said. "You cut it off because it's sinful."

"No one needs to cut off any hands," Corinne said. "Or feet."

"It's a metaphor."

"I know."

"It's from Matthew."

"I *know*."

Mercy's voice was soft, supplicating. "I'm sorry, Corinne, I know you were friends, but maybe—"

"Maybe what?"

"Well, maybe it's good for you to see . . . that Enoch Miller is sick with sin. Maybe it wasn't ever about *you*, you know?"

"Mercy . . ." Corinne was staring at her steering wheel.

"I don't mean to bring up bad memories."

Corinne turned to her. "Mercy, Enoch Miller is a good man. He's God-fearing, I know it. Anyone who says any different is wrong."

Mercy looked taken aback. "I'm sorry, Corinne. I shouldn't—"

"He didn't stumble me. I stumbled myself."

Mercy nodded and looked away. She didn't want to hear that. That it was Corinne who had been wicked and immoral all along. Not with her baby strapped into the back seat of Corinne's car.

They drove in silence. Corinne turned on the radio, to make it less stark, but Mercy looked panicked, and Corinne quickly turned it off.

⁓

Corinne couldn't stop worrying about Enoch the whole time she was at her mom's house. No one noticed she was checked out. She smiled and listened to their stories. She played Candy Land with her nephews and one of her stepsister's kids.

Then she left early, with a covered plate of ham and macaroni and cheese for supper. For Enoch. She walked into his kitchen, calling his name.

"I'm in here." He was in the living room, playing video games. He was still wearing his dress clothes. His suit jacket was on the coffee table.

"Hey," she said.

He glanced up at her. His eyes were glassy. "Hey."

"Did you have lunch?"

"No."

"I brought you some ham."

"Okay." He kept playing.

Corinne set the plate down on the table. She picked up his jacket. After a second, she took it into the bedroom to hang it up. When she turned away from his closet, Enoch was standing in the doorway to his room, taking up the whole thing.

"Hey," he said. "I'm sorry." He held a hand out to her.

Corinne went to him. Into his arms.

"Hi," he said.

"Hi. Are you okay?"

"I'm a little off my game."

"I'm sorry I surprised you," she said. "After church."

"Don't be. It was nice to see you."

"It didn't seem nice."

"It was like . . ." He hugged her. "Remember when you were a kid, and you'd see your teacher at the grocery store?"

Corinne nodded.

"It was a little discombobulating."

"You should eat," Corinne said. "You should . . ." She loosened his tie.

"Yeah," Enoch said, taking off the tie. He walked past her into his room, unbuttoning his shirt. "How's your family?"

"Good. The same. Shawn and Alicia went to Chicago for their anniversary."

"That's nice." He was standing in front of his dresser. His shirt was still half buttoned.

Corinne went to him. "Let me help you." She reached for his buttons.

He caught her hands. "I've got it. I can undress myself."

"Enoch. What's wrong?"

"Sorry—I told you, I'm off my game."

"This is about seeing me. At church."

"It's about feeling lost, Corinne." He sighed. He let go of her hands. He leaned past her to get clothes out of the drawer. "When you're not here—when you're with your family—I'm not with anyone. I start to feel *lost*. I'm sorry, I wish I didn't."

Corinne let him move away from her to change.

"I thought you were happy," she said.

He glanced back at her. "Come on, that's not fair. I am happy."

She frowned.

"Just usually not on Sunday afternoons," he said.

"Do you want me to stay home with you?"

"No! Jiminy Christmas. I don't want that." He sat on his bed and put his head in his hands. After a second, Corinne sat down next to him. "I want to go *with* you," he said.

"I know," she said. "I'm sorry."

"The Sundays stack up. I start to think about my nieces and nephews, birthdays, Christmas . . ."

"I thought you said we weren't there yet," she whispered. "At the hard place."

"We're not," he said. "I'm just . . . I'm off my game, I'm sorry. I don't want this to hurt us. The fact that I'm having an off day."

"Do you want me to go home?"

"*No.* Please don't. I never want that."

Corinne leaned against his side.

His face sank into her hair. "I'm sorry I'm so dependent on you. It isn't sustainable."

"What does that mean?" she asked. "Practically speaking. That it isn't sustainable?"

"I don't know, I'll make some worldly friends. I'll join a book club."

Corinne winced. "Your life was so full before me . . ."

"That's patently untrue. I spent every night alone."

"You worked with friends and went to church three days a week."

He sat up straight. "We're not having this conversation again."

"Why not?"

"Because it's not real! I don't want my old life back, and also I *can't* have it back."

"Yes, you can."

"*Corinne.* Please. Just let me have a hard day."

"If you're having a hard day, we're already at the hard place."

"We were always at the hard place!" he snapped.

Corinne stood up.

"Corinne."

"I'm not going anywhere," she said. "I'm just giving you a minute. I'm taking a minute."

He nodded.

Corinne walked out into the hall. There was a closet there. She opened it. Sheets. Towels. A bag of dog food. (Why did he have dog food?)

There was another closet by the front door. With Enoch's coats and boots. Umbrellas.

Maybe in the guest bedroom . . .

Corinne had only walked past this room before. She went in now and opened the closet.

Jackpot.

"What are you doing?" Enoch had come in behind her. He was standing on the other side of the spare bed.

"Waiting for you," she said. "I can't reach Hüsker Dü."

⌒

Enoch was sitting on the couch. Corinne knelt on the other side of the coffee table, laying out the Monopoly board. The same old board. (When she went looking for some sort of game, she hadn't expected to find their whole *trove*.)

"I can't believe you threw out Simon," she said.

"Japheth threw it out—he assumed it was broken."

"That's very convenient, Enoch Miller."

"He was about to take the rest of these to the Goodwill."

She looked up at Enoch over the game board. She imagined him carrying boxes of old and unwanted things out of his mother's house—Matchbox cars, *Reader's Digests*, a stationary bicycle—but setting this stack of games aside. Cleaning out his closet to make room for them.

Corinne laid out Candy Land. Then Clue.

Enoch watched her. "Is this a good idea?"

She glanced up at him. "As good as ever."

Enoch picked up the Monopoly box. He took out the top hat and the horse and rider. "What are the rules?" he asked gruffly.

"If Simon is out, so is Operation."

"I'm very good at Operation."

"Don't I know it."

Corinne was arranging the weapons for Clue. All the pieces were still here; it was very satisfying. Enoch grabbed her hand. She looked up at him. His eyes were shining. His nostrils were twitching.

"I love you," he said.

"I love you," she said. "I always have."

"Come sit next to me, Corinne."

Chapter Eighty-one

Corinne's title when she left the ad agency was "assistant director of global strategy."

It was a very fancy title, and she was proud of it.

Before that, she'd been a "senior planner."

Her specialty, her boss always said, was breaking insightful bad news.

Some planners wouldn't pitch something that the client didn't want to hear. Corinne always felt like she had to be honest—that they were paying her to be honest. And that real insight was impossible without honesty.

She'd tell clients that their customers didn't like them. That the logo they'd spent a fortune on was confusing. That the public image they'd spent twenty years building made them seem cold or even corrupt.

If she could get in the room with them, she'd tell them all of this in a way that made them see the hope on the other side of it.

She was a firm believer in making sacrifices. And tough choices. Cutting losses. She loved a cost-benefit analysis.

Her last promotion came after she fired one of her favorite people at work. Corinne had volunteered to do it. Not because she wanted to hurt her friend, but because she knew she could make it hurt less. She knew she could make this person, a junior planner, see how much happier they'd be somewhere else.

When Corinne decided to leave the agency, her boss—her best friend, Kyle—had accused her of being rash.

"*I'm not being rash,*" she'd said. "*I'm weighing my options.*"

"*You're on track to be a VP.*"

"*If I leave and do well on my own, you'll hire me back for more money.*"

"*I might not be here.*"

"*You'll hire me somewhere else. Someone will.*"

Corinne had been very realistic about what she could expect from her family, if she moved home. How she'd have to compromise. How much she could swallow, and what the rewards would be. What she could take, what she would get.

Corinne didn't shy away from difficulty.

She was willing to make sacrifices.

"*You know why you're so good in a room?*" Kyle had said once, on the way home from a pitch. They were on an airplane. He was drinking gin.

"*Is it my natural charm?*"

"*It sure as fuck is not. It's* despite *your natural charm.*" He had a mouth full of ice. He tilted his glass at her. "*It's that you're not scared to lose.*"

"*I'm scared to lose,*" Corinne had argued. She'd been rolling her eyes and half laughing. "*I just know I'll live through it.*"

Chapter Eighty-two

"This is Enoch."

"Hi."

"Corinne." He was surprised she was calling so early. "Hey there, what's up?"

"Do you feel like taking a walk over lunch?"

"It's pretty cold . . ."

"Sunny though. The trail will warm us up."

"Up north?"

"Yeah."

"All right," he said. "I brought a sandwich for lunch . . ."

"Eat it on the way."

"Yeah, all right. I'll see you in an hour—I love you."

"I love you."

Chapter Eighty-three

She met him in the parking lot. His truck was already there.

Corinne was wearing her warmest coat, her down coat. She had a baby-blue stocking cap with a giant yellow pom-pom. She brought coffee.

Enoch got out of his truck when she pulled in. He looked tired. They'd stayed up late last night playing their game. Corinne had wanted to play until Enoch's forehead relaxed, but they never quite got there.

Maybe the game itself was too heavy on him. Too much.

She'd sat next to him on the couch, and they'd made up new rules. They worked with what was available—Enoch didn't have a Parcheesi board, and he had a very stupid edition of Trivial Pursuit. (The Millennium Edition.) It was so much fun. Enoch was having fun, too, even if it wasn't enough to make him forget everything.

They left the game spread out on the coffee table when they went to bed. And when Corinne got up this morning—almost four hours after Enoch—it was all still there.

That's when she'd called him.

"You look tired," Corinne said now, holding out his coffee.

"Wild night." He kissed her cheek. "You sure it's not too cold for this?"

"We can turn back, if it is."

It was different on the trail. Than it used to be. They held hands. Enoch braced her even when she didn't really need it. They didn't talk much. He was tired. And Corinne was scared. It did warm up though, once they started walking. With the sun shining down on them through bare branches.

They walked beneath the tunnel of hedge apples and got to the pond. It was iced over and gray. They threw their empty cups away and walked to the edge of the water.

"If you brought me out here to kill me," Enoch said, "you picked a good day. No witnesses."

"Nah." Corinne bumped his hip. "Pond's too shallow. How would I dispose of the body?"

They looked down at the ice. It was beautiful, really. The whole park felt wider in winter. More open. Corinne put her foot on the edge of the ice and listened to it crack.

"Do you want to sit down?" she asked.

He glanced over at the stone bench. "No, I'll stand. It's warmer."

She nodded. He let go of her hand to put his arm around her shoulder.

"Enoch?"

"Corinne." His voice was so low and soft, she could hardly hear it.

"I've been thinking."

"I can tell."

"When you said that we're always at the hard place—"

"I'd had a bad day," he said.

"But you were right. We are always at the hard place. We're already there." She looked up at him. His eyes were closed. "There's no magic wind that's going to blow through and untangle us," she said. "So maybe . . ." She unzipped his tan work coat and slipped her hand inside. His chest was warm. "Enoch . . ."

He opened his eyes.

"Will you marry me?"

His head jerked back. "What?"

"Will you marry me?"

"But you just said . . ."

"I know."

"I'm not following."

"Because I'm not saying it right." She made a fist in his T-shirt. "I just—I don't know what we're waiting for, Enoch. A sign? A shift? We have all the information we need. We know that it's going to be hard, it always has been—I'll take it. Anyway. If you'll give it to me." She pressed her fist into his chest. "I want it. This life with you. I want it more than anything."

Enoch's eyes were shining. His eyebrows were down. He was pushing his tongue into his bottom lip. "Corinne . . ."

"Marry me, Enoch."

"Corinne, you wouldn't want *me* to propose to *you* just so that I could get back into the church . . ."

"That's not what this is."

"I know you're worried about me . . ."

"I am. Because I love you. But that's not what this is."

He reached up and touched her cheek. His fingers were cold. "Honey . . ."

"I love you," Corinne said. "Nothing is going to change that. Nothing ever has. What are we waiting for?"

Enoch thumbed her cheek. His glasses were fogging up. "I was waiting for you to decide . . . Can you be happy?"

"Can *you* be happy?"

"Only with you," he said.

"Enoch . . ."

He huffed a laugh. He took off his glasses to wipe his eyes. One side of his mouth was tweaked up. "Yes," he said.

"Yes?" Corinne's voice was all treble.

He lowered his eyebrows and nodded.

Corinne laughed. She was crying.

Enoch wrapped his arms around her and yanked her close. She laughed again.

"Yes, I'll marry you. Dream girl. Yes."

Chapter Eighty-four

In the end, it had been a cost-benefit analysis.
She couldn't live without him.

Chapter Eighty-five

They held hands on the way back to the parking lot. They kept stopping to kiss and laugh into each other's mouths.

"When do you want to get married?" Enoch asked.

"Tomorrow? Yesterday? We just need our birth certificates to get a license, and then we can make an appointment with a judge." She'd looked it up online.

"All right," he said. "Let's go get the license."

Corinne laughed. She felt like she was bubbling over. Spilling over the top of the glass. "Yeah?"

"Yes. Unless—should we take a few days to think about it?"

"No," Corinne said. "I'm not going to change my mind."

Enoch took the day off work. They went to the courthouse to get their license and made an appointment with a judge in two and a half weeks, then they went back to Enoch's house and stared at the paperwork while they ate pizza.

"I guess this makes us half married," Corinne said.

"I already felt half married," Enoch said, knocking his shoulder against hers. He was eating a piece of pizza with one hand, and holding a napkin under it with the other. "Maybe three-fourths. That's the deal I made with Jesus."

"What are you talking about?"

He looked over at her. "I told you that I didn't feel bad about what we were doing . . ."

"Because you secretly married me without my consent in the eyes of Jesus?"

"Because I was treating it like a sacrament," he said matter-of-factly. "I was all in."

Corinne shook her head. She tried to be weirded out by that—and not deeply moved. "I don't want any part of your internal machinations with God."

"Fair enough. But I talk to Him about you all the time."

"We need to get you more friends."

Enoch laughed. He was still giddy. They both were. "Have you thought about where you want to live?"

She hadn't.

"I mean," Enoch said, "we're going to live together, right?"

"Yeah. Of course. I guess . . . here?"

"It doesn't have to be here. I could move in with you."

"That would be dumb."

"We can get someplace new."

"Maybe . . ." Corinne said. "We could live here in the meantime, and see how it goes?"

"All right," he agreed.

"Is it weird that I'm more freaked out by moving in with you than marrying you?"

"A little . . ."

"It just seems like a huge step."

Enoch's chest quaked. He was giggling hard. Silently.

She shoved him with her shoulder, and he let himself fall onto the arm of the sofa, still giggling.

He pushed himself up with his elbow. "You can have the spare room for an office if you want. We could put your table in there. And probably your couch."

"That might be nice," Corinne said. She could move in with Enoch, and no one in her family would even notice. Because they never came to her apartment. "Are we going to tell our families?"

He leaned against her. "Do you want to?"

"They'll find out eventually. When you get let back in."

"That's a long time to wait."

Even after they got married, it would take months of elders' meetings for Enoch to prove his repentance.

"Let's tell them after we do it," she said. "So they don't have a chance to make us feel bad about it."

He nodded. Solemnly.

"I wish it could be good news," she whispered.

"It will be," he said. "It means neither of us will be sinning, in their eyes. I'll be able to talk to my mom again in six months."

"Yeah, but she'll be disappointed—you won't ever be an elder again. Have you thought about that?"

He nodded again.

"Have you thought about all the difficult things? Have you thought about what happens if we have kids?"

Enoch sighed. "Yes."

"*Really* thought about it?"

"Corinne. You're the one who proposed here. I thought you wanted this."

"I do—I just don't want you to regret it later."

"You act like . . ." He shook his head. He was irritated.

"What?"

"You act like there's a version of my life that's easy. There isn't. I'm not trying to make it harder—I'm not a *martyr*." He said it like someone had said that he was. "I'm trying to have the best life I can, the most happiness available to me, knowing it will be hard, no matter what."

"Oh . . ." Corinne said, struck a little dumb.

"Oh?"

"I actually completely agree with that philosophy."

"Don't sound so surprised."

"I thought you were more of a romantic, Enoch."

"You don't think it's romantic that I see you as 'the most happiness available'?"

"Well, when you say it that way . . ."

"I *did* say it that way."

Corinne took a second to think, then said, "I feel like we take turns talking each other down."

He shoved his pizza crust into his mouth and wiped his hands, putting an arm around her. "It's why we're going to be so good together."

Chapter Eighty-six

Corinne was working on a big project this month—a pitch for her old agency. Kyle wanted her to come to Boston for the client meeting, but she told him she couldn't. It was a struggle even to focus on work, she was so busy being engaged to Enoch Miller.

She hadn't told anyone she was engaged.

There was no one she could tell who would understand.

So she went around her apartment, telling herself:

You're going to marry Enoch Miller. You're already half married. To Enoch. (Enoch, Enoch, Enoch.) You're going to fall asleep with him. And wake up with him. And fall back to sleep after he leaves. You're going to move in with him. Make plans with him. Ruin his prospects.

You're probably going to have to talk to his mother someday.

You're going to have to listen to him talk about Jesus for the rest of your life.

The rest of your life, with Enoch Miller. Standing right next to you. Taking up entire doorways. Holding your right leg up by the back of your knee.

Corinne packed up her things. Half of them had never been unpacked. She listened to the oldies station and felt like it was a sign of good luck when they played "My Cherie Amour."

La la laaa-la la la
La la laaa-la la la

⌒

Corinne went to Noah and Mercy's house on Thursday afternoon. Mercy didn't mention their conversation about Enoch. And Corinne didn't mention that she was engaged to him. That they were half married already. Maybe three-fourths, if you asked Jesus.

She brought her clothes over to Enoch's house in suitcases and boxes. He cleared out half his closet to make room for her, even though she didn't really need a closet the way he did. Corinne didn't own things that needed to be ironed.

She hung her clothes up next to his. This was probably Shannon Frank's half of the closet. Shannon Miller's. If Corinne changed her name, all three of them would have it.

She packed up her kitchen. Her pizza stone. Her tea.

Enoch came by one day after work and loaded almost everything into the back of his truck. Corinne was going to donate her bed to the Goodwill. The two of them carried her couch down the stairs—it was a terrible idea. Corinne could hardly manage her half, and Enoch hurt his back. A guy walking by her building took pity on them and helped Enoch get the couch into the truck.

When they got to his house, they got it as far as the garage.

"Let's just leave this here for now," Enoch said.

"Agreed," Corinne said, dropping her end. (She was already mostly dropping it.)

Enoch set his side down, and sat down on the couch, groaning.

Corinne sat down in his lap and kissed every part of his face and neck that was available. She unzipped his coat to get more.

"I live here now," she said. "Officially."

"The couch made it official?"

"Whither the couch goest."

His chest hitched.

"I live here," she said. "With you."

"With me," Enoch said, holding her.

La la laaa-la la la
La la laaa-la la la

Chapter Eighty-seven

It was Wednesday night, and Shannon Frank's truck was parked in Enoch's driveway.

Corinne thought about driving right past it.

But Enoch was expecting her, and Corinne was going to have to get used to this, to Shannon, eventually. Shannon and Enoch still had lunch. She still stopped by to borrow things. Apparently, sometimes, he watched her dog.

Corinne did drive by. Twice. Shannon's truck was still there.

On the third loop, Corinne parked on the street behind Enoch. She still went in through the garage; it would be excessive to go to the front door and knock. She wasn't just a guest—she lived here. (In Shannon Frank's house.) She opened the door to the kitchen as slowly and squeakily as possible, so that no one would be surprised to see her.

They were in the kitchen. Enoch, Shannon, and an extremely attractive woman who had to be Shannon's girlfriend. Enoch was standing by the sink with his arms folded. His face was red. Shannon was on the other side of the room, with her hands on her hips. When Corinne walked in, she dropped them. "Corinne."

"Hi," Corinne said.

Enoch always took his shoes off in the house, but Shannon had hers on, so Corinne kept hers on. (She wasn't going to bend over in front of Shannon Frank. She wasn't going to let Shannon Frank see her socks.)

Corinne walked over to Enoch. "Hey."

"Hey," he said gruffly, unfolding his arms to touch her shoulder.

"Hi," the beautiful woman said. "We haven't met."

"I'll introduce you," Shannon said sharply. "I was going to introduce you."

"I believe you," the woman said.

"Corinne, this is my girlfriend, Natalie."

Natalie held out her hand. "It's so nice to meet you, Corinne."

Corinne took her hand. "It's nice to meet you."

Natalie really was extraordinarily pretty, with asymmetrical dark hair and olive-colored skin. She had big brown eyes and a nose ring, and she was smiling warmly at Corinne.

"Congratulations," Natalie said.

Corinne glanced up at Enoch, and his forehead tensed apologetically, or maybe just regretfully.

"Enoch told us about your engagement," Shannon said. "We're really happy for you." She didn't sound happy.

"Thank you," Corinne said.

"We were just talking about your wedding plans."

"Oh . . ." Corinne glanced up at Enoch. His jaw was shifted to the side, and his tongue was in his cheek. "We're not planning a wedding."

"Is that because you don't *want* a wedding?" Shannon asked.

"Um . . ." Corinne glanced at Enoch again.

Enoch was frowning at Shannon. "Shannon . . ."

Shannon was seething at Enoch. "I'm asking *Corinne*." She turned to Corinne. "Is it because you don't want a wedding?"

"I want to marry Enoch," Corinne said.

"And he wants to marry you," Shannon said. "That's what makes this worth celebrating." She didn't seem very celebratory.

"When are you tying the knot?" Natalie asked, smiling in a very deliberate fashion.

"In about a week," Corinne said.

"Plenty of time to plan a wedding," Shannon said.

"Shannon—" Enoch warned.

"*Is* it?" Corinne asked.

Shannon put her hands on her hips again. "Corinne, do you really want to get married at the *courthouse*?"

Corinne shrugged.

"In between arraignments?"

Enoch raised his hands. "All right, enough!"

"Is that what you want, Enoch?"

"I said, *enough*!" he shouted.

"Is that not what you want?" Corinne asked him.

"Corinne, I'd marry you in a sewer."

"I don't want to get married in a sewer."

"That's not what I meant."

"What he means," Shannon said, "is he'll do whatever you want." She turned her viciously pretty face on Corinne. "Do you really not want a wedding? Or is it that you think you don't deserve one?"

"Enough!" Enoch roared.

"You!" Shannon pointed up at his face. "Promised! Not! To shout at me!"

"I promised you that in marriage counseling!" Enoch bellowed. "It was dissolved with the rest of our vows!"

Natalie was watching Corinne with a soft, almost apologetic smile. She raised her eyebrows like, *Yep, this is happening.*

"I'm trying to help you, Enoch!" Shannon shouted.

"I didn't ask for your help!"

"You asked me to be your witness!"

Enoch asked his ex-wife to be his best man?

"Only if I can't find anyone else!"

"Shannon." Corinne stepped between them.

Shannon was still pointing at Enoch. She looked at Corinne and dropped her finger.

"We can't have a wedding," Corinne said. "No one would come."

"I'd come," Shannon said.

"Me, too," Natalie offered.

"Well, great," Corinne said. "This sounds like a super fun and not at all depressing party. Maybe I could invite my college boyfriend and a few people who bullied me in junior high."

"Your wedding should be a *celebration*," Shannon said vehemently. "You deserve a celebration."

"We can't help the fact that no one wants to celebrate with us."

"But that doesn't mean that they get to set the tone! That all the people who have rejected you get to decide what kind of wedding you have. They don't get to turn this into a walk of shame—fuck them!" Her voice broke. "Fuck them, you know?" She looked up over Corinne's shoulder at Enoch. "You deserve to be happy."

Natalie was standing behind Shannon. She smiled at Corinne again and raised her eyebrows. Then she touched Shannon's back. "Babe."

Shannon's posture wilted. She rubbed her face and turned away from Corinne and Enoch.

Corinne looked back at Enoch. He was staring at the floor, kneading the back of his neck.

"What would that look like?" Corinne asked.

Shannon lifted her head. "What would what look like?"

"A wedding."

Shannon stood straight. She looked careful. "However you want it to look, Corinne."

"If I try to picture it," Corinne said, "all I can see are the people who won't be there."

"You should give yourself something beautiful to remember," Shannon said.

Enoch's hand fell on Corinne's shoulder. "It will already be beautiful enough. I don't care about all this."

"But you *do* care," Shannon argued. "You're letting the shame in— you both are. You think you have to make this as austere and grim as possible. As part of your repentance." She pointed at Enoch again. "You'd get married in a hair shirt if you could find one."

"What would it look like?" Corinne asked again. "What are you proposing?"

"She doesn't get to propose anything," Enoch said.

Corinne turned to him. "Oh my God, Enoch, you're the one who apparently asked her to be your best man."

"I was going to talk to you about it, Corinne."

"You should have talked to me *first*," she whispered.

"A park," Shannon said.

Corinne looked at her. "It's February."

"We could rent a nice room."

"For the four of us?"

"There's a beautiful Unitarian church by our house," Natalie said.

"We can't get married in another church," Enoch and Corinne said, at the same time as Shannon said, "They can't get married in another church."

Natalie tried again: "My parents have a really pretty sunroom."

"We could do it here," Enoch said.

Corinne looked up at him, into his soft brown eyes. She just barely shook her head. Enoch nodded. He put his arm around Corinne's waist and pulled her close to him.

"There should at least be flowers," Shannon said sternly.

Corinne felt a rush of heat in her face. Her eyes were stinging.
Flowers . . .

She could have flowers.

It was her wedding day.

She was marrying Enoch Miller, and she could have flowers.

"Okay," she whispered.

Shannon's lovely face lit up. "Okay?"

Corinne nodded.

"Ha!" Shannon said, looking at Natalie. "Flowers!" She looked back at Corinne. "And a pretty dress?"

"All right," Enoch said, "it's time for you to leave, Shannon."

Shannon grinned at Corinne. "See how bad he wants you to wear a pretty dress?"

"It was so nice to meet you, Corinne," Natalie said. "Congratulations again. Congratulations, Enoch."

"Thanks, Nat."

"It was nice to meet you," Corinne said.

Natalie pulled Shannon toward the door. Shannon pointed at Corinne. "Flowers. I'm going to call you."

"Are you really . . ."

"Good-bye!" Enoch shouted. "Go!"

Chapter Eighty-eight

Enoch followed them to the door, locking it behind them. As if Shannon Frank didn't have a key.

Corinne sat on the big leather couch.

Enoch walked into the living room, his posture almost completely defiant. "Before we talk about this, please hear me: This is about Shannon, not you. It's about her feeling like she had a picture-perfect wedding with me and now isn't allowed to have one with Natalie. And it's about her own guilt, for marrying me and staying married to me for so long. This isn't even about you and me, Corinne."

Corinne looked up at him. "That doesn't mean she's wrong."

Enoch ran one hand through his hair and huffed out a breath.

"Will you build a fire for me?" Corinne asked.

He looked confused, but he nodded. He reached for his coat and put his work boots back on, and went outside for the wood.

Corinne stayed on the couch, barely moving.

Enoch came back in, shaking snow off his coat and the firewood. He kicked off his boots and glanced at Corinne on his way to the fireplace. She hadn't moved.

It took him a while to build the fire.

She loved his hunched back. The way his thighs spread when he knelt. She loved the snow melting in his fox-brown hair.

When he was done, he came to sit next to her. He was being careful.

Corinne slid her arms inside his coat and hugged him tight. She kissed his mouth, her heart completely open to him. Enoch relaxed. He wrapped his arms around her, he sighed.

When Corinne pulled her mouth away, she was leaning across him. She let him keep holding her. Cradling her. She rested her head on his chest.

"I should have talked to you first," Enoch said. "I'm sorry. I just wanted to tell someone. And I knew she'd be happy for me."

"It's okay," Corinne said.

"I didn't ask her to be my best man—but I told her I was worried about finding a witness, and she offered."

"I think it's genuinely okay."

"You *think* so?"

Corinne nodded. "That's all I can manage at the moment."

"Fair enough."

She rubbed her face in his T-shirt. He had a sweet smell. It was almost cloying sometimes. When the house was warm. When the door to his bedroom was closed and he'd been sleeping under his down blanket. It reminded Corinne of his mother's house. Of the baskets of laundry sitting in the basement, not far from Corinne's sleeping bag. His brother's sleeping bag.

Corinne looked up at Enoch. He still seemed anxious.

"Do you want a wedding?" she asked.

"I already had a big wedding," Enoch said, every word measured, "and it didn't help my marriage." He wound a piece of Corinne's hair around his index finger and tucked it behind her ear. "Do you want a wedding, honey?"

"I'm not sure," she said. "I never really thought that was an option."

Enoch kept stroking her hair. Finding new wayward tendrils to tuck away.

"I always knew I wasn't going to marry a brother," Corinne said, "even when I was a little girl. I couldn't imagine that happening. We'd go to those big church weddings—I remember Lynette Green's wedding—and I knew that wasn't going to be me."

Enoch was shaking his head, but he knew by now not to argue.

"And once I was cast out, I knew my family wouldn't come to my wedding. If I had one. I figured I'd have some sort of civil ceremony . . . Maybe a reception with my friends. Marc wanted to get a band."

"Marc?" Enoch said.

She sighed. "Marc."

Enoch kissed her forehead.

"When I think about you and me," Corinne said, "and some sort of dream wedding . . . it isn't happy." There were tears in her eyes. Her nose was scrunched. "Because the people we love wouldn't come. Are we going to throw a big wedding for ourselves? That's even more pathetic, isn't it? Wouldn't it just make us sadder?"

"I want you to have the wedding you really want," Enoch said.

"I don't get to have that," she said. "That's what I'm trying to explain."

Enoch frowned, his eyebrows a heavy ridge.

She reached up and ran her thumb along one. "But I get to have you. And I never dreamt that was possible . . ."

Enoch caught her hand and kissed it.

"I think," Corinne said, "that I've spent so much time thinking about the sort of wedding we *couldn't* have . . . I didn't really consider what sort of wedding we could." She looked in Enoch's eyes. She tried not to cry. She failed. "We could have flowers, couldn't we?"

Enoch exhaled, smiling painfully. "Yeah."

"And a cake? A small cake?"

"We could have a huge cake, Corinne, and eat it all ourselves."

She laughed. "Do *you* want a cake?"

He was smiling. "I really do."

"What else do you want, Enoch?"

"Rings," he said softly. "And a dance."

"A *dance*? Like, with a band?"

"I want *a* dance. With you."

"Dancing is against the rules," Corinne said, a little shocked, despite everything.

"What are they going to do, kick us out?"

Corinne sat up to kiss him. She was crying freely now. Enoch held the back of her head. She pulled away far enough to ask, "Where are we going to *dance*?"

"I don't know . . ."

"Shannon was right. I hate that she was right. I hate that she was here. And that she knows you so well. And that she was right."

Enoch sighed. He couldn't help any of it.

"You deserve to be happy," she said. "You deserve to celebrate."

"Corinne," Enoch said, "so do you."

———

They couldn't think of anywhere good to get married. It was too cold to do anything outside, and Corinne really *couldn't* get married in Enoch and Shannon's house. She could live here, she could love it. She could make it her own eventually—or deal with it, if she couldn't. But she wanted their marriage to start somewhere fresh. The county courthouse was at least neutral ground.

They could definitely have a reception, though. Even if it was just the four of them. Corinne had already decided that making peace with Shannon Frank was preferable to asking a stranger to sign her marriage license. She'd thought about inviting a few friends from college, but it would be so much to explain—why her family wasn't there, why Enoch's family wasn't. They didn't have to explain any of it to Shannon; she was made of the same fabric they were.

They could have a tiny reception. They could have a small cake. Corinne could try to find a dress. And she could have a bouquet, with any flowers she wanted. (She wanted hydrangeas.)

They could dance. At least once.

They could plan their wedding around the people who were going to be there. Not the people who weren't.

Chapter Eighty-nine

"I need you here in person."

"I can't be there in person, Kyle. I put together a deck for you."

"Yeah, I saw the deck. It's a good deck. But, Corinne, I need *you* to present it."

"I could maybe call in?"

"I don't want you to call in!"

"Okay, I won't."

"This is such an important pitch," he groaned.

"I know. I'm sorry."

"I'm *not* going to double your hourly rate."

"All right."

"Because then you'll know I can double your hourly rate, and it will wreck our working relationship."

"I am definitely putting a pin in that thought."

"I could get you a bonus."

"It doesn't matter—I can't come. I have a thing."

"Unless it's a wedding or a funeral, you can reschedule."

"Yeah . . ."

"Oh, God, Corinne, is it your mom? Shit."

"No. It's not my mom. She's fine. Everyone's fine."

"Then it's . . . Is someone getting married? Because, actually, you *can* skip a wedding. The bride and groom won't even know you're there."

"I can't skip this one."

"*Corinne . . .*"

She sighed. "Kyle."

"Mother *fuck,* Corinne."

"Yeah . . ."

"Are you fucking kidding me here?"

"Assuming we're on the same page, no."

"When?"

"Friday."

"This Friday?"

"Yeah.

"You were going to get married this Friday, and not tell me?"

"I'm still getting married this Friday."

"Fuck you, Corinne!"

"I'm not rescheduling my wedding for your pitch, Kyle. Fuck *you.*"

"That's not what I meant—I meant, fuck you for not inviting me!"

"I'm not inviting anyone!"

"Why not?"

"It's not that kind of wedding."

"What kind of wedding is it?"

"A small one. An intimate one."

"Oh, fuck that, Corinne. Don't be one of those people. Everyone hates those people."

"What people?"

"You know. Those 'just the two of us' people. Weddings are celebrations. They're declarations!"

"Look—I'm getting married at the courthouse. There won't be guests. It's all going to be very . . . legal."

"You're not even inviting your mom?"

"My mom wouldn't come."

Kyle was quiet. Uncharacteristically. "Corinne . . . are you in trouble?"

"No. I'm in love. And I'm getting married. To a really wonderful person."

"Person?"

"Man. I promise that I'm not in trouble. There's just a bunch of religious stuff between my family and me, and you don't need to fly to Kansas to bear witness to it."

"I thought your family was Christian."

"They are."

"Are you marrying into Islam?"

"It's really hard to explain."

"It wouldn't be so hard to explain if you weren't so fucking closed down and repressed, historically speaking."

"Yes," Corinne agreed. "That's true."

Kyle sighed. "You really don't want me to come?"

"No."

"Will you bring him to Boston to meet me?"

"Yes."

"I'm sending you a very expensive gift."

Chapter Ninety

Corinne was picking out a wedding cake with Enoch Miller.

They could have gotten away with a package of cupcakes, but here they were at a bakery, flipping through photos of cakes.

She kept feeling like this was ridiculous. Like someone was going to show up and laugh at her, or pull the rug out from under her. But it wasn't going to be this bakery employee, and it wasn't going to be Enoch.

Enoch wanted two tiers, so that they could get two different flavors.

"We'll have so many leftovers," she said.

"It's *cake*," he said.

"Cake freezes well," the bakery worker said.

"Cake freezes well," Enoch repeated.

They chose white cake because it tasted like wedding cake, and chocolate, because Enoch liked chocolate. And Corinne didn't ask him what kind of cake he had the first time. (His mom probably made it.) (She probably made cream cheese mints, too. Church weddings always had cream cheese mints.) Corinne and Enoch's cake was going to have buttercream frosting with pink and yellow roses.

Corinne's bouquet was going to have blue and green hydrangeas. And Enoch was going to get a pink rose for his lapel. The florist said she could make it all match. Corinne didn't care whether it matched.

She felt just as silly at the florist as she had at the bakery. But she wanted these flowers; she *wanted* them, even if it was all a bad joke.

"I should have been bringing you flowers," Enoch said, on the way out. "All along."

———

"I'm going to say something you probably won't like," he said one morning. "So I'm only going to say it once."

They were getting married this week. In four days.

Corinne lived with him now. She worked at his kitchen table. She needed him to get better internet service.

Enoch sat on his bed. (Their bed?) (Not quite.) "I think we should have our reception at Natalie's parents' house."

"I don't even know Natalie," Corinne said. "Never mind her parents."

"It's a nice room. It will feel special."

"Have you been there?"

Enoch shrugged. "I went to their Christmas party two years ago."

"You're a conundrum, Brother Miller."

"I know you don't like Shannon," he pressed on, "and maybe it *would* be too much. You can decide. But it's a nice room. It's the right size. And then we could just stop worrying about it. I feel like we're going to end up having our reception here, and it won't feel special."

"Would we have to, I don't know . . . decorate the room?"

"Nope. It's like the Conservatory. In Clue. With windows and plants. Shannon will set up a table for the cake, and I'll bring a boom box. And that's it, we're set."

"I guess Shannon and Natalie will be there anyway . . ."

"They don't have to be."

Corinne sighed. "I don't want to have to ask someone who's at the courthouse for their arraignment to sign our marriage license."

"We could just eat cake and dance in your apartment," he said. "Just the two of us. There's plenty of space."

"No." Corinne made up her mind. "It's fine. We can get married in the Conservatory. With your first wife. And the revolver."

"Hey." Enoch laid his big hand on Corinne's thigh. Over the blanket. "Stop calling her my wife."

"I'm just kidding."

"You're not," he said. "You're venting anxiety maybe, but you're not kidding."

"I'm just stating a fact," Corinne said, lying. "She *was* your wife . . ."

"She was. She's not anymore."

Corinne didn't argue.

Enoch squeezed her leg. "Okay?"

"Okay."

～

They picked out rings, too. Gold bands. Corinne was going to wear hers all the time, and Enoch would put his on after work, so that he didn't accidentally "deglove" himself. (A concept just as horrific as it sounded.)

Corinne told Enoch he could choose a song for them to dance to. Enoch cared more about music; he'd had to fight harder for it.

Corinne bought a new dress. It wasn't a wedding dress. It was a dress from the plus-size corner of a department store. But it was pretty. It was flowered silk, burgundy and blue, with a high, buttoned neck and gauzy sleeves. And she bought a very twee pair of high heels that she would never wear again. (Royal-blue leather with a T-strap. She bought them at a store aimed at young goths.)

Enoch was just going to wear one of his church suits. He asked Corinne which one, and she picked the brown one. She bought him a dark green shirt to wear with it, one that he could never, ever wear to church.

"With the pink tie, Corinne? Are you sure?"

"You're going to look like the king of the forest."

～

On Friday morning, Corinne got ready in the bathroom, with the mermaids, and Enoch got ready in the basement.

Corinne took time to actually put on makeup and to pin her hair back properly. She should have gone somewhere to have it done, but it was too late now. She put on lipstick the same shade as her lips.

And dangly earrings. Then looked at herself in the mirror—she was completely recognizable. She looked the same way she always had. Unremarkable. Round. Disgruntled.

How could she look so much the same, when she was so changed?

Maybe she hadn't changed at all. Maybe the world had changed around her.

"Corinne?" Enoch called from the hall. He'd gone to pick up the flowers. He must be home now.

Corinne walked out of the bathroom. Enoch raised his eyebrows when he saw her. "You sure clean up nice."

She shook her head.

Enoch himself looked very nice. Like he'd spent a little more time on his hair than usual and shaved a little more carefully. The green shirt was a good choice. And he was already wearing his pink rose boutonniere.

"Come here," he said.

Corinne went to him. He took her hand and kissed her cheek. "You look beautiful."

"Thank you. You look very, *very* handsome."

"I look like a tree."

"King of the trees," she said.

His voice dropped: "You nervous?"

"Yes," she whispered. "Are you?"

"Yeah." He hunched lower. He smelled like Polo aftershave. "I'm so nervous."

She laughed out a breath and rested her cheek against his.

"I feel like Pinocchio," he said. "At the end, when the fairy makes him real."

Corinne shook her head. It was too much. "I need to get my shoes."

"Hold that thought," he said. He dropped slowly to his knees.

"Enoch—" Corinne tried to hold him up. "—be careful." He was already down. She looked at him, confused. "We already did this."

He gazed up at her. "You did it."

"And you said yes. We're locked in."

"Let me have this, Corinne . . ."

She looked down at his long face, his long nose, his wire-framed glasses. She cupped a hand under his jaw. "All right. Fine. Go for it."

"Corinne?"

"Yes."

"I love you completely, and I want to share my life with you. Will you have me?"

She brushed her thumb over his chin. Time was trying to stop on her. Time was trying to slip and spin. Her brain wanted more frames of this. Enoch Miller on his knees for her. Enoch Miller offering himself up. It was different from him consenting; she was glad she'd let him drop.

Corinne thumbed his chin again. She nodded. "Yes." She brought her other hand to his face—she kept nodding—and bent over to kiss him.

"Yes," Enoch agreed, nodding with her. He backed up, reaching into his pocket.

"Save the rings for the wedding," Corinne said.

He shook his head and held out one of the velvet boxes. "I know we skipped over the engagement pretty quick; you don't have to wear this, but—" He opened it.

It was a gold ring with a clear violet stone and two smaller gems that were probably diamonds. It was nothing Corinne would have picked out for herself, but once she saw it, she wanted it. She held out her left hand, and Enoch slid the ring on. It fit perfectly.

"It's lovely," she said. "How did you know what size to buy?"

"Honey, we picked out rings together . . ."

Corinne crunched up her nose. She was blushing. "That's right, we did—that was sneaky of you. It's beautiful." She held out her hand to look at it. She felt overcome for a second. She should have painted her nails. "It's beautiful, thank you." She looked at his face again. "Come up here and kiss me."

Enoch stood up. His knees cracked. He kissed her. "Let's go get married."

Chapter Ninety-one

It was strange being all dressed up with Enoch. It felt like they were on their way to church together.

They had to park in the county parking garage and walk quite a ways to the courthouse. Corinne felt clumsy in her heels. She left her coat in the truck because it spoiled the effect of the dress. (The effect for whom? Who would even see her?) (The effect for Corinne.) Enoch held her hand—his palm was sweaty—and Corinne held her bouquet. Enoch had the rings and the license. He kept touching his pocket.

The courthouse was full of lawyers and clerks, people picking up forms, tired people in trouble . . . Most of them smiled at Enoch and Corinne. It was obvious why the two of them were there. Corinne took probably too much comfort in these strangers' smiles. She was tearful by the time they got in the elevator. Enoch put his arm around her. "You good?"

Corinne nodded. "I love you," she said, fizzing over.

He kissed her forehead. "I love you, too. I like this dress."

"Thank you."

"And I like your shoes. I like anything that makes you easier to reach." He kissed her cheek.

Corinne smiled, and the elevator doors opened. Shannon and Natalie were standing there. Shannon was wearing a very smart jacket and pants with a lovely blouse. (Damnably pretty, that woman.) Natalie was wearing a sweater and a casual skirt. They both smiled.

"You look so beautiful!" Natalie said. "Both of you!"

Shannon and Natalie had stopped by Enoch's house again this week to make plans. It was nice, it was fine. It had shown Corinne how Enoch and Shannon were together. Like siblings almost. Or people who had served in a war together. Natalie was easy to like. Patient and generous. An elementary school counselor. Raised by Unitarians. She'd offered to bring her camera today, and she had—she held it up now. Enoch slipped his arm around Corinne for a picture.

"There is an actual sentencing happening in your courtroom," Shannon said after the flash went off. "It's not too late to plan something more appropriate."

"Yes," Corinne said, "it is."

"Fine." Shannon scowled. "Have it your way."

That shocked a laugh out of Corinne.

Shannon turned to Enoch, her pretty face pinched. "Hey, I need to run something past you—"

Enoch glanced away from Corinne. "Does it have to be now?"

Shannon looked unusually unsure of herself. "Um, no—we can go in. We just have to sit in the back and be quiet."

Enoch pushed open the heavy wood door. There was a sentencing—or something—happening. The room was mostly empty, except for the defendant and two people who were probably attorneys. And except for Japheth Miller, who was sitting by himself in the back row, in his church suit, looking up at them.

Enoch stopped. They all stopped.

Japheth was frowning. He nodded at Enoch, then turned to face the front of the room.

Enoch looked at Shannon. Her arms were folded, and she was squinting up at the judge. Natalie was smiling at Corinne, conspiratorially. Corinne turned back to Enoch. He looked a little bit undone. She placed her hand on his lower back. His arm contracted around her.

"Could we ask the wedding party to please sit down?" the judge asked. "Court is in session."

They all quickly moved toward seats. Away from Japheth. (Who really was huge now.) They sat down in benches like long pews. Enoch held Corinne's hand tight.

The sentencing ended. Corinne couldn't focus enough to understand what was happening. She felt bad about being so festive while someone was having such a miserable time.

"All right," the judge said, looking up at them. "Miller-Callahan?"

They nodded.

"Come on up."

Corinne stood up too quickly on her three-and-a-half-inch heels. She teetered. She glanced at the back of the room. Where Japheth Miller was sitting—

Where Corinne's mother was sitting now, with Mercy and Alicia. All of them dressed for church. Corinne's mother was crying. Alicia waved.

Enoch was touching Corinne's back. "Come on, honey."

Corinne moved. She moved even though time had stopped, and everything should be frozen. Everything should at least be slowing down. Like an instant replay. Time had stopped, but only for Corinne. The rest of the world was moving. The judge was talking. Enoch was listening. Enoch was swallowing, his Adam's apple bobbing. His long face somber and pale. He was holding Corinne's hand. She was holding an absurdly large bouquet with big sprays of out-of-season hydrangea. Somewhere behind her, Corinne's mother was weeping.

Corinne was standing at the courthouse.

She wasn't standing outside by the flagpole.

Or at the bottom of a tornado slide.

Corinne was standing in front of a judge. Enoch Miller was holding her hand.

Corinne wasn't good. *She had never been good.* There was a narrow path, and she wasn't on it. There were sheep and goats; she was a goat. She was cast out. She was out of grace. Out of favor. She didn't believe in soul mates. She didn't believe in souls. She didn't believe in heaven.

Corinne . . .

Corinne, Corinne, Corinne.

Corinne was standing next to Enoch Miller, her almost husband. He was holding her hand. Her mother was here. The judge was looking at her. Enoch was looking at her. Russell Stover eyes. Cherry cola hair. With his big nose and his concerned forehead. "Honey?"

"I'm sorry?" Corinne said.

The judge was giving her a stern look. "Corinne," he said, like he was repeating himself, "do you take this man to be your husband, to live together in matrimony, to love him, to honor him, to comfort him, and to keep him in sickness and in health, forsaking all others, for as long as you both shall live?"

Forsaking all others, yes. "I do," she said.

"Enoch," the judge said, "repeat after me."

Enoch did. He stacked up a bunch of promises. About loving and cherishing Corinne 'til death did them part. She knew that he'd made these promises before, and that they'd fallen through. But she still believed him. She looked up into his serious face. Her ankles wobbled, and she believed him.

"Corinne," the judge said, "repeat after me."

She did: "I, Corinne, take you, Enoch, to be my husband, to have and to hold from this day forward." *From this day backward, for all the days that have ever counted.* "For better, for worse"—*for worst, probably*—"for richer, for poorer, in sickness and in health, to love and to cherish, 'til death do us part."

"Do you have rings?" the judge asked.

"Yes," Enoch said.

"Well, get 'em out."

Enoch fumbled with the boxes. Corinne took the larger ring from him and slipped it on her right thumb. She held out her left hand. Enoch's voice was so deep, Corinne could hardly make sense of it. "I give you this ring as a token and pledge of our constant faith and abiding love." He pushed the ring onto her finger—he squeezed her hand. There was a tear on his cheek. He must have been desperate to wipe his glasses.

"All right, Corinne," the judge said.

Corinne repeated after him. She handed Enoch the flowers, so she could hold his left hand in both of hers. Her fingers were trembling. She slid the ring onto his long, blunt finger. It got stuck on his knuckle; he had to push it down the rest of the way. *Constant faith,* Corinne thought. *Abiding love.*

The judge was talking about virtue and authority. "I now pronounce you man and wife." He was signing their marriage license
while he talked. "You can kiss the bride," he said, "but you don't have
to—it's already legal."

Enoch looked down at Corinne, and the corner of his mouth
twitched up. He hunched over her. She almost stopped him—*My
mom is watching, Japheth will tell.* Enoch pressed his lush mouth
over hers. His lips were parted. He held on to her elbows. Corinne
stood as tall as she could to make it easier for him. Her heels left
the floor.

"Do we have witnesses?" the judge was saying. "Come on up.
Come on."

The clerk had come around the bench with their license. "Bride?
You sign here." Corinne signed. "Bride's witness?"

Alicia was standing next to Corinne, tearful and beaming. "Can I?"

Corinne nodded. Alicia signed, then pulled Corinne into an embrace.

"Groom?" the clerk was saying.

Enoch signed. His brother signed next. When Japheth was done,
he squeezed Enoch's arm and walked past him, back down the aisle.

"All right," the judge said. "Congratulations. We need to clear the
room for the next case."

Enoch led Corinne away and out through the heavy doors. Alicia
hugged Corinne again. And then hugged Enoch. Corinne's mother
was standing a few feet back, with Mercy. They were both crying.
Everyone was crying. Even Natalie. Even Shannon, standing a few
feet in the other direction.

Corinne looked at her mom.

Her mom took a step forward, and Corinne met her more than
halfway. Her mom hugged her. "I'm so happy for you," she whispered. "God works in mysterious ways."

He sure as fuck did.

Did Sister Miller give Corinne's mom a Bible tract so that Corinne
could meet Enoch Miller? So Enoch Miller could meet her? So they
could fall in love and have sex on his mother's couch and ruin their
families' lives and break each other's hearts? So that Enoch could
ruin Shannon a little bit? And Shannon could ruin him back? So

that Enoch could turn away from the only world he ever knew? Just to have *this*? This promise with Corinne? This door finally opening?

Was that Jesus's work?

Maybe it was.

Corinne didn't care anymore; she'd take it.

She'd take this hug. She'd take her mother's blessing. She'd take Mercy, just being here, too scared to make any eye contact.

Her mother didn't congratulate Enoch. He was cast out. More recently and radically. But Corinne could tell that her mom approved of him. Approved of this. Enoch Miller was still an elder's son. People wanted to forgive him.

Shannon had stepped closer to them, while Corinne wasn't paying attention.

"We're going to celebrate now," Shannon said. Bravely. Generously. (She was even more radically cast out than Enoch. No one wanted to forgive Shannon Frank.) "With cake."

Corinne's mom shied away. "I have to get Mercy back to Ruth," she said.

Corinne nodded.

"I'd love some cake," Alicia said. Bravely. Generously.

"I'll write down the directions," Natalie said.

Corinne pulled Alicia toward her. "You don't have to do this," Corinne whispered. "I know it's against the rules."

"Shut up, Corinne. It's a conscience matter."

"It's cold," Enoch was saying to Corinne. "Do you want me to go get the truck?"

"What?" Corinne said. "No. I want to go with you."

Their eyes caught for the first time since he'd kissed her. Corinne threw her arms around his neck. (Literally "threw" them.) Enoch hugged her so tight, he lifted her into the air. A flash went off. "Corinne . . ." Enoch sighed.

Chapter Ninety-two

In an elevator with Enoch and Alicia and Shannon and Natalie.

Walking to the parking garage in heels she never should have thought she could keep on for more than five minutes.

In a filthy garage elevator with Enoch Miller, her husband. Her husband. All six-foot-who-knows-what of him. Her husband.

Enoch Miller trying to hold her close because she'd left her coat in the car.

(No one had spoken to him. Because he was cast out. But they would let him back in someday soon. And then it would just be Corinne on the outside. Corinne and Shannon Frank.)

Climbing into Enoch's truck. Watching her new ring throw purple flares around the cab. Enoch, Enoch Miller. *Enoch*.

A stranger's house. An actual fucking conservatory. So many flowers—on the table, hanging on the door. An extremely beautiful woman whom Corinne hardly knew taking photos.

Two different kinds of cake. And coffee. And Alicia un-burping a Tupperware container of cream cheese mints. "They're so easy, Corinne, honestly. You could make them. It's just cream cheese and butter and powdered sugar. Oh, and peppermint extract. It's a good thing Shannon called me yesterday morning—they have to chill overnight."

There were no speeches. There was music. All of Enoch's not-quite-country indie rock. Corinne and Enoch, relieved to be sitting. Relieved to be married. Relieved to have finally pulled the trigger. To have crossed from one hard place over to a new one. To have settled something, finally, that had started between them when they were too young to sort it out.

"We don't have to dance," Enoch said. "I know it's awkward."

Corinne stood up. "I'm not denying you the only thing you actually asked for."

"I asked you to spend the rest of your life with me."

"Only after I already said that I would." She pulled on his arm. "Come on."

He went to cue up the music. Corinne waited for him.

"I've never been to a wedding with dancing," Alicia said eagerly. "This is just like in the movies."

Enoch had chosen "The Luckiest" by Ben Folds, something they could just sway to. It was extremely awkward, with only three people watching. When Corinne glanced over at them, Shannon and Natalie seemed lost in their own thing, thank God. Alicia was crying again.

"Is this song all right?" Enoch rumbled.

"It's perfect," Corinne said. (She couldn't tell him that she would have chosen a Stevie Wonder song that he'd roller-skated to with someone else.)

"I'm so happy . . ." Enoch whispered. And it occurred to Corinne that he hadn't had this the first time. That he hadn't been to a wedding with dancing either.

"You're all I want," Corinne whispered back. And it was absolutely true.

There wasn't any reason to stay long. No one had much to say. They all ate too much cake. Corinne ate so many mints.

Alicia hugged her for the tenth time when she left. "I'm taking credit for this," Alicia said.

"Alicia, I've known Enoch for twenty-five years."

"I'm still taking credit."

Natalie went to pack up the extra cake. Enoch carried the card table back to wherever it came from.

That left Corinne with Shannon Frank.

"You should take all the flowers," Shannon said.

"You and Natalie should take them."

Shannon was unpinning a swag hanging from the door. "Don't be stupid."

"Shannon, I—"

"Corinne, we don't have to have a moment. I swear."

"I'm sorry I slept with your fiancé," Corinne spat out anyway.

Shannon slowly turned toward her. Looking genuinely surprised. "I thought you were going to thank me."

"Also, thank you," Corinne said. "But mostly—I'm sorry."

Shannon's mouth was flat and mean. (Corinne always thought Shannon looked mean; maybe that was just her face.) "Corinne," she said, "I'm sorry I married the love of your life."

"That's not really on you," Corinne said. "You can't apologize for that."

Shannon cocked her head, taking that in. It really *wasn't* on her. Marrying Enoch had been a mistake, but not because Corinne had any claim on him. "All right," Shannon said, "how about this—I'm sorry I talked so much shit about you at church."

Corinne pointed at her. "I knew it!"

Shannon laughed and shook her head.

The moment was over by the time Natalie and Enoch came back, and Corinne wasn't ever expecting to have another one. Corinne thanked Natalie profusely. She thanked Natalie's parents, who emerged from the kitchen to offer their congratulations.

She carried the leftover cake on her lap on the way home.

Home with Enoch Miller.

Her husband.

Chapter Ninety-three

Enoch let them in the front door, and Corinne staggered through it, leaning over. "I can't wait to take these shoes off. Jesus *Christ.*"

Enoch hooked his arm around her waist, pulling her upright. "Whoa, whoa, whoa," he said.

"Sorry," she said. "*Jiminy Christmas.* That's my wedding gift to you. No more blasphemy for the day."

Enoch drew her in, turning her to face him. His eyes were narrow. His forehead was tense. "I need you to keep the shoes on, for just a little while longer."

Corinne raised her eyebrows, she went still.

Enoch hunched over to kiss her neck. To kiss the hinge of her jaw. "I like this dress," he said. "I like these shoes."

"Thank you," she murmured.

"Can I just . . ." He was maneuvering her backward. Into the living room. His arms around her waist, one hand on her bottom. Until she bumped into the arm of the couch. "Corinne," he said, biting her neck, pushing forward.

Corinne rested on the edge of the couch. She set her bouquet down behind her, so she could put both hands in his hair. It wasn't slippery today—he'd put gel or something in it.

Enoch was sucking on her neck. He was holding her hips.

Corinne let her head fall back. She closed her eyes. "Is this how you want to consummate our wedding vows?"

"No," Enoch said. "I want to bend you over."

"Oh," she said. Weak. So weak. Such a fool. "Okay."

"Wait here a second?"

Corinne nodded.

"Don't move," he said.

"I won't."

Enoch stood up. He disappeared down the hall. Corinne stayed perched on the arm of the couch. She hardly had a chance to feel silly before Enoch was back, kissing her again. Mumbling sweet nothings. Actual nothings: "this dress" and "my girl."

"Your wife," Corinne ventured, and he lifted her off the couch, hugging her. Holding her. Taking bites out of her.

"I love you," he said, pulling up her skirt. "I want you. Can we—"

She nodded. "We can do whatever you want, Enoch."

"Turn around," he rumbled.

Corinne turned. She didn't lean over. She let him bite the back of her neck and rub her hips. She let him bend her. "I love you," she said, "I love you."

Enoch dragged his big hands from her shoulders to her ass. He lifted up her dress and palmed her cheeks through her burgundy tights. "Corinne, I promise we can do this later, looking into each other's eyes."

"I don't care," she said, bracing her elbows on the arm of the couch. "I've seen your eyes."

"*Ha,*" Enoch laughed, and Corinne grinned. She *didn't* care. She wanted this. She wanted forever of this. Of him.

He pulled her tights down to her thighs, and she stood up on tip-toe, and he was right, the shoes did make it easier. She heard his belt buckle and looked over her shoulder to watch. Enoch dove forward for a kiss, then made her look away, so he could put on the condom. Corinne listened. She smelled the latex, she lifted her hips. Enoch had fetched the spermicide gel, too. Corinne was not getting pregnant on her wedding night—her wedding afternoon. She was getting fucked over a couch by the love of her life. (That's what Shannon had called him.) (Whatever, it was true.)

Enoch pushed into her, and Corinne felt her spine start to un-spool. He pushed into her hard—he knew now that she didn't mind, that she liked it. Corinne shook her head to deal with the sudden burst of pleasure. The buzzing in the base of her back, in the base of her skull. Enoch held her by her hips. He bounced against her ass. He said her name, and it sounded like blasphemy.

Corinne made ugly noises she never would have allowed herself in her twenties.

She was loud, and it didn't matter—Enoch Miller lived in a house, and his neighbors wouldn't hear. Corinne lived here, too. She cried out. She loved it like this. She liked it better than coming, and she didn't even have to choose. She loved him. She loved him. She told him so.

"*Corinne . . .*" Enoch said, holding himself still inside of her like he was trying to stop something. He couldn't stop. He pumped a few more times, and Corinne closed her eyes and took it.

Enoch remembered to hold the condom on the way out. He leaned over and kissed her bottom. His belt buckle clinked.

Corinne stayed just where she was, catching her breath, waiting for the buzzing to dissipate. She felt Enoch taking off one of her shoes. "Is there blood?" she asked.

He touched the inside of her thigh. "Did that hurt?"

"On my heel," she said.

"Oh . . ." Enoch bent her leg at the knee. "A little bit. Ouch." He took her other shoe off. "I can't believe I made you keep these on."

"Worth it," Corinne said. "Never mention it again."

He peeled off her tights and underwear. "Ouch," he said again. "Come here." He pulled Corinne to her feet. Her skirt felt whispery on her bare legs, and the ground felt strangely close and flat. She had blisters on the back of both heels. Only one was split.

Enoch's mouth was four inches farther away again. He hunched over to kiss her. And then he bent down and put his shoulder in her belly.

"Jesus Christ!" she said. "Not again!"

He lifted her up with a grunt. "Jiminy Christmas, you mean."

"Enoch, your back. Your knees. Your everything."

"I'm carrying you over the threshold," he said, lurching down the hall.

"This is the last time, and I fucking mean it!"

Enoch heaved her onto the bed. "Do you need some peroxide?"

"No. I need you to stop giving yourself a hernia. And I need you to touch me."

Enoch's eyes were dancing.

"Come here," Corinne said.

She took off his jacket. She loosened his tie. She set the pink rosebud on the bedside table, on top of his Bible. Were the angels and the demons still watching them, or had they lost interest?

Enoch touched her . . . (She still didn't have a good word. She was just never going to say it.) He whispered so much nonsense in her ear that Corinne started crying even before she came. He wouldn't let Corinne take the dress off. "Let me have this," he said.

"I'm constantly letting you have things," Corinne said. She was rubbing her clit. He had two thick fingers inside of her. He was doing whatever she asked.

When she started to come again, he kissed her right hand.

Were the angels and the demons watching? Or did they only pay attention when it was a sin?

Chapter Ninety-four

Enoch made dinner.

They ate more cake.

Enoch helped Corinne take off her dress. He wanted to take a honeymoon soon. And he was going to have to call his mom to tell her the news, even though she might not want to talk to him. And even though Japheth had probably already told her. His whole family probably knew. Could Corinne believe that Japheth came?

She couldn't.

Did Corinne think her mom would invite her to dinner next week? Corinne wasn't sure.

Enoch was already thinking ahead to the Sundays when he could go with her.

It would be the only place they could go together. The only church people who would associate with them both.

Enoch took Corinne's hair down, one pin at a time.

Chapter Ninety-five

It was Sunday morning.

Enoch Miller had an elders' meeting after the service.

Corinne lay in bed waiting for him.

She waited in the church lobby with her mother.

She waited by the flagpole.

She waited for thirteen years.

Corinne was waiting in her own bed. In his bed. The bed they shared.

She wondered if Enoch was in the church basement right now, repenting. If he was laying himself low . . . She'd made him promise that he wouldn't say he regretted it.

———

It was Sunday morning, which meant Corinne was alone.

She was home in their bed, waiting for him.